PRINCE OF THEN

JUNO HEART

Prince of Then: A Fae Romance

Black Blood Fae Prequel

Ebook: ISBN: 978-0-6483392-9-8

Paperback: ISBN: 978-06456242-0-5

Hardcover ISBN: 978-06456242-1-2

V221028

"... the end is another beginning."

RUMI

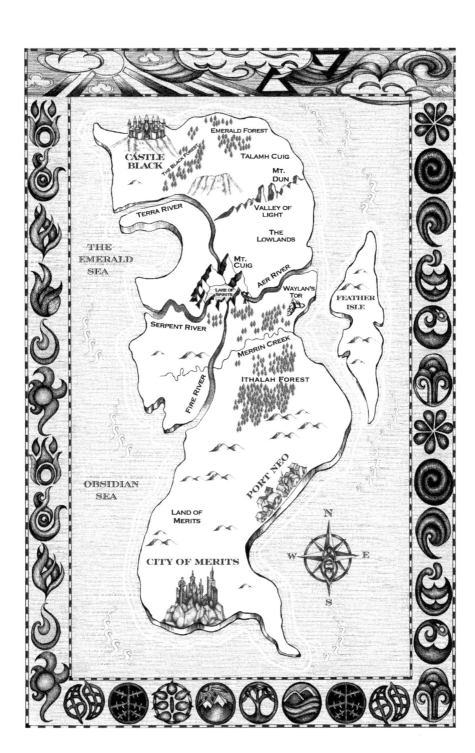

Prologue – The Beginning

O nce upon a time, the Faery city of Talamh Cúig was a place of peace, where the Elements co-existed in perfect harmony and gifted the people with their ancient nature magic.

Sisters—the Elements were five in number.

Ether, the soul who bound them together.

Terra, who loved to play in the dirt.

Undine, bathed in blue.

Salamander with her hair on fire.

And Aer, who longed to rule over all, but none more so than Gadriel, the raven-haired prince with eyes of brightest sapphire blue.

But what will a shunned air mage do when she learns that love cannot be forced?

Seal the prince's fate.

Poison his blood.

And curse his line forever.

1

The Cursed Prince

Gade

"Gadriel, I see you at the water's edge. Surely you don't wish to hide from me," calls a voice, soft as the summer breeze and just as sweetly cloying.

I know exactly who that voice belongs to, and I definitely want to hide from her.

Scooping my sword from the ground, I duck behind a tree trunk and quickly tie my belt around my hips. When I glance up, she's in front of me—Aer, standing in the forest, her impossible golden beauty shining as bright as the midday sun.

"Hello, Gade," she says, smiling and blushing like the maid I'm well aware she isn't. Far from it, for she is as old as the earth beneath my feet, more lovely than the sky, as tempting as a cool lake, and more terrifying than the wildest of flames.

"Kiss me," she breathes, pressing her palm against my still-wet chest.

To balance my powers, I've bathed in the Lake of Spirits—the source of our kingdom's magic—and now, the six-pointed star glyph on the back of my hand glows brightly, fully charged, Aer's hungry gaze fixing on it.

"I knew you'd come soon," she says, the thin straps of her creamy gown slipping halfway down her arms. "I knew you couldn't stay away."

A wry smile twists my lips. "Of course I couldn't. It's been a month since I last visited the lake, and my powers were ebbing."

She steps closer, crushing pine needles underfoot, the smell invigorating. "How old are you now, Gade?"

Why she asks when she already knows the answer is beyond me. "Eighteen."

Her fair brow rises. "A man now, and so tall and strong. I predict that today will be the day you'll finally kiss me."

"You're an Elemental mage, not a faery. Me dallying with you would be like a forest stag trying to win the heart of a princess in the highest tower. Or the dark sea longing to hold the moon in its slippery embrace. Ridiculous and impossible."

The pine trees groan. Limbs and twigs snap as her gold eyes darken; the first signs of her anger. She steps back, her long fingers curling into fists. "I've been patient, young princeling. I have court-ed, and I have waited, and my desire for the great king you will one day become has been my only sustenance these long years past. And you repay my dedication and steadfast love with insults?"

A sour taste fills my mouth as I recall her past attentions, the lavish presents she gifted me each celebration of my birth, the precious jewels, the poems. The many times her regard made me feel akin to an insect drowning in a pot of the sweetest honey.

For many moons, I've thought nothing of her lingering touches, her heated stares. Why would I? She is a mage. I am a prince. Never in the history of Faery has one been interested in the other.

"Oh, Gadriel, how I tire of this game."

"What game? If you play one, I do not know it."

Her brittle smile twists into a snarl. "Are you really so naive, handsome Prince of Five?"

I'm not. It is only with Aer that I pretend to be.

Her knuckles bleach white around a thin branch as she snaps it from the ash tree behind me, leaning too close. "I am ready to be yours and can wait no longer for this to be done. But I can't force you. You must choose me, and the time has come to do so."

My frown grows. "Choose you for what?"

"To be your bride, of course." A sly smile spreads over her face. "In all the seven realms, there is no one who will love you as I do. I shall be your forever queen."

With those words, the first tendrils of fear snake through my stomach.

She is deadly serious, and a *deadly* Aer is a grave problem.

I draw a quick breath, then force a smile. "You're an Elemental mage. It cannot be. What about your sisters? Think of Ether, Terra, Undine, and Salamander."

"What of them?"

"It would put the Elements, no, it would put *everything* out of balance—the whole kingdom would be at risk. You, the air mage, cannot rule over your sisters. It is impossible."

Translucent yellow eyes turn opaque, and she strikes, pulling me close as her sickly sweet lips coax mine to open.

The air mage kisses me.

Fingers digging into her shoulders, I shove her away. "I do not want you, Aer. What you wish for will never be."

Thunder shakes the sky as her fury surges through the air, an acrid scent. I have made a grievous mistake. A terrible error of judgment. I should have taken more care with my words and let her down gently.

"I insist that you *do* desire me." Her gown wavers then melts away, and she stands before me naked, her body luminous, glorious, and a bizarre contrast to the ugly contortion of her features. Eyes squinting. Brow lined. Teeth bared and elongating.

It's such a strange sight that laughter explodes from me.

Aer's gold eyes turn black as she covers her chest with her arm, and then the gown appears, enfolding her curves again. "You dare to laugh at me? You ignorant, ungrateful fool. Do you not realize I hold your fate in my hands?"

My blood rushes through my veins, and I shake my head, stepping backward. "Aer... You misunderstand..."

She opens her mouth, and a screech like the sound of a thousand wailing harpies shreds the air as I fall to my knees, clutching my chest.

Then there is only pain.

And more pain.

Agony is my blood, my soul, my very name.

I am agony.

"Aer..." The word croaks out of me, the taste on my tongue like bitter poison, thick as it slides down my throat. "What have you done?"

Silver fire licks over her arms, the wind whipping her hair around her shoulders like serpents seeking prey to strike. Purple clouds race above, then explode with a thunderous boom. Lightning flashes. The forest floor shakes.

"I curse you, Gadriel Raven Fionbharr and all the future heirs of the Throne of Five. In your blood, the blackest poison will bloom, gifting you the cruelest death. You will burn, and you will moan, and pray to all the gods that love will find you fast. Your pure heart will turn to coal heartbeat by heartbeat, breath by breath. You will hate and, finally, you will love, but find your true mate you must—or die a slow and painful death."

My every muscle taut and trembling, I struggle to my feet and face her, my hand crushing my sword pommel. "You must truly loathe me."

"No, fair prince, it is the opposite. I will love you beyond the veil to the depths of the underworld and back. This is the price you'll pay for not surrendering your heart to me as you should."

But the punishment isn't equal to my supposed crime. Aer's revenge is savage. Never-ending.

"Punish me if you will, but not the innocent souls in my line who come after me. In what way will my children's children have wronged you? Your curse is unjust."

"All is fair in matters of love and rejection. But I am not without mercy. You are the most fortunate of your line, for you will keep your Powers of Five. Future princes of your land will rule one element only, yet I'll allow you to retain them all. See? Am I not a merciful mage, Gadriel?"

There is only one answer to that question, and she would not like to hear it.

"And you still *live*, Gadriel. I could slay you this moment with one breath, but I do not. And I've given you part of the key to easing your misery—to remain alive, you must find a mate before the poison has run its course. It won't be an easy task because the mate I select may not be fae and may view you as a monster, just as you view me now."

"Not fae? What else could she be?"

"Perhaps a troll. Or a human."

"No, wait, Aer. Please do not—"

Closing her eyes, the mage begins to chant, softly at first, then growing louder and louder until blood trickles from my ears.

Through the pain, I can only make out a little of what she says: "*Black will fade to gray, gray to white, and white to never. Never was the darkest taint and never will it ever be.*" Then she mutters in a low, guttural voice, the words an incoherent song that splinters my bones and grinds them to dust.

Clutching my head, I drop to my knees again. "Please, Aer. Stop!"

The sky clears as she turns away, her billowing robes dissolving into the forest until only her voice remains. Floating on the breeze come whispered words of ruin—*a halfling, a king, dark and light, and Faery born.* They all mean naught to me.

"Farewell, Black Blood Prince, first of your cursed line. Your pain will one day cease, but your kingdom's suffering will be endless. My gift to you is the Black Blood poison. This gift is your curse, and when your bones are ash, your son's curse to bear, and so on and so on. Until the end of time."

Like a volley of poisoned arrows have pierced my chest, agony shoots through my veins and settles in my skull. And then there is no lake. No forest. No warmhearted Prince of Five.

Only blackness remains.

And then nothing.

Nothing.

Nothing.

2

Many Years Later

Holly

The ancient forest that enfolds my village is not only my oldest friend but has an abundance of comfrey, my favorite herb for treating burns and swellings. This morning, I've gathered so much that its leaves spill from my basket, obscuring the plants resting beneath it—spotted St John's Wort to keep the devil from our door and foxglove for my mother's weak heart.

On the whole, it has been a successful foraging trip, but I cannot leave the forest until I have the root that eases Mother's nerves and brings her restful sleep, which means I must go deeper into the woods to where a patch of wild valerian grows in the damp soil near the river's edge.

With the sun warming my shoulders, I cut through tangled vegetation and hasten down a gentle slope, calling greetings to robins singing from gnarled branches.

It's a perfect spring day, yet worry dampens my mood. My sweet, gentle mother grows weaker with each day that passes, and when I look into her wise gray eyes, it's clear she knows she's running out of time.

"It's all right, my darling Holly," she told me this morning. "We'll meet again one day in the Otherworld."

A comforting notion, but in reality, a gigantic pile of pigs' swill.

As the daughter of the village wise woman, I have faith in the healing power of plants and herbs and respect the spirits that imbue them, but I don't believe in a faery tale land beyond the grave where our loved ones wait joyously for us to join them.

Life is too unfair.

With all that Mother has suffered—my father's death in a riding accident when I was a babe, losing her two sons to malignant fevers three years later, the constant bellyache of poverty—it's beyond me how she still believes that with her last breath, she'll be transported to some misty island to dance and feast alongside ancient kings and queens forevermore.

All Mother has left in the world are her daughters; me and my older sister, Rose. Not that good-hearted Rose is much help since her main interests are flirting with her beau, Liam, and collecting pretty threads and ribbons to decorate her well-worn gowns. These pursuits occupy her days and seem to satisfy her, but I can't imagine a greater waste of time than kissing the baker's son in the storeroom for an entire afternoon.

The young men of our village are loud and foolish and rarely speak a sensible word. My black hen, Nellie, has more sense than all of them put together, so I count myself lucky that whenever I stand next to Rose, most don't spare me a second glance.

The trees begin to thin out, a bright sail of blue sky appearing above thin alder branches as I gather my damp skirts in my fist and pick my way down a hill to a section of boggy grass and wildflowers near the riverbank. Squinting in the dappled light, I peer around the lush vegetation, spying the white flower heads of my quarry above a patch of wild carrot and hemlock.

I hurry over, pick a leaf, and crush it between my fingers, a strong earthy smell releasing. Bending, I put my basket on the ground and harvest the valerian plant, roots and all.

A crack sounds, followed by a high-pitched piping noise, the leaves to my right shaking as if an animal passes through the scrub, then a strange, heavy silence falls over the forest.

I glance around the gold-lit trees, listening for movement. If a bird or a creature is injured, I aim to find it, take it home, and nurse it back to health.

A silver mist appears from nowhere, swirling along the forest floor. It eddies and forms a thick column, a tall blonde woman stepping out of it—a young noble lady by the fine fabric of her billowing white dress and clear, glowing skin.

"Good morning," I say, covering my shock at her sudden appearance with a friendly smile.

She gives me a brilliant smile back, and a silver aura vibrates around her body as if she's back lit by bright sunshine. But that doesn't make sense—the sun is behind *me*, not her.

"Good day, child," she says. "How fortunate I am to meet you here today."

Child? I am almost twenty years old. Perhaps her eyesight is defective.

"I'm very glad to find you passing. I need your assistance. My sister has fallen, and I cannot manage alone. Your basket is full of healing herbs, so I assume you are the type who longs to help others. Assist me and your efforts will be rewarded with something all humans seek but cannot easily find." A graceful arm beckons me forward.

This woman speaks strangely, which makes me wonder if she's a wealthy traveler from a town very far from ours and perhaps a poet or philosopher. The ways of the rich are a mystery, but if I help her sister, she may pay in gold coin that will see us through next winter.

"Do you live nearby?" I ask. "Or have you a cart waiting?"

The road back to the village is long, and there aren't any houses on this side of the forest. Between the two of us, we won't be able to move her sister, but I can ease her pain at least before going for burlier help.

"No, girl, I live far from here in another time and place. My sister has arranged return transport but needs assistance to rise."

I wonder if this sister might have fallen and hurt her head. She sounds moonstruck and is possibly mad. Regardless, I will never refuse to help the injured, so I follow the white lady into a small clearing.

She links her arm through mine as we walk. "See over there? My sister rests beyond the hawthorn tree."

A woman lies under a dark cloak, a cloud of white hair and long limbs protruding from the material.

"Yes, I see her."

The injured girl sits up, then stands, her movements slow and graceful. Brushing leaves from her clothes, she walks toward me, her bearing regal, the light behind her dazzling, and her steps too sure to be injured.

A cold tendril of fear curls through my stomach as I realize I've made a terrible error of judgment.

The woman's smile is wide, but her dark eyes glitter with something inhuman and frightening. She looks unhinged, not entirely normal, and I have a sinking feeling that following them into this glade was not only a silly mistake, but a fatal one.

Rose always warned me that my desire to save all creatures, be they vicious or friendly, would be the death of me. Right now, I really hate to think she might have been correct.

"Hello," I say as I take two steps backward, stumbling over stones. "How is your ankle? Are you in much pain?"

Her laughter echoes through the trees. "Thank you for coming. Look down and check the path you tread upon."

"Pardon?" My gaze drops to my brown boots positioned in the middle of a ring of gilled, white-capped mushrooms that glow beneath the hawthorn tree. A *faery* tree. Fear tightens my throat muscles.

Still smiling, the lady offers her hand. "Come, my name is Ether. You can trust me. I will ensure you arrive safely."

"Arrive? Arrive where? I can't leave here."

"Talamh Cúig, the Land of Five. A girl like you is needed, and what is owed must be paid."

Paid? Good grief, what nonsense this demented woman speaks. My heart pounds as I shake my head and try to lift my feet to flee for my life—first one foot and then the other—but my boots are stuck in the mud and I cannot move an inch.

"I'm trapped," I say, my voice trembling despite my best efforts to tamp down panic.

"Yes," she says calmly, pointing at the circle of mushrooms. "Indeed, you are."

Unlike most residents of my village, I don't believe in the stories of faeries *dancing in the moonlight*. I'm practical minded, and most of my fears are based in reality—the pain of hunger, the grief of losing a loved one. But I do believe in humoring lunatics if it will keep them calm and buy me time to escape their delusions.

"But the ring is broken, you see? When I entered it, I trampled on an edge. Doesn't that break its power? You have no authority to take me anywhere. And besides, my mother is sick and needs me to return home."

"It matters not, human. Our hawthorn tree secures the boundary of the sacred circle, and your mother's time is nearly done. There is not a herb or tincture in the seven realms that could divert her from her course."

Eyes shining with as much compassion as flat, black stones are paired with a soothing smile. She touches my cloak, hand delving underneath the rough material until she finds bare skin at the base of my throat. This close, she is beyond beautiful. Unearthly. But her grip is merciless and choking.

As her fingers squeeze my neck, the birds begin to chirp, the song wild and frantic.

The lady's hand tightens.

I cough but find I have no strength to fight. My vision darkens, sweat beading my skin. "Please... My mother..."

Then the voice of the first lady who approached me, the golden sister, wafts over me. "The girl is not as horrible to behold as I would wish but certainly no great beauty. She will do fine. The bargain I made was a good one. What is your name, girl?"

My name... my name.

What is my name?

I do not know it.

Perhaps I never had one.

The light grows dimmer, and the other sister speaks. "Aer, are you absolutely certain this girl is the one you seek? I would not like to seize the wrong mortal."

Nausea overtakes me, darkness unfurling in my mind and swallowing me whole, then a wash of starlight bathing me as I fall into a spinning tunnel.

Down.

Down.

Down.

White light explodes inside my head, and I remember... I remember who I am. "Holly," I whisper. "My name is Holly..."

"Oh, yes, Sister," the lady called Aer says. "She's most definitely the one."

The wave of blackness crests, slips over my head, and pulls me under, drowning me in midnight.

And then I'm no longer Holly.

I'm no one.

No one at all.

3

The Oak

Gade

Seven hells. The foretold witch has finally arrived in my land.

I survey the dark shape lying face down, possibly unconscious, beneath the twisted oak tree, near certain it's the malevolent being I've been waiting for. I sniff the air. Yes, the creature is most definitely female.

An insidious invader. A sorceress.

Of all the infernal days for the prophecy to be fulfilled, why must it be today?

I'm in no fit state to deal with meddlers from lands beyond the veil. I've spent the last sennight stumbling through the Lowlands and have somehow managed to lose my horse, Wren, and my golden eagle, Lleu, and am now alone with my mind in tatters.

The timing of the witch's arrival could not be worse.

Old stories tell of a hostile sorceress, predicted to appear beneath the Crystalline Oak, her mind full of schemes and set upon the downfall of my home, Talamh Cúig.

I've not given much weight to these tales because why would a sorceress come to these lands? What could she hope to gain from a city in decline?

Since my parents' death three years past, the air mage who cursed me has withdrawn from the capital, her absence weakening the Elemental Power of Five that my people rely on for their magic. And now, without a king and queen, the Land of Five slowly decays.

Perhaps the witch beneath the tree is a spy sent by the Merits, the southern Unseelie fae who've long been obsessed with building machines, time devices called clocks and steam pumps to move water through their dark city, in the pursuit of evermore power.

Why bother with such laborious distractions when they could employ nature magic as we Elementals do? As *all* fae creatures are meant to do.

No doubt they're planning to march on my kingdom while my land and powers are weak. Ruling as prince, the only surviving son of King Bryar and Queen Aisheel, I can't be crowned king until I marry the fated girl the air mage has chosen for me, the girl who will stop the poison's deadly flow through my blood.

I must find this girl before it is too late, marry her, and claim the throne. If only I knew where in the Elements I'm meant to find her. But today, with rage and bitterness clouding my mind, instead of searching, I must waste time ending the life of a witch. Once, I shunned violence at every opportunity. Now, the poison makes me long for it.

Damn the curse and its progression.

The wind on top of Waylan's Tor tears at my cloak while crazed thoughts swirl through my mind, jumbled and chaotic; they make no sense. It's the poison's fault, pulsing through my blood like liquid fire, turning me into a monster day by day.

Squinting, I fold my arms over my leather breast plate and run my gaze over the Crystalline Oak—its gnarled roots and branches covered in glittering dark crystals—and then the girl beneath it, lying wretched and unconscious.

The witch I must kill.

Kill her, the curse's voice snarls inside my mind. *Finish this girl at once, or she will be your downfall. The end of your precious Land of Five.*

Heaving a sigh, I unsheathe my sword and stalk down the rocky hillside, clouds of orange dust exploding with every thud of my boots. The wind continues to lash without pause, and the sun above is scalding hot.

I check the sky, searching for Lleu—my bonded creature and when it suits him, also my loyal companion. Where in the realms has he gone?

The oak's branches creak in the wind, but still the witch lying beneath the dust-covered cape, her hair streaming around the hood like ragged sand-colored ribbons, doesn't move. Perhaps she's already dead and I won't need to bother shedding her blood.

Before the curse, in the blink of an eye, I could turn her into a pile of shattered bones and gore, using any one of the elements I control. But these days, I find a manual form of elimination more satisfying and take pleasure in my victims' accelerating heartbeats, the fear swirling in their eyes, their pleading whimpers—all of it a sensory delight to me.

As a boy, I hunted only for sport and the opportunity to study my prey at close quarters, but it was against my nature to kill without reason. I practiced swordsmanship for fitness and to protect my family in case my magic was ever disabled.

Now dark, twisted thoughts sustain me like air. They are the food that nourishes my body. The earth that cushions my feet. And the water that quenches my thirst.

Should a court member laugh or speak out of turn, I picture all the worst ways to end them. Strangulation. Suffocation. Burning. Drowning. Chopping and rending bone and sinew limb from limb. Fellow fae crushed to dirt.

Yes, my mind is broken, but my body grows harder, more un-yielding as each day passes and the poison thickens in my veins. With each moon's turn, the suffering of others becomes more intoxicating and addictive.

In the beginning, I fought hard against the poison's insidious pull, but now that it has thoroughly ravaged my mind and body, there's no point in struggling. It's over. The curse has won, and I will be its bound slave until I marry my chosen one. Then the poison will lie dormant until my death when it will transfer to my heir. This is the sorrowful song the air mage sings, and since she cannot lie, it must be true.

I roll my shoulders, then crack my neck. No more delaying; it's time to deal with the witch.

Stalking forward, excitement spikes through my veins, the curse baying like a wolf deep in my chest. If this girl—this trespassing witch—hopes to meddle in my land, then she will be the unfortunate recipient of all my pent-up rage.

My steps grow longer, harder, each thud of my boots a small earthquake that vibrates the ground. Strangely, even as I move closer, the witch doesn't stir.

Boom. Boom.

No response.

Boom. Boom.

Still nothing.

A distant bird screeches, and then it happens—the brown cape ripples like a wave as the witch's head rises. I stand five short paces from her billowing gray skirts and watch her body tremble and her hands make fists. A frown creases her forehead, and fear forms wet pools in her light-colored eyes.

For a witch, she doesn't look very powerful. Perhaps the journey through the portal to our lands depleted her strength.

Now three paces away, I halt, my sword tip pointing toward the ground.

"Don't come any closer," she says, scrambling to her feet.

I blink at the melodious tone of her voice, the sound far from malevolent.

The bones in my spine crunch as my shoulder blades draw together. I grunt, preparing to speak through burning throat muscles and a dry tongue, which haven't formed words in days.

"Distance won't save you. I could kill you with a single thought while standing on top of that tor. My sword is an amusement. I favor the feel of it, the weight, and admire its brutal efficiency."

She takes a slow, shuddering breath. "Killing is sport to you, is it?" Her pointed chin lifts, the hood falling to her shoulders and exposing broad cheekbones, yellow eyes, and a mouth too wide and decorous for her solemn features. She has the hair of a sorceress—the golden color changing, shifting shades from light to dark as she moves. "Then you must be the devil himself and this land the hell you rule over."

A laugh rattles my chest as I sweep my sword in a broad arc around the plains, heat blazing over my shoulders. Anger never fails to bring the power of fire crackling over my skin. "You think *this* land is the hell realm?"

Yellow eyes stare back, unblinking and defiant.

I grip my blade's hilt tighter. "This part of my land certainly resembles that place, and I may appear similar to the dark guardian who rules over it, but you're mistaken. You have ported into the Land of Five, witch. We've been expecting you. So do not bother feigning ignorance. I know who you are."

I take two steps forward. She takes one back, and her spine hits the crystalline bark of the tree trunk, her hands thrusting out in a futile effort to protect herself. I summon a shield of wind and brace for a blast of the sorceress's power.

None comes.

I flip my palm up, and a trickle of blue light spins into two strands that twist around each other, becoming a vortex. Before the curse weakened me, I could summon a storm of lightning, a raging flood, or a wildfire large enough to destroy an entire forest with ease. But that was *before*, when I was much more than I am now.

Expelling a harsh breath, my confidence wavers. Perhaps in my current weakened state, I cannot beat this witch.

No.

I am the prince of Talamh Cúig, heir to the ancient Throne of Five—of course I can crush the stranger. Let her do her worst.

My teeth grind together as I step forward and fist her hair with one hand, the other pressing my sword's edge to her white throat.

"Please," she says, gripping my forearms, the contact flaring the star glyph on my hand. "My mother…"

"What?"

"Don't kill me. My mother is ill. I'm needed at home to care for her. I'm all she has. Have mercy. Please."

"Why should I grant mercy to a demon who wants to stop me from healing the sickness of this land?"

Her eyes, the color of light amber crystal flecked with gold, widen. Her lips part, but she says nothing as I stare into her dilated pupils.

"That's right, little sorceress. I know exactly why you're here."

"How could you possibly know why I'm here when I have no idea where I am or how I arrived at a place where strange and unnatural men such as you exist?" Her skin reddens as my sword scrapes it and my gaze fixes on the dancing pulse at her throat.

"Please." Her weak fingers rise to grip my bicep. "Wait. Think rationally. *Look* at me."

Grimacing, I relax the pressure of my blade.

"First, consider our differences," she says. "Although it seems impossible, I can think of no other explanation… *you* are the magical creature, not I. You're the strongest man I have ever laid eyes on. Your clothes seem fashioned from fantastical dreams, and power and madness burn equally in your gaze."

I snarl, and she flinches, then licks her lips and continues. "The ears that part your hair are pointed, not rounded like human ears are, like *mine*. And a moment ago, I witnessed magic forming on your palm."

She tugs my wrist, but my sword arm doesn't yield.

"*Look closely*," she begs. "I'm a powerless human, and you are something else entirely." She shakes her head. "Or perhaps I'm asleep and dreaming. Yes, hopefully, that is true."

She's human? No. It cannot be. She lies. Sorceresses have been known to bend truth; fae cannot.

"You're not human. Your arrival in this land has been foretold. You are a sorceress."

"I'm not. My name is Holly O'Bannon. I swear it on my life. I live in the village of Donore. It's a simple place by the sea. My people fish, and I forage in the forest for food and herbs to help sustain my family. I promise you I'm no threat to any person or place."

She lives by the water as do my people. I wonder if her ocean is as wild and untamed as the Emerald Sea and as full of deadly creatures.

"My mother lies dying in pain, helpless, while she waits for my return. This morning, I was in the forest picking herbs to ease her sleep when two women accosted me—otherworldly, both bright and shining—one gold, one silver."

The air mage and her sister, Ether. It can be no others.

Pain lances my chest as I step backward. Why would Ether bring the witch here? I refuse to believe that the High Mage of Talamh Cúig is a traitor to our court. It's impossible. But if it is true, then the witch's arrival heralds my downfall and the ultimate destruction of my kingdom.

"You lie," I say. "You are not *human*. It is said mortals are goblin-like creatures covered in hair who emit a scent of rotten bog marshes. You smell like herbs—just as a witch does."

"I promise I speak the truth." She attempts a small smile. "What is your name?" She lifts her chin while I glare at her, my fingers flexing on the hilt of my sword, readying to finish this. "Please. Which city do you call your home? Take me there. Someone will understand. They'll know I'm not a witch. No doubt your people will want to help me return home. Whatever breed you are, you're not monsters devoid of empathy, are you?"

My eyes roll back into my skull as I call on the power at the center of the six-pointed star—spirit—and transform, instantly dissolving to mist. A moment later, I reform in a solid state, amazed at my sudden boost of power, chest to chest with the witch, and my fingers wrapping around her slender neck.

Breathing hard, I consider my options. I could let her go. I could leave her here, a tasty meal for the draygonets. Or take her prisoner and haul her home to the Black Castle. But I know I won't do either of those things—the cursed blood will not let me. It speaks to me as it pumps through my veins and vital organs, rushing through the chambers of my heart, the ratio of poison to blood growing every day.

Flames burst from the star on the back of my hand, wrapping around our bodies as a word sounds on repeat in my mind—firm and urgent.

Wait.

Wait, dark prince.

Wait.

My muscles freeze, and I strain to hear more, to understand. This is not the voice of the poison, nor Aer's voice, or my own madness speaking. It is her sister, Ether—the High Mage. *This* is a voice of reason. A voice I trust.

I loosen my grip around the witch's neck—but only a little.

She hisses like an animal pierced by an arrow.

A sudden wind howls, tangling our hair together, my black strands with her wheat-colored locks. Our gazes clash and hold—blue with yellow, then an ear-piercing shriek sounds above. I look to the sky, knowing what, or rather *who*, is coming. A rasping laugh escapes my lips.

The girl screams once—short and sharp, then falls silent, staring agog as the golden eagle lands, his broad talons braced upon my shoulders so his head looms over mine.

"About time, Lleu. Where in the Elements have you been hiding?" I say.

He spreads his immense wings, claws digging into my leather spaulders to reprimand me for scolding him.

The girl's mouth opens and closes repeatedly. "What... what is that?"

"Now you pretend you don't know an eagle when you see one. Your lies are not only astonishing, but foolish."

Sweet breath pants over my face. Step back, I tell myself. Instead, I press closer.

Kill the witch—the curse-maker's voice rasps inside my skull. *Kill her.*

Lleu's beak is rough against my ear as he chirps loudly. I don't happen to speak eagle, but his meaning is obvious. He agrees with Ether and tells me to stay my hand.

To wait and restrain my violent impulses. Control them.

But then the madness of the poison whispers through my blood.

Remember, it says. *Always remember, Black Blood Prince.*

You are mine.

As she is yours.

Kill her.

I cannot let this girl walk away.

I cannot let her live.

"Please…" she says, her body shaking. "Won't you at least tell me your name?"

I can't disclose that I am a prince of the land she seeks to destroy, but there is a name I can give that isn't a lie—the name those closest to me, my sister and cousins, use.

My eyes narrow as I draw a long breath.

"Some call me Gade," I say, and squeeze her throat tighter.

4

The Boar

Holly

"I'm a sworn protector of the Land of Five and the city of Talamh Cúig," the man says in his deep, rasping voice, a perfect match for his beastly size and fierce demeanor. "Do you still claim this place was not your intended destination?"

So, the man who is about to strangle me and wears a giant vulture on his shoulders like a well-worn cloak is a soldier or a guard.

"Of course, I claim it because it is the truth. I've never seen nor heard of this land until I woke up under this tree with a mouthful of red dirt and an insufferable headache."

Keeping my eyes on the bird whose sharp beak hovers far too close, I tug the man's wrist again, but I might as well be attempting to move a stone statue's hand from my throat for all that it moves, which is not a bit.

The male's striking eyes of deep sapphire narrow, but he doesn't speak a word.

"In all honesty, I cannot say it's a pleasure to meet you. However, a name for a name is a fair exchange, and as I mentioned earlier, mine is Holly."

"I don't care what you're called." He grimaces and looks off to the side, cocking his head as if listening to some distant noise. Then he growls, causing my head to jolt back and hit the tree.

"No," he says, his gaze focused on the red dirt. "I cannot *wait*. Why should I take such a risk?"

The bird screeches and flaps its large wings in a disgruntled fashion. Perhaps it's the one the man converses with. In appearance, the creature is similar to a sea eagle, only larger, with beautiful iridescent feathers of black and gold shimmering in the harsh light.

An enormous sun burns low in the teal-colored sky behind the prince. Therefore, it must be late afternoon in this strange land—Talamh Cúig, I believe he called the city. I shift my gaze sideways but don't find any buildings.

I clear my dry throat as well as I can while in the middle of being strangled. "Did you give me the true name of your home?"

Gem-bright eyes narrow as he shifts his weight from one heavy black boot to the other. "My kind cannot lie. But you already know that, don't you?"

I do *now* thanks to him declaring it so.

Attempting to calm my trembling, I take slow, shallow breaths and ponder what he might mean by *his* kind—surely he's only a

29

human who's mastered the dark art of sorcery. Is he a warlock or a druid?

Other than the sharp, crystal-covered tree that currently bruises my spine, as far as the eye can see, the land is a dazzling wash of red, yellow, and orange, the landscape as barren as a desert.

On first inspection, the kingdom this man guards is not particularly attractive.

Where are all the plants and flowers?

Despite the lack of greenery, a herb and citrus scent cuts through the overpowering note of leather and horse, teasing my senses. Plant aromas are intoxicating to me, and this man's body smells like the deepest part of the forest.

I inspect his long, shiny dark hair, the strong and strikingly handsome features, his muscled body dressed in the gold-embellished, molded leather of a warrior, and decide that the beauty of his people likely makes up for the plainness of their land.

"Will you let me go? It's clear I'm no threat to someone of your size who possesses a deadly weapon." Plus, there are the strong, callused fingers poised to snap my neck.

He glowers. "*Enough.* Be quiet."

His gaze drops away, and he mutters at the ground, then nods sharply. Unless he can communicate silently with his eagle, he must be addressing an unseen entity. Or he's insane. I'm not sure which option I prefer.

"Who... who are you talking to?" I ask, swallowing twice to moisten my throat.

Gritting his teeth, he presses his flawless face and eyes of blue wildfire even closer. His skin is a marvel, fluctuating with his emotions from tanned to the polished white of marble. Never before have I seen such breathtaking angular perfection in a man's features. And never have I been so frightened and, at the same time, determined to hide it.

"I'm battling with the chaos of my mind, witch. Isn't it obvious I am mad?"

I would like to agree, but think it's best to humor him instead.

"Well, I hope you aren't because it might be hard to talk an irrational person out of murder."

"You're out of luck. I have a sickness in the blood, a poison. If my suspicions are correct and you're in league with the wind sorceress, you will be familiar with the likes of curses and hexes."

My pulse roars in my ears. Why does he think I'm in partnership with the sorceresses who dragged me into his world? Or even more ludicrous, believe me to be a witch?

Iolite eyes search my face. "This poison I bear rots my mind. It darkens my heart and soul and brings constant cravings for violence and death."

The eagle shifts its weight from talon to talon on Gade's broad shoulders, chirping softly in his ear as though to calm him. I wish the beast great success in the endeavor.

"That is unfortunate for you," I say, trying not to squirm under the bite of his blade. "But I swear I've never met those ladies until today." I gesture helplessly at the sky. "If indeed, it is *still* today. Who knows how long I've been lying under this tree? Do you know, Gade?"

"Your words sound soft and laced with sweetness, but your pretend innocence doesn't fool me. All you need to know is *this* is the day you'll meet your end. And—"

A high-pitched screech followed by a rumbling growl sounds behind us, growing louder as it comes closer. The eagle swivels its head, then crouches low before launching into the air in the direction of the horrid noise.

"No, Lleu!" Gade releases me, stalking several paces behind the tree to peer after the bird. I look around the trunk and see a large red-skinned boar disappearing over a hill; the eagle flying above it.

Seizing my arm and dragging me along in a trail of dust, the man says, "You have a reprieve, witch. Your life has been saved by a wild pig."

"Where are we going? Somewhere terrifying no doubt."

"To the northern section of Ithalah Forest."

Well that means nothing to me. "Is it far? And don't you have a horse?"

"Yes, and that is precisely where we shall find him, somewhere in the forest making himself sick on birch bark. He's a glutton for it. We'll follow my eagle, Lleu. He has a vendetta against the sacred boar and hopes to kill it. I must follow and stop him from doing something foolish."

We crest the hill, and the man stops and scowls toward a distant line of trees, while I pant and wipe sweat from my brow.

His eyes fix on me. "What ails you? You sound close to death."

I fan my face with the hood of my cape. "I'm half-strangled and thirsty. Humans can't survive in intense heat for long without water."

He huffs and holds out his right hand, the strange tattoo on the back of it glowing brightly before he flips it over. "Here," he says gruffly as water spins in a tiny vortex on his palm.

I stumble backward. "How did you do that?"

"Magic, as you guessed earlier. How else?"

Sweat beads my lip as a shocking realization settles in my chest. This man isn't a human warlock. He's a monster. A devil from the old tales. My limbs tremble, and I force them to still. "Is this safe to drink?"

"Of course. Do it now before I take it away to punish your ingratitude."

"But how do I—"

He looks to the heavens. "Simply bend and take a sip! Do witches need special devices in order to complete basic tasks?"

"Are you deaf? I'm not a witch. Stop repeating that ridiculous idea."

"Whatever you are," he growls out, leaning close, "you'd do well to stop telling me what to do."

The thought of drinking from his palm appalls me, but raging thirst soon overrides my disgust. I cup my hands around his, a jolt of energy sparking over my skin, and I drink and drink and drink under the scorching heat of his focused attention.

"That's enough," he says gruffly, ripping his hand away as the water vanishes. "You'll make yourself sick if you guzzle it like a dying kelpie."

A kelpie? He speaks of the mythical water horses I've heard spoken of in village tales as if he rode one only yesterday. "Are you a man or a magical creature?" I ask.

He gives me a strange look, then tugs me up the barren hillside. "Surely you've heard of the sidhe, the Tuatha de Dannan."

I know what he speaks of—those devious beings made of magic and mischief—and I shudder to think one of *their* kind might hold my life in his hands.

He takes my silence as a sign of ignorance. "No? Then mayhap you know of us as the Fair Folk or the Good People." He laughs. "Of course, the second description is absurd. We are anything but *good.*"

"So, then you're a... *faery?*"

He looks sideways, studying me with suspicion. "For a witch, you appear to know very little. What else did you think I might be? A leprechaun?"

"Certainly not. For one, you're far too large to be one of *those.*"

His gaze lingers on my mouth, then with a sneer, he dismisses me and strides ahead, clouds of red dirt exploding under his heavy, knee-high boots. I have no choice but to follow in his wake, stumbling to keep up, my skirts dragging in the dust as I go.

We walk until my feet ache, blisters swelling on my skin, the distant trees growing ever closer. Even trailing about ten paces behind the man, I can hear him muttering to himself.

I run to catch up. "What does your bird have against the boar?" I ask, hoping to distract him from the dark thoughts that enrage him. I need this supposed faery guard calm so he doesn't swing his sword back and slice my head from my shoulders.

The leather-crossed muscles of his upper-back stiffen, then a long silence passes. Curses are spat out, then, finally, he says, "Many years ago, the red boar shook my eagle's fledglings from their nest, killing his mate in the fight that ensued. Lleu yearns for revenge, but the boar is sacred, and if Lleu murders the beast, our laws decree he must be put to death. And that, I cannot allow."

Before the birch and ash trees of the forest swallow us, the squeals and screeches of a battle assault my ears. The self-declared faery darts off, leaping over logs, pushing through brambles and branches, and I stumble through the undergrowth, trying my best not to lose sight of him instead of running in the opposite direction.

This man has vowed to kill me, but even so, he might be my only chance to survive in this strange land I know little about.

Finally, I come out into a small, mossy clearing to a horrifying sight.

Gade stands with his chest pumping, fists clenched at his sides, watching the eagle and boar tumble in a blur of feathers and talons, tusks and drooling fangs.

"*Wait*," I call as he dives into the fray with a guttural battle cry.

I lurch backward and hide behind a silver birch trunk, my heart pounding, unsure whether to run for my life or wait to see the outcome of the brawl.

Three creatures roll and roar before my eyes, smashing across the forest floor as they attempt to tear each other apart—one a faery beset by madness, the other two, raging wild creatures. There is a sudden explosion of heat, and a wall of flames leaps high, then the eagle bursts through the blaze into the trees above.

When the flames clear, Gade has his arm locked around the squealing boar's neck. Struggling to his feet, he throws the animal into the air, and it lands in the distance with a crack then a loud thud.

The eagle screeches from a branch, crouching low as if preparing to take flight, and the fae whips around, glaring at it.

"Stop," he yells, clutching his side as he lies on the ground, thick blood dripping between his fingers. The eagle turns his yellow eyes on the fae, its tawny head canting to the side.

"Lleu, do not forget you have bound yourself in my service. Have we not been companions and the best of friends since childhood? I forbid you from chasing the boar, vile creature though it is. It has done you and yours the greatest of harm; I know this. But vengeance will only bring about your death, and I cannot face life with this curse without you by my side."

The eagle bows its head, the great glossy wings drooping.

"Please, my friend, don't go after the boar. Look—my lifeblood drips from me. The wound is deep. Take word to the castle. Bring help."

For long moments, the bird watches the fae pant, then in a loud rustle of leaves, he launches into the sky.

"Come," grunts Gade, beckoning me toward him. "Lleu won't forsake us."

When exactly did he and I become an *us*?

Standing in front of him, I wring my skirts with my hands. Should I help this unhinged man who not long ago held a blade to my throat? Or is this the perfect opportunity to escape him?

If I run, I might get eaten by a wild animal. Or worse, be captured by a fae who's hale, instead of weak and injured, strong enough to torture me for all eternity.

I've heard the stories about beautiful faery monsters who capture humans for their own evil devices, exchanging our newborn babes for misshapen changelings. Even though I never believed the tales, they captivated and terrified me. And now, here I am...

trapped in Faery with a real-life fae who is bleeding out before my eyes.

This is my last chance to run.

Right now.

With a loud sigh, I kneel beside him, the rough ground scraping my skin as I unstrap a panel of his armor. I inspect the wound, and he hisses out a breath. A gash as long as my hand runs across the lower left side of his belly where the boar's tusk gouged through a slit in the layered leather, the edges of the wound a ragged, bloody mess. His vital organs appear to be healing slowly with magic, but infection could be his undoing.

"Can your power heal me, witch? I've used my reserves of magic to mend the worst of the damage and can summon no more." Narrowed with pain, his eyes search my face. "If you choose to heal rather than harm, I vow that when I'm able, I shall take you to my kingdom. There, you can plead your case of innocence and seek assistance. Fae cannot lie, so you must know I speak the truth."

All the tales about his kind agree. Fae cannot lie. I believe he speaks the truth. My chances of surviving in this place without him are slim. I glance around the forest floor carpeted in thick moss, perfect for dressing a wound.

I will help him. It's my best chance of finding a way home.

"As I've been trying to tell you, I have no magic to call upon. But luckily for you, I do know plants and herbs and will do my best to assist you."

Brushing off my skirts, I make my way over to a pale-green cushion of moss. I extract two large plants, pluck debris from the layers of withered stems, then return to the wounded faery.

"Lie back," I tell him, ripping a strip of thin muslin from my underskirt to wrap the moss in.

"Swear you'll do your best to heal my wound, and we will call a truce until we arrive at Castle Black."

Does he not know how little most humans' vows are worth? Not mine, though. I'm a woman of honor, and I keep my promises. "I swear it. Every move I make will be to help you and never to harm."

"On your ailing mother's life?"

My heart pounds. "Yes. I will do as I've promised. I swear it on my mother's life."

He nods, and I quickly pack the wound, then bandage his torso with more strips of material from my skirts. As I work, his warm breath pants against my ear. Magical tattoos bloom over his skin, flaring blood red one moment, then disappearing.

"This will staunch the bleeding and disinfect your wound. How long before your eagle will bring assistance?"

"A few days, not many more. Soon it will be dark, and we need somewhere safe to sleep. I'll use the last of my powers to find my horse." He winces, pushing dark hair off his brow. "There's an abandoned shepherd's hut nearby, kept stocked with wood and some dried food. We'll go there."

"All right. I can see no better option. Hurry, call your horse."

His eyes close, his breaths deepening. He whispers guttural words I can't decipher. With a grunt, he falls backward against the ground, panting as if he expended great energy.

Several moments pass.

"Nothing's happening," I say, looking around us. Trees sway in a gentle breeze, and a few creatures scrabble through the brush.

"Shush," he says. "I'm concentrating."

After another moment, his glowing eyes open, and he smiles over my shoulder. A chestnut horse with the glossiest coat I've ever seen is silently picking its way over fallen branches toward us.

"How was the birch bark you abandoned me for, Wren?" the fae asks. "Tasty?"

The horse whinnies and bares its teeth as though laughing.

"Very funny. Now help me rise, my friend."

The beast lowers its head. Gade wraps his arms around the muscled neck and staggers to his feet. With a grunt, he swings into the saddle. "Mount behind me," he commands.

After a brief struggle with the difficult angles, I manage to haul myself up behind him, blood from his leather armor slick on my fingers. Wiping it on my skirt, I shudder at the sticky feel of it.

"Be at ease," he tells me. "'Tis old blood. Your moss has stopped the flow for now." He clicks his tongue, and the horse moves forward.

As the sun lowers, our pace is slow and steady, the sounds of creatures settling in their forest beds comforting. My nerves are rattled by my body's proximity to this supernatural being—a ruthless fae creature who, even injured, if he set his mind to it, could finish me off with not much effort.

Everything about him disturbs me. The breadth of the chest I cling to, his heat, his heart's thud against my palm, and the worst thing, his scent—metallic blood, musky leather, and the pungent tang of the woods.

I breathe slowly and concentrate on staying in the saddle as we head down a steep incline crossed with fallen trees and boulders.

I rack my brain for more knowledge of the Fair Folk. The tales told are varied and often contradictory. Are they petty, vengeful creatures who delight in causing crops to fail if a farmer displeases them? Fallen angels cast from heaven? Or devils forged in the fires of hell? Whatever the answer, I know I'm in grave danger and must stay alert to survive.

As the trees grow thicker, a solemn atmosphere thrums in the air, as if the dark mood of my injured companion affects the environment we travel through.

Questions plague my mind. If I can escape the fae, how will I find a way to return to my realm? What do my mother and sister think has happened to me? They must be beside themselves with worry.

"Why is the forest so quiet?" I ask to distract myself from my spiraling thoughts.

He sighs. "The creatures of mud and feather sense the taint in my blood and fear it. They fear *me*. But lo, the trees are not afraid and speak to us as we pass. Can you not hear them?"

"Of course not. How many times must I tell you I have no magical abilities for you to believe me?"

"Who knows? Five thousand times or ten," he answers sulkily.

I snort. "What do the trees say to you?"

"Each one has its own tale, and they gladly tell it to any traveler who cares to listen. A mortal's senses must be quite deficient if you can't hear them."

I bite my lip, swallowing my rude reply. I need to humor him and stay alive—find my way home to Mother before she passes to the Otherworld, which after today, I find myself believing in a little more. I must help her. I must say goodbye.

In the dimming light, we travel onward, the unnatural hush of the forest creating an uneasy sensation in my belly. Gade speaks to the horse every now and again but only grunts if I dare ask how much farther we have to travel or inquire about the plants I see, some of which I don't recognize. The journey seems never-ending, and wounded or not, the faery guard proves to be an insufferable, intolerant companion.

After a time, we break through thick brush into a clearing, the golden dusk setting our skin aglow.

"We're here," says the fae.

Nestled halfway up the cleft of a shallow valley, a stone hut comes into view, a ring of fruit trees embracing it. It makes for a pretty scene to be sure, but the cottage looks tiny, and I shiver at the thought of being cooped up in there with the fae for even one night.

He brings the horse to a stop by a four-stall wooden stable at the side of the house.

"Get off," he says in a low growl. "In case you've forgotten, I'm injured and cannot dismount until you have done so."

I slide to the ground and glare up at him. My eyes sweep over the structure that is soon to be our refuge. "How many rooms does this hut have?"

"Seventy-five," he says, then winces and curses. "Actually, only one." Throwing a leg over the horse, he groans and lands on the ground less than an arm's length away from me.

Too close.

My heart kicks against my ribs. "How many beds?"

A wicked smirk plays over his lips. "There is a bed for each room."

"So only one?"

"That's what I said, didn't I?"

By the maggots. How will I cope in such close confines with this maddening creature? Perhaps I'll renege on my promise and let him die after all. Or hasten his end along.

Right now, I'm so glad I can lie and he can't.

"Come," he says, pushing through the vine-covered door.

Squaring my shoulders, I take a deep breath and follow.

5

The Healer

Gade

The hut looks exactly the same as last time I was here, only covered in several more layers of dust. It's dark and claustrophobic, the very opposite of the light-filled palace overlooking the wild Emerald Sea that I'm known to prowl around, seeking rare shadows to hide in.

In truth, this desolate hut perfectly matches my soul's dark yearnings.

I wonder what type of living quarters the witch is accustomed to?

Whether it be a forest cave or a fiery pit, I shouldn't waste my energy thinking about her. If the mortal species is as far beneath faeries as I've been told, then this girl is like a rat in a cellar compared to a prince accustomed to reigning on a throne of gold.

Gazing around the hut, her teeth worry her bottom lip, then she squares her shoulders and turns to me. "Lie down. I'll start the fire."

I stumble toward the bed, then collapse onto it, grateful to be reclining again. She watches me pant, pity etched on her broad, even features. Longing pangs in my chest for my magic to be as it once was—powerful and unconquerable.

I despise being weak in anyone's presence, and for unknown reasons, more so in *hers*. I guess because she is only a lowly human, it grates me, a prince, to be at her mercy.

"There's a freshwater well behind the hut and dried meat in the larder. It will soon be dark. Do not waste the last of the light."

With a brief nod, she sweeps a shrewd yellow gaze over me, and then hurries through the door, a wooden pail swinging from her fingers. I close my eyes and release the groan I've been suppressing. A few days' rest is all I need to restore my powers to their base level, which unfortunately while I'm curse-affected, isn't very impressive.

I refuse to die in this hut.

I cannot.

And I won't.

I must live to save my kingdom.

As a reward for tending me, I won't take the little witch's life until after the Court of Five has assessed her. This is fair, but since she might also be my only hope for survival, it's the wisest course of action. I'll curb my desire to wring her fragile neck and watch her closely in case she breaks her vows and tries to finish me off at the first opportunity.

The witch makes three trips to the well for water, followed by a lengthy expedition to gather plants and grasses, then returns and starts a fire in the hearth. Since I can't raise even a tiny Elemental spark, I resign myself to lie still, grateful for the warmth.

I roll onto my side and stare at the flames dancing across her body as night's fingers creep over the floor and shadow the hut's rendered walls. With each breath I draw, the fire transforms her from a shadowy wraith to a demon with her hellish eyes ablaze. It is unsettling, and although I long to look elsewhere, I cannot tear my gaze from the feverish vision.

"Lie on your back so you don't strain your wound," she orders.

I obey, then turn my head and watch as she boils water in the pots that hang over the flames.

She takes tubers from deep pockets in the apron tied over her skirts, peels and slices them quickly with a herb-cutting knife produced from one of her poor-quality boots, and places them in the larger vessel before tossing the grasses and herbs into the smaller pot.

While she works, she keeps her back turned and gaze fixed on her tasks. "Tell me about your people's magic," she murmurs. "How does it work? Will you turn into a beast at any moment and rip me to shreds? Before you waste what little energy you have, know this: first, nothing you do will make me cower. And second, the last thing you'll see is me crying in front of you."

"I wouldn't be so certain of that. Anyway, I'm not interested in your tears at present. Perhaps when I'm feeling better."

For a moment, I consider telling her as little as possible about my magic, then decide it doesn't matter. *Knowledge* won't help her overcome me. I am still a prince of the Land of Five. For now, while

I'm injured, she has the advantage. But soon, I'll heal, and then the witch will be at *my* mercy.

"In my land, we have Elemental magic. Most fae control only one element, but I can manipulate all four at will and sometimes even the fifth, which is spirit."

She waits for me to elaborate—but there are two things I cannot tell her. I control the elements because I am the heir to the Throne of Five. And as a result of the curse's progression, my control of them weakens daily. These things are none of her business.

After washing a wooden mug, she fills it with herbs then boiling water. A pungent smell fills the room, watering my eyes.

"But you can't perform this magic while you're injured, am I right?" She passes me the brew. "Drink this. It will ease your pain, ward off infection, and help you sleep."

Sleep? I do not wish to sleep while in *her* company. This human sorceress will likely smother me.

The first few sips of the potion are hot and bitter, then warmth seeps into my muscles and settles my body's tremors.

While I drink, she searches through the larder followed by every drawer in the hut. I could point out where certain items are stored, but I don't. I prefer to watch her grow frustrated, huff, and click her tongue. It provides me with a much-needed, albeit petty, form of entertainment.

Finally, she finds strips of dried meat and adds them to the pot of tubers, allowing the mix to simmer. After a time, she wakes me from a doze by holding a steaming bowl of food under my nose.

"Here. Eat." She helps me sit against the bed's headboard, then takes a seat at the rectangular table in the center of the room and sips from her own bowl.

"I'm not hungry." My words are thick and slurred, likely the effect of the herbal potion. After drinking a whole mug of it, I cannot stomach a full meal as well.

"Human bodies require food to heal properly," she says. "Surely this is true for fae or whatever mythical species you claim to belong to. If you wish to recover quickly, I recommend you swallow every mouthful."

I sigh and begin to eat, wincing at the bland flavor. Rather than doing what she bids, I'd prefer to argue the point, but my thoughts move through my mind like sludge, and I can't think of one comment to annoy her with. I am tired, and my energy wanes with each labored breath.

To prevent my eyelids from closing, I concentrate on the firelight flickering over my odd companion. Writhing flames turn her locks blood red and twist her generous lips into a sneer. As I swallow my last mouthful of food, my lids defeat my will and close.

I drag them open. "Tell me, sorceress..." My words trail off as smoke clouds my head.

"Good," I hear her say. "The herbs have done their job."

Then her words run together, sounding like an incantation, a dark spell, barely audible over the spit and crackle of the fire.

"Don't kill me until I wake," I slur as sleep drags me into the abyss.

6

By the Creek

Gade

When I wake the next morning in searing pain, for a moment, I wonder if the witch is slicing me into pieces to add to one of her putrid-smelling stews. If she did, she'd find no fat upon my bones, only muscle, and I would not be very tasty.

Cracking my eyes open, I peer around the hut, searching for the girl. Pale light streams through the sole, high window next to the door, faintly illuminating the room.

The ash-filled hearth, long table, narrow bench that runs along the rear wall, and tall larder positioned next to it, all look as they did last night. The only thing missing is the witch.

The girl may not have hacked my head from my shoulders while I slept like the dead, drugged by her potion, but it appears she has unwisely used the time I was unconscious to escape.

Fury clouds my vision, and for three heartbeats, all I see is red, a river of blood, not mine—hers.

All is well, says the poison in my veins. *If she still lives, she is yours and can never escape you.*

The curse is right.

She's likely already dead, her small body lying cold in the woods, a tasty meal for wolves and the wilder fae creatures who'll happily consume any weak being they chance upon—dead or living.

Why does the image of her broken bones and gnawed flesh strike dread through my entire being?

With a grunt, I brace my wound with my hand, leap out of bed, and prepare to hunt her down.

As my feet hit the packed-dirt floor, a wave of nausea engulfs me. Pain burns deep in my gut and in the marrow of my bones. I'm accustomed to the agony of my cursed blood coursing through my veins, but these sensations nearly bring me to my knees.

Lifting the edge of the bandage around my stomach, I see a neat row of stitches. How did I manage to sleep through *that*? The room spins around me, ash and smoke coating my throat as I choke and cough. I wheeze like a changeling rattling their last breath, revolted by my weakened state.

The door slams open, and the girl strides through it, a skinned rabbit dangling from one hand and a pail of water from the other.

A frowning glance near slices me in two. "What are you doing out of bed? Lie down. *Now*, please, if you will, or you'll start the bleeding off again."

Another wave of sickness strikes, and I reach for the bed, collapsing back onto it.

"Thank you," she says.

"Of course," I say in my haughtiest voice. "Don't hesitate to inform me how else I may be of service. I am eager to please you."

My fingers grip the blanket as I brace for the stabbing pain from uttering a lie, but even though I spoke the words aloud, none hits, which baffles me.

Scratching my chin, I consider how my words might be true. Deep down, I must know she is likely the only thing saving me from a slow death, and that in my current vulnerable state, I would be wise to humor her. To *help* her even.

Yes. That explains it nicely.

I draw a sharp breath, preparing to test my theory and, hopefully, ruffle her feathers at the same time. "I would love nothing more than to satisfy your every whim with haste."

Pain strikes my temples, drawing a curse through my lips. I suppose that's what I get for stretching the truth to a ridiculous degree. I deserved that. No more mocking comments from me today. Or at least until after I've survived lunch and whatever horrid-tasting concoction she might choose to feed me.

I rub my temples, and she smiles smugly before setting wood in the hearth, then lighting the fire with speed and skill. "It hurts when you talk balderdash, doesn't it, fae? Serves you right for lying, then."

"Addressing me by the name of my species is not only ignorant but insulting," I say, changing the subject swiftly.

"Is that why you do the same to me, then? To insult me?" Pots clang as she hangs them on hooks above the fire, then she turns and scowls at me. "Would you prefer Mister Fae? Or perhaps Commander Fae? I'm assuming by your arrogant personality that you hold a fairly high rank in your royal guard or army."

Well, I can't really comment on my rank without giving too much away. In the Land of Five, the heir to the throne is not *in* the army, he's the head of it.

Sighing, I slump backward, and my skull thumps against the wall before sliding down onto the pillow. "Just Gade will do." I wince, then smirk. "And I shall continue to call you *witch*."

"Do it out loud again, and I shall acquaint your ballocks with that hot poker over there."

I have no doubt she would. She seems a vicious enough female to follow through with her threats.

"How in the realms did you manage to catch the rabbit?" I ask as she prepares a stew with brisk movements, breaking bones and tearing flesh and sinews from the animal with practiced movements. Perhaps she was a servant in the mortal realm.

"The usual way. I set a trap."

I grunt and pull my weight onto my elbows to ensure a better view of her as she buzzes around the room like an angry bee.

"My father and brothers are dead. My mother is sick and my sister uninterested in getting either dirt or blood beneath her nails. I learned how to hunt to survive. But royal guards who live in palaces likely have no idea of the trials humans who aren't members of the gentry face. Keeping our bellies full is constant and exhausting work."

"Human lives have never been of interest to me. If indeed you are one, as you claim," I say, affecting a disinterested tone, even though I find my curiosity kindling hot.

Like me, this girl has only one living sibling, but thanks to the Merit fae, I am worse off than her, since neither of my parents are alive.

Painful memories assault me.

Many moons ago, King Bryar and Queen Aisheel embarked on a diplomatic journey to the dark kingdom and never returned. The Merit king, El Sanartha, claimed they disappeared before they arrived, wiping his hands of any responsibility and blaming wild Unseelie fae outside the borders of their city, who he claims no authority over.

Since the Merit cannot lie, elements of truth must exist in his story. Still, I'm certain he was involved in their demise. If not by action, then at least by design. It must be so. And when I gain control of the curse, marry my fated one, restoring my strength and power, I will make the Merit king pay.

Forever.

You may never find your bride, the curse whispers. *And if you do, she may not think you worthy of her.*

Nonsense. I will never stop looking for the fae who is destined to rule by my side. And the curse tells lies—I know that.

I remind myself that I was an obedient, if somewhat reckless, son who was always faithful to the crown. Those traits may not have served my parents well on the day of their demise, nor my kingdom in the years that have followed, but I believe they make me a worthy mate.

When I find this girl, I will know her, for she will love me instantly, just as a fated one should. And I'll repay her with my honor and a queen of Faery's crown.

When my parents disappeared, the high mage forbade me from marching the Court of Five's army onward to destroy the Merits. Instead, she counseled peace.

She refused to risk my death and the crown falling to my cousin Elden, the fae closest in line to the throne. Although, he's a little too fond of revels, tricks, and ruses, I believe Elden would do a decent job of ruling. But since Ether is the spirit, the key to our Elemental magic, her word must always be obeyed.

It took twelve moons for my parents' bones to be found and returned to us and thirty-six more for my heart to fully rot in my chest. But when the curse is quelled, I will have my revenge. I vow it with each and every sunrise I greet.

"Are you still awake?" the witch asks, jolting me from my morbid thoughts.

"Of course. You were explaining why you have the skills of a huntress. And I was over here showing little interest."

"Then allow me to finish boring you. In my world, villagers are hungry and many of us die from starvation. Most humans are poor. No doubt that makes us pitiful in your opinion."

"Mortals are beneath my notice. Why should I care? There must exist a noble class, well placed to assist."

"That's not how it works. Wealthy folk only care for lining their own pockets and ensuring enough villagers remain alive to perform tasks they don't want to do themselves."

"Fascinating." I grunt as pain strikes my temples. "Where did you sleep last night?" I ask, wondering if she had dared to rest beside me on this narrow bed.

"Mostly, I stayed awake, sewing you up, cooling your fever, then chopping wood by lantern light. Close to dawn, I took some rest by the fire."

"I admit I'm surprised you didn't attempt to flee while I was asleep." Emphasis on the word *attempt*. Even in my current state—wounded, weak—I would never *allow* her to escape from me.

She sighs. "I'm not so foolish. If I had tried, I'd be dead already."

Or worse than dead. Captured by any number of wild creatures, at this very moment, she could be enduring the most unpleasant of tortures. Forever pain, devised by fae who feed on the screams of their victims is not a very good way to die, but it's most certainly one of the longest.

"I won't run. I promise." She hands me a bowl of fragrant rabbit stew. "My only way to return home is likely with help from your people."

"Why don't you use your witch's powers and locate a portal?"

She crosses her arms over her chest. "Because I don't possess magic, and I couldn't transform this gown from shabby to fine to save my life, let alone locate a portal in Faery. When will you realize that I'm exactly what I say I am—a human, not a witch?"

I study her long-limbed, supple body. She is taller than tales told of human women, but height alone does not a sorceress make. I am not often incorrect. But could I possibly be wrong about this? About *her.*

Squinting in the smoky light, I study her carefully. The smooth brow, broad cheekbones, uncompromising pale-gold eyes, and her unsmiling wide mouth are all attractive enough for her unremarkable species, I suppose. And her rough hands and brusque manner tell me she is competent and used to hard work.

In contrast, enchantresses often possess ethereal beauty, soft skin, and clothes woven from magical fibers—the very opposite of this girl before me. I suppose I must take her word and accept that she is mortal. A young one at that.

Still, I cannot forget it was Aer who brought her here. Aer, the being who is the root cause of all my troubles and of all that ails my kingdom. Therefore, the human is not to be trusted. Under any circumstances.

After we finish our meal in silence, she cleans my wound and applies a foul-smelling poultice, the firelight casting an orange glow over the walls and her lightly tanned skin.

Time flows slowly while I lie unmoving, lost in delirium, and watch her bustle in and out of the door, prepare meals, and tend to my wound. I begin to wonder if perhaps two, three, or even more days have passed. I cannot tell.

Each moment spent in this hovel blends images of the girl into one continuous, feverish nightmare. Her brisk movements. Her impatient sighs when I don't move my limbs fast enough for her to perform her ministrations. Her palms, scalding my flesh. Somehow it is both horrifying and strangely pleasurable to be so completely and utterly at her mercy.

She works efficiently, only speaking if necessary, and I'm at least grateful not to be subjected to constant mind-numbing prattle. But there is one problem with her tight-lipped, reticent nature, my senseless curiosity cannot be satisfied, which makes her all the more intriguing.

Why should a prince of Faery be fascinated by a lesser being? Boredom likely explains it.

Without warning, she pushes my shoulder, jarring my attention from the thatched roof above the bed to her steady, honeyed gaze. "Come, fae. It's time to get up."

"What?" I ask, confused.

"I said, get up," she repeats.

"How many days have we been here?"

"We're nearing the end of the second, and it's time you bathed."

"Only two? What? *Bathe*? Unlike what I have heard about humans, fae do not sweat, and we don't require daily washing. We only bathe for pleasure."

A sandy eyebrow rises. "Well then, for the sake of your wound, it's time to take your pleasure."

My mouth falls open as I replay her words, stuck on their double meaning. Her cheeks darken, and I chuckle. "Ah, frail human, there's no need to fear me in this state. Any tryst with you could not be categorized as a *pleasure*. You are safe from me for now. I vow it." I shuffle to sit on the edge of the bed and point at my chest. "Do you perhaps have designs on *me*? Human men are no doubt lacking in many ways. I'm sure I am rather... *stimulating* to your senses."

Scowling like an irate pixie, she visibly tamps down anger.

I give her my most annoying smile.

"In any event, water will revive your mind and clean your wound. Stop your prattling and stand up."

Me? Prattling? I shoot onto my feet, then stagger sideways, my skull thudding against the top of the door frame.

From behind me, the girl wraps a blanket around my bare back and ushers me through the door into blinding daylight. "Wait, I'll retrieve your boots."

"There is no need. I could easily run up the side of an erupting volcano without them," I boast.

"How pleasant for you," she says in a mocking tone. "I send congratulations to your manly pride and condolences to the skin on your feet."

I harrumph, then give her a wicked smile. "I see you've relieved me of the burden of my clothes," I say as she scurries along to keep up with me. "How daring of you."

"Only your top section. I promise I didn't enjoy the task," she says in a tone that suggests I am hideous to look upon, which is *absolutely* not true.

"Well, humans can lie," I say, tripping over a rock and quickly righting myself. "I'm sure you delighted in it."

She takes my arm roughly. "Here, let me help you. You're still weak. I don't want you to fall and me have to carry you all the way back."

"Are you sure of that?" I tease. "You seem the type who might enjoy a challenge." Fighting nausea, I shrug her off and lengthen my stride toward the narrow creek that winds through the valley behind the hut. "Have you been caring for Wren?"

"Your horse?"

"No, my tiny faithful bird." The sky spins around me, and I stop to swallow bile, vowing to forgo sarcastic taunts until I am at least a little stronger and to visit Wren on the return journey.

"Your horse fares well. To maintain his condition, I rode him along the valley this morning."

"Another lie. Wren only allows *me* to ride him."

"And now me, proving you are perhaps not the most important being in the entire world. He has a lovely temperament, and you're very fortunate to own such a magnificent and obliging beast."

Wren obliging? No. She is mistaken. Did she dream it? I cast my gaze along her body, wondering what she's made of—foolishness or courage? Certainly something sturdier than most human girls.

We pick our way down a lightly treed slope and stop on the mossy edge of the creek bed. The six-pointed star glyph on my hand flares as I breathe deeply, the sun on the back of my head providing energy.

Yes, the human is right. A swim is a fine idea. I shuck off the blanket, work the buckle on my belt, and then unfasten my leather pants.

The girl yelps. "Wait until I turn around."

"For what reason? I don't care if you look upon my body."

"Well, I *do*. And I'd rather not endure the sight, thank you very much."

"Your loss. I am well built and agreeable of form. You should hold back your thanks until *after* you've enjoyed the sight."

A choked noise escapes her.

With difficulty, I peel off my trousers, toss them into the air, and then stagger into the water, using reeds and tree roots to stay upright. As I sink to my knees, water rising to my chest, a burden lifts from my mind, then deep peace flows through me as I lie back and float.

"It is quite safe for the overly modest among us to look now," I say, watching her kick stones from the bank, then search beneath them. For what, I have no clue.

"What do you seek?" I ask.

"A type of healing moss." She swings around and meets my gaze. "Do you feel any better?"

Sifting my hands and arms through the water, I grin, gratified to see her cheeks darken. "Yes, human. This was a worthy idea."

"Good. I'll refresh the poultice and your bandage as soon as we return."

"I have no doubt." My hair splays across the creek's surface as if it has a mind of its own, her gaze tracking the sinuous movement.

"Gade?" she says.

Shock courses through me at her use of my name, her gentle tone.

"When will your people come for you?"

"By the fourth day at the latest."

"Quite soon, then?"

"Yes. Unless something prevented Lleu from arriving home." Knowing the impulsive nature of my eagle, this is, unfortunately, more than possible. Fear settles like a block of ice in my gut.

Lleu may well have risked a detour to chase his enemy, the golden boar, and as a result, been captured by the dark being that protects the creature—the antlered annlagh who rises from hibernation when the boar is near death.

I swipe hair from my face. "My sister will come soon and provide a much-needed power boost to my magic. This will make the journey home safer for us. If she doesn't come, we'll have no option but to travel regardless of my lack of power."

"Then I hope Lleu is safe and your people are on their way," she says, inspecting my chest as though cataloging the scars and dark-colored glyphs marking my skin.

A surge of power licks through my veins. I stumble onto my feet, the water now up to my thighs. The girl screams and covers her face with her arm as I send a bolt of water magic across the creek. The surface sizzles, turning a deep shade of purple before clearing.

"Did you see what I did? Perhaps my power is returning," I say, hope blooming inside me.

"No," she says, peeking through her fingers. "I didn't want to risk an eyeful of... other things."

Laughter rumbles in my chest. I drop back into the water loudly, then spring up silently. "I have gone under the water again," I announce.

No pain blinds me, because my words are true. I *did* go under. And now I am out of it.

Pointing to the blue aura swirling near the bank in the distance, I say, "This is a sign of my healing."

I fight a grin as I wait for her to turn around. She does and emits a bloodcurdling scream. I lose my footing on the slippery stones and plunge backward into the creek, the cold fingers of two wraith-like river maids pulling me into the deepest part of the creek.

"Gade!" the human cries as I flail against the nymphs' hold.

Drawing on magic as I'm dragged beneath the water, I wrap my hands around a thin, blue neck and tug the black-eyed face closer. "Recognize your prince or die in ignorance, naiad," I say, bubbles rising to the surface.

Green hair strokes my face and chest as the river maids retract their claws, then bow to me before swimming away with haste, my name upon their wet indigo lips.

When I surface, spitting weeds and slicking long hair from my face, the mortal breaks into a wide, genuine smile, stunning me into silence.

"You are awful," she scolds, unaware that I was nearly made a meal of beneath the water. "Have you injured yourself in your attempt to embarrass me?"

"If I had, it would be worth it because now you know for certain that faeries are perfect in every way."

Scarlet washes over her cheeks.

Taunting her requires little effort, and I have no idea why it is so gratifying that I immediately begin to search for another way to make her blush.

Perhaps she has little experience with mortal men, which might explain why the sight of an unclothed body discomforts her. In this regard, we fae could be of service and teach her the many ways to enjoy her physical form. Not me, personally, of course. But in general, my species has much to offer her.

I bend and splash water on my chest to cool the heat igniting under my skin—likely, my fever is returning.

"All right," she says, dusting her hands on her skirts. "Since you're so perfect, you should be fine to return to the hut without my aid."

With her arms swinging, she marches up the hill, leaving me to wonder why the sight of her departing form fills me with bitter melancholy.

I climb onto the shadowed bank and attempt to summon a glamor of clothing, failing miserably. Then I don my trousers with clumsy movements and hurry after the girl.

How dare a mortal leave before I have dismissed her. If we were back at my court and she abused fae royalty in such a manner, she would be severely punished.

I laugh, thinking of the many ways I could make the mortal pay, then curse as the edges of my wound pull tight, all the while walking faster to catch up with her.

7

Mad Fae

Holly

The faery is mad.

Day and night, he raves about mages, magic, and a black poison that supposedly runs through his veins. He frightens and fascinates me in equal measure, and if it wasn't for my mother, rather than spend one more hour in his presence, I would tear into the woods—and risk death at the hands of an even more diabolical creature.

If I can't be there to ease Mother's suffering, I must at least arrive home in time to help her transition through the veil from this world to the next. Since I now reside in the realm of Faery, I can no longer deny that this Otherworld she believes in likely exists.

Today is the third day confined in the hut, and I long for it to be over. Not only is the fae frightening—his size, his every movement inspired by irrational thoughts—but he exudes a magnetism that prickles my skin and keeps my gaze lingering on his form and hard, masculine features.

As I finish scrubbing our lunch dishes, I turn at the creak of the bed, surprised to see the fae on his feet and stretching his arms as he yawns.

"I cannot endure this hut a moment longer," he says, settling on the edge of the mattress. "But every time I stand, I lose my balance. What poison do you feed me?"

"Poison? I wish. But had I done so, you'd already be dead, along with my chance of surviving this horrible place."

Slumping over his knees, he grunts.

"Come, let's get you outside. Fresh air and exercise will strengthen your muscles." I jam my hands under his armpits and heave. He doesn't budge. "Please don't resist. You're as heavy as three horses."

"When was the last time you carried a horse?" he says with a smirk.

"Just stand up, will you? Lean on me if you must."

"Your rough handling is turning my mind to indoor activities," he says, straight-faced and staring into my eyes. His ragged breath breezes over my mouth, and I jolt backward, shocked at how close our faces were.

"You ate enough lunch to feed an army, so you should exercise lest your muscles turn to jelly."

He laughs, those beguiling blue eyes sharpening, like a dog's when scenting prey. "Never. Pinch my flesh, stroke my skin. See for yourself how fit I am. Besides, there are other ways to burn energy than hiking over mountains and battle training."

Who said anything about battle practice?

"Goodbye, then," I say smoothing my skirt. "Enjoy your peace and quiet." With a wave of my hand, I head through the door. "I'll visit Wren, and then take a walk by myself."

"Wait," he calls out, his boots scuffing over stones as he follows close behind. "'Tis an excellent idea. I'm eager to see how Wren fares."

"If you pay attention," I say. "You'll find I have many wise ideas."

He grunts, lumbering up beside me. "Time will tell if that is so, mortal."

"Why do you take that everywhere?" I ask, indicating the long sword belted to his lean hips.

"Why? Because I'm not a fool. Would you prefer I had no weapon to protect you with should an assailant strike?

"That's unlikely—out here in the middle of nowhere."

He laughs, adding an unsteady swagger to his steps. "You're not in the human realm anymore. Out of the two of us, don't you think I'd know more about what is *likely* to happen? As I've told you before, if anyone comes to the hut while I'm asleep, slam the door and wake me immediately. They'll take advantage of my weakness, try to kill me. And, mortal, their plans for you don't bear contemplating."

"Of course I won't let anyone in."

"Good. Your healing drafts produce a heavy slumber. I would not wish to sleep through your demise."

No. He'd probably prefer to take an active role in it.

We cross the yard and duck into the small stable, both laughing at the scolding whicker Wren greets us with. The fae rubs the horse's neck and leads him out of the stall, murmuring in a foreign tongue.

He tucks the reins loosely into the horse's saddle bag and walks on, allowing Wren to either keep pace with us or stop to feast on grass as he wishes as we descend a hill toward a line of willow trees that graces the river bank.

I stop now and then to stuff my pockets with pungent self-heal, and the fae waits patiently by my side, circling his arms or lifting medium-sized rocks as if to improve blood flow through his limbs.

Color is returning to his cheeks. He looks much better than when we first arrived in this valley and Lady Death's hot breath dampened his neck.

"Don't lag too far behind in case you faint without my knowledge," I say as I skip ahead through an arch of silvery leaves hung from golden branches.

He glances back at Wren who is busy nibbling on birch bark, and then holding his wound, he jogs to my side. "When I've returned home, you'll bear witness to how fast I can move. How much stronger I am," he boasts.

A shadow crosses his face, his brows pinching together.

"What's wrong?" I ask.

"At least, I hope to be restored. Since the boar's strike, the curse seems to have gained the upper hand and triumphs more easily over my will."

"Do you think that's why your fever keeps spiking? It responds to my teas and breaks as it should, only to return over and over.

Yesterday morning you looked deathly, and then went on to chop wood in the afternoon. Human fevers don't behave this way."

"The poison in my blood works against my healing. It longs for my demise."

I snort. "The poison does? That's ridiculous. It isn't a sentient being with hopes and dreams."

"*Humans* clearly have little experience with curses; otherwise, you would understand this concept. When curses are conjured, ripped from the Otherworld by their creators, they squall like newborn brats and are indeed alive, seeking sustenance from your soul, as though it were mother's milk. They take over their hosts' minds, destroy their flesh and bones, but worst of all, their good hearts. Curses are parasites. For your information, I didn't always have a taste for violence."

"Many of my neighbors believe in curses and use protections against the meddling of *your* kind. They hang marigold garlands over barn doors in the hopes of preventing the Folk from riding our horses to death in the night. Some wear their coats inside out, sprinkle salt everywhere, carry iron nails in their pockets, or chime bells the moment their children take their first breaths to keep you faeries away."

He crosses his arms over his chest and looks me up and down. "These actions are naught but foolish games. If a fae wishes to meddle with a human, believe me, they will meddle. Besides, there are worse things than faeries; the creature who inflicted me with this curse, for example. All the bells and whistles and iron in the realms would not save you from *her* should she wish to cause you harm."

Up ahead, the purple flowers of vervain dance on the light breeze. They make a good tea for pain and insomnia. I stop and collect both blooms and leaves. The fae joins me, ripping a whole plant from its roots and passing it to me.

"Thank you," I say, stooping to re-cover the roots with dirt. "I have enough. These shouldn't be flowering yet. Plants behave oddly here and grow in strange places."

"Odd to *you* perhaps, but not to fae."

As we walk up the hillside that overlooks the winding river, Gade tugs my arm, his touch tingling all the way to my belly. A strange heat kindles there, filling me with a pleasurable guilt.

"Sit a moment. The view is pleasing here," he says, dropping to the ground and resting his elbows on his knees in a relaxed fashion. His eyes narrow as he presses against his wound, and I'm displeased to see it still pains him.

Inspecting his pointed ears, broad shoulders, and muscled arms, I feel the opposite of relaxed and make sure to sit a safe distance away from him. Although, perhaps I shouldn't be too worried. Since we've been in the hut, he hasn't tried to hurt me or expressed a serious wish to do so.

Sighing, I look about the landscape. The sky above is blue, the breeze mild, but storm clouds gather in the distance. I hope they're not headed our way anytime soon. I'm not thrilled with the idea of drying out soaked clothes while I potter about the hut dressed in my undergarments.

"We should return," Gade says, pointing at the clouds. "Storm's coming."

"Not yet," I reply, not sure if the reason I want to stay longer is to listen to the pleasant hum of insects or to do the opposite of his bidding. "Let's stay a while and hope for the best."

"You're an optimist." His lips make a sour shape as if positive people make unbearable company.

"I prefer to fret when I have cause to, not beforehand. And what makes you a proud pessimist? Life cannot be so bad for a magical creature, even a cursed one."

"Are you so sure of that?" Sighing, he lays back on the grass, clasping his hands behind his head.

Black hair forms a halo on the ground around him, like a puddle of spilled ink that I long to stain my fingers with.

I choke on an in-drawn breath. What a strange thought. Touching any part of this fae guard other than his wound would be foolish and dangerous.

"Talamh Cúig was once the most splendid city in all of Faery, but alas, my home slowly fades. With the heir to the crown weakened, the castle and its land are tethered to a dying magic. The royal family is cursed. The Court of Merits, our enemies, may rise against us at any time, taking advantage of our vulnerable condition. Only our High Mage's wards protect us from them, for the current Prince of Five is in no position to do so."

"Another cursed fae? It's beginning to sound like more faeries are afflicted than not. Take me back to the human realm as soon as possible, please. Faery land is not so nice a place as many humans have dreamed."

I pluck blue daisies from the grass and try not to admire the strong lines of Gade's handsome face. No man or woman I've looked upon comes close to possessing the beauty of this fae. How did I fool myself, even for a moment, into believing he was human?

"You mention the prince, but what about the king and queen?"

Dirt crumbles as his hand claws into the earth beside him. "They're deceased. Only a son and daughter survive them."

"And this prince, will he help me return home?"

Glowing arrows of blue pierce through me. "Perhaps he will. Perhaps he won't."

I suppose that is fair. How could a palace guard predict the behavior of his kingdom's ruler?

My stomach tightens as I think of my sister, Rose, then of Mother, huddled in her bed, in pain. Dread weaves through me at the thought I may never see either of them again.

Thunder growls in the distance, the rumble moving closer. "How did the king and queen die?" I ask.

"By the hand of evil," he growls out. "That is all you need know and all I will say on the matter."

"But, Gade—"

"Enough questions. Let me rest in peace."

"Where I come from, we say that when someone has died, so if I were you, I wouldn't use that turn of phrase and—"

Thunder booms, cutting me off, and the ground rolls beneath us. "What the devil is that?" I ask as lightning strikes the valley below, opening a chasm in the earth from which rocks and dirt explode.

Another blinding flash hits the ground to the left of us, and my companion makes a strangled sound. I leap to my feet, expecting to find the fae standing beside me. But instead, he's still lying on the ground, now in an awkward position, legs twisted and an arm frozen in mid-air above his belt, as if in the act of reaching for his sword.

"Gade! What's wrong?"

A terrible sound roars from the valley below, so loud my ears ache from the assault. It's as if a group of wounded bears all groan in pain and misery together.

I blink three times, barely able to believe what I see. A creature has risen from the upturned turf and now strides with malevolent purpose up the grassy incline toward us.

It is at least seven feet tall and has the body of a well-muscled man, the angled face of a fae, only more twisted and grotesque. Drool coats its wolf-like snout, and from a mess of dark, bushy hair, an enormous pair of golden antlers sprout, strung with delicate crystals that glint in the light.

"*Gade*, please hurry. Why don't you get up?" My eyes flick to the fae guard, finding him in the exact same position as the last time I looked, except for his eyes, which are wild with desperation and fixed on mine.

"That fae is no help to you, human," rumbles a voice that pricks the hairs on my neck. "I have cast a paralysis spell over him, and your fate is in my hands."

A wave of nausea spins my head. I face the creature and stare into a pair of yellow eyes. He's now standing only a few paces away.

"Who are you?" I ask. My voice is clear and steady, even though I might pass out at any moment, and part of me wishes I would hurry up and do it.

"I am known as the Annlagh, young mortal. And that, is what you shall call me."

An annlagh? I've never heard of such a thing. But whatever it might be, it's disgusting, and I think it's about to kill me.

8

The Annlagh

Gade

Circles of dark magic ring my body, burning my flesh, while I lie like a corpse on a funeral pyre, my heart still beating. My sight and hearing function normally. But no matter how hard I try, other than my eyes, I can't shift a muscle to protect the human against the ancient power of the annlagh.

She will be crushed. Or worse, dragged underground to the creature's lair of narrow, twisted passages of packed dirt that snake forever down to the hell realms.

The mortal will be tortured. Broken. Remade. And then broken again.

Forever.

I draw on my reserves of power and attempt to transmit a message to the girl with my eyes, my energy, my very being.

Speak wisely, I tell her silently.

Promise nothing.

Run.

Run fast and do not look back.

My gaze shifts sideways, scanning the birches that circle our hut on the hilltop. A bank of swirling clouds looms over the trees, a gray dragon of smoke and fury coiled as if ready to strike. If only I could reach out with my power and control it. Weaponize it.

But I can't. I may as well be a block of marble for all the use I am to her.

The girl's calm voice draws my focus.

"What is an annlagh?" she asks, swooping low like a trained assailant and sliding my sword from its sheath against my hip.

Fire licks from the annlagh's mouth. "You dare draw a weapon against me, mortal?"

With the sword clenched in her hand, the tip pointing down, the human stands firmly, projecting a brave but foolish front.

"You've told me that I'm at your mercy, therefore, I'd be a fool if I didn't try to protect myself. Can you truly fault me for not rolling over and waiting to die?"

The annlagh inclines his head, the jewels tinkling merrily from its antlers, a strange contrast to the violence brewing in its eyes. "I cannot. You are brave at least, a trait worthy of some respect."

My breathing labored, I study the annlagh's grisly limbs, the drool dripping from its maw. An unusual thing to notice considering the circumstances, but its yellow eyes, at least in color, are a near match for the girl's.

In a final, desperate bid for assistance, in my mind, I call to the High Mage of Talamh Cúig, even knowing it's a futile endeavor. I'm too far away, too weak to be heard. I can't even reach and touch my garnet ring, which strengthens my connection to Ether.

The mortal lifts her chin. "You haven't answered my question, Annlagh."

"You wish to know what I am? Very well. I am a nightmare made flesh and bone, as old as time itself. Not a combatant for you to face, child, simply your death sentence."

"A terrifying description. But if I'm to die anyway, will you at least tell me your purpose here?"

The creature nods. "As the only one of my kind, I live a lonely existence, so I must rise once a century to take a mate and slake my demon's appetite. But thanks to the fae who lies before you and his wretched eagle, I've been awakened early, forced to protect the sacred boar to which I am bound."

The girl draws a sharp breath. "You've killed Lleu?"

"The reckless bird flew away, mortal. It lives, unfortunately. For now."

Dragging the sword tip through the grass, she circles the annlagh, forcing the beast to pivot to keep her in his sight. I cannot fathom why it hasn't blasted her to dust yet. Perhaps it's as confused and fascinated by the daft human as I am.

"Why didn't you kill the eagle?" she asks. "You could easily have done so."

"And, behold, now a compliment!" Deep laughter grates like rocks tumbling in an avalanche. "You're not as foolish as I first suspected and have guessed the obvious. The bird lives because I did not wish to end it. But its time will come."

He lunges forward, and the human steps in front of me, brandishing my sword with a shaking arm as if the weapon is as heavy as a tree limb.

My eyes flare wide.

Move away.

You cannot protect me.

Run.

Run now.

The annlagh grins. "Do not fear for your companion. No matter how badly I long to hurt him or speak his true name—I cannot. Such are the rules that bind me when I ascend from my earthly mound when it's not my season. Here in the Above Realm, that fae on the ground has amnesty, but after it maimed the boar, his bird did not. I may have toyed with it a little, but I didn't kill it. And as for your fate, human, well, I am undecided, but confess the many options delight me."

As the annlagh reverses their positions and stalks a broad circle around us, Holly grips the sword with both hands.

"For now, I think I shall allow you to live. You are insignificant, but remain of interest to me." Drool drips from his fangs as he leers, breath steaming from his mouth in fetid tendrils. "I am curious to know how you would fare in a coupling with me. Before long, I shall need another mate. I've never had a human. How loudly would you scream, I wonder. And would you survive the ordeal, pet?"

Holly's gaze doesn't break contact with the creature's eyes.

He snarls and snaps his jaws close to her throat. "I look forward to the future hunt. Today, you will live, and my servants and I will keep watch on you."

Holly's shoulders rise and a visible shiver undulates down her spine. "Your servants? And who might they be?"

"Never mind, mortal. Only know that your deeds in Faery will not go unseen. Act accordingly. I cannot kill your friend today, but I can hurt him and impede his healing, which in time, may have fatal consequences. What would you give to have me leave him be?"

Their heads bow together as they whisper.

No. Do not promise him anything. Not one thing. Nothing.

The girl gives a sharp nod, then steps away from him, her eyes flicking briefly to mine. If I'm not mistaken, trouble brews in their depths.

What has she done?

Bid him farewell, I try to impress on her mind. *Do it now. Bow and walk into the trees where the shadows are dark and long. Hide.*

But, of course, she cannot hear me.

Her jaw clenches. "If you're not interested in murdering us, then why are you here?"

Back to that stupid, dangerous question.

The annlagh steps forward, his claws gripping her stubborn chin. "First, I smelled your blood, earthy and delicious." Leaning close, he inhales, his whiskered snout slobbering along the side of her neck. "Yes, very nice indeed. Perhaps I shall sample you now."

Mottled fangs lengthen as his mouth opens. The girl shrieks, slashing the sword at the creature's bowed legs. This distraction weakens the immobility spell, allowing me to break free of it.

Fury lending me speed, I leap to my feet and tear my blade from the human's grip, pushing her aside and raising it vertically in front of my face.

The Laws of Five prevent me from killing the beast here and now, but I have every right to inflict damage to stop it from hurting my human. A growl parting my lips, I prepare to slice it to pieces and leave only its vile heart beating.

Holly grips my arm, and I jolt as magic shudders through me. Energy explodes from the center of my chest in a flash of white, sending the beast flying across the ground. Roaring, I raise the sword and run toward him, then draw back the blade, picturing his head lying on the ground, separate from his body, his blood dripping down my wrists.

"Prepare to have your head cleaved from your shoulders," I growl out.

"Gade, control yourself," says Holly, coming to stand beside me. "He was leaving. Think of the laws he mentioned, the rules you'd break. Please, let him go."

"Peace, fae," says the annlagh getting to his feet and picking rocks from his antlers. Smirking, he walks slowly backward, palms up in surrender.

"If you ever go near her again, I will kill you, rules or not. Do you understand?"

"I do." He chuckles. "You couldn't possibly make yourself clearer." He bows his head and spins around, flapping a clawed hand over his shoulder in a dismissive gesture. "And *that* was the second thing I wanted, mortal—to know if he would fight for you. And the answer is, yes, with passion and fervor."

Passion? That's not right. *Honor* might be a better description. I may be curse-ridden, but my sense of right and wrong hasn't completely deserted me. *Yet.*

We watch the annlagh disappear underground in a flash of dark-green light and a spray of dirt and rocks.

"Well, that was interesting. What an unusual creature," Holly says, raising a brow at me.

"Indeed. And a dangerous one. Given his interest in you, we must take great care to avoid his minions."

"And how will we do that?"

"Flee to the safety of my home as soon as my people arrive. Then I must keep you well guarded. Come, let's return to the hut before another beast springs from the soil."

"Speaking of beasts, where has Wren got to?"

"In accordance with his hermit nature, he has no doubt returned to the stable." For some reason, I smile at her over my shoulder as I stride up the hill. "Breaking out of that immobilization spell nearly killed me, and now I need food and lots of it. Will you cook something tasty for dinner with the leftover rabbit?"

"Certainly," she says, puffing as she reaches my side. "As long as you help me."

My brows snap together. "Me?" I point at my chest. "Cook?"

"You're a guard, aren't you? You must need to make food while out on your various postings."

I grunt and stride ahead to avoid answering her question truthfully. I still don't want her to learn my true identity. Not yet. Not until there is no other option.

Why? Unlike my courtiers, she doesn't sweeten her words or walk on eggshells around me. She says what she thinks and seems to mean what she says, and I'm not ready to give that up. It is... *entertaining* to say the least.

Back at the hut, she makes me chop meat and wild onions, then start a broth over the fire while she searches for thyme in the overgrown rear garden.

When the food is ready, we eat in an uncomfortable silence. Uncomfortable for me, because I must constantly work to stop myself from asking questions about her home, her life in the mortal world.

Why should I care? I ask myself again and again, my gaze tracing tendrils of golden hair that curl damply about her face as she finishes her meal.

"Clean the bowls, please," she says, getting up to tend the pots.

I look behind me as if there might be a servant hovering nearby.

Shaking her head, she puts her hands on her hips. "Try not to look so shocked when you're asked to do a simple task, Gade. It's not an admirable trait. Despite the close call with the annlagh, the walk today did your health good. You need to move around to heal properly and build up muscle strength. Washing the dishes will be good for you." At that, she glances at my bare arms, likely admiring the glyphs that circle them. She clears her throat. "You don't want to remain an invalid, do you?"

"Of course not," I snap.

Gritting my teeth, I push off the seat and carry the dishes to the bench where a pail of warm water waits. Slowly, I clean the plates and spoons with a frayed cloth and answer her many questions about the annlagh with short, sharp replies.

How often does it rise? Once a century unless the sacred boar is in danger.

What kind of magic does it have? Old, dark, and powerful.

Could it destroy me? Yes, possibly in my current state. Curse free and in full health—no, absolutely not.

Am I afraid of it? A little, but only for what it might do to those I care about, such as my sister, my cousins, and... *her*—the foolish human.

Why didn't it have permission to kill me today?

I throw the cloth on the bench and squeeze between the table and the fireplace she's busy fussing over, making sure my body brushes hers. Only to distract her, of course, so I don't have to answer that last question and make her wonder if I'm more than a simple palace guard. At that thought, pain shoots through my skull.

Why? Because it's a rotten lie. And even thinking one hurts like a lashing of iron.

Disturbed by my passing, she clangs the ladle into the pot and emits a surprisingly ripe curse, then sweeps hair from her cheek before scurrying in the direction of the outhouse, no doubt to get away from me.

"Take care outside," I yell through the open door, leaning on the frame. "I'd hate for you to run into a boggart. They love to wander around unclothed by the river, and I know how naked bodies upset you—covered in excess hair or not."

Receiving no word of reply or thanks for my warning, I sigh and shut the door.

Although I'd prefer it if she were, this girl is no fool, and it's getting harder to keep my true identity from her. But it's vitally important it remain a secret.

And *again* I ask myself—why?

Well, the uncomfortable truth is... who knows what liberties she might allow an honorable palace guard? But a faery prince? Likely none. Heat burns through my body.

And, yes, there's likely something wrong with me for wanting to touch her in that way, I know it. But lately, I cannot stop my mind fixating on wild images of her body and mine that would scare the living wits out of her.

When she returns, I'm lying under the bedcovers in a perfect position to watch her rebuild the fire that I should have thought to tend myself, but didn't. Next time, I will do it and impress her with my ability to undertake *simple tasks*, as she called them earlier, without her bidding.

After her task is completed, she sits by the hearth and forms her usual makeshift pillow from a tablecloth, then curls up under her cloak, snuggling into its warmth.

A foreign pressure fills my chest. With dawning horror, I recognize it as guilt because I lie here comfortable, and she sleeps on the cold, hard ground. This bed may be small, but surely there is enough room for one small human girl.

I cough once to clear my throat. "Why don't you sleep up here on the bed? You would achieve a much better night's rest." My voice is low and husky, anticipation for something I dare not ponder smoldering through my blood.

Lit by flames, her tawny head rises from the rags. "You'd be willing to give me the bed?"

"I did not say that."

"If you expect me to share it, then you're more touched in the mind than I imagined."

"Touched?" I ask.

"Deranged. Demented. *Unbalanced* of mind."

"I see." I flip onto my back, interlinking my hands behind my head. "I'm merely practical. And as it turns out, surprisingly merciful to creatures below my station."

"Creatures like me, you mean?"

"Like humans, yes."

She snorts and shuffles to face the fire, giving me her back. "Go to sleep, Gade. You're insufferable. I'd never share a bed with you. I wouldn't get a wink of sleep."

"Oh? Why is that?"

"Because I'd be too busy wondering when to throttle you."

"You don't trust me," I say, a statement, not a question.

"All faeries are untrustworthy."

"That is untrue, and your assumptions are offensive. Since you're human, *you* are in fact the one who spills falsehoods from your lips with ease, not I."

"It's not your words I'm fearful of. I'm not ignorant. I've heard the tales of what fae do to humans, how they trap them in Faery for centuries and use their bodies until they're spent. I'll never willingly be a faerie's plaything."

"*Never* is a long time. There is an old saying about that: never say never. It's wise because in this realm, as you will soon learn, anything is possible."

Except, perhaps, for a fae to care for a human—to want to bed her, yes, that is more than possible. But a prince could never bond with a human. I shudder at the very idea.

A terrible thought crosses my mind.

Why did my power surge and break the annlagh's spell only so I could protect her?

It makes no sense. The answer is implausible. Unbearable.

Because, no, I don't truly care about her.

I couldn't.

I wouldn't.

Why didn't I just let the annlagh whisk my mortal-sized problem to the Underworld? He would have done me a service. I am healed enough and could survive without her gentle ministrations.

Why should I concern myself with her fate? The beast admitted that Lleu lives, and this confirms my sister will soon come for me. I no longer need this *Holly* person's help.

But still, I rose to fight for her...

Ice slides down my spine as I think over my actions today and all the days since we've been confined in the hut. I contemplate the pleasant heat that burns through my chest whenever she is close, the way something claws inside me like a living entity, striving toward her, seeking the forbidden.

What is this madness? The curse twisting my thoughts so I no longer recognize my emotions?

Shuffling onto my side, I stare at the shadows dancing on the wall instead of the outline of *her* lumpy form beneath her cloak, self-disgust curdling the food in my gut.

Why did anger at the thought of the annlagh touching her leave me willing to break sacred laws, an action that would've had dire consequences for my kingdom?

Horror knots the muscles of my stomach.

Thank the Elements she didn't accept my invitation to share this bed. I might have started something we would both sorely regret.

Hurry, Mern, I think. *Please come before it's too late.*

Too late for what? I wonder foolishly.

My eyes squeeze closed, and I'm assaulted by images that answer my question with stunning clarity.

Soft kisses. Tumbled bed furs. Mortal eyes of orange aflame with desire.

Never, I whisper, the pain of a lie ricocheting through my body.

I bite back a laugh, then a groan, the bitter tang of blood coating my tongue.

I'd bet all the gold in my kingdom that tonight, sleep will be a long time coming.

9

Kiss of Power

Holly

I t's after lunch on the fourth day. No fae rescuers have arrived yet and likely never will.

I can't stop thinking of Mother and my sister, Rose, who has little patience for tinctures and compresses and no love of wandering through forests in search of herbs.

If we're not going to be guided back to Gade's kingdom shortly, then I'll need to seek a way to return home by myself. It must be possible. And it makes no sense to wait here in this hut forever, staring at the faery like a besotted fool.

The fae has spoken of portals and the mages who control them and also admitted that these doorways sometimes form naturally, and a person has only to stumble through one to be transported somewhere in the seven realms.

It would be risky to leap through time and space to an unknown destination, but also cruel of me to leave the still-healing fae alone in the middle of nowhere. But if I want to see my family again, what choice do I have?

Images of Gade's strong features spring to mind, his intense blue gaze, the tiny dimples that frame his mouth on the rare occasions he forgets to be fearsome and smiles. The brisk, hard movements of his warrior's limbs, powerful even in their diminished state when he chopped wood this morning, after first making me wrap his wound up tightly.

Restored to full health, he would be a vision to sustain me during the long years of spinsterhood that likely stretch before me when I return home. Half of me hopes I get to witness it, and the other part quakes in fear of his replenished beauty and power, and I'm not sure which outcome I prefer.

The polished wood of the table is smooth and comforting as I stroke it slowly and stare at the flames leaping in the hearth.

"What are you thinking about?" comes a deep voice that jolts me from my daydream.

I look over at him lacing his boots on the edge of the bed. Other than a loose bandage, his torso is bare. Doesn't he notice the cool air?

"Nothing that would interest you." Never have I been so glad to expel a lie as easily as a sneeze. "You should put your shirt on."

"I don't feel like it. And you're a liar. You seemed to be pondering something delicious, a sweetmeat dripping honey and sprinkled with candied sugar. Or perhaps you were ruminating upon my form. Living in such close confines with a fae must be overwhelming to a human's senses."

"Now you're fishing for compliments. Don't be desperate. If you must know, I was thinking about finding an open portal in the forest. Of going home, seeing my family."

"And here I was certain you were thinking of my charming face." Boots thud rhythmically as he paces across the room, rubbing his stomach in a distracted manner.

"Yes, I was imagining the joy of never having to see it again." I rise from my seat at the table and grab the ointment from the cupboard. "You need more cream. And a large slice of humble pie."

"I'm fine, and I'm not hungry. When did you bake a pie?"

"There's no dessert. It's just a way to say someone's too arrogant for their own good. If you want the wound to turn foul again, then, yes, I agree, it is fine." I reach for his arm to stop him pacing. "Here, Gade, let me—"

"I can do it." He snatches the clay pot and sits on the bed, scraping his nail across the contents, barely collecting any.

I watch him dab it on his wound. "That's not enough," I say.

Iolite eyes hold my gaze as he smears ointment over his skin more roughly.

"Are you *trying* to annoy me? That will only stretch the stitches. If you're not going to do it properly, then, please, let me."

The pot hits my boot then rolls over the floor. "Did you throw that at me?"

He smirks. "No, I just dropped it on purpose."

Don't react. It's what he wants.

I collect the pot, sit beside him, and scoop out a large dollop of comfrey-infused lard. I move the bandage lower and apply the cream, the material of my dress scratching my hot neck.

"We need to leave here soon before we murder each other."

"Agreed," he says, his chest rising and falling with uneven breaths.

Sitting so close and touching his skin has a peculiar effect on me, causing my own breaths to be short and ragged and the warm buzz in my chest to scare me senseless. But it's as if he has mesmerized me like I'm prey, and I don't want to move away. Not yet.

"Does this hurt?" I ask, wondering if pain makes his stomach muscles clench under my touch.

"No," he snaps, his gaze dropping to my mouth. He moves closer, only a hairsbreadth, but panic spikes through my veins.

My breath snags in my throat. "What—"

"Do you realize, *Holly*, how fortunate you are that you weren't found by a less honorable fae than I? One who wouldn't let your sharp tongue and somber nature deter them from taking what they want, using you for their pleasure."

The bed frame protests as I jolt backward. "That's a *horrid* thing to say. That you even think such things is very revealing."

"Revealing?" His stare penetrates, peeling through layers of clothing until I feel bare before him.

His gaze tracks from my throat to my chest, spreading unwanted heat along its path. "I have never met a human before you," he says in a husky whisper. "I'd been led to believe they were plain, even disgusting creatures. But I admit you are not without your charms."

Heat scalds my cheek as he strokes it lightly, the room spinning around me. I should slap him for the insult. Push him away.

"Do not fear me, little human. I never take more than what is willingly given."

Fire emanates from his body as he gently, carefully, folds me in his arms, his lips meeting mine in a kiss that shocks and sears.

My heart stutters, blood rushing to pool in my stomach. I can't think. I can't move. I can only melt like hot candle wax, butter left out in the sun, honey on warm bread.

Heavens, what is happening to me?

His lips press warmth and sweetness into my mouth and a strong emotion akin to joy. It's the very opposite of what I should be feeling. I must be under a spell because instead of stopping this madness, I melt further into his embrace, relishing every moment of my first kiss.

The heat. The heady, giddy sensations of desire.

My first kiss... with a supernatural being...

No, this cannot be. I've started down a path that can only lead to madness and ruin.

"Stop." I push his chest. "Please. This isn't right."

Wet lips parted and his eyes glazed, he asks, "It was... unpleasant?"

"Yes. I mean no. Well... it's not appropriate for a fae and a human to... It's not natural."

"Be quiet," he snarls out, staring wide-eyed at the pulsing star tattoo on the back of his hand.

Muttering incoherently, he flicks his fingers in front of his bare chest, and a stream of water shoots from his palm into the pot over the fire. "Draygonets, what sorcery is this?" he says, leaping off the bed.

I stare in silence, the sight as shocking as the first time I saw his magic, when he captured me by the oak and conjured water to quench my thirst, then again at the creek, and with the annlagh.

He flexes his hand again, and this time, water only drips down his arm. He curses under his breath. "Come here, mortal."

"No. Absolutely not." I scramble off the bed and scurry behind the table, not at all liking the direction of his thoughts.

He takes two large steps and grips my shoulders, pulling me against his body. Warm hands bracket my face, and his head dips. Then he whispers against my firmly closed mouth. "I am sorry for this, but I must test a theory. You have my word no harm will come to you."

Then his lips take mine and pleasure winds through my stomach again, coiling in on itself until it's as tight as a strung bowstring.

His kiss is featherlight and slow—until suddenly it's not. I cling to his forearms as fever claims me, not to drag them down and away from my face, but to keep them there forever.

He tilts my head, deepening our kiss. The sounds of our ragged breathing, his soothing whispers, weaken my legs, and a tremor builds over the fae's body, the scent of burning flesh filling my nose as he begins to shudder hard.

Without warning, he breaks away, leaving me swaying on my feet.

"Son of barghest," he says. "Holly, look. Look at this!" The outline of the star symbol on his hand glows like molten silver, tendrils of smoke rising in the air. With both hands, he reaches toward the fire, and the flames disappear.

"You... you put it out," I say. "What's a barghest?"

"Indeed we did." He casts a distracted glance in my direction. "A what? Oh. It's a fae-eating hound." Those rare dimples sparkle as he laughs. "This is extraordinary. My power stabilizes when we..."

He moves his palm between us. "Kiss. Is that what humans call it, too?"

"Yes. That's the correct word." My skin blanches, then flushes hot.

He steps closer. "Do not worry. This is a wonderful development, human. We've found something that stimulates my power—physical interaction between us—and if you're willing to test how long it lasts, we may be able to travel safely tomorrow, whether my people arrive or not. Don't you see? We're unprotected while I have barely any magic, but this gives me hope."

What? Might I have to kiss him all the way back to his city? I reel backward on my heels, panic muddling my thoughts.

"Come with me, Holly."

"Can you please put some more clothes on first?"

"No. I cannot."

A warm current sizzles over my skin as I take his hand and follow him into the sunlit clearing in front of the hut. The air is still and cool. The sounds of the creek, frogs croaking in muddy bogs, and the fragrance of pine leaves travel up the valley, a pleasant and comforting mix.

"Stay there and don't move," Gade commands, striding ten paces away before turning to face me.

With his arms spread wide, he tilts his face toward the strange, purple clouds feathered over the sky. Insects with pink wings, little green faces, and long elven ears swoop from the direction of the trees and fly around his limbs. He clicks his tongue in annoyance, and they flee, the sound of tiny laughter tinkering in their wake.

A flash of silver light arcs between Gade's palms, forked like lightning and quickly fizzling out. He spits out a curse. "I'd hoped the charge would last longer. Take three steps closer to me. Hurry up."

I trudge forward. "Yes, sir. Whatever you say."

He smirks. "At last you address me in a respectful manner."

"Used to other castle guards following your command, are you?"

"Yes, you could say that," he answers, staring off into the trees. He takes a big breath and spins in a circle, his arms lifted again. This time, when silver shoots from his palms, the light is weaker and doesn't meet in the middle in an arc of power like it did before.

Scowling, he stalks forward until his sword hilt presses into my stomach and his hand cradles my head, pulling me in close. The scents of leather and smoke wrinkle my nose. It's intoxicating. Stupefying. I should step back, but I'm too flustered to move.

"Pardon the trespass." He kisses me, and the land spins, tumbling me in a barrage of wild emotions that I don't understand nor attempt to escape.

The frightening truth is I have no desire to run from this feeling, and I want to stay in his embrace for as long as possible.

Soft, warm lips tease mine until they part, gentle, but insistent. A hoarse noise sounds in my throat as the fae's teeth graze my skin. I'd like to imagine it's an expression of disgust. But, of course, it's not.

My fingers twist into the pliant leather of his sword belt at his hips, and I lean closer, eager to learn the rhythm of this new dance. My body trembles as if what we do is too much and at the same time, not nearly enough. My stomach coils tighter and tighter, seeking release from the agony—from the joy of each sensation.

Without warning, pain sears across my skin where his body touches mine, my stomach, shoulders, the back of my neck and head, all burning, the worst scald on my lips and inside my mouth. With a yelp, I spring backward, gaping at what I see—Gade transformed into a magical creature, an aura of golden light pulsating around his body as if he is the sun itself.

"That hurt," I say, rubbing my lips.

He grins. "I'm sorry. I didn't expect such an incredible surge of power. Next time, I promise to take more care. But look what we did together."

The glyph on the back of his hand flows bright orange as he turns it over to show me. His body appears taller, his features elongated and eyes glowing a bright green. "Fire—heed me," he says, and knee-high flames leap, making a circle of fire in the grass around him.

"Your eyes have changed color," I point out.

"Yes." He beams a smile, flashing sharp teeth. "Because the elements course through me."

"Impressive."

"Earth, form for me," he booms. Unpolished crystals shake their way from deep in the soil and swirl in the air above Gade's head. He snaps a finger, and they crumble to flakes and float onto his palms.

He steps over the flames, strides up to me, and paints a line of sparkling dust from my forehead down to my bottom lip with a single stroke of his long finger. "Now you look ready to attend a fae revel, pretty human."

Pretty? The power surge must have scrambled his senses and confused his mouth into emitting an accidental compliment. In the short period I've known him, he's spent most of the time frowning and curling his lip at me. I don't believe he finds me the least bit attractive.

A preternaturally beautiful faery flirting with a human that no villagers ever bothered to gape at is a ridiculous notion.

If it's so ridiculous, my conscience asks, *then why do faeries steal humans and trick them into prolonged dalliances in their realm?*

I study him as he walks away, then spins in a slow circle, tiny vortexes of wind twirling in the air above his hands, dissolving almost as soon as they appear. The fae scowls and shakes his arms, attempting to reignite the magic.

I clear my throat. "Gade?"

"What?" He draws his sword and marches toward me, slashing it in a complicated pattern, the final flourish ending with the tip pointed at my heart.

"Do fae ever take humans as partners?" I ask.

His lips twist. "Partners, no. Lovers? Yes. Many fae do so if they can find willing mortals or ones who are susceptible to our trickery."

"So the tales of stolen maidens and youths in their prime are true?"

"Indeed they are."

"No beauty surpasses a faerie's. Why would you do it?"

Harsh laughter sends chills down my spine. "Why? Because we *can.* And it is fun."

"I see. Have you captured a human before?"

"Before you? No. And while I have you, I have no interest in any other."

I glower and try to decipher his meaning. Am I to become his plaything? A pet that he plans to torture to death when we return to his city?

Exhaling hard, he folds his arms over his bare chest. "Why do you ask? Has the *kissing* made you worry about what might be in store for you?"

"Perhaps," I admit.

"Well, push that idea from your mind, and know this; when I want something, I take it. If you become prey, mortal, there is no speed you could run or place you could hide that would prevent me from finding you." He leans close, and whispers in my ear. "Or from having you."

I shove him away, and he taps my nose as if I'm a child. "Best to not think about it. Be glad that right now, I have no interest in torturing you." He smirks. "Nor do I want you, little human." He winces and stumbles over an indent in the ground, righting himself quickly and rubbing his temple.

Strange. From what I saw, he didn't injure his head. Perhaps he has a headache from using magic.

"In my realm, I'm not thought of as *little*," I say.

The fae sheaths his sword and grins. "Do not look so dour. If you will give me a little honey from your lips in exchange for my protection on the journey, we will soon be at Castle Black and celebrating our triumph." He rubs his hands together. "All we need to do now is some more tests."

My shoulders slump. "You mean more kissing?"

A crooked smile flashes over his face. "Of course."

"Let's get it over with, then." I roll my eyes and move closer to him, disturbed by the warmth in my belly, the erratic beat of my heart. *Pull yourself together*, my brain orders my body. But my body has a mind of its own and refuses to listen.

This testing business goes on for an excessive amount of time, and it's only when the sun's rays slant low through the nearby lattice of tree branches that he concludes our work with a soft, lingering kiss.

He has the audacity to lick his lips as he moves away and with the flick of his wrist, spins leaves of every color, weaving them in a beautiful pattern around me. He shoots them into the air, shapes them into a fire-breathing dragon, an eagle in flight, sets them alight, and finally dissolves them in an iridescent bubble of water magic.

"I think we can call our experiment an outstanding success, mortal."

As far as testing how long a kiss powers his magical abilities for, I would have to agree. The effect seems to be cumulative—the more closely spaced the kisses, the more inner heat they create, the longer his power lasts. But as for my determination to remain un-affected by his attentions, well, in that regard, I failed completely. And even now, I feel heat rise to my cheeks, no doubt painting them deep scarlet.

Unconcerned by my humiliation, he paces back and forth, grin-ning. My eyes catch on the gold and garnet ring he wears on the middle finger of his left hand, the stone glowing as if alive.

"This is brilliant," he exclaims proudly. "I can recharge my magic as needed. We could leave tonight, should we wish to."

"I don't think you've thought it through properly," I say. "If we come across danger, an enemy, for example, you propose to stop regardless of what's happening around us, kiss me, and then go on to save the day. Do you know how ridiculous that sounds?"

"Granted. There will be challenges. Still, it is better than lying in bed waiting to be attacked, is it not? The annlagh could have flayed you alive yesterday and currently be sucking the marrow from your bones. Is that a more appealing alternative than kissing me several times a day?"

"Possibly."

"I have a theory that the more often I kindle the force between us the longer it will last."

"Why would a kiss affect your powers, Gade?"

"Why?" He squints at me. "Are you really so naive?"

If he's referring to the mysteries that lie between a man and a woman, then, yes, I most definitely am. I shrug and kick stones with my boot, refusing to meet his haughty stare.

A loud sigh draws my attention back to his face. "The force that drives attraction, craving, and desire is the most powerful, creative energy that exists. It generates life and all forms of magic—dark and light. Trust me when I promise I can return us safely to my home if only you will bear my kisses when I request them. If you do this, then I will vow to take no more from you. I am fae—for us, bargains are a pleasure to make. Strike one with me, name your price. Please, Holly. Will you do this for both our sakes?"

There he goes calling me *Holly* again. I'd be lying if I said that hearing him use my name and beg in that deep, earthy voice didn't affect me. I shake my head and snap out of it. The fae has offered to bargain, and I'd be a fool to squander the opportunity.

But if I can ask for one thing and one thing only, what should that be?

A breeze blows a golden pear leaf into my hair, and inspiration strikes. Above all else, getting home is what matters. "Fine. I agree to kiss you as many times as needed without complaint if you'll vow to allow me to return home to my mother."

Dark eyebrows knit together as he puts his hands on his hips. "But not before we've made it to Castle Black."

"All right. Not before then."

"Consider it done."

"So, you promise you'll let me leave?" I ask.

"I do."

"Say it out loud," I order, knowing he cannot lie.

Aggravated, he scowls at the sky, then fixes me with a steady gaze. "Human who calls herself Holly, I, the fae who stands before you, do solemnly vow to allow you to attempt to return to your mother once you have resided at Castle Black for seven days and seven nights." He smirks and flourishes his hand as if he has done me a great honor. "There. It is done. Our bargain is struck."

"Wait a moment. Seven days and seven nights? That wasn't part of the deal."

"It is now. Take it or leave it. Make up your mind quickly and state your wish before the chance to do so closes."

"For what possible reason do you want me to stay there for that period of time?"

"That's my business. And if you do not like the terms, I shall rescind them immediately and take what I require from you regardless." He spins on his heels and marches off, black hair flowing behind him like a sheet of rippling midnight sky.

"Wait! Gade, please." I bolt after him and tug on his arm. He keeps walking. "You stupid, stubborn fae. Stop. Please. I'm begging you."

Slowly, he turns, arching a raven brow at me. "Do continue. I enjoy the sound of a female begging. And after insulting me so severely, you have much to atone for. *Now begin.*"

I'd love nothing more than to punch the smug smirk off his face. Instead, I draw a breath and swallow my pride. "I'm sorry for what I called you. It was impolite of me. Please, Gade, I beg you to listen, and I promise I'll accept your bargain and the terms exactly as you've spoken them."

The smile twitching the corners of his lips turns sly. "Good. Let us seal the contract." Before I know it, his mouth is on mine, pressing a rough, quick kiss that is over before I can even think to shove him away.

"That was unnecessary," I say.

"I agree. Unnecessarily *delightful.*" Laughing, he strides up the hill in the direction of the hut.

He glances over his shoulder to check if I'm following along like a lost lamb, which I am, then his voice echoes through the valley. "Don't tarry. We must prepare for our journey. We'll leave at first light. And do try to look a little happier or at least somewhat grateful. You're considerably closer to seeing this ailing mother you're forever going on about. That is, if the sorry tales you've spun happen to be true."

"Of course they're true."

As I reach the top of the hill, our little hut comes into view, along with two unfamiliar horses tethered outside the stable—a tall brown and white roan and another whose tawny coat shimmers like gold in the dusky light.

Gade curses as I come up behind him.

"Do you know who the horses' owners are?" I ask.

"Yes. Be at ease. They belong to my sister and our cousin."

Hope quickens my pace, and for once, I manage to keep up with Gade's long steps. "A rescue party, then? Finally, some good news." Especially if it means I won't have to kiss him again.

He shrugs and pushes on the door to the hut. "That remains to be seen. You haven't met my sister yet."

10

Mernia of Castle Black

Holly

Eager to view our rescuers, I elbow past Gade, jerking to a halt when my eyes adjust to the smoky darkness of the hut. Gade's chest slams into my back, and I grunt, then gape at the new arrivals as if I've never seen a faery before.

The girl, who I assume is Gade's sister, is busy roasting a green-skinned bird on a spit over the fire. She turns to us wearing a trouble-maker's grin, and I gasp a little too loudly at the sight of her and her travel companion, a male who flashes me a bawdy smile from where he sits on the floor.

The female fae is shorter than me and waif-thin with long black horns that curve high above her head. In the poor light, her eyes glow a rich hazel-green, a mesmerizing contrast to the gold tones of her shimmering skin. She's beautiful and difficult to look away from.

"What took you so long?" My grumpy companion asks her. As he speaks, I catch him lifting a finger to his lips in a gesture that looks suspiciously like a keep-quiet signal, directed at her, not me.

What secret is Gade hiding?

"Brother." The sister swaggers over. "It's splendid to see you alive, but I expected you might be a *little* more grateful."

"Of course I'm grateful." Gade crosses his arms. "Thank you for coming."

"Lleu returned yesterday morning," continues the fae, "and from that moment, we worked tirelessly, combined our stores of magic, and drove our horses at reckless speeds to arrive before you perished. Perhaps we should have struck a more leisurely pace."

Gade laughs. "I appreciate your efforts, Sister. I only thought Lleu might have been swifter."

"Lleu did his best, and if he hadn't returned," she lifts her chin toward me, "at least you wouldn't have died alone. That is some comfort to me." She nods at Gade's hand. "You couldn't contact Ether?"

His gaze slides from his sister's, and he twists the garnet ring on his finger. "It likely wasn't working."

Frowning, Mern opens her mouth to speak, and Gade silences her with a shake of his raven head.

Outside, a bird of prey calls, the sound eerie in the hut's smoky gloom. Gade ducks his head through the door and whistles. A moment later, Lleu glides onto his bare shoulder, and they greet each other with obvious pleasure—pats and low murmurs from the fae and trilling squawks from the eagle.

I stare at the bird's razor-sharp talons, wondering why they don't seem to cause Gade pain. Points of blood bead around his shoulder, but he keeps smiling and stroking the eagle's head, oblivious to the injuries.

The ways of faeries are baffling indeed.

"Lleu, I knew you wouldn't fail me," says Gade. "But the next time you disobey me and chase that brainless boar halfway across the land, I'll lock you in a cage for a sennight and cut off your goldfish treats. That beast will be the death of you one day."

"He couldn't wait to return to you, Cousin," says the fae sitting cross-legged on the floor. He pulls a large water bladder from a satchel and drinks deeply, then coughs and wipes his mouth. "He flew too high and too fast and kept showing Mern gruesome images of your wound. We knew speed was critical." He gives me a lewd grin. "But we didn't realize you had such interesting company."

Gade glares at his cousin, and the fae takes another swig from the bladder, somehow nodding to me at the same time. "You've found yourself a stray mortal. I've never seen one in the flesh. It's quite a curious looking creature. I expected something a little more disgusting, such as no teeth in the mouth, only gums. Lord Serain told me they have pink skin, like a young hog's, but this one contradicts my assumptions. Call me fascinated. May I touch her?"

"Certainly," says Gade. "If you're comfortable with my knife embedded in your neck, go right ahead."

Shocked, I snort out a nervous laugh.

"Behave," Gade whispers near my ear, as if *I'm* the one saying outrageous things, and shoves me farther into the room. "Human, this is my sister, Mernia, known to all as Mern, and my cousin,

Elden. They won't help you escape, so don't bother appealing to their better natures, for like me, they do not possess them."

"Speak for yourself." Elden laughs, his yellow hair ruffling like a lion's mane around his angular features. With needle-sharp ears and eyes that tilt dramatically upward, his appearance isn't quite as startling as Mern's, but near enough. "So... is it safe to call you Gade in her presence? If I've erred by mentioning it, allow me to wipe her mind of the memory."

Gade shifts his weight and nods, cutting me a furtive glance. "That name is fine."

So, it seems Gade's secret has something to do with his true name, the one the annlagh mentioned he wasn't allowed to use in the Above Realm.

I force a smile and a teasing tone of voice. "Your cousin doesn't seem to trust me, Gade, even though I've spent days tending your wound, hunting for you, and cooking for you. I've had ample opportunity to slip a poisonous herb in your stew and haven't taken it. I've even promised to comply and return to the castle where you work as a guard and—"

Water spurts from Elden's mouth, the pouch flopping on the floor as he narrows his feline eyes. "Human, your knowledge of my cousin surprises me. And what you say is true—he does *guard* the palace extremely well. And the safety and happiness of every fae within its walls are always foremost in his mind."

"Do shut up, Elden." Mern turns to her brother. "Does your *human* have a name, Gade?"

"It's Holly." He spits the word out like it's bitter medicine on his tongue. "She may be mine, but doesn't yet know it."

"I'm definitely not yours," I say, my statement making Elden cackle. "People don't *own* each other. That's called slavery."

A shudder racks my body. Why does Gade think he has a claim on me?

"I haven't decided what purpose you'll serve. But I have no need for a human slave or lover with an irritating, quarrelsome temperament like yours." Gade rubs his forehead and curses.

Watching him closely, Mern laughs. "And yet... finders keepers. You are stuck with each other." She directs green and gold eyes and a warm smile on me. "Hello, Holly. I've never met a mortal before. Heard stories, of course. If you find me staring at you at times, please don't be alarmed. I'm merely curious."

"Likewise," I say. "I've only seen the rare sheep or cow with horns as beautiful as yours..." I let my words trail off, realizing how rude they sound.

Gade may be happy to regularly offend everyone around him, but I'm not.

"Sorry," I say. "I meant that in the nicest possible way. You're the most beautiful person I've ever seen." Except for your brother, I think to myself. "I'm glad to meet you. You mentioned you have magic. Can you use it to get us out of here quickly?"

"Unfortunately not," she replies. "My magic is elemental, earth based and depleted at present. My power involves transmuting stones and glass into other crystals and forms. I can manipulate plants and trees and sometimes see fragmented visions of the future."

"Sister, the girl will not benefit from hearing the entire Book of Mern and a detailed inventory of your numerous skills." Gade crosses the floor and bends to kiss Mern's cheek. "Granted, you do love to boast."

"As you well know, there is no harm in it." She points the fire poker at me. "Given our circumstances, I've never been more envious of the Merits' power to transfer, but I'm afraid riding faster than the wind is the best we can do for the return journey."

"What does transfer mean?" I ask.

Gade frowns. "The ability to disappear and reassemble your body in a location you set your mind to."

"A very useful power," I admit. "What are the Merits?"

"You mean *who*?" Mern grins. "The less you know about the Unseelie fae whose kingdom lies in the south of this land, the better. Best you forget their name."

Unseelie fae. I've heard that term used to describe the dark fae, those like the annlagh who are even more monstrous than the creatures I share this room with.

"So, who's hungry?" Mern asks. "We've brought your favorite rosemary bread, Gade."

We all agree we're famished and huddle around the table to eat a tasty pheasant stew. The atmosphere is jovial as the fae update Gade on news of their court and tease each other mercilessly. Despite Gade's grumpy greeting, he appears to be rather fond of them.

While they talk, I find my gaze lingering on this smiling version of my abductor and patient, especially on his luminous chest, highlighted by the flickering flames. Before dinner, I was pleased to see him throw on a shirt, but now I sorely wish he'd fasten the buttons. Rather than the protector of a kingdom, he looks like a marauding pirate, and it's putting me off my food.

At one point, I feel his attention on me as I lick my spoon, and Mern says something strange. "That's right, Gade, if your heart's wish is to be as bald as a newborn chick, keep staring at the girl."

I glance up to see him leaning forward, rotating a lit candle between his fingers, a lock of black hair about to burst into flames.

"Son of a troll!" He lurches out of his slouch, shoves the candle into the clay holder, and thumps it back on the table.

Mern and Elden laugh, but Gade doesn't. He just scowls and asks to hear good news from home.

Stories of a newly built falcon mews and of the cook's puff dumplings exploding in the earth mage's face during a recent dinner return a smile to his handsome face.

The conversation turns to matters of a kingdom in decline, weakened by the deaths of its rulers. As they speak of a magical sea, tribes of forest creatures, and court politics, curiosity grips me, and I long to view the city of Talamh Cúig with my own eyes.

"Why hasn't a new king been chosen yet?" I ask, chewing a tougher piece of meat.

The fae fidget with their cutlery, and Gade's knee bounces at the corner of my vision, a sure sign he finds the subject uncomfortable.

Mern clears her throat. "We Elementals already have an heir, a prince, but before he can be crowned king, he must meet his foretold mate and marry her."

"Oh." I mop up stew with a hunk of Gade's favorite bread. "Why is that?"

"It's complicated." Her gaze slides away. "When the prince came of age, he offended a powerful mage, and she laid a curse on him, its sole purpose to torture him cruelly. It dictates that he needs this mate to rule, but it also makes the chosen girl hard to find."

I sigh. "Really? Another curse? Your brother told me he's also afflicted with one. Is that all the fae do? Run around cursing each other?" I push my empty bowl away, knocking a mug of water over.

"You seem overwrought," proclaims my abductor, passing me a cloth. "In Faery, curses are ordinary things—small ones, large ones, hilarious, and heinous. We're quite accustomed to them. Besides, these things are not your concern."

Gade jumps up to stoke the fire, then settles himself on the edge of the bed, prodding at his wound.

"With all this talk about curses, I wouldn't be surprised if a vampire attacked us in the night. I think I have good reasons to be overwrought."

"No one mentioned a vampire, human," says Gade. "Whatever that is."

"*Holly*," I say. "My name is Holly."

"Yes, yes. I'm well aware. I don't know why you're so proud of the name. There are better ones to possess." He winces and palms his bandaged side.

"Are you still in pain?" Mern asks. "Let me try easing it." With graceful movements, she rises from the table and sits beside him.

White light pulses from her hands, dissolving into Gade's stomach. After a few moments, she leans back and scrapes hair behind her horns. "Any better?"

"Well, it tickled," Gade says, straight-faced.

Mern huffs. "And?"

He fights a grin. "It feels quite warm."

"That's not funny. I'm worried. If my magic has no effect on your wound, it won't do much to boost your power. You'll be an easy target on the journey home."

Gade picks at a stitch on his sword belt. "Do not fret. I've found another power source."

Mern's jaw drops. "You have? What is it?"

"I'll tell you tomorrow," Gade says, sliding under the bedcovers and lying down. "For now, we should get some sleep. We need to leave at first light."

"Fine. Elden and I will take the floor by the fire. There's not enough room for three, so you and Holly can..." Mern sweeps her arm toward the bed, her forearm's golden bracer flashing in the firelight.

"We can what?" I say.

Gade remains silent, his hands curling into fists on his thighs.

Mern sighs. "Do I really need to spell it out?"

The fair-haired cousin snickers as he shakes out a bedroll in front of the hearth.

"Yes," I say. "Please do."

"Holly, you'll need to share the bed with Gade."

"No." Gade stands, rolling his shoulders. "I'll sleep in the stable and keep Wren company."

"Sit down." Mern pushes his chest, and he slumps back onto the bed. "Have you been allowing the girl to sleep on the floor?" She points at my blanket and makeshift pillow of bundled rags folded to the side of the fire. "Our parents raised you better, and it's too cold in the stable for you to get a good night's sleep. Grow up. The bed is big enough for two, so get in, Holly."

Gade grumbles as he moves closer to the wall, making room for me.

Sparks leap from the fireplace as Mern lays a blanket over her still-clothed body. Perhaps she's anticipating trouble tonight because she doesn't even remove her boots.

Shuffling toward the bed, I remember Gade asking me to sleep beside him last night. He seemed quite enthused by the idea. What has changed to make him so reluctant now?

I stare at him lying on his side, his head resting on his forearm and ink-black hair spread over the pillow that he has pushed to the edge of the bed for my use.

I swallow hard.

Long lashes flick up, indigo blue flashing as his eyes fix on me. "Stop sulking, human, and get in." He pats the pillow and makes a show of wriggling closer to the wall, as if a few inches between us will protect me—from *what* I hate to imagine.

When his lids fall closed, I slip my boots off, flip the covers back, and slide beneath them. Heat engulfs me. The fae is as hot as a furnace, yet I shiver as if I lie next to a block of ice.

Gade's eyes crack open.

They're too close. *Much* too close.

He clicks his tongue as if I've displeased him and rolls over, facing the wall.

"Goodnight," I whisper to the room's inhabitants.

Only Gade answers with a grunt.

I force my breathing into a steady rhythm and pray that the dreamworld takes me quickly. I'm exhausted but unlikely to get much sleep tonight with my senses on high alert.

Because of *him*—the fae who I have to kiss all the way back to his home.

11

Secrets

Gade

Wake, fool. Reach out and touch what is yours.

A voice as dry as old bones hisses through my skull—the curse, come to torture me, refusing me a moment's peace.

Take, it commands.

Take what lies in front of you.

"Shut up," I whisper back.

Inhale the scent of innocent flesh. Take her soul. Bend it to your will.

She is yours and your blood knows it well.

Do it now.

I jolt awake and blink at the human's sleeping form. She faces me, her hands folded under her cheek, a strand of honey-colored hair moving in front of her lips in time with her breathing.

Last night, as the girl slept, I inched closer, allowing her earthy, human scent to fill my senses and the pad of my fingertips to trail over the silky skin of her face, along her shoulder to her wrist. Silently, I begged her to feel me, to open her eyes and witness my desire to possess her, to own her as no man has before.

But alas, she slept on.

Now, in the firelight, I slowly raise my hand to tuck the errant lock of hair behind her ear...

Wait... Firelight?

I lift my head and look over the girl's shoulder, the room coming into focus. A fire blazes, lighting up my sister and Elden packing for this morning's journey.

How long have they been working, while I've lain here cozying up to the mortal?

"Gade, you're finally awake," says Mern, her words informing me they've been busy for some time. "Since the curse allows you little rest these days, and you looked so comfortable, we decided to let you sleep."

How *thoughtful* of them, allowing me to spend longer lying next to the mortal as though we're bonded lovers. They've obviously lost their minds.

I grip the girl's shoulder, my fingers sinking through the blanket into soft flesh and breakable bones. I give her an abrupt shake. "Wake up. We're leaving soon."

She stirs, and before her gaze can arrow through me, I climb over her body, taking care not to touch her.

Standing with my shirt unbuttoned and feet bare in front of the fire, I stretch my back and greet Mern and Elden. I ignore the mortal as she rises, coughing from the smoke, and then shuffles to the outhouse that Queen Mab made for the human shepherd who guarded her sacred flock many centuries ago.

Faeries don't produce waste. We utilize all we consume, even toxins, which are transformed into energy that helps fuel our magic, more proof that we are superior beings and that humans are base and disgusting.

Porridge bubbles in a pot above the flames, the smell conjuring fond memories of past hunting trips with my father and Uncle Fyarn.

Elden drops spoons into two bowls, passes one to me and the other to Holly as she walks through the door, an icy draft slipping into the room alongside her.

"Thank you," she says, taking the bowl. "Good morning." Her eyes flit everywhere except toward the corner I lean in.

"Mern, come with me." Still shoveling porridge in my mouth, I usher my sister outside, walk across the yard, and press my shoulder against the rough bark of an ancient pear tree.

A cold wind rustles the silver leaves on the ground, but all else is silent. So quiet I can hear the trees whispering to each other.

"You won't like this," I warn Mern. "But you and Elden must leave now." I cram a particularly large spoonful of porridge in my mouth and chew slowly while my sister gapes at me. "I'll travel alone with the human."

Mern scratches the base of her left horn. Something she does when she's angry and trying to hide it. "And why is that?"

"I have my reasons."

"Stupid ones that likely involve slaking your lust for the pretty mortal."

"Pretty? I would call her no such thing." But I'd most definitely *think* it.

She laughs. "Then you fool yourself, Brother. I've seen the way you watch her."

I shrug a shoulder. "And, still, I ask this of you."

The pear tree's roots curl and buckle, Mern's frustration affecting the earth beneath our feet. "No. It's too dangerous. You're still weak. The magic I transferred to you last night had almost no effect. You admitted as much yourself."

"But I've found a way to access power, limited though it may be. I assure you I'll be safe, and you and Elden will not be far ahead. Give me your golden horn. I promise to summon you with it should trouble find us." Its magical call can be heard over greater distances than the physical ear can detect, fae or not.

With a sigh, she removes the horn from around her neck, hidden beneath her clothing, and places the chain over my head, tucking it beneath my shirt and fastening two buttons around it.

"Thank you."

"How do you think the girl came to be in Faery?"

This is where I should admit that according to what Holly described, it's more than likely the mages, Ether and Aer, were involved. "I'm not certain," I say instead.

Mern takes my empty bowl, and the hut door swings open. We both watch the girl stride purposefully in the direction of the stable. I unfold my arms and push off the tree, standing straight.

"Where's Holly off to?" Mern asks.

"Where do you think you're going, human?" I call out.

Without faltering a step, she yells back, "To visit Wren, as I do every morning."

My shoulder sinks back against the tree trunk.

Mern stabs her finger into my chest. "Gade, wipe that smug expression off your face and tell me how you're accessing power."

"I wasn't feeling smug. More like pleased with myself."

"Same thing. Now hurry up and tell me."

"I know I said I'd explain last night, but I'd rather not speak about it. It might ruin it, cause it to stop working."

"Gade, I don't like this."

"Riddle me this, Sister, who will one day rule our kingdom? You or I?"

"Very funny. To become king, first you need to find your fated queen. So for now, we are equal, and because you love me, you'll give me an explanation."

Smiling, I tug her close and kiss her cheek. "Dearest Mern, thank you for not revealing my identity. She thinks I'm a palace guard, and I'd prefer to keep it that way."

Mern's brow rises, and she shakes her head, nearly taking my eye out with a horn. "You never ask much of me, so I won't refuse you this request, no matter how baffling I find it." She paces back and forth, arms folded tightly across her leather chest armor. "A castle guard? How did you manage to speak such a lie?"

"I didn't. She assumed it was so and spoke the words herself, and I didn't see the value in correcting her. It is my duty to protect our kingdom and the castle. The role of guard is close enough to the truth."

"That explains a lot."

"What?" I push my weight off the tree. "What do you mean?"

She strokes hair from my eyes. "Simply that a picture is beginning to form."

"Of what?"

"The foolish game you're playing." Then she turns and stomps off toward the stables.

"Mern. Wait!" I march after her, skidding to a stop near the entrance to the ivy-covered barn. I grip my sister's arm and swing her around to face me. "I'm playing no game. What do you speak of?"

She nods toward Wren's stall.

My horse whinnies loudly. At first, I think he's greeting me, and a smile tugs at my mouth in response. Then I look closer.

The girl strokes his nose as she grooms him, and I realize it's *her* presence he's delighted by, not mine. Heat lashes my chest, not from anger, but from something much worse—*jealousy*.

Holly hooks the brush on the wall, adjusts Wren's saddle and bridle, sloppily I note, then leads him past us, not once glancing to the side, ignoring me as if I'm an insignificant stable hand.

Mern and I watch her mount clumsily then trot my horse around the yard, smiling like a child at play.

Disgusted, I click my tongue. "She cannot ride very well. Look how she's abusing my Wren, bouncing around on his saddle, treating him like a child's pony instead of a warrior prince's steed."

Mern laughs, slamming her elbow into my ribs. "How is she to understand Wren's importance if you haven't told her who you are? She may not ride like a fae, but she seems perfectly capable to me."

"Well, whatever she thinks she's doing, I don't like it. I shall insist she stops." I take a step forward.

"Gade, wait a moment." My sister's forest eyes hold me firmly in place as she looks me up and down, her gaze shrewd. Mern has always seen more than I've wanted to reveal, even when we were children.

Stepping back, I lean against the stable's rotting door frame and push stones around the paving with my bare foot.

Mern squeezes my arm. "You're troubled by the girl's presence. Perhaps she should ride out with me now, and you can follow behind with Elden."

My head snaps up, cracking against the door frame. "What? Absolutely not." Stones crunch, turning to dust beneath my heel. "Trust me, that wouldn't be wise."

"Why not?"

I ignore her question and ask one instead. "Why didn't you bring a horse for her? That was a mistake," I say, tipping my chin at the girl.

She eases Wren into a walk and bends over his neck, stroking his red coat. I am beyond amazed to see my traitorous steed tolerating affection from a stranger.

Mern shrugs. "The images Lleu showed us didn't include Holly. We saw only that Wren was with you and in good health. Come, Brother, tell me why she discomfits you."

"She's *human*. Isn't that enough?"

"No, Gade. It really isn't. I never thought of you as prejudiced, but I suppose the curse has changed you and—"

"My power surges when I'm physically close to her. For this to be possible, an enchantment of sorts must have been placed on her. I don't understand it, nor do I trust her. But at present, I *need* her. I can't make this connection when others are around."

And that is only because I don't wish my sister and cousin to witness me *interacting* with the girl. That would be mortifying—a future king of Faery gaining power from a human girl's kisses.

"But this is marvelous." Mern grips my forearms and shakes me. "Do you think she's the one?"

Panic surges through me—flame and ice on repeat until I push Mern's hands away. "Don't be ridiculous. I would know my mate on sight, and though she once threatened it, Aer would never dare match me with a mortal."

"But, Gade, she—"

"There is something else I must tell you," I say. "The day before yesterday, the annlagh appeared to us. I believe he rose from the earth solely because he sensed a human's presence and was curious. The creature rendered me immobile but didn't hurt either one of us, though he could've. He confessed to an ongoing interest in the girl. There's power in possessing her."

One of the stable sparrows flits down from the rafters and lands on Mern's shoulder, ruffling its gold-speckled wings. "The annlagh? Now I *really* don't like this situation. We should shove her through the first portal we can find and send her back to wherever she came from."

"Not yet. I need time to understand her power over my magic."

"Fine." Mern nods, her expression blank enough to make me suspicious.

"Really? Your lecture is concluded?"

Mern pinches the tip of my ear. "We're ready to leave and have prepared supplies for your saddlebags. Since you've decided to shun our company, we'll make a start now and leave you to your human." The hug she gives me is quick and brutal, a sure sign she's anxious.

"I'll take care. I promise," I say, pulling her back for a gentler hug. "See you at home."

"I'm unfortunately familiar with your version of *taking care*, Brother. Think how you came to be injured in the first place." She sighs. "I'll leave glyph messages in the rocks as we scout ahead. Make sure to pay attention."

"Don't I always?" I walk backwards in the direction of the human, grinning at Mern. "On second thought, don't answer that question."

Elden stumbles out of the hut, arms laden with supplies. He tips his chin at me. "Good travels to you and your mortal, Gade."

"And the same to you and my overbearing sister."

Laughing, Elden continues toward the stable.

Wren trots forward, the human frowning and muttering to herself in the saddle as they cross Elden's path. He grabs the reins and pulls them to a halt.

"If I were you, I wouldn't call Gade a *fecking-feck-less-fae-who-thinks-he-owns-you* too loudly," he tells her. "He has a terrible temper."

She reels backward. "I whispered that. How did you hear me?"

"My element is air. And just as I heard Gade's travel plans from inside the hut, not a single tree's whisper escapes me. I say this to help you, Holly. Mind your words when I'm about. Gade, too. When his powers are firing, he hears everything around him."

Elden clicks his fingers and multi-colored leaves appear, spinning around the girl's head. She looks impressed by his cheap trick—one that even I, a future king, couldn't perform in my current state.

Unless I kissed her stupid first. At that thought, flames lick along the skin of my arms and chest—and possibly a few other places.

Smirking, Elden winks and mounts Neem, his sturdy brown and white roan.

Within moments, Mern and Elden are cantering through the yard, then disappearing into the trees. And once again, I am alone with the mortal.

I march over to my horse and snatch the reins from the girl's hands. "Dismount. We need to get ready to leave."

As she swings a leg over Wren and slides to the ground, I swipe an ax from the woodpile and walk in the direction of the creek, planning to restock the hut's firewood. She skips to catch up with me.

"I thought you said we were leaving straight away. Why didn't you want to travel with Mern and Elden? Is it because of the kissing thing?"

I roll my eyes.

Yes. Of course that's why, but I refuse to say it out loud and admit I've changed my plans because of *her* and the wildly disturbing effect she has on me that I have no wish for my family to witness.

"I have some things I need to do first," is my only reply.

Such as waste a little time to give my sister a decent head start.

"Now stop plaguing me with questions and help me put the hut to rights before we leave."

12

Only One Bedroll

Gade

"I wish I'd dressed more elegantly for traveling through your land," says the human behind me in the saddle, her fingers digging into my sides like tiny claws. "Even the deer in Faery are wearing jewels in their antlers as they trot along through the scrub."

I grunt. "Wait until you see the bark and leaf capes on the badgers that roam the woods near the castle. They're a very cunning design."

"You're joking," she says.

"Not at all. But even though they pay the moss elves who are fine nature weavers to make them, they look fairly ridiculous. Please don't tell the badgers I said that. They're very sensitive creatures."

Warmth infuses my chest as she laughs, its uplifting effect on my mood disturbing. I straighten my spine and remind myself I should be contemplating how to find my fated mate instead of trying to entertain a mortal, no matter how intriguing she is.

Late-afternoon sunshine illuminates the overgrown path through the darkening woods. My eyes ache from sifting through the shadows for threats, and my ears ring from the constant assault of the mortal's endless questions about the land and the kingdom she'll soon be entering.

Since her proximity produces a subtle but constant charge of power that helps me navigate and bend the forest to my will as we travel, the benefit of her body pressed against mine far outweighs any disadvantages of being distracted by it.

"I'm so exhausted I might fall off Wren's back," she says, strangling me as she tugs hard on my cloak.

"Then wrap your arms tightly around my waist. We'll soon make camp on the eastern bank of Fire River, where Merrin Creek crosses it."

I don't know why I tell her this information because it is as useful to her as the location of her village well is to me.

"Lleu, scout ahead," I command. "Check for signs of trolls. We don't want to encounter them during hunting season if we can help it. And I'm too tired to put up much of a fight tonight."

From his perch on the bronze plate of my shoulder armor, he lifts into the air with a strong flap of wings that makes the girl gasp, then soars above the trees, heading in a north-westerly direction.

Holly sighs and presses her cheek between the blades of my shoulders, and before long, her slow, rhythmic breathing tells me she has fallen into slumber. Perhaps she, too, struggled to sleep in that narrow bed last night.

I dig my fingers into the collar of my tunic, seeking relief from the sudden uncomfortable heat that scratches at my neck and chest.

When we arrive at a small clearing by the creek, the sun is a molten red and purple ball burning low through the trees, and Lleu's hunting calls cut through the air as he catches his dinner in the last of the light.

"Dismount," I say as Wren draws to a halt. "This is where we'll stop for the night."

Surprisingly, she swings her leg over his back without an argument and slides to the ground. I jump down after her, check Wren's temperature, and then hang a bag of oats around his head, rubbing his neck as I murmur my thanks for his exertions today.

I glance at the girl. "If my magic was stronger, I could set up camp in no time." I turn and stare without blinking, waiting for her to offer her lips as a recharge source, but she remains silent and unmoving.

Such a strange girl. Most humans would leap at an excuse to kiss a faery prince. I huff out a breath, recalling that she thinks I am a lowly palace guard. Even so, she should still find me irresistible.

"Unfortunately, without magic, we'll have to do the tasks the hard way," I say. "*Manually*. I shall collect wood for the fire, and when Wren is finished eating, you can lead him to the river to drink his fill. Then bring him back and clear this area of sticks and stones." With my finger, I draw a circle above the ground around us.

Instead of leaping into action, she only stares as if my directions are nonsensical.

Grinding my teeth, I say, "We need a clear space for the fire and a smooth area of earth to sleep upon. Do you think you can assist? Or must I do everything myself?"

"If you think you can trust a human to complete the tasks to your exacting standards, then certainly."

I grunt and begin to walk away, then stop in my tracks and peer back at her. "What did you say?"

She swats a hand at me like I'm an insect. "Nothing. I'm tired and grumpy and the jibe is beyond you, I'm sure."

Shaking my head, I leave her guzzling from a waterskin and walk into the thicket of trees that glow silver in the dusk. I focus my mind on the rising breeze, attempting to control it with my thoughts. The wind howls, buffeting me hard against a dryad whose body rests inside the trunk of a massive oak.

"Forgive me," I tell him.

He folds in half, bowing his bark-crowned head to his feet as I pass, and says, "Of course, my king," in a rasping voice.

I'm not your king yet, I think. *But soon. All I need is the girl who will make it so.*

When I return to the clearing, my arms filled with small logs and branches, Wren and Holly aren't there. I shrug and commence work.

After I finish setting the fire, I stroll to the creek and find my horse eating grass by the bank and the girl up to her knees in the water with her skirts hiked up and her stockings and boots strewn carelessly over the mossy rocks near the edge.

Too busy splashing her face and shrieking at the cold, she doesn't notice me arrive, nor does the silly girl realize she has just alerted half the creatures in the land of our presence.

As I draw a sharp breath to admonish the mortal, Lleu swoops low over her head, making her long sandy hair fly in the gust of air. For a moment, I'm transfixed by the sight, then jolted out of my daze when she falls face-first into the water, emitting another loud yelp.

In a burst of churning froth, a kelpie's dark head surfaces, its black mane a tangle of weeds and its teeth chattering as it spies what it imagines will be an easy dinner—my human.

Not while I am here, demon. Black fury clouds my mind and grips my muscles. If the kelpie touches even a hair on the girl's head, I will destroy it.

"Holly, get out now," I yell, leaping down the bank and into the water.

She stumbles to her feet. "What... why?"

"Get out now or be eaten by a water horse."

She peers over her shoulder. The beast rides toward her on a violently surging wave of river magic, hoping to sweep her under and away from me forever.

Over my dead body.

"Gade," she cries out, scrambling toward me.

I catch her around the waist and cradle her skull, pulling her close. She nods, knowing exactly what I need. Our lips lock together for three heartbeats, and sweet, heady power rushes through my veins.

I push her behind me. "Quickly, go. Get on the bank. *Now.*"

Cracking the bones in my neck, I face the shrieking creature. My palms shoot out, and I focus my energy on the cresting wave, forcing it to recede. Stunned at the strength of my renewed power, it takes barely any effort to subdue the beast's magic.

The kelpie's body sinks below the surface, its thrashing head still visible. With my hand raised to keep it immobile, I stride through the water, seize its bridle of matted reeds in my fist, and drag its head close to mine.

I whisper in its flattened ear, "Bow to your prince. Do it now, and if you execute it well, in this instance, I may spare your life. You have one chance to survive, kelpie. And if you ever... *ever* try to touch what is mine again, you will pay a terrible price for the pleasure."

It bows its head low, the dark mane swirling through the steaming water. "Prince of Five, stay your hand, for I will pledge allegiance to you and none other for a thousand cycles of the moon, but not one day more."

Fisting its hair, I shake it hard, its rotten teeth clattering in the long horse-like skull. "And this girl behind me?"

"She is yours and always will be. Never will I seek to touch your property, Gadriel Castle-breaker."

"Good enough." I let the slippery bridle slide through my fingers. "Be gone. And if you come near these banks again, I'll know it."

It whickers softly, backing away with downcast eyes before disappearing beneath the water with a thunderous crack of its tail.

"What in the fiery pits was that?" the human asks, her voice breaking as she shivers in her soaked-through clothes.

"A kelpie." Intrigued by the way the wet fabric of her dress embraces her curves, I wade out of the creek and join her on the bank.

Fae lords and ladies are more often than not reed thin and ethereal of body. This human is solid and voluptuous in an earthy way that for some reason, sets my mouth to watering.

"I've heard of them," she says. "They can shapeshift and appear as beautiful men or women to seduce mortals... they're myths."

"They also eat them. And as you saw with your own eyes, they are as mythical as I am. You were stupid to enter the water alone, human."

"You could have warned me."

"I didn't think you'd be foolish enough to bathe in the gloaming. All fae know it's the favored time for wild creatures to attack."

"I'm fae now, am I?"

My fists clench as I shoulder past her toward the camp. Wren follows me immediately, but of course the human stays behind for the sheer pleasure of being difficult.

I stop walking and call over my shoulder, "When the cannibal eydendric elves come out of the woods to bid you good eve, give them my best, then waste no time drawing your herb-cutting knife because I promise that you'll need it. I hope it's up to the task of keeping you alive."

A yelp pierces the air, then footsteps pound the earth as she quickly catches up to me.

Back at the camp, I remove some of the food Mern packed from the saddlebags for our dinner, a thought nagging at me. Why did the kelpie call me Gadriel Castle-breaker? It's an odd name and one I've never been called before.

I sort through memories, songs, and poems and find nothing that explains the strange moniker. Blowing out a hard breath, I decide to let it go. Likely the creature just hoped to rattle me, and I shouldn't allow such base trickery to affect me.

The girl catches the dried meat and bread I throw at her, and I tip my chin at the log I've drawn close to the fire, directing her to sit on it.

Kneeling in front of her, I twist my fingers into her hair, causing her to emit a loud gasp. "Apologies," I say as I tug her face close and press my lips to hers before she has a chance to protest.

Heat blisters my skin, and I rise quickly, flicking sparks from my fingers toward the kindling, flames roaring to life. She scowls as if I've done her grievous harm, when in fact, it's the exact opposite. I, the prince of Talamh Cúig, am taking *care* of her—a mere mortal—a remarkable occurrence, since the curse ensures I barely give a fig these days about anyone or any*thing*. She should be crawling in my wake and thanking me profusely.

"You need to get warm before you freeze to death," I mutter by way of explanation for stealing her kiss.

Placing the food on the log beside her, she shuffles closer to the fire, her movements slow and quiet, indicating residual shock, hopefully due to the incident with the kelpie, not from my kiss.

When I hand her a blanket, she thanks me and wraps it around her shoulders.

I frown. "No. You must take your clothes off, and then put it around you. Otherwise, the blanket will become damp, you'll generate no body warmth and freeze to death. Truly, human, 'tis a wonder you've survived all these years without me. How old are you, by the way?"

"Almost twenty years."

Fire-lit amber eyes stare back at me, framed by a star-studded mantle of black sky, but she makes no move to follow my directions. This one is not only stubborn, but foolish and ridiculous to the point of endangering herself.

I sigh. "Do it now or suffer days in a sick bed with only me to tend you."

"Fine, then. Turn around."

With a shrug, I go over to Wren, rub him down, remove his tack, and then check his hooves. As I work, the slap of clothes hitting the grass pricks my ears, but I keep my back turned. My mouth waters with a strange hunger, but I breathe slowly and dispel it.

"All right. You can turn around now," she says, as if I need a mortal's permission to do anything.

We eat our meal in silence, staring into the flames, the forest's shadows, and the net of stars floating above—anywhere but at each other. A fox cries in the distance, followed by the more unsettling sounds of wild fae on the hunt.

After promising not to go far and taking Lleu to watch over her, she disappears into the trees to perform her lowly human functions, returning as I bid Wren good night. Lleu flies into the tree above us, settling in to watch for danger as we sleep.

Wringing her hands, the girl grimaces at the single bedroll I've spread out near the fire. "Gade, where's mine?"

"Your *what*?" I take a drink of water before packing the skin away.

"My bedding."

"Unless you choose to kiss me all night long, I don't have the strength to keep the fire ablaze, therefore, you must take warmth with me in my bedroll."

"With you? But my clothes haven't dried yet."

As I picture the blanket falling to the ground and what she might look like unclothed, a sudden breeze whips my hair across my face, tangling it around my throat. I frown at the unbidden flash of air magic and the surprising effect this human has on my powers.

A smug smile teases my lips. "You must be naked so we can exchange body heat. Normally, I sleep clothed while traveling. It's safer in case I need to leave in a hurry or rise to fight. But tonight, to keep you warm, I will make an exception and sleep unclothed."

Even by firelight, I see the color blanch from her cheeks. My fingers go to my sword belt, working it loose.

"*Stop.* I can't imagine anything more mortifying than to lie naked next to you."

"Could you not?"

"I'd rather die."

"Then you may very well get your wish."

The chattering of her teeth makes my jaw clench hard. She must be made warm and quickly, too, if she hopes to be well enough to stay on Wren's back all day tomorrow.

Looking miserable, she pulls the blanket more tightly around her shoulders and shifts her weight from boot to boot. "Do you promise you won't touch me?"

"Impossible. We'll be lying side by side, my body warming yours, keeping you alive, in fact."

"But no more of the... kissing business you claim feeds your magic."

Claim? As if I would make up a story to justify putting my lips on hers. If I want to kiss her, I will, and she will beg for more. "Fine. There will be none of this kissing business, as you call it."

"Do you promise?"

"Yes." I throw my hands up, then rake them through my hair, tugging harder than necessary. "By the Elements Five, I swear that I will not only keep my trousers on, but I vow not to touch you any more than is necessary for our comfort and survival. Is that sufficient?"

"Yes. Thank you. Now turn around while I take my shoes off and get in."

Fireflies dance through moonlit branches as I hold my breath.

Waiting.

And waiting.

Turn, the poison says. *Do what you wish. You are a prince and will soon be the king.*

But I have promised to be good, and good I must be. At the very least, I will *try* to be so.

Snarling, I banish the curse's voice, form images in my mind of locking it behind the cage of my ribs, then passing the ancient key to the human, placing it in her warm palm.

What?

No.

What a stupid thing to imagine. Why would I ever give *her* anything of importance?

Rolling kinks from my shoulders, I concentrate on the fireflies. Their bright streams of light trail through inky darkness, winding around branches, as rustling sounds tell me the human is making herself comfortable in my bed.

I clench my fists, but I don't turn around, visions of what she might look like torturing and taunting me.

Rosebud lips.

Dusky skin.

More sweet buds on her chest, and elsewhere... soft, dewy petals unfolding.

Stop it, I tell myself. *What you want is impossible.*

Swallowing hard, I drop my sword belt on the ground, still not looking, still obeying her.

This is foolish. I am acting the fool. Who is the ruler of this land? Me or a fragile parcel of mortal flesh and bones?

"I'm turning around," I say, beginning to unbuckle plates of leather armor, unstrap knives from my waist and chest, all the while keeping my gaze on the ground as if I'm an obedient, humble slave and long for nothing more than her approval. I huff a laugh out.

What is wrong with me?

I unfasten the top strings on my pants.

"But you said—" she begins, obviously watching my every move. As I long to watch hers.

"Calm down. To please you I shall leave the trousers on. I have no plans to ravish you... tonight."

No, no plans, only a barrage of images assaulting me, showing me every detail of what such an endeavor might entail. How well I'd need to restrain and control myself. The way I'd need to treat her like a precious, irreplaceable object to keep from breaking her.

Carefully, I climb in beside her, my limbs sliding against her shivering body. She tries to shuffle away from my bare chest and draw her hips back, but it's no use. There's nowhere she can go in this bed of sewn-together blankets to escape my touch. And she needs my warmth to survive the shock of her encounter with the kelpie almost more than she needs air to breathe.

That is what I tell myself, at least.

Shudders rack her frame, the chattering of her teeth unbearable to my ears.

"Holly, if you will allow me to kiss you... only for a moment or two, I can keep the fire going longer and make you warmer."

"No."

Sighing, I press my chin against the top of her head and draw her into my arms. "Then you will have to suffer my embrace."

"Gade, I don't think—"

"Shush. Relax. I won't hurt you."

Her fists curl against my chest, her heart beating like a caged robin's as her panted breath dampens my skin. Touching her like this arouses a buzz of power, which I wrangle from the debauched direction it wishes to flow in and instead focus, using it to calm her, soothing her to sleep.

After a while, her muscles loosen, her breath slows, and just when I think she is drifting off to sleep, she looks up at me and touches my face.

"Why do fae have such long, pointed ears?" she asks. "Do they feel like human ears?"

"Touch them and find out."

Her cold fingers tentatively stroke the edge of my ear.

"Does the shape mean you can hear better than humans do?"

"Of course. Faeries surpass mortals in all ways."

Sharp nails pinch the tip of my ear with ruthless vigor. I hide a grin, and she massages the place she pinched, cringing and no doubt wondering if I'll retaliate.

"I'm sorry if I hurt you. I was curious to know if they're sensitive."

I grunt. "They are sensitive but... not to pain."

She blushes at that and snatches her hand away, tucking it against my chest.

Firelight flickers over her face, and I trail my fingertip down her nose. "I have many questions about your features. For example; why do humans have flat faces with cheekbones like juicy apples?"

"I've never thought of my face as flat before. But compared to faeries, I can see how you might think mine bland."

"Bland? No. In truth, I'm rather taken with your features. They are... charming."

Elements, please freeze my rambling tongue, for it has developed an alarming mind of its own.

I study the crescent moon above, flashing yellow as though it mocks me with a wink. When I first saw the mortal beneath the Crystalline Oak, if I'd known she would cause me to speak such drivel, I would have run at great speed in the opposite direction.

"Sleep now," I say, trying to glamor her into submission before I do something I'll regret. "Tomorrow we'll travel toward Mount Cúig where the four rivers of my kingdom originate from. Picture them in your mind as you drift off, winding north, south, east, and west from the Lake of Spirits cradled in a wide volcanic mountain, a sacred place to our people. Let your mind flow along with these magical waters and carry you to the realm of gentle slumber."

To my surprise, she follows my instructions without protest, and within moments, she is asleep in my arms, her flesh warm and long locks of hair a silky torment against my skin.

Like a babe, she sleeps tranquilly, believing she is protected and safe. But little does she understand the danger she will be in as we travel closer to my kingdom.

In Faery, humans are not safe.

Never have been.

Never will be.

And certainly not with the greatest monster in the land developing an unhealthy obsession with her—that is *me*—the cursed Black Blood Prince of Five.

13

The Merit King

Holly

After a second long day of travel, we camped at the base of Fire River at the point where it begins its climb up Mount Cúig toward the Lake of Spirits.

I spent another harrowing night sleeping close to the fae by the fire, but at least I had my own bedroll. Strangely, I slept much worse than the night before when I lay in his arms, the beat of his heart as soothing as a potent sleep tonic.

So far, Gade has kept his word and hasn't touched me without reason during the night, for which I'm both grateful and, if I'm honest with myself, more than a little disappointed.

The men in my village are wary of me, a healer versed in the old ways, and because of this, I fear that I may never experience a man's most intimate touch. But if I asked Gade, I'm certain he would not hesitate to show me.

This morning, after a quick breakfast of cheese and dried fruit, we packed Wren's saddlebags and headed up the mountain through a forest of shimmering trees, the pungent smells of pine, damp earth, and decomposing leaves perfuming the air.

As we travel slowly upward, Gade describes the view from the obsidian towers of Talamh Cúig's castle—the wild ocean, black cliffs, and the distant mountain ranges. Stories follow of the nine sacred hazel trees that the sea witches guard during the city's seasonal rites and of the wide variety of fae species, the vibrant images making my head spin.

When he asks about my world, I speak about my sister, then my mother and how desperate I am to return home to care for her before she passes. I remind him of our bargain, how he agreed to help me find a portal after I've visited his court for seven days and seven nights. I even ask why the duration of my stay is so specific, but he talks around the issue and refuses to elaborate.

After a while, I dismount to take what Gade calls one of my human time-wasting breaks. Contrary to his opinion, I complete the task promptly and head back, cutting through a thick undergrowth of ferns, when I spy him waiting on the path, scowling from his place in the saddle at a flock of rainbow-colored birds that flit around him.

"You had better not be contemplating going back on our bargain," I call out. "You look extremely devious at the moment."

"What?" His head swings in my direction, dark hair flying over his shoulder armor. "No. There's something tracking us." He thrusts his palm toward me. "Here. Mount quickly."

As he's about to pull me up behind him, a rumbling growl comes from the bushes. It turns into a roar as a large wolf leaps at Wren's head. In a blur of rapid movements, Gade's knife blade is embedded in the beast's throat, sticking out between its matted fur.

Gade dismounts, his boots thudding on the ground beside a nightmarish creature—a wolf with a distended, round stomach and two ugly heads with fang-filled snouts jutting from two thick necks. He withdraws his blade from one of the throats and stabs it three times into the beast's heart.

One, two, three.

Squelch. Squelch. Squelch.

"Just to be certain," he says, glancing up at me as he wipes his knife on a bank of moss under a pine tree.

"What was that thing? Did you have to dispatch it so violently?"

"It's an othrius. They are not the most malevolent of creatures dwelling in these woods, but I thought it best not to wait for it to grab you and steal you away. They eat their meals rather slowly, and I didn't want you to become its next course."

"That's a surprise. I thought you'd quite enjoy witnessing my gruesome death," I say, bending over the corpse and peeling back two sets of lips to inspect the sharp fangs.

Gade's bright eyes flick to the sky as if he's asking his favorite deity for patience, and he pushes me toward Wren. "Get back in the saddle, Holly. Don't tarry. There may be more of them lurking about."

Oh, so now I'm *Holly*, am I? He rarely calls me that.

"Of course, Your Royal Highness." I perform a mocking bow. "Just as you command."

He flinches as if I've struck him, then picks me up and deposits me on Wren's back without a word, quickly mounting in front of me.

Broad sunbeams push through fluttering leaves and twisting branches as we pick our way beneath soaring firs toward the summit of Mount Cúig.

The plants and vegetation seem to adhere to their own rules here in Faery, all manner of species growing when and where they shouldn't. In fact, everything is odd, the purple tinge in the sky, the silvery hue of the sun, and especially the grumpy fae I'm nestled against.

Birdsong echoes through the forest, along with Lleu's haunting calls as he flies high above the treetops, regularly swooping down and landing on Gade's shoulder to whistle cheerfully and almost take one of my eyes out with his massive hooked beak.

Wren gallops up a steep section of land, and then we burst through the trees into a glittering wonderland. We stop on a flat section of bank that surrounds a rainbow-colored lake, shining as if a magical mirror has been placed across the crater of the mountain. Fir trees dot the landscape, tall sentinels swaying in their uniforms made of every shade of green.

We dismount and Gade points out the other three rivers that trickle magically uphill from the bowl of the lake before flowing down to the east, west, and north. "Shortly, we'll follow Terra River northward to my home. But for now, you should rest and eat."

He tosses a parcel of food into the air, which I catch against my chest.

"I must bathe to restore my powers," he says, then grimaces. "Thanks to the curse in my blood, it won't do as much good as it should, but may spare you a few of my kisses."

"In that case, take your time," I say, heat traveling from my chest to my neck. I turn away, pretending to inspect the view. "And please take care of your wound while you swim."

Wren nickers and commences eating grass, the sound suspiciously like laughter. If it is, I'm glad we're amusing him.

Gade grunts, unfastening his belt, and I keep my gaze averted as he undresses quickly. Bracers, weapons, and bits of leather armor and clothing thud against the ground.

"Don't move from there lest you get eaten by trolls," he commands, his voice growing distant as I imagine him strolling down the slope toward the lake.

I open an eye in time to see him disappear under the water up to his neck, dark hair floating over the surface. A gust of wind startles me as Lleu lands beside me and taps his beak on my thigh, emitting a shrill noise.

"You're right, Lleu, I shouldn't be looking. What do you suggest I do to occupy my time instead of gawking at your master?"

As if he can understand my words, the eagle hops around the grass under Wren's belly, picking up colorful stones with his beak and depositing them one by one into my palm.

"Why, thank you. These are lovely." Crossing my legs, I make pretty gemstone patterns over the grass, looking through the bigger, translucent stones at the sky and inspecting the unusual pink and purple clouds streaking the horizon.

I consider a venture into the woods in search of plants to add to my healing pouch, taking Lleu with me for safety. Then I remember the two-headed othrius and decide to obey Gade's instructions and remain exactly where I am.

Lleu and I are busy sharing chunks of bread when Gade strides up the hill, naked as the day he was born, and making me choke as I twist around to face the forest. At least, I presume faeries are born in the same manner humans are. If not, I hate to think by what method.

A rumbling chuckle sounds behind me, then the rustle of clothes and clang of weapons being affixed to belts and straps as Gade dresses, all the while murmuring to his horse.

I'm a curious person by nature and long to take a peek at his body. But I'd have trouble hiding my awe, and I refuse to increase his already over-inflated ego by drooling like a desperate old maid.

When it sounds like Gade is finished, I risk a glance, surprised to see a wavering overlay of fine golden armor, a barbed circlet, sharper ears, and more extravagantly chiseled features flashing over his traveling-soldier's garb.

"What's happening to you?" I ask. "A kind of magic weaves itself over your image."

The hand tightening his sword belt stills, and he raises a single black brow.

I point at his body. "You look different, as if you're two different people at the same time and your body can't decide which one it wishes to remain."

"It's nothing to be concerned about. The Lake of Spirits has renewed me, so my power is asserting itself in a corporeal manner, that's all."

Lleu suddenly starts hopping from foot to foot, whistling. Picking up the gemstones on the grass one by one, he throws them at

Gade, hitting his legs and stomach. Muttering and side-eying the eagle, Gade does his best to ignore him.

"Why is Lleu doing that?" I say.

"Don't ask," the fae answers.

"I already did."

"Stop it, Lleu. You've made your thoughts quite clear," he admonishes.

Lleu makes a piping noise, hops over to me, and snuggles under my arm. I stroke his golden head. "What was he trying to tell you?"

"Oh, you wouldn't be interested."

"I'm sure I would be. Tell me—"

"Be quiet." Gade whirls around, squinting toward the trees. He draws his sword a heartbeat before a flash of blue lights up the bank below us.

"Kiss me, Holly, and do it quickly." He yanks me into a hard embrace and ravishes my mouth cruelly. "I'm sorry, but danger comes." Then he pushes me away, an aura of gold light radiating from his body. "Go to the trees. *Run.* Lleu, go with her."

Before I can object, a man's head, crowned by a wild mop of silver hair, appears from thin air, followed by his lanky, translucent body. On his shoulder, sits a black raven with emerald eyes and a long bronze beak from which it emits a horrible caw. The bird, like its master, is as transparent as a phantom and both look exceedingly unfriendly.

The man smiles without warmth or humor. "Gadriel, what a surprise to meet you here."

Gade's spine stiffens as he stands tall. "Since you've transferred directly into our territory, to our most sacred of places, you must have expected to meet an Elemental, El Sanartha. Although... perhaps not me."

The newcomer called my companion Gadriel—a more regal name than Gade. Fae must shorten birth names for convenience and to show friendship and affection as humans do.

Gade flicks the sword hilt in his hand, spinning it in warning. "What do you want?"

The stranger stops several feet from us, and my eyes bulge as I inspect him from head to toe.

A crown of spiked, rainbow obsidian sits atop a shock of white hair. Fingers tipped with black claws are braced against his narrow hips, the color matching the row of curved fangs poking between his gray-lipped smirk. Dark green eyes glitter in his pale, pinched face. His expression conveys a touch of madness and a nature cruel and dangerous.

"Come now, is that the proper way to greet me?" the stranger asks, a metallic cape flowing around his slender form.

Gade slides his body in front of me, and I peer around his arms to get a better view of the strange fae. "I address you as you deserve. Murderers forfeit any title of respect." Gade's tone is taunting, unafraid, which seems unwise considering the circumstances.

"Perilous words to speak to a king," says the fae called El Sanartha.

"Can you deny their truth?"

The fae laughs, spreading his upturned palms by his sides. Since he doesn't refute Gade's claim, he is very likely the villain in this piece. And if he is indeed a king, he's most definitely a deranged one.

As their body language grows more hostile, a wall in my mind crumbles, opening space for the idea that something in this scenario doesn't ring true. The king speaks to Gade in a familiar manner, tinged with a note of uncertainty or fear, and it's not at all how I'd expect royalty to address a palace guard. How would a foreign king come to know a soldier's name? Who are they to each other?

Alarm prickles over my skin.

Gade points his sword tip at the ground. "We are both busy, Merit, so let us not waste time. Tell me now what you hope to gain here." These words, spoken softly but filled with subtle power, startle the king's gaze from a slow perusal of my body back to Gade.

The king flicks his chin toward me. "Our High Mage sensed the human enter the Tuatha realm. My sole purpose here is to see her for myself. I am pleased to note she is able bodied and suitably attractive. Therefore, I wish to make her my property."

The ground shakes beneath my feet, thunder rumbling above. "Why?" Gade growls out, raising the jeweled hilt of his sword, fury pulsing from his trembling limbs.

"We Merits believe humans have much to teach us. As a species, they embrace change and their toil over new inventions is both admirable and fascinating. We wish to learn from them. What will you accept in exchange for her?"

"Let me see..." Gade pretends to think, then snarls like a wolf. "First, your snow-white head displayed on Castle Black's tallest spire. And second, *nothing*. Nothing and no one could take her from me. If you don't believe me, draw your sword and let me prove it."

The king smiles. "I am glad to hear your much-touted sense of humor has not completely deserted you, even as the famed poison progresses through your blood."

"And if you believe I would bargain with the fae responsible for the death of my parents, you're clearly as mad as the tales my courtiers tell about *you*."

The king shrugs. "Every single item in all the realms has its price. What is yours for the girl?"

"The life of every Merit and the return of my parents' souls as your punishment for asking, and still, I wouldn't give her up."

"Then it is a pity I cannot comply and test your high and mighty resolve."

"I repeat: if you gave me every jewel or power in existence, I still wouldn't let you have her. *Never*, do you hear me? The mortal is mine."

"Perhaps. Unless I kill you now."

"Impossible. You stand at the Elemental seat of power where your magic lies dormant. Somehow, you've transferred here, but not in a solid state. Do you not realize I can see straight through you?"

The king's body flickers, one moment flesh and bone and the next, as incorporeal as a spirit's.

"True, Gadriel, but my senses tell me you're injured, not fully recovered, and unable to access your power. My sword is as solid as yours, and my skill with it is not to be underestimated, even in this state."

"Nor is mine." Gade lifts his blade, then without turning, whispers. "Take Wren. Follow Lleu into the trees. If I fall, ride north until you can go no farther. Do not disobey me."

Lleu screeches and takes flight, and I watch where he lands.

My fingers dig into the bracer on Gade's forearm. "Wait. Should I...?"

"*What?* Speak quickly."

"Kiss you to enhance your—"

"No time." He shoves me away and slashes the blade in front of his chest in a cross pattern, then looks back at me briefly. "For Dana's sake, Holly, go!"

"Oedgar, my dear, you may watch my victory from the trees," El Sanartha says.

It takes me a moment to realize he's speaking to the bird whose black wings give a metallic creak as it flies away.

Without warning, the Merit roars and takes off at a run toward Gade, his body flickering and solidifying. Cursing, I grip Wren's reins and make a dash for the line of trees, running alongside the horse as fast as I can. By the time I hide behind a tree trunk and peer around it, the Merit fae is far too occupied to care where I am.

Gade's hand grapples around his neck as if he's searching for something, possibly the horn he wears on a leather strap, which seems to have disappeared. Grimacing, he raises his face to the sky and bellows, "Mern!" like a battle cry, and a bolt of lightning strikes the ground behind the king.

I look around to see if Gade's sister will answer the cry and magically appear from the ether as the white fae did, but unfortunately, that doesn't happen.

A sharp zing of steel on steel rings through the air as the fae slash back and forth, crushing wildflowers beneath their boots like heroes in the traveling pantomime shows I loved as a child. But this is no choreographed performance—far from it.

The scent of blood tainting the breeze is real, telling me that flesh has been opened, hopefully not Gade's. I don't trust him, but I'm certain that out of my two possible captors, he is the safer option.

Gade fights well, so much better than should be possible, considering his still-healing wound. Magic flows through the Elemental guard's limbs in visible flashes of silver hoops that circle his body, quickening his movements. Lightning bands his arms, granting them strength and power. He grins as the Merit curses, likely proving a more formidable opponent than the king had hoped.

Two blades come together again, one black one silver, both sliding to their hilts. With a grunt, Gade pushes away, spins and feints a mid-chest cross cut, instead slicing low along the gap between one of the king's thigh-high boots and the edge of his armor. Blood gushes from the wound, proving the Merit is a flesh and blood creature after all and not a phantom.

El Sanartha's voice rings out across the grassy bank. "Give me the girl," he demands, "and I vow I'll leave your court in peace for the remainder of your lifetime—however long that shall be, Gadriel Lake Eyes."

Lake eyes? Is that some kind of fae slur?

Gade growls. "You'll have to end me first."

El Sanartha bows. "So be it. I shall do my best."

"If you harm a hair on her head, I'll hunt you until the end of time."

"*When*, not if I harm her..." El Sanartha pants. "You will already be dead."

"Then I'll haunt your nightmares until your body's last breath and rattle your bones forevermore. Touch her and rue the day you first looked upon her lovely amber eyes."

"Lovely, you say?" says the king, renewing his attack. "Who..." Lunge. Stab. "Owns..." Slash. Smash. "Who?"

Gade roars, then in frantic paces, the fae range back and forth—toward the bank, then closer to the trees I'm hiding behind—grunting and panting in a blur of powerful limbs and flashing metal.

Pine needles lift and whirl around their legs, the fresh scent mingling with the bitter tang of blood. Even in their weakened states, both fighters are ruthless, savage, and I can only imagine how vastly more terrifying this battle would be if both males were at their full power.

They turn widdershins in an ever-narrowing circle of violence. The king stumbles, tearing his claws across Gade's face. Gade's sword slashes back with renewed vigor, curses spitting from his lips. He thrusts, feints, making his opponent stumble again, then spins with his sword raised high, using the force of his momentum to strike hard from above.

The Merit blocks the strike, but his black blade cleaves in half, and still he slashes with the jagged metal left jutting from the hilt gripped in his claws. With his broken blade, victory is impossible. Gade will triumph. He has to.

Gade redoubles his attack, slashing mercilessly and driving El Sanartha back toward the forest until his spine slams against the trunk of a tree. The tip of Gade's blade pierces the Merit's throat as he flails like a stuck insect, a dark ribbon of blood trailing his pale skin. Gade's gusting breath blows the Merit's white hair from his face.

But why doesn't he move to kill him?

I grit my teeth against the horror of the words I'm about to speak, but say them anyway. "Finish it."

End it now, before the roles reverse, and the fae I have no bargain with kills Gade and carries me to a land where they buy humans to study and experiment on. If this Merit wins, my instincts tell me my life will be that of an abused pet locked in a cage. Perhaps forever.

The raven called Oedgar swoops down, pecking at my scalp and then my cheek before flying toward the king. Squawking, Lleu chases after it, keeping it away from Gade.

"Gade, finish it," I shout, something telling me that the Merit won't stop until Gade and his people are destroyed.

Gade looks back over his shoulder at me, staring long enough for the Merit king and his horrible bird to disappear, leaving nothing but swirls of dark smoke in their place and a stench of burning hair in my nostrils.

14

Arrival

Holly

"What happened?" I rush to Gade's side, pulling Wren along with me. "Where did the king go?"

"King? That son of a draygonet doesn't deserve the title." Gade crowds me against a tree, his palms above my head, his eyes wild and terrifying. "Did I tell you that you could move while the battle raged?"

I open my mouth to answer, but his fists curl into my hair, the shock of his roughness cutting off my words.

"No. I didn't," he says against my lips. "You could have got yourself killed. I sorely wish you would *listen* to me and follow my instructions."

For a moment, I think he's going to kiss me, but instead, he pushes away from the tree, cursing under his breath.

Crouching, he wipes his blade on the grass, then slides it into its scabbard hanging from his sword belt. "The Merit has likely transferred nearby to recover before he returns home."

"And he won't come back to fight?" I ask, my fingers twisting the material of my skirts.

"Come here. Let's go." Strong hands grip my waist and hoist me onto Wren's back. "I doubt the Merit will return, but in Faery, anything is possible; quite often the very thing you least expect. And we don't want to run into him off the summit, where I'll be weaker."

Gade whistles for Lleu, and the eagle swoops onto the perch fixed above Wren's neck.

"That raven bird tried to kill me," I say, looking down at Gade as he fusses with the bridle then rearranges the position of my legs. Even through my skirts, my skin burns at his touch.

"Doubtful. If Oedgar had wanted you dead, then dead you would be. The creature is fortified by magic and metal, a deadly combination," he says gruffly as he scans my face, then my collarbones. "Your mortal flesh and skin are soft and weak." He speaks the last part in a husky whisper, some rare emotion darkening his eyes to indigo.

I'd like to argue, but my mind, overheated by his touch, swims in residual shock from the battle.

He gulps water from a skin, and then in his usual feat of magical acrobatics, mounts gracefully with me already in position on a rolled blanket behind the saddle.

"Are you all right?" I ask as he wheels Wren around and jerks him into a trot, then a canter.

"Fine."

"You weren't wounded in the fight?"

"No."

"What about your stomach? I hope you didn't reopen the wound."

"I said I'm fine, didn't I? Listen, this may be asking the impossible, but can you at least *try* to stop talking for a while? If we're to arrive home before nightfall, I need to focus the little power I have left to boost Wren's speed. I recommend you hold on to me tightly."

The thought of arriving at his kingdom sends twin bolts of fear and excitement branching through my veins as I wonder if the kingdom's rulers will murder me on arrival. They haven't sworn to protect me like Gade has.

As we fly down the mountainside, I press my cheek against Gade's back and stare at the violet-tinged sky peeking through the treetops. If I'm going to be thrown in a dark dungeon, this may be my last opportunity to soak in beauty.

In a matter of hours, we're off the mountain and following Terra River as we race across a flat plain that Gade calls the Lowlands, an expanse of grassland, broken only by the two tall peaks of the Dún Mountain range growing ever-closer in the north-east.

When we reach the mountain pass and start through the thin valley that snakes between soaring black cliffs, Wren's pace slows to a walk, the comforting clip-clop of hooves against stones a calming sound as we travel through the narrow passage.

Fighting my drooping eyelids, I wrap my arms tighter around the fae's waist, hoping I don't fall asleep and tumble off Wren's back. "So, is Lake Eyes your family name?" I ask in an effort to stay awake.

"Absolutely not."

"Then why did the king call you that?"

"It was a taunt, the same as if I were to call you something foolish, such as honey eyes because your eyes are amber. Or sweet lips because when I kiss you, it tastes like…" He clears his throat, then clicks his horse into a trot.

"Do go on," I prod, eager to hear the end of *that* fascinating sentence.

"Be silent. I'm listening out for bird signals."

I don't hear any birds. In this dark mountain pass, there are no trees for them to rest in, nor any nooks and crannies etched into the sleek stone cliffs. "Oh? And what do you expect they might tell you?"

"Likely they'd advise me not to murder the human in my care before we arrive at Castle Black."

"*Before?* Wait… We struck a bargain. You promised you wouldn't—"

"Enough prattle. I keep my vows, so you can calm down. I was making a jest."

I blow out a breath. "Well, it wasn't an entertaining one."

"If it's diversion you seek, then look over your shoulder. The Valley of Light is putting on quite a performance."

"What?" I grip his sword belt and swivel around, blinded by a river of light that flows along the path behind us, giving the illusion we've been riding over liquid silver and making the cliff walls sparkle like jewels. "Spectacular," I grudgingly admit.

"Indeed. Now don't let go of me. We'll ride the rest of the way at breakneck speed."

"Yes, sir," I whisper, hugging him tightly.

"I heard that," Gade says as he leans over Wren's neck.

The horse breaks into a gallop. A creature of air, his hooves are so silent I suspect they barely hit the ground as we speed along, at one with the wind and the elements around us.

After a while, two riders appear in the distance, their horses growing larger as we advance toward each other.

The silhouette of a large mountain spans behind them and what looks like white waterfalls gushing down its rocky sides, a pink and blue sunset above it.

The riders turn out to be Gade's sister and cousin—Mern's magnificent horns and Elden's mop of shaggy hair clues to their identities.

Steamy breath blows from the horse's nose as Mern stands in the stirrups, laughing and waving her arms recklessly above her head.

"What took you so long?" she asks, trotting her golden horse up to us, then swinging it around so they're riding beside us. "We've been home since morning."

"Wonderful," rumbles Gade's voice against my chest. "Shall I present your medal now? Or would after dinner suit you better?"

"Oh, shut up, Brother." Mern leans in and plants a loud kiss on his temple.

With a laugh, he drops the reins and seizes Mern's chin, kissing both her cheeks in turn. "It's good to see you." He grins at Elden. "And you, Cousin."

Elden rides close and wraps Gade and me in a rib-crushing squeeze. I groan as he releases us, and the horses snort and stamp in impatience, their bridles jangling merrily.

"You had an uneventful journey?" asks Mern.

Gade laughs. "Not exactly. We met El Sanartha at the Lake of Spirits. Our swords tussled, but he wasn't at full power, and I had no trouble beating him."

"*Elements*, why didn't you use the horn to call us?"

"Because I seem to have misplaced it."

Mern's golden skin blanches white. "And Holly wasn't harmed?"

"No. I would've died before I allowed him to touch her."

Mern cuts a sharp glance my way. "How... protective of you, Gade," she says in an amused voice.

"But of course, the Merit was extremely interested in her. We haven't heard the last of it. The war council must be ready for anything, even war." His tone is ruthless and bloodthirsty, as if he's happy about the prospect of battle, rather than disappointed or even frightened by it.

"I'm right here," I say, digging my fingers into Gade's sides. "I wish you wouldn't speak about me as if I'm already dead."

"That's fair," Gade agrees. "As long as when you are deceased, we're allowed to gossip about you often."

"Funny," I say.

A low chuckle comes from his throat. "Not many would agree with you, human." He nudges Wren into a trot. "Now let's get a move on. I'm famished."

"Is the secret out yet?" Mern asks, tipping her head in my direction.

Gade's muscles stiffen. "No."

Mern and Elden laugh. "Well, it soon will be."

"What secret?" I ask, my jaw clattering shut as the horses gallop side by side, cutting off the conversation and hurtling us toward the majestic mountain where the fae's city must be located.

A violet night falls around us as we start across an ornate bridge that transports us high above the mountain's waterfalls and onto a path that spirals upward toward a pair of grand gates. A full orange moon floats above them as they slide open on Gade's command, flashing a deep jade color in the moonlight.

The horses move forward, and Mern nudges me with her knee. "Holly, most fae in Talamh Cúig have never seen the likes of you before. Prepare for unwelcome attention. Faeries aren't shy creatures. They'll want to touch. Prod. Many won't like the presence of a human. Do your best to endure it with a smile on your face or risk getting it bitten off."

A shiver rolls down my back. I'd prefer to retain my face if possible. I only hope the palace guard I've struck a bargain with has the authority to keep me safe, as he promised.

"Will you hand me to the authorities as soon as we arrive?" I ask Gade.

He looks back at me, his lips compressed. "We shall see."

"Can't I stay with Mern, wherever she lives? She seems kind and caring. I think we'd get along very well."

"Impossible."

"Why?" I tug Gade's cloak.

"That will soon be apparent," Mern replies ominously.

Our horses tread up the winding pathway in a cacophony of jingling bridles and clip-clopping hooves, the sound of waves crashing below us.

"There's an ocean down there," I say. "I can't see it, but I can hear it."

"Yes." Gade's head turns toward the noise. "One day, we'll build a second stronghold on the expanse of land we're passing now and enjoy a better view of our enemies as they travel through the Lowlands to break peace with us."

"If it's a good position for defense, why didn't you build there first?"

"Castle Black sits on sacred ground, forged from volcanic rock that rose from the sea by command of the sea witches, with whom we maintain an Elemental alliance."

"Also, our land suffers since the death of the king and queen," says Mern. "We need a new monarch to take the throne and fortify our land before we can build again. Every day, I beg the Elements to help the heir find his true power so this can be done."

"What's stopping him from—" I begin.

"Enough," Gade says. "Our political problems are the least of the mortal's concerns."

Arriving home has put the fae in an even sourer mood than usual. Perhaps he dislikes his work as a castle guard and doesn't want to return to it, which would be odd, since he seems rather fond of violence.

We travel east along a path through woods that Elden calls the Emerald Forest. Tiny faeries peer out from behind trees, their wings aglow as they fly in front of us as if lighting the way for our party. Other creatures, their bark-covered bodies peeling from tree trunks, bend in deep bows as we pass.

A song of lilting pipes drifts from somewhere in the valley below, growing louder until sparkling light circles our horses and our bodies, then disappears in a tinkle of bright laughter.

"Ignore the pixies," says Elden. "They're hoping you'll leap off Wren and chase after them. Best you don't, though. We may never see you again."

"Duly noted." Shivering, I nestle into Gade's warm back, my thoughts drifting and growing slower, as thick as treacle.

"Time to rest, little human," Gade's voice rumbles against my cheek, an incantation lulling me to fall into the dream realm. It feels like magic, but I'm too tired to bother fighting it.

When I wake, we're in a large courtyard, softly lit by floating lanterns, and Gade passes me from the saddle into waiting arms. Something strokes my cheek, and Elden's softly accented voice says, "Her vulnerability is rather charming, don't you think, Gade?"

"Put her down," he replies. "*Now*. She's awake and quite capable of standing without *your* cloying assistance."

Elden chuckles, and Gade dismounts, rainbow-hued light outlining his body. By some magic, he looks taller, his shoulders broader, and an impressive crown of multi-colored crystal spikes glows softly on his forehead, casting moon-sparked flashes on the dark paving.

I glance at Mern and Elden, wondering if perhaps crowns are a compulsory fashion accessory for every fae in the city—guard or not.

Mern wears an ornate silver and ruby circlet that curves across her forehead and winds around the base of her horns, but Elden's head is bare.

From the edges of the courtyard, elegant fae bow low as we pass by them and up the stairs that lead to a foreboding castle, shining the color of wet tar in the moonlight.

I side-eye Gade as he walks beside me with his head held high, and I realize I've been a gullible fool.

He isn't a palace guard. He's someone important—perhaps a high councilor or a war commander.

At the top of the stairs, gigantic black and green doors open, creaking on their ancient hinges, and a woman bathed in pulsing silver light appears on the threshold.

"Ether," Gade says, smiling.

All three of my companions bow low to the magical creature. When Gade rises, he presses his forehead to Wren's, and an armored fae takes the reins and leads the horse away.

"Gadriel. You've returned safely, just as I promised Mern days ago that you would." She opens her pale arms, and Gade leaps up the last two steps and plants a kiss on her luminous face.

"High Mage, look what we've brought home for you to study—a mortal girl named Holly," Elden says as we enter a cavernous foyer.

Precious metals and jewels set in fanciful designs cover every surface, the richness blinding to my eyes that are more accustomed to plain and practical interiors.

Gade stares at his cousin with violent intent. "The girl is mine, not yours to give away like a trinket you found on your journey. As yet, I haven't decided her fate. But on pain of death, no one is allowed to lay a finger on her."

Ether laughs. "No one but you, of course."

Gade fixes her with an imperious look. "I don't know what you mean."

"I am only reassuring you, Your Highness, that the bond between you is clear. No one would dare take her from you."

"Bond?" Gade glares. "What bond?"

"*Your Highness?*" I splutter. "What... Are you a *king*?"

"He is a prince and heir to the Throne of Five," says Ether, turning her black gaze on me.

My head spins as recognition hums through me. "I know you. We've met before," I say, a blurry image of the forest near my home wavering in my mind.

"Do you think so, dear? It is unlikely. I am spirit and flow through all that exists. Perhaps we've met in a dream."

My mouth opens to contradict her, but my words drift away, my mind as light as cotton candy. "But I—"

"Yes, Holly?" says the mage. "You have something to tell me?"

Frowning, Gade grasps Ether's wrist, his lips parting as if he has an urgent question to ask. Then his eyes glaze over too.

"I do, but I can't seem to recall what it was. It was important..."

The mage strokes my shoulder, and I notice her ring and little finger are longer than the others and webbed together with a shiny flap of scale-covered skin. "The thought will return to you. Promise me that when it does, you'll find me without delay and speak of it to no other."

As if I'm hypnotized, I nod. "Yes, I'll do that. I promise."

"For now, you need rest, as does Prince Gadriel."

Prince Gadriel. I can't believe it, but then again, it does make unsettling sense—his arrogance, the way he speaks and holds himself as if the entire world must obey and revolve around him.

A white halo of hair moves around the mage's head, bristling and flowing as if it responds to her emotions. I would love to run my fingers through it, test its weight and texture, but wisely, I don't give in to the urge. Best not to risk offending her.

"Elden," says Gade as he unstraps his weapons and passes them to servants. "Take the mortal to the cells. After I've slept a while, we'll meet with the council in the Great Hall and discuss her fate."

With my heart in my throat, I step forward and tug Gade's arm roughly, a hiss traveling through the gathered courtiers at my mishandling of their prince. "Are your vows worth so little? You promised to help me, that no harm would befall me at your court."

"Not precisely," he counters, jerking his arm away. "You agreed to remain here for seven days and seven nights, and I vowed to allow you to attempt to return home to your mother. That is all. If you didn't think to add words into our bargain that safeguarded you, then you cannot blame me for your own failure."

"Then you're nothing but a monster who bends the truth to your advantage. Admit you swore to protect me."

The courtiers titter, and cries of "burn the human" hiss through the air.

Cruel fingers grip my shoulders, and Gade pushes me against a wall, snarling down at me. "I swore *nothing* of the kind. Since it is impossible for me to lie, your accusations are baseless."

"Gadriel." Ether places a hand on his back. "Control your rage. Do not allow the curse to command your nature. Has your injury weakened you so much that you now stoop to terrifying the wits out of a girl who stands helpless before you?"

He sighs and steps back. "As always, you're right, Ether. But I must know... is this mortal the foretold witch?"

"No. She is not that. But know this: harm your healer at your peril."

Color leeches from Gade's face, and he drops his head, eyes downcast. "Your will is mine, High Mage."

"Good. The girl must have a well-appointed room of her own, not a cell in the dungeons. See to it."

"But—" begins Gade.

"But nothing. She is a guest in our land and will be treated thusly. Call me after you have rested." The mage gives me a sly smile, then dissolves into the air, leaving a shower of golden petals in her wake.

I'm the only one who gapes at her dramatic exit.

With a series of brisk commands, Gade offloads me to a servant, who nods sourly, and then leads me up one of the two sweeping carved staircases that provide access to the castle's many levels. From where I stand, I count seven landings and seven thin towers with chambers circling their perimeters, spiraling ever upward.

"Wait a moment." Gade takes the stairs three at a time and stops on the one below me.

My heart pounding, I meet his glowing blue gaze and try not to cower under the magnificence of his true appearance, free from the glamor that diminished his fierce beauty.

I raise my chin. "Yes?"

The maidservant moves away, and Gade leans close to me, his breath stirring my hair and speeding my pulse. "Trust no one," he whispers, which strikes me as strange since his command before ensured that he's the only fae in the city who has the ability to harm me.

If he's convinced his subjects are a danger to me, then I'd be a fool if I didn't take extra care over the next seven days, while I hope and pray with all my might that the prince remains true to our bargain.

In the meantime, I plan to pay attention to everything I see and hear, so that when the opportunity to return home presents itself, I'll be more than ready to take it.

15

The Black Castle

Holly

Thanks to Ether, my quarters in the south-eastern tower are luxuriously furnished, swathed in dark green and gold silks and tapestries, with an enormous four-poster bed fit for a queen to sleep in.

Set deep into the black and jade curved walls are seven arched windows that overlook the Black Forest and the soaring mountain peak where the future city of Talamh Cúig will one day be built.

Surprisingly, the gilded doors aren't locked, and I spent yesterday, my first day in residence, wandering through the castle and grounds with Mern and her attendants, doing my best to ignore the dark prince whenever I found myself caught in his orbit.

Whenever our paths crossed, Gade looked cold and distant and refused to meet my gaze, and I got the distinct impression that he wished he had never stolen me from beneath the crystal tree, where I had the misfortune to arrive in Faery.

In his own land, Gade's dazzling true nature is revealed. From his crown of multi-colored gemstones that Mern tells me represents the five elements, to the hard, beautiful lines of his glamor-free body clothed in materials that change with the light and environment—embroidered with gold, tipped and cuffed with feathers and furs—he's a breathtaking sight to behold.

Returned to his castle and stripped of all artifice, Prince Gadriel appears to grow stronger with every breath, his sky-blue eyes reflecting power and a frightening intensity that stems from the curse burning madness like a contagion through his blood and illuminating his supernatural nature.

How did I ever convince myself this spectacular, dangerous creature was a mere palace guard?

I've spent the morning with Mern and her group of raucous courtiers, watching them compete in an archery competition, where no less than three fae left the tournament grounds with elaborately fletched arrows pierced through their hearts. In Faery, sporting skill is a matter of life or death.

After the games, which the Prince of Five neglected to attend, we meander toward the Great Hall, taking the long way around the city, so I can gape at the sights. My new friends laugh at my awe, but if they could only see my home—the ramshackle village, my tiny cottage, and the nearby forest and ocean that conform to the laws of nature—they might better understand my astonishment.

Talamh Cúig's castle is a dazzling, light-filled structure made of black and green stone with an abundance of arched windows lining its walls, through which refreshing briny breezes blow in from the Emerald Sea below.

The ground floor houses the Great Hall, kitchens, and the sprawling quarters of most fae who live in the city. Subsequent floors hold smaller but no less grand reception and meeting rooms, quarters for the fae of higher station, and the imposing sky-high towers where the royal family and their retainers live.

The city itself sprawls over the mountain, and the outdoor areas contained within its jet-black walls include a dairy, wild gardens, no less than three forges, and quaint stores that ramble up and down the hillside. All paths lead to the oval tournament ground at the bottom of town, nested between the cliff edge and the wall of shiny black rock the castle sits upon.

Everywhere I look, magic abounds. Creatures seem part animal, part forest. Beautiful cruel-eyed fae command the elements with a flick of their hands. Indescribable colors of flora and fauna delight my senses, and floating lights follow me unbidden. Strange music calls from afar, beckoning me to join a dance that Elden says might keep me twirling into insanity or death. I do love to dance, but it might be best to avoid joining a faery reel if I can.

Mern links her arm through mine and pulls me up the stairs into the Great Hall for lunch. Even though the midday sunlight pours into the hall from tall windows, and flames from thousands of candles burn from sconces and candelabras, a strange fae light dusts everything with the sparkle of stars, the effect both charming and unsettling.

I stare at the flashing jewel-toned colors of the faeries' clothing, their skin, eyes, horns, and wings, all a sumptuous feast for the eyes.

"Close your mouth, Holly," says Elden, holding a wine goblet up to his wide grin.

His brother, Blade, blows on his palm and sparks dance around me, landing on my clothes. I yelp, shaking out my fur-lined tunic. He winks, then disappears into the crowd in a flutter of red and gold velvet, his chestnut braids swinging.

Mern's hands brace my waist, and she spins us in a tight circle. "We won't see Blade again for days. He and his band of trouble-makers hold revels that last a whole sennight."

"That's fine with me," I admit. "Your cousin's fangs make me nervous."

Mern laughs. "Oh, he only bites those willing to receive. Remember, this is the Seelie Court; we aren't entirely wicked."

"You have no idea how glad I am to hear that."

Today, the hall is only half full. Most fae gather around the long tables that heave with the weight of food and trailing vines, loading up their gilded plates as they chatter loudly. We join the rabble, collecting elaborate dishes and utensils of our own.

I snack on fruit and sip water from a golden goblet, Gade's presence calling to me from the dais, but I keep my eyes averted from the throne and hope he doesn't notice me.

After Mern's tour of the Great Hall yesterday, I can easily picture the throne in my mind—multi-colored crystal spikes set in a grand pattern to match the Crown of Five. I haven't allowed myself to look at the prince, who is no doubt lounging upon it, but I have no trouble imagining his regal magnificence.

My flitting gaze snags on a fae huddled in the corner closest to the dais with its bony knees drawn into a narrow chest. Leathery flesh hangs from a skeletal body, and sunken eyes glare from a hollow face, topped with a puff of bright-green hair. The creature seems barely alive.

"Who is that?" I ask, pointing at the wretched faery.

Mern glances up from the golden pear she is eating. "That's Nestera, a changeling who was thrown out of the human realm centuries ago. Although she has moments of clarity, if not wisdom, the poor thing has lost her senses. Take care not to go too close, Holly. Unlike Blade, she bites without permission."

"Perhaps she needs help. Is she sick?" I ask, my healer's conscience making me ignore Mern's advice and move toward Nestera.

Voreas, Mern's best friend, who appears neither male nor female, but something glorious in between, tugs the rust-colored cape hanging from my emerald tunic. "The changeling's fractured mind connects her to dark forces. It is best not to attract her attention."

For a moment, I pause and consider Voreas's words, but it's too late. Nestera has already noticed me. Creaking and clacking, her limbs unfold, and she rises to her feet, then hobbles toward me.

A full head shorter than me, the creature paces a circle around me, cackling and moaning. She stops and gathers my hands between hers, her nails clawing at my skin as her flat, brown eyes rake over me.

"Nestera, leave Holly be," says Mern. "She has done our kind no harm."

"As yet," rasps the changeling as she pulls me closer. "There is still time for much mayhem."

"Release the girl," booms Gade as he approaches the edge of the dais, the points of his black and gold shoulder armor flashing as if covered in tiny diamonds. The armor matches his ornate arm bracers, and he is dressed in leather that displays the contours of his lean, strong body to great advantage. "Now. Or your next breath shall be your last."

Nestera bows her head, shuffling away from me. She stops moving when a tall, lanky fae with long braids that skim his calves stands next to Gade. "Come now, Gadriel," he says, lifting a highly polished staff carved from a white branch. "Your subjects have a right to meet our mortal visitor. Nestera will vow to do her no harm, isn't that so, my dear?"

Kindness infuses the fae's voice, and his pale gray eyes resonate deep peace and contentment. He reminds me of the priests who pass through my village on pilgrimages to the nearby holy springs.

Another fae steps down from the dais, his black braids trailing behind him and his black eyes cold as he fixes them on me, sending a shiver down my spine. Crow's wings sprout from his shoulders, their midnight hue matching the intensity of his dark smile.

The changeling grins, bowing to the gray-haired fae beside Gade. "Lord Fyarn. "I mean no harm to the lass. It won't be I who attempts to cause her downfall; I vow that much to our Prince of Five. Fate long-woven works through the girl, as it is with all creatures—fae or mortal."

"That's our father's brother, Uncle Fyarn," says Mern. "Elden and Blade are his children. Their mother, Sheanna, died in childbirth—a stillborn daughter with roots for arm and legs. Our legends say that Fyarn is part dryad, a creature of the alder trees, and speaks their language like no other can. The fae next to him is my brother's chief adviser, Lord Serain. The nature of his work demands a suspicious mind, so don't fret if he doesn't seem to warm to you. He disapproves of nearly everyone except for Gade."

The smiling Fyarn is handsome and his bearing stately, but he wears drab-colored robes of brown and gray, and his skin appears papery, like young bark, lending credence to the story that his ancestors once grew in forests.

Voreas tugs Mern backward, leaving me standing alone with the changeling. A hush falls over the courtiers surrounding us as they watch the proceedings with interest.

Stern-faced, Gade descends five broad stairs onto the marble floor and comes to a halt quite close to me, the position of our bodies forming a triangle with the changeling's.

"As my uncle wishes," he says. "Speak your piece, Nestera, and know this: if you harm the human by word or deed, before my court, my blade will slit your throat. I protect what is mine and suggest you heed my words as you never have before."

In alarm, my gaze cuts to Mern. She shakes her head, warning me to remain silent.

"Fear not, princeling," says Nestera. "I have no desire to harm your precious things. But I would like to admire her honeyed eyes and come to know her a little better. Will you allow it?"

A muscle jumps in Gade's jaw, but he nods consent.

Nestera grasps my hands and focuses her attention on me, breathing deeply. A vibration of magic sparks in my forehead, traveling to my stomach. I consider calling out and asking her to stop, but my stubborn nature keeps me quiet, my muscles frozen and expression calm.

Finally, Nestera speaks. "All the forest beings recognize your name, mortal. Tiny spiders and the smallest beetles cower as you pass. They *know* you." She faces Gade, letting my hands drop.

"They all know her, Your Highness. And there are some who wish her harm."

Gade seizes Nestera by the shoulders. "Tell me what you've seen," he commands. "What could the ancient forests of Faery know about a mortal girl?"

The changeling laughs. "Ask your High Mage. Does she not see all things in all realms?"

I scan the hall for Ether but cannot find her.

"Is there anything else you can tell me?" asks the prince. "No matter how small the detail, I must know it."

"Only this: there are some who hope to use the mortal to their advantage. Do not give them the opportunity. I have an amulet bargained from Morgana, a powerful sorceress from the mortal realm, long dead. It will alert the girl to danger when it crosses her path. Will you allow me to gift it to her?"

Gade opens his palm, and the changeling drops a chain onto it. His eyes close, and a heavy silence thrums through the hall.

With a rough sigh, the prince looks in my direction without meeting my gaze, then he beckons Mern over with an impatient gesture. She covers his palm with her own and stares at their hands, concentrating. Several moments pass, then her eyes flare open, the irises glowing a fiery green. "It is fine, Gade. Not cursed nor spelled to harm. Protection resonates at its core."

"That's what I felt, too," Gade says.

He nods at Nestera, passing the necklace back, and the changeling closes in on me.

"While you wear this necklace, dear one, ill will shall be revealed to you."

A pendant of stormy teal labradorite dangles from her fingers, and as I reach for it, she snatches it away.

"Not too fast, Holly Cure All," she says under her breath. "Gift givers must be rewarded with a blessing of equal worth. What will you give me in exchange for it?"

"Nothing," announces Lord Fyarn. "Gadriel, will you stand by and let your mortal bargain with a changeling? Nestera's visions are the deceptions of an unstable mind. She returned from the human realm damaged. I sanctioned a greeting, but do not trust her to bargain fairly."

"And yet my sister and I sensed no harm in the gift." Gade's eyes fix steadily on mine for the first time since we arrived at Talamh Cúig. "Ask Nestera what she desires for the pendant, mortal. And don't agree to her terms until I approve them."

"I only wish for simple things," says Nestera. "Nothing costly of coin or cunning of meaning."

"Then tell me what you want." I give her a warm smile.

"At my time of need, you will bring me twenty-three arm lengths of the orb spider's web, the same of our weaver's golden twine and her silken rope—one of which can hold my weight—a crested pigeon, and a biscuit soaked in the old queen's favorite honey."

"But how will I find such things?"

"Every item is easily obtained within the castle walls. You merely need to ask. Is that not true, Prince?" she says.

"Yes, quite true," Gade agrees. "As a safeguard, I will order that no one at court can refuse your request."

"But what if, for some reason, I can't deliver them at the time you need them? If I was sick and bedridden or... no longer in this realm."

Gade frowns, then smiles his approval, sending a rush of warmth through my blood.

Nestera inclines her head. "If it is in your power to bring these items, then you must, but if not, you will be free of the bargain and may keep the pendant."

My eyes search Gade's, and he nods. "That sounds fair," I say. "I'm very grateful for the gift and accept the price as you have stated."

Nestera spins three times in a circle, like a giddy child. "So be it." She presses her cheek to mine and whispers in my ear. "The jewel will heat and become uncomfortable to wear when you are in danger. Heed its warning."

The gold chain is cool on my neck as Nestera drops it over my head. The moment it's nestled under my tunic, Lord Serain gives me a tight smile and retreats with Fyarn back to their matching chairs that are shaped like exploding stars and set the same distance apart behind the throne.

Elden and Voreas sidle up and lift the pendant from my chest, cooing over its setting of gold and silver eagles' wings.

Something about Lord Serain strikes me as amiss. A heavy sensation fills my chest as I watch him speak with the lesser court advisers who stand by his side, disdain dancing at the edges of his smile. He is a faery, a species that believe themselves superior to all others, and arrogance is likely the least of his bad traits.

"Is all well with Lord Serain and Lord Fyarn? Serain in particular seems unhappy," I say, glancing at each member of our party—Gade, Mern, Voreas, and Elden—to check their responses. Their faces remain clear and relaxed, no worry or fear flickering over them.

"They're fine," answers Mern. "During last night's meeting, when we discussed you, Holly, our Uncle Fyarn argued the most vigorously for you to stay. In fact, he hoped you'd remain in Faery for longer than the period of time agreed with my brother. He likes you. And as I told you, Serain is difficult to please, but nonetheless he is our land's greatest defender."

I scowl at Gade, who steps closer, hoping he wasn't swayed by his uncle's appeal to keep me in Faery for any longer than we bargained. Gade promised to help me return home after seven nights and seven days, and he must stick to it. After all, a vow is binding, even more so in Faery than in my world, or so Mern tells me.

"Don't worry about Lord Serain," says Gade. "You must promise not to go anywhere without a guard. Serain may be troubled by your presence, but he wants you safe. Whenever he senses danger, it is nearly always present."

Mern swipes a creamy pastry from a tray that a winged fae carries past. "Holly spends most of her time in our company, Brother, and you know we can protect her. There's no need for guards."

"Must you talk with your mouth full?" Gade says, laughing as he turns to me. "Heed me well, when you're not with Mern or Elden, you must have no less than two fae guards beside you. They will deliver you from your room into my sister's or cousin's protection. And don't bother arguing. This is not negotiable. The alternative is having guards posted outside your room with you locked inside the chambers for the duration of your stay."

"So despite my efforts to save your life in the hut, you would still imprison me?" I ask.

"Only for your protection."

"Any other instructions before I take my leave, Your Highness?" I say, mocking him with a false expression of eagerness that he fails to notice.

"Yes, I'm glad you asked. You must attend tonight's feast."

"What?" I'd much prefer to eat in my chambers and avoid the sight of him lording it over his court in all his obnoxious gorgeousness. "Why?"

As he opens his mouth to reply, Voreas slings an arm over Mern's shoulders, his shiny silver locks swinging out and whipping the prince's face.

Gade pushes him away. "Watch out."

Voreas grins. "'Tis only hair, not a blade."

Gade rubs his cheek. "Braided through with rusty barbs, no doubt. Strike the mortal with that ridiculous hair of yours and see what happens."

"My pardon, my Prince. Would a dance with your captive improve your mood perhaps? The musicians have taken up their instruments."

Gade's lips compress. "As you know, I rarely bother to dance, so what makes you think a human would inspire the effort?"

"That isn't precisely a no," whispers Mern. "If you had a dance card, you would scratch his name in it for certain."

I ignore her teasing and smile stiffly at the prince. "You haven't told me about last night's meeting with your mages and council. Did you inform them that with your help, I'm leaving in five days' time?"

"Six," he corrects. "Come to tonight's revel and we shall speak more of it then."

"I'll think about it." I incline my head and back away. Just before I turn around, he raises an eyebrow at Mern and Elden and tips his chin in my direction, no doubt bossing them into following me.

Holding my head high, I stride toward the stairs that lead to the east tower where my room is located, the sounds of my friends' footsteps striking the marble hard behind me.

As I weave through the crowded hall, pieces of material are torn from my fine tunic, faeries' sharp nails scratching my skin. Elden shoos them away, and they cower for a moment before pressing closer again, chanting rhymes and snickering amongst themselves.

"Are you being a bore and returning to your room?" asks Mern when she catches up.

"I can think of better things to do than watch your brother smile smugly from his throne while his courtiers attempt to pinch my flesh off," I say, tickling her ribs.

"Oh, don't worry about him. He's confused at the moment, and that doesn't sit well with him. We need to let Gade adjust."

"To what?"

"I'm sure we'll find out soon enough," says Mern mysteriously as we start up the stairs. "I have a wonderful idea—let's visit the apothecary. You must be curious to see how our healer works with plants and magic. Gade says you're very skilled with herbs yourself."

Surprised at his compliment, I feel my cheeks warm.

But Mern is right. I'd love nothing more than a visit to the town's healer.

Grinning, I retrace my steps down the staircase. "That sounds excellent. Which way do we head?"

Mern laughs, linking her arm through mine. "Turn left."

"Wait, we're coming, too," says Elden, he and Voreas catching up.

I hope the healer is a little more welcoming than the rest of the fae in this city. Most seem to view me with a mixture of curiosity and fear, which is ridiculous. They're the ones who possess formidable power and magic.

As we step into the Great Courtyard, I glance over my shoulder and meet a pair of narrowed cerulean eyes. Gade stands in the doorway to the hall, arms crossed over his chest, an elaborate ruff blowing in the breeze around his neck and chin, so black I can't tell the fur apart from his silky, raven hair.

I give him a mock salute, and he shakes his head and strides back into the hall.

As I skip down more stairs, I can't throw off the feeling that out of all the Court of Five fae, their ruler fears me the most.

16

Blessings and Curses

Holly

"Tell me about the curse." I elbow Elden as our gang of four meanders down the stone paths that wind through the town, passing dwellings and storefronts tucked into the hillside, their glittering stone and crystal facades blinding my mortal eyes.

Since we left the hall, the weather has taken a gloomy turn. Puffy clouds, the color of darkest amethyst stones, gather on the horizon, and gulls cry in the distance over a restless sea. Shivering, I wrap my cloak around my body.

"You mean Gade's curse?" says Elden, battling the winds lashing hair over his face. He snaps his fingers, and the breeze untangles his yellow locks.

"What other curse would she be referring to, genius?" asks Mern as she leaps from the top of one low stone wall to next, her steps light as a feather.

"No need to show off your magic, Mern," says Voreas, flitting over the walls in a similar unnatural fashion. He lands beside me with an ungraceful grunt. "I'm sure Gade has already shown Holly his many talents. No doubt she's quite bored by magic."

Mern and Elden snicker as I huff in response and kick a stone out of my path.

"Small, incidental curses are common in Faery," Elden says. "But those like our prince's shape kingdoms and often lead to the death of the afflicted."

"What? You mean the curse will kill him?" I blurt out.

A haunting song floats from over the ocean, and I stop walking and peer out to sea, searching for its singers.

"Don't mind the sea witches." Mern tugs me back into motion. "The Sea Court recently lost their newest babe to a kraken. They'll cry out their grief for at least a sennight."

"The poor things." I grimace, longing to cover my ears and block out the noise. "It's such a heart-breaking sound."

"Oh, this is nothing. Their revenge song is a thousand times more terrifying." Mern pats my shoulder. "But you'll likely be home by then and won't have to hear it."

"I hope so," I say. "All going well, in five days' time, I'll be leaving."

"Six," says Mern, sounding like her haughty sibling.

I glance up the hill at a lone, hooded figure lurking in the shadows of the castle, possibly glaring down at us. The drape of the hood makes it hard to tell.

"Is that Lord Serain up there gawking at us like a bitter, old crow?" I spin Mern around by the arm so she's facing the figure.

She looks up and laughs. "Yes, it is. He often skulks about spying on everyone. Don't think you're special, Holly."

"He's creepy."

"He probably thinks the same about you." Elden jumps off the wall that he's been reclining on while picking his teeth with the longest rose thorn I've ever seen. "Humans are strange."

I push him down the hill a little, and he laughs as his pointy boots slide over tiny stones.

"Is Gade really cursed to die?" I ask, a feeling similar to sadness filling my chest.

Mern links our arms, quickening my steps. "Not if he can find his fated one."

"Fated what? Sword? Boot?"

"Mate," all three fae answer, their eyebrows twisting at me as if they think I'm daft.

"I'm sure we mentioned Gade's fated-mate dilemma back in the hut," says Elden, scratching his sharp chin.

"Oh, do you mean when I thought you were talking about some unknown heir and didn't realize you meant Gade because you were all lying to me?"

"Fae can't lie," says Voreas. "They were probably being careful with their words and circling the truth."

I sigh. "I'm learning to pay more attention to what faeries *don't* say rather than what actually comes out of your mouths. So, Gade is searching for a mysterious partner?"

"A chosen bride," confirms Mern, leading us through a tall, quartz-lined tunnel in the hillside that comes out into a wild cottage garden teeming with medicinal trees and shrubs.

A small rendered cottage with a dark thatched roof squats against the far wall, hewn from the same black stone the cliffs and castle are made of.

"Who chooses this bride?" I ask. "And how does she stop Gade from dying?"

"It's a long story," says Mern, bringing us to a stop under an oak tree. "The short of it is this—since we are Elemental fae, our kingdom and magic are fortified by our five mages, Ether, the High Mage whose spirit unites all, Terra, who rules the earth, Undine, water, Salamander, the fire element, and Aer, the Sorceress of the Seven Winds. It is the last of these sisters who cursed my brother, solely because when he came of age, he rejected her love and refused to make her the Queen of Five."

Voreas dances around us, further explaining the curse in a lilting voice. "If Gade finds and marries the mate whom the air mage has chosen before his poisoned blood kills him, he will be free and may even live a long and healthy life. But the curse will lie dormant in his first-born son, and upon Gade's death it will be revived to destroy the power and mind of the next Heir of Five."

Dawning horror chills my blood. "Why would one of your mages do such a terrible thing? Risk your kingdom like that?"

"For a simple reason. She's insane," says Elden. "Most Seelie fae resonate toward the light. But not Aer."

"Where is this horrid Aer and the other mages you mentioned?"

Mern shrugs. "Everywhere, Holly. The breeze that caresses you now—that is Aer. The fire that warmed you in your chamber last night—Salamander. And the water you enjoyed at luncheon—Undine."

My skin crawls as I scan the nearby shrubs, searching for a pair of wicked eyes.

"Do not worry," calls a soothing voice.

In the cottage doorway, stands a creature no taller than my waist. "Close your mouth, girl. Haven't you seen an elf before? Come closer so we can inspect each other better."

I obey immediately.

She leaps onto a log that rests beside the door, which raises the top of her head to my collarbones, then takes my hands in hers. Her skin is brown, her curls black, and tiny horns curl at the side of her intelligent face.

"I am Mapona, matriarch of the clan of moss elves, and as you'll soon see, a giantess among them."

"Nice to meet you. I'm Holly, a human captured by Prince Gadriel—"

"Captured?" Her golden eyes narrow. "*That* part of the tale is news to me. I heard you saved our future king's life, and for that, I'm most grateful to you."

Mapona ushers us through the cottage door, and Mern has to stoop to fit her horns through without catching them on the frame. The moment I step inside, an atmosphere of calm and order envelops me.

The white-washed walls and ceiling are barely visible through the drying racks, herbs, and healer's tools that hang from them, but the round, pungently scented room is clean and tidy.

Light from the rear garden flows through a circular window, illuminating the measuring scales and bowls on the long, rectangular table in a wash of molten gold. The ceiling is high, but the furniture is set low to the ground to accommodate the elves' height.

It's a beautiful space, and I could easily occupy many hours here, digging through drawers, opening pots and jars to investigate their contents.

"Good afternoon." Mern squats down in front of the table, greeting seven moss elves who are smaller in stature than Mapona, but wear similar bark-textured, gray-green clothing, have the same adorable curved horns, and peer out of matching curious golden eyes.

The elves speak fast, bantering happily with my friends who joke back in the same strange tongue, their gazes regularly catching mine as they openly discuss me.

"Please sit," the healer says.

We perch on a wooden bench pulled up to the table facing the fire, our knees jutting high from the odd angle of our low seats.

Mapona sends the elves out to weed the garden, and then sits opposite us. "Holly, Aer cannot harm you within the city without risking exile. She may be unstable, and she often puts her own desires before our people, but she has recently sworn to protect all who live behind Talamh Cúig's walls. But you must take care when you are beyond them."

"Thank you," I say. "That's reassuring to know."

With a flick of her fingers, Mapona sends an arc of green light spiraling around the room. Open-mouthed, I watch its dazzling path, my jaw dropping as the ladles in the pots hanging over the fire begin to stir themselves.

The healer chuckles, leans toward me over the table, and plucks my new necklace from the folds of my clothing. "Ah, I see you're wearing the Morgana pendant. Nestera has protected you well. Be sure to heed its warnings."

"She will," says Mern, reaching into a bowl of nuts and seeds, stuffing a handful in her mouth. "Gade says she isn't stupid."

"Must you always talk with your mouth full?" chides Elden, shoving his own pile of nuts in his mouth. "I alone have been given leave to be so uncouth."

"By who?" asks Mern.

"Myself."

Mern throws a dried berry at Elden, and he opens his mouth and swallows it whole.

"I'm glad your brother acknowledges my mind is sound," I tell Mern. "At long last, I can rest easy."

Voreas bursts into laughter, thumping my shoulder and nearly shoving me off the bench. "You are jesting, human—"

"I have a name," I remind him. "It's Holly, and you should try using it."

"I find your words very amusing," he replies.

Elden shakes his yellow head. "We can see that."

"They're reversed truths," says Voreas. "Too close to a lie for fae to easily duplicate the style, but nonetheless, entertaining."

"I'm glad to be of service," I say, dishing out another serve of the sarcasm he's so fond of.

Voreas claims it's difficult for fae to speak in mocking ways, but I recall hearing Gade do it more than once, but never without painful consequences.

"So, you are a healer," says Mapona.

"Of sorts. My mother is remarkably skilled with herbs, and I've done my best to learn as much as I can from her."

The elf snorts, shuffling over to her cutting bench. "What are these?" She points to dried plants hanging from the rafters.

"That's mugwort."

She sniffs and rubs her long chin. "Used for?"

"Among other things, it aids digestion and improves energy."

"Yes, and this?" A bunch of dried roots are thrust into the air, dirt spraying everywhere.

"It looks like valerian, for sleep and to calm the nerves."

"And this?" She shoves a mortar filled with crushed pink leaves under my nose, the sharp scent stinging my eyes.

I wrinkle my nose. "I haven't smelled anything like it before. It's unpleasant, but also rather appealing."

"Good. For a human, you are truthful. This here is bone's blush. With the right dose, it will bring a man to his knees. It has no effect on females, but if there is a certain male you wish to enslave... well, it is very efficient."

Leering, she wraps three generous pinches in a square of muslin and presses it into my palm. "Take this. If I told you the exact quantity required, would you eagerly sprinkle a measure in some lucky fae's goblet at tonight's revel?"

I shake my head, placing the package on the table. "You're very kind, but I wouldn't use it."

Mern laughs and pats Mapona's hand. "Holly has no need for attraction magic. I know of at least *one* male in our city who is already enchanted by her natural charms."

I frown at Mern, wondering if she might be referring to Elden. He's very friendly and takes every opportunity to touch me in an incidental but, I suspect, likely innocent way.

Voreas folds his arms over his silver-studded leather jerkin, grinning slyly at me. Could Mern mean him? It wouldn't surprise me at all if the mischief maker wanted to bed a human and satisfy his curiosity.

Gade's advice upon arriving at Castle Black flashes through my mind: trust no one, he said. But my instincts tell me that Voreas, Mern, and Elden's friendship is real and they would never hurt me on purpose.

Mern lifts a bowl of mixed herbs, passing it to the healer. "Care to show Holly your remarkable skills, Mapona?"

"Of course, Princess."

Holding the bowl in her right hand, Mapona closes her eyes and raises her left. She cocks her head and sniffs the air. "Ah, Holly must view my tricks another day. The prince comes."

"What?" I quickly scan the room, searching for somewhere to hide.

I'm not ready to see Gade again so soon. The business in the Great Hall earlier was enough face-to-face prince time to last me until the end of my visit.

"Mern, Elden, Voreas, come and help me in the garden," says the healer, beckoning them toward a door covered by a thick tapestry curtain.

My friends troop after her, disappearing into a room beyond, and I follow. Mapona stops me on the threshold and pushes me backward. For an elf whose head only comes to the top of my pelvis, she's remarkably strong.

"Not you, Holly. Someone must remain to greet the prince."

"But why me?"

She smiles. "Because it is *you* he wishes to see."

Before I can object or question her ludicrous statement, the curtain whips closed on her backside.

A moment later, a bell chimes, and the prince strides through the door alone, no attendants or courtiers in sight.

Instead of the formal, fur-embellished midnight doublet he wore at luncheon, he is dressed in heavy fighting boots, black leather trousers, and a vest studded with metal spikes that could take my eyes out if I happened to get too close—which I don't intend to do.

"Prince Gadriel," I say, dipping my head.

Since he's practically a king, a curtsy would be a more appropriate greeting, but I can't bring myself to fawn over the fae whose brow I spent sleepless nights wiping herb-infused cloths over.

His dark hair flies like raven feathers as he surprises me with a dramatic bow. "Greetings, human," he says, a smile flickering on the edges of his mouth.

"How many times must I tell you to call me Holly? Would you like it if I called you by the name of your species all the time?"

"When first we met, you did *exactly* that. But likely, I wouldn't mind what you called me as long you were thinking of me." He smirks and struts around the room, hands clasped behind his back. "Seven," he says, nonsensically.

"Pardon?"

"Seven more times you must remind me to call you Holly. After that, I will try very hard to never call you *human* or *mortal* again." He goes over to the bone carvings and pots of medicine dotting a shelf and gives them a thorough inspection.

When it becomes clear he's not going to explain his presence, I finally ask, "What are you doing here?"

Ignoring the question, he points at his chest and indicates his clothing, drawing my eyes to the black and gold tattoos of ivy that circle his muscular biceps, then the long black sword hanging from his hips, his tousled dark hair, and the dirt smeared across his cheekbone. At present, a plain circlet of twisted, black metal graces his brow.

"I was training by the smithy and saw your party pass by in the distance," he says.

"So you followed us here, then?"

"No." He stares at the fireplace. "I came by my own pathway across the battlements, then through the coral hedges."

Interesting. It's not exactly a denial. But it is likely he saw us pass and could tell by our direction where we were headed. Also, it would be impossible for him to deny following us if he hadn't paid close attention to which path we took to the apothecary. To me, it sounds very much like he did follow us.

"I see. And you've come to ask Mapona for a tincture to promote your healing?"

"Not exactly."

"Perhaps you're here to make your own tincture, then," I suggest, teasing him with my words and a challenging grin.

"And risk dismemberment?" He returns my smile. "Certainly not. I wouldn't dare encroach on the healer's sphere of excellence, nor upon yours, Holly of Donore, since you undoubtedly possess similar skills."

I don't recall telling him the name of my village. But at some point during our time together in the shepherd's hut, I must have done so.

My mind races. I'm not comfortable with a future king of Faery knowing how to find me after I leave his realm. I could pretend my village is far from Donore. I could lie. But I don't.

The tattoo glyphs on his hand and arms flare to life as he steps closer. I walk backward until my calves hit the bench.

"I came here because I wished to see what Mapona made of you," he says, his husky voice almost a whisper.

"She doesn't appear worried by my presence in your kingdom, if that's what you mean."

"But did she name you a blessing or a curse?"

"Is she in the habit of making such pronouncements?"

"Frequently. In fact, she is known for it."

"Mapona called me neither to my face. I suppose you must ask her directly for her true assessment," I reply.

"Strange, but she isn't here," the prince says, looking over the walls, and then ducking his head under the table in a pretend search.

I swallow a laugh. "After announcing your visit, she swiftly disappeared. What reason would a healer have to hide from her prince?"

"Good question." He taps his chin. "Perhaps because my magnificence is too painful to look upon."

This time, my laughter escapes me. "Well, I certainly agree with part of that sentiment."

Surprising me, he laughs too. "Let us ask her, then." He lifts his chin and bellows, "Mapona, show yourself."

"Your Majesty," says the moss elf as she appears in front of Gade, bowing low. "It is rare to have the pleasure of your company in the apothecary. How may I be of service today?"

"I'd like to know your opinion of this mortal who helped me in my time of need."

"As her name suggests, she is a bringer of peace, luck, and protection, a blessing if ever I've seen one made of flesh and bone."

"But holly berries are poisonous, are they not?" Gade asks.

Mapona smiles. "Only if they are ill-used. The wise among us know how to bring out Holly's best qualities."

Gade turns to me. "So, it seems you have received Mapona's approval."

I raise an eyebrow. "What did you expect? Here you stand, living proof of my good nature. And should you wish to demonstrate yours, you can tell me what you and your councilors have planned for me. And while you're granting favors, you can give me leave to be absent from tonight's feast."

"Unfortunately, at this moment, I can satisfy neither of your requests." He cuts me a short bow. "I'll see you at dinner. And do not be late." Then he disappears through the front door in a blur of motion.

"Did he just vanish into thin air?" I ask Mapona.

"No," says Mern as she enters followed by Elden and Voreas. "My brother can't transfer like the Merits. But while he's here in the kingdom, his power is stronger than when he's traveling, and he can move with extraordinary speed."

She dips her fingers into a bowl and flicks silvery powder on my face. It stings.

"Ow. What was that for?"

"A charm, so you can eat our food, including the fruits and treats that are known to beguile humans, and remain unaffected."

"Very useful. Thank you."

Mapona pats my hip. "I'm sure Gadriel will answer all your questions at tonight's revel. But I warn you, you made a tactical error showing your eagerness to know of your fate. Never give a male power to manipulate you for his own schemes if you can help it."

I cross my arms and shift my weight. "Which in his case are?"

"Our prince's foremost wish is likely the pleasure of your company this evening, Holly. But after that, I cannot say what he wants from you because he doesn't yet know himself."

And *that* is precisely what worries me.

17

Only Mortal

Gade

"So, you chose not to heed my warning." I glower at Holly as I slide into the seat beside her at the far end of the high table.

Perhaps in protest of the mortal's presence, tonight, three members of my council dined with courtiers on the tables set around the edges of the Great Hall, and others have joined the post-dinner dancing, leaving the dais presently rather empty.

Except for the mortal and me.

"What warning?" she asks, glaring back at me as if I don't have the right to sit next to her at my own table in my own hall. "If you gave me one, Gade, I don't remember it."

That's an outright lie. Anger heats my blood, but I suppress it, telling myself it is typical for a human to shun the truth to avoid discomfort. And I cannot blame her. If I had the skill, I would employ it regularly.

"You're late," I say, filling Mern's empty cup with wine, then swirling the ruby liquid around the sides. "*And* you missed dinner."

"No, I didn't." She takes several hearty gulps from her goblet and points to a bowl in front of her. "As you can see, I arrived in time for dessert. And since you seem fixed on monitoring my every thought and movement, yes, I enjoyed every mouthful."

"If the scent of your blood is any indication, you also enjoyed a large quantity of mulberry wine."

She huffs, pours more wine, then visibly startles, thudding her goblet against the gilded table. "You can no more smell my blood than I can read your thoughts."

"Your blood near enough *tells* me your thoughts." I run my nose along her neck and inhale deeply. "And tonight, both are rather mouthwatering."

Frowning, she shifts sideways in an attempt to put distance between us, proving she knows little of faeries or fae princes. We are not so easily deterred. If I wish to be close to her, then close to her I will be.

She fixes her gaze on the crowd of writhing fae below us, mesmerized by their slick wings and sharp talons slicing flesh and air as they dance to the chaotic beat of fiddles and drums.

"At least fae don't *drink* blood," she states in a wavering voice.

"Some do. Steer clear of the fae who bear fangs and cry blood instead of tears. Personally, I prefer wine." I flash my sharp incisors in a grin. "However, it is never too late to experiment with new pleasures." My teeth aren't exactly fangs, but close enough to make her skin turn the color of fresh milk.

Tapping my nails against the arm of my chair, I slouch back and survey the revel below, wondering how it appears through her eyes, a young mortal in a strange land who is as uncertain of her fate as I am—the fae who happens to be master of it.

Tonight, the Great Hall is on fire. Restless flames burn from one thousand and twenty-three sconces lining the black stone walls, the six hundred and thirty-three candelabras hanging from the vaulted ceiling, and three hundred and ninety-three fire pits bordering the edges of the dance floor.

Four mages stand as sentinels in the corners of the hall. The High Mage, Ether, who's usually by my side, is in Aer's position because I banished her to the forest and banned her from attending revels.

Since my return, Aer has become more unstable, and I don't trust her to leave the mortal in peace. And Holly is already in enough danger at Talamh Cúig—mostly from me.

With her careless speech, over and again she has made herself my possession and unknowingly released me from my vow to send her home.

Her expressions of thanks, her gratitude, have made her my property to do with as I will.

Forever, if I so desire it...

She is mine, and no one has the right to touch her—not my courtiers, the wild fae, Aer, or even her benevolent sisters.

No one but me.

Releasing a sigh, I soak in the mood of the revel, at once dark and light, lush and decadent, and as with all Faery celebrations, both joy and danger flavor the air simultaneously. Should I allow it, the crowd could turn on the beat of a wing against the vulnerable human healer who calls herself *Holly.*

To my mind, it's a rather peculiar name for a mortal. Brimming with magical meaning, it feels more fae than not. I roll the sound of it around my mind, taste its texture on my tongue.

Holly light.

Holly green.

Holly Cure All ever mine.

How does she feel, surrounded by fangs, feathers, and the fiendish natures of creatures who have lived in mortals' nightmares since the beginning of time?

I allow my gaze to trail over the gemstones glittering in her coiled hair, the colors matching my ceremonial crown, the eagle feathers and crystal wands that spike from the ruff around my collar and shoulder guards.

Of course, as Talamh Cúig's ruler, my clothing is more elaborate in splendor and detail than any other fae present. As it ought to be, since I am the future king of the Bright Court.

I cannot help wondering what the mortal thinks of me dressed in such finery.

Brushing my lips against the soft shell of her rounded ear, I murmur, "How do you plan to apologize for disobeying me?"

She laughs. "I don't plan on it at all."

"Well..." I take a sip of wine. "We'll see about that."

"Will you *make* me apologize?"

"Contrary to your narrow view of us, violence isn't the foremost thought on all faeries' minds. Certainly not mine. Instead of murdering you, I propose we strike another bargain, Holly of Donore."

"Why, so you'll have another one to break?"

I shrug. "Any vow I make is forged in flames and set in stone, ice, and sky. You want to know your fate at my court, and I want to punish you for your defiance, but without causing you lasting harm. Our problem is unique, but not unsolvable."

The glow in her yellow eyes indicates the idea excites her, but her trembling smile says she mistrusts my motives.

Smart mortal.

"I'm curious to hear your terms and to know if your councilors will let you stick to your original bargain and let me leave. What do you want in exchange for information that should already be freely mine?"

"It shouldn't. You bargained to be allowed to leave, not to be informed of my councilors' opinions about when and how you do so."

Her lips compress. "Just tell me what you want, then?"

"A dance of my choosing." I lick a drop of wine from my lips. "With you."

A sugared biscuit freezes halfway toward her belligerent, bewitching mouth. "What?" Then she throws the sweet in her dessert bowl. "Fine, I accept your ridiculous terms. I gave up trying to make sense of your fickle ways several days ago."

The wine has loosened her tongue and made her reckless. She has foolishly agreed to the terms without request for clarification.

The many ways I could abuse her trust swirl through my mind, heating my poisoned blood. My withered heart aches to ignore what's left of my better nature, to possess her tonight and every night until I overdose on her cries of ecstasy.

My startling thoughts confuse me into smiling at her. And for a moment, I am lost. Unsure of my purpose. My direction. And wondering why, instead of trysting with the pixie twins who knocked on my door last night, I tossed and turned alone, reliving my time with the mortal in the shepherd's hut.

As disgusting as the truth may be, since I've returned home, *she* is all I can think of.

A frown furrows her brow, and her rosy lips part. "Gade?"

"Yes?"

"Your hand is on fire."

"What?" I look down.

Sparks shoot from the six-pointed star glyph on the back of my right hand, tiny flames rippling along its outline. I cover it with an empty plate and will the magic into submission. Even thinking about touching the human flares my power.

"Are you all right?" she asks.

"I'm fine." The pain of a part-lie stabs my temples. I fight a grimace and rub the black diamond nestled in the tip of my ear. "So, are the terms of our agreement as spoken acceptable to you?"

"Yes. Let's get the dance over with as soon as possible."

"Now?" I ask foolishly.

"Right away... Unless you're afraid I might be a better dancer than you."

"I believe I am only afraid of one thing, mortal, and it's certainly not your dance skills."

Thankfully, she doesn't ask what trembles the marrow in my bones and keeps me up at night. Neither of us would benefit from hearing the reason spoken out loud.

Her brows rise. "Tell me what your council decided."

I take another slow sip of wine and feel her impatience bristle against my skin. "Regarding your return home, my council agreed to put your fate in my hands."

"Including your uncle and Lord Serain? What did they advise?"

I consider her question. Specifics were not part of our bargain. She asked what the council decided about her going home—that is all. Why is she concerned about my advisers?

Since the death of my parents, my uncle has been a constant supportive presence in my life. I trust him without question. And Serain's loyalty is as steadfast and enduring as the tides.

"My uncle urged me to do as I see fit, and Serain knows I will always do what is best for my kingdom."

"And what did *you* decide?"

"I will keep you close over the next six days—"

"Five."

I smile slowly. "And if no person or event prevents it, I will likely have to adhere to the terms of our first bargain."

Joy lights her face as dread spikes in my blood.

"I should point out that wasn't our first bargain," she says. "And we've made many since. For example, when you were wounded, you promised not to kill me in exchange for my assistance."

"You are right. Others were over small matters, but still, they were bargains."

"So you'll help me return home?"

I bow my head to indicate agreement, but say nothing. Foolishly, she accepts the gesture, affording it equal weight to words that are spoken aloud. In Faery, this is a fatal mistake.

"Thank you, Gade. I am in your debt."

Worse and worse—the human is too innocent for this realm of cunning tricks and glamors. At her reckless acceptance, saliva fills my mouth.

I cannot believe how little care she takes with her speech, the liberties she gives me without a single thought. If she keeps it up, before long, something terrible will befall her. When it does, I only hope she'll let me save her.

"Indeed," I say, rising and offering her my hand. "You are mine, little human, to do with as I wish. And for now, I want to dance with you."

Unsteadily, she stands and places her hand in mine. "Two things: I'm not that small, and I'm not yours and never will be."

"To be precise, that's three things. But unless my hearing fails me, you just claimed to be in my debt—*out loud*." Before she can ask what that means, I change the subject, inspecting her clothing from her head to her glitter-painted toenails. "Mern chose well."

"I beg your pardon?"

"Your dress of gold, the gemstones sewn through your hair... all of it suits you well. You look..." I grit my teeth to stem the flow of compliments that strain against my lips.

In truth, I can hardly believe how fair she looks this eve—more than human, less than fae, but something in between. Luminous. And *better*.

Better than what? I ask myself.

Than everything, whispers the curse. *This girl is everything you secretly want and all you need, and yet you refuse to see it.*

"Yes, Gade? How do I look?" she prompts.

"Better."

My hand tightens around her fragile bones as I lead her down the stairs to the marble floor. I release a slow breath and force my grip to soften. I'm furious, but I don't want to hurt her.

The curse is deceitful and tries to sway me from my true course by tempting me with a human. But it will fail. For years, I have known my fate... to be joined with a stranger of Aer's choosing for the sake of my kingdom. For me, there can be no other path, but that doesn't mean I relish it. Or can't enjoy a dance with a baffling, but enchanting, mortal.

Shining disks of gold cover Holly's sleeveless gown, the long train chiming as she moves, mocking me like laughter. When we reach the dance floor, she holds her hands out, waiting for me to take her into my arms.

The drums and fiddles reach a frantic pace as dancers move around us. Translucent wings and long, gnarled limbs blur past, my courtiers' lust thickening the air and making breathing difficult.

I click my fingers, and the music shifts to a more soothing tempo.

"Not here," I say as I snatch up her hand, towing her through the sea of fae, then the arched doorway that leads onto the patio that runs the length of the Great Hall.

As the crisp sea breeze assaults me, I inhale deeply and spin her along the balcony away from prying eyes. Where it is quiet. Where we are alone.

The noise of the revel seems muted and distant. No drums. No fiddles. No raucous singing. But what need is there for music when we have the rhythm of our wild heartbeats, the crash of waves, and the applause of the stars above?

There is nothing else I want.

As long as I have her.

She laughs as we move in an elaborate pattern across the slate floor. Harnessing all the air magic I can muster, I turn us faster and faster until a deep flush paints her cheeks, and her blood flows in sync with mine.

Then I notice the glaze of her pupils, the coolness of her fingers, and turn in ever-slower circles, bringing us to a halt.

"You are unwell," I say.

"Absolutely not. I'm fine."

Her words are slurred, her feet unsteady, and in two breaths, I realize the problem. Faery wine has a potent influence on humans, and nobody has warned her to take care and drink less than she would in the human world.

"Don't imbibe any more mulberry wine tonight. Your constitution is too weak for it."

Anger sparks in her eyes. "If you hope to rule a kingdom successfully, I suggest you learn the skills of diplomacy. For a prince, you're far too rude to visitors."

"And for a guest, *you're* very objectionable. Can you not just accept friendly advice gracefully?"

"If it is given with grace, of course I can. But *that* wasn't, and I very much doubt you're trying to be friendly. And while I'm listing your faults, there is another that bears mentioning; you, sir, do not like to be challenged."

"On the contrary. I greatly enjoy a challenge." *Especially from a girl with fire in her gaze.* "Opposition on the battlefield and in my bed chambers is invigorating, but I admit not always so welcome from my courtiers."

Holly nods sagely. "Do you enjoy living like this?"

Appearing mesmerized, she glides near the entrance to the hall and sweeps her hand at the dais and the dancing fae visible through the archway. She takes another step closer to the door-way.

I turn her to face the opposite direction, moving toward the balustrade, hoping to keep her out here with me longer. "You were saying," I prompt.

"Oh, yes. I was saying that you live your life on a pedestal before your court, worshiped and never disagreed with. Being born fae royalty must be an odd way to grow up, and what I'd like to know is this... Do you love it above all else, being treated like a god?"

"If I were insane and irrevocably infatuated with myself, cer-tainly I would be thrilled with it. But as yet, I'm not either of those things. What is your point? You wish to tell me I'm vain and arrogant?"

"Well... you *are* fae. From what I've seen so far, the stories about your kind are true—you're all fickle and conceited."

"Do you judge Mern, who calls herself your friend, so harshly? What about Elden?"

"No. They're different."

"Then your assumption is wrong. Faeries are not *all* the same. And you don't yet know me well enough to assess my true charac-ter."

"What I know so far has led me not to trust you. But your answer to my next question will help me form a more accurate opinion. Since your advisers have placed my fate in your hands, will you swear to do as you promised and let me go?"

"Go where?"

"Don't pretend to be dense. *Home.*"

"Well, I've already answered this question tonight."

"And if I recall correctly, you used the word *likely* instead of definitely."

I release a loud sigh. "Because you're disagreeable and argumentative, I should want you gone as soon as possible."

"That's not an answer." She swipes hair from her face and stumbles, clutching the stone balustrade for balance. Clearly as drunk as a leprechaun, she laughs and pushes my chest. "Oh, Gade. Gade. Gade."

My brow rises. "Yes?"

"What would you do if I said that instead of returning home in a few days, I'd prefer to gaze upon your horribly handsome face a little longer?"

"What?" At her shocking words, blood rushes through my veins, roaring in my ears. Has she lost her mind? What about her ailing mother, who she professes to be eager to return to?

I clear my throat. "You mean, out here, tonight?"

"No. I mean if I wanted to stay in Talamh Cúig for longer than the seven days of our bargain."

"Since this is my castle, my kingdom, if I said I wished you to leave, then leave you must."

Her eyes narrow. "So, you'd like me to leave sooner rather than later?"

A rough sound comes from my throat. I dare not speak. I cannot give a true answer that will please either of us, so I simply stare back, wondering what to say to divert her from this dangerous game she's playing.

Several topics cross my mind. Human courtship rituals? No, too fraught with double meaning. The weather? Far too boring. The artistry of my fine clothing? Certainly not. To *her*, that would only confirm my conceited nature.

I click my tongue, clasp my hands behind my back, make a strange humming noise, and then say, "Ahhh... how do you like Faery so far?"

Again she laughs, pressing her palm against my chest, this time gently. "About as much as any mortal who fell through a portal into a strange land to be captured by a mythological creature who dragged them unwilling back to his castle would."

"You dislike it, then?"

"No. I'm rather fond of it."

I laugh, a strange warmth flooding my chest.

"And you must enjoy my company, Gade," she says with a teasing smile. "Why else haven't you agreed to let me leave in five days' time?"

"Six days," I say, correcting her error.

"Oh, five, six, pick up sticks," she says, swatting at me as if I'm a wasp buzzing around her head.

Tonight, she speaks in riddles that befuddle even me—a prince of Faery, master of tricks and ruses.

"What are you talking about?" I ask, worried now that someone has put a spell on her. As I grip her arms, fire rushes through my veins and thunder rattles the sky—the Elements inside me overreacting to the touch of a mere mortal.

"Seven, eight, lay them straight. It's a children's rhyme, Gade. Don't look so worried. I haven't lost my mind entirely." She rubs her eyes, then pinches her cheeks. "You're right. I have drunk too much faery wine. But I still need to know, will you let me leave when I ask to go? Answer me straight."

I can't, because the truth is, when it comes to this human, I don't know what I want, let alone what I'll *do* about her.

I'm drawn to this girl like a bee to sweet pollen, and part of me longs to drink her down deeply, and the other, to destroy her and the hold she has over me.

A stray curl of hair tickles her lips. I cross my arms to stop myself from brushing it aside. "Human, you're an inconvenience. A blight upon my tranquility and peace. And a pest to be dealt with accordingly."

"Dealt with?" Excitement, instead of fear, blazes in her eyes.

Stupid, stupid girl.

Then she asks, "How do you propose to do that?"

18

Temptation

Gade

"**A**t present, human, there are many ideas drifting through my mind, one more persistent than the others."

"*Holly*," she says, her chin raised. "And that makes two."

For several moments, I am silent, entranced by her formidable expression, then my mind catches up to her words.

"Pardon? Two what?"

"I've had to remind you not to call me human twice since our meeting in the apothecary today. When you nearly knocked me over near the falcon mews this afternoon and just now."

"You were busy laughing and staring goggle-eyed at Voreas, and you bumped into *me*."

"Either way, I only have to remind you five more times, then you'll address me correctly as you promised. Apparently."

"Would you like me to repeat the term many times over and get it over with?" I ask.

"No, I actually look forward to catching you out."

A chuckle rumbles in my chest. "I see."

Although I barely know my mind around this girl, there is no doubt she amuses me.

I step closer, frame her face with my hands, and brush my lips against hers. When she gasps, I take her mouth and inhale her shock deep into my lungs. Power licks along my skin and over my scalp. I slit my eyes open to watch our hair; long locks of black and dark gold, rise and intertwine like dancing serpents.

With a groan, I draw her body closer, mold her soft curves to the hard angles of the leather armor I wear over my ceremonial tunic, inflicting, at the bare minimum, discomfort, if not pain. But still, she doesn't shy away from me.

A warm floral scent infused with human earthiness infiltrates my mind, sweet, musky, and intoxicating. I draw back and stare into her desire-filled eyes. Every part of my being gravitates toward her, longing to merge and join with her in every way possible. To take everything her body, her alluring eyes, offer.

But it is the last thing I should do.

Fae lead humans astray, often with fatal consequences. We cannot help but use their flesh and bones until they tear, and snap, and break, and then crumble to dust. It has been this way ever since the first fae stumbled across a human and found their short lives, their fragility, addictive and enthralling. But not me. I've never derived pleasure from another's tears.

More fool you, the curse snarls in my mind.

You pretend you are different and deny yourself unnecessarily. Take her. If the mortal is anything, she is yours, for you are the descendant of Mab herself, and permission to take what you desire is woven into the fabric of your being.

You are Seelie.

Soon to be king.

Why hold back?

Why, indeed?

I grit my teeth against the poison's taunting voice, desperate to give in, longing to obey.

Feel the way her body trembles at your touch, feverish desire addling her mind to your advantage. Now is the time, Gadriel, to take what you desire, just as the Prince of Five should.

Take.

Take her.

Silence, I tell the poison. Be silent.

But what stops you, Prince? The fear that you will break her?

You should not care what happens to her. After all, mortals are faeries' playthings. Keep her as a pet for thirteen moon turns or until her little heart slows and her empty mind bores you. She is entertainment, and you, the Black Blood Prince, shall have your fun.

No.

I cannot.

I will not listen to the curse's whispers. That way lies madness. Regret. And a first for me—shame.

And yet... what would happen if I took a small sip, no more, of the girl's sweet nectar?

Nothing, the curse answers.

Not a thing.

If I want to, which I most *definitely* do, I could kiss her again, control my urges, and not take too much, not harm her. She is mine, and this is what I choose, not the *poison* that burns in my blood.

As I inch closer, I slide my hand through her hair and cradle the base of her skull. The moment our lips meet, power surges through me again. White light explodes, surrounding us, accompanied by a pulsing, droning noise that makes her break our kiss and stare up at me with dilated pupils.

"That noise—" Her body sways in time to the magical pulse. I cup her shoulders and steady her.

"Discharged Elemental magic. I won't let it harm you."

As the drone fades away, a bolt of connection arcs from her heart to mine, likely invisible to human eyes, but as real as her bones beneath my fingers.

Why does my magic rise like the tide toward the moon at her body's command? It makes no sense, contradicts fae and natural lore, and is beyond dangerous for a human and fae ruler to be inexplicably magically bonded. For what purpose?

She isn't a sorceress as I initially suspected—that idea was a figment of my imagination—but it's possible she possesses latent magic and is unaware of it. Another reason for me to remain close by and watch her carefully.

Gently, I let my hands fall away from her body, but she curls her fingers into my tunic and attempts to draw me closer, her lips seeking mine.

"Gade, why did you stop?"

If she knew of the violent desire simmering through my veins, she would not ask such torturous questions.

"One kiss was not enough for you?"

"Not tonight," she replies.

I clench my jaw to trap the dangerous question hammering behind my teeth, then ask it anyway. "Tell me, Holly, how much would you let me take from you?"

"At this moment, everything. Ask me tomorrow, and I'm sure my answer will be less generous. So, hurry up and kiss me while I'm in the mood to dally with the enemy."

"Enemy? You are too harsh. We are not *that* to each other."

"No? Then what are we?"

Good question. Another one I cannot answer.

The breeze flutters the spikes and feathers of my ruff, and she smiles, caressing it briefly, her lips plump and tempting. Internally, I shake my head at my foolishness. I must stop thinking of her this way—as if she is fae and about to become my lover.

Holly is human—inexperienced and vulnerable. Unimportant and insignificant.

Pain, equal to spoken lies, scorches through my blood, lust such as I've never felt before instantly eclipsing it. I grit my teeth, searching for a way to diffuse my reaction to her and end the torment of temptation.

"You are wine struck," I say, employing the bluntest weapon available—cruelty. "You don't know what you're saying, let alone what you ask of me. A fae's definition of *everything* is likely lethal to a mortal."

"I'm not as frail as you think, and if I know anything, it's this—if I live to be one hundred years old no one will ever kiss me that way again—as though I'm beautiful and worthy of desire."

Rage clouds my mind and tightens my fists, knuckles cracking.

"Has someone told you that you aren't these things? Who? Mortals from your village? If so, tell me their names, and before they come to the end of their insignificant lives, I will correct their bad opinions. These pitiful human *men* are wrong. And they must be deaf, blind, and ignorant to be immune to your appeal."

Her jaw drops, her chest laboring with ragged breaths. "Gade—"

She lifts her fingers to my cheek at the same moment a tribe of wild faun flock in from the hall, dancing in a sinuous line along the balcony and weaving slowly around us.

They flick Holly's hair as they writhe past and brush their slick-skinned chests and twisted horns against her bare arms.

"*Begone.*" I snarl. "Take your cunning pipes and entice a faery into your game. Have you not heard? This human is mine."

A mischievous youth with more courage than sense, named Liefnarn, bows as he passes, his tongue greasing Holly's cheek when he rises. In a breath, my blade is at his bobbing throat, the balustrade crumbling behind his back. "You wish to die tonight?" I growl.

The stench of fear pulses from his trembling body. "No, Prince Gadriel, I do not. Please... please accept my humble apology."

"For *what*?" My hand squeezes his throat as I bend him backward over the railing, my control slipping along with my reason.

"For daring to touch what belongs to you... the girl... I should never have—"

I snarl into the faun's white face, each word punctuated with a hard shake of his body. "Never. Touch. What is mine. *Never.*"

Warmth presses between my shoulder blades; Holly's hand, then her voice. "Gade, you must let him go. He meant no harm, and he has said he's sorry. Do it now."

As if compelled, I step back, setting Liefnarn on his hooves and sheathing my knife.

"My Lady, My Prince," he says and scampers away, joining the crowd of gaping faun near the entry to the hall.

I force a smile and clap loudly as I watch them disappear back into the revel.

Holly raises a brow. "You nearly kill one of them, and then praise their dancing with effusive applause? You confuse me."

"I was celebrating their departure," I say.

She huffs a laugh. "After what you just did, I really shouldn't find that funny. I've heard stories of goat-like men with hooves, but I never suspected they were true. They're quite... unnerving."

"You're wise to fear them. Although, they're not as bad as actual goats. There are a few bearded beasts here in Faery that I wouldn't trust as far as I could hurtle them."

More laughter from her lips, and something akin to happiness spreads through my chest, shaking me to the core. The old Gadriel longs to dwell in the sensation, but the curse whispers for me to crush it. Crush the mortal and her beguiling smiles and straight-forward, nurturing nature. Squeeze her until she cries. Screams. Then breaks.

No, that is the curse's wish, not mine, and I will never give in to it.

Then hurry up and find your mate, it replies. *Time is running out.*

"I hope you don't throw goats around on a regular basis."

I grin back at her. "No. Not very often. But if you would like me to demonstrate... I'd happily oblige."

Her laughter chimes like Beltane bells, and I marvel at myself—jesting merrily as if I'm the lighthearted youth I was long ago.

Before the curse.

When my parents lived and loved and all was well in Faery.

Behind the girl's shoulder, a dark shape swoops over the forest, and Lleu flies past three heartbeats later, the breeze from his wings tearing our hair and tangling it together.

We laugh as my fingers work to separate our strands—dark and light—and I press a handful of tiny gemstones that fell from her locks into her palm.

The crash of the waves below keeps time with our breathing, the revel fading farther and farther away until nothing exists but the two of us. I tuck a lock of hair behind Holly's ear. "Is it true what you said earlier? You think I'm handsome?"

"Without a doubt, all fae are a feast for the eyes," she says.

"That is a highly unsatisfactory answer."

"Well, Prince Gadriel, it's the only one you'll receive from me tonight. And since you're refusing to provide any further entertainment, I must bid you goodnight."

She dips her head, slipping out of my arms and moving quickly through the archway, melting into the crowd of courtiers before I can recover. She left without my permission.

Fool, hisses the curse. *She was yours for the taking, and you let her drift through your fingers.*

"And yet she is still mine and always will be," I mutter.

I roll my eyes at myself.

By the Elements, must I bed the human to exorcise her from my thoughts?

I push away from the balustrade and take the winding seaway stairs down to the tournament oval, fireflies lighting my way as the moon retreats behind a thick bank of clouds. I wink at them, and they form elemental symbols in the sky.

Sylphs and sprites hover around me, their breezy whispers of *my king, my king* fraying my nerves.

"Not yet," I tell them. "I am not your king yet."

"Soon, soon," they reply. "Soon you will be the King of Five."

"Be gone. I wish to brood alone this eve."

A blast of my air magic sends them racing up the hillside, snickering and screeching as they go.

Musing on why my power recharges in the human's company, I force my tense muscles to release, and I breathe the briny air deep into my lungs.

A group of sea witches senses my presence and draws closer, singing as they dive over the waves towards the cliff I'm perched upon.

"Beware, Prince of Five," they cry. "Danger seeks you from many directions."

Shooting to my feet, I cup my hands around my mouth and shout, "Then name my enemies. Tell me what you know."

Pain strikes immediately, a bolt of dark power throwing me backwards onto the grass before I have a chance to raise a shield. A whorl of magic slides along the point of my ear, then into my mind, and I lose consciousness, entering a dreamworld where the landscape is dark and bleak.

The abrasive voice of the annlagh echoes through my head. "Your air mage has taught me a verse, Princeling. A very interesting one."

Mocking laughter grates against my skull. I attempt to sit up but can only move my limbs, my torso pinned to the earth.

The voice continues. "Let me see... I believe it went like this: *If by another's hand the chosen dies, then before their blood fully weeps and dries, black will fade to gray, gray to white, and white to never. Never was the darkest taint and never will it ever be. Or... take the chosen for a bride, and the poison ceases deep inside.*"

My knuckles crack as I dig my fingers into the earth beside my body, long-hidden memories of the day Aer cursed me and the words she spoke rushing over me.

Yes.

Now I remember.

I remember her speaking similar words.

"I've heard it before," I say aloud. "Your recitation is boring. Go away, and let me slumber in peace."

The annlagh snorts. "But you haven't heard the whole of it, Prince."

"Well, then, if you think yourself so clever, tell it to me."

"Alas, I cannot. The air mage prevents me from revealing the whole."

"Then why are you here? How did you invade my mind?"

"You doubt my strength because I am of the wild fae and you are royal? Your cursed blood does not make you better than me. Look at you, weakened by your own mage's curse. Whereas I am older than the rocks your castle sits upon, more ancient than the dusty bones buried under your faery hills."

"When you finish boasting, perhaps you'll deign to answer my questions."

"First, as you guessed, I am here to gloat. And, second, I will tell you the how of it. When I rose from the earth and met your mortal, I witnessed something of great interest—your magic bonded with hers. While you were under my spell, in exchange for leaving you unharmed that day, I asked to borrow a sliver of this power so I could reach your mind at a future time to relay an important message, and the little human agreed."

A memory explodes in my mind, my jaw cracking with the force. I see Holly's head close to the annlagh's, her nodding, and then stepping away. This is what she gave in exchange for my safety.

The first rule of Faery is to never bargain with a more powerful creature than you. Does this not apply in the human world? Where there is great power imbalance, extreme caution must reign in all dealings.

"What power do you speak of?" I snarl. "The girl doesn't have any."

"Does she not? Well, if you believe that, Prince of Five, then you're far more foolish than I suspected."

"Fine. If you won't explain yourself and have performed a sufficient amount of gloating, release me or I will make it my life's sole purpose to hunt for your sleeping mound and seal it off forever."

A shriek sounds above, announcing Lleu's arrival. The moment he lands on my chest, his talons sharp even through the leather, the annlagh's spell is broken and my mind freed.

"Thank you, my friend." I stroke his golden head, relieved to feel no residual trace of the annlagh in my mind.

Lleu emits a series of angry noises, bouncing on my stomach like a newborn eaglet.

"Yes, yes," I reply. "You are right. The annlagh risks much by meddling with a prince of Faery, as did you when you interfered with his golden boar."

"Watch out, Prince," shriek the sea witches as an arrow of purple light shoots from behind the sacred hazel trees that ring the oval, skimming Lleu's feathers and sending him screeching into the sky.

As I sit up, Aer slinks from the shadows of the trees.

"If you've hurt him, you'll pay dearly, air mage," I tell her.

"Lleu is but a coward."

"You couldn't be more wrong," I reply.

As she steps lightly over the grass, a vision dressed in gold to match her traitorous, coin-colored gaze, she mocks me with an insincere bow.

I don't bother rising to greet her. "Harm my eagle and exile will be the least of your fears," I say.

In a blur of movement, she sits beside me, her knees folded against her chest like a youth, and far too close for comfort.

"I would never hurt you, Gade, only what stands between us. You should know that by now. And besides, you would require all four of my sisters' help to cast me from your land forever. They would never forsake me."

"Perhaps I know them better than you do."

She flicks her gold hair over her shoulder and laughs like a flirtatious imp. The air mage is no such innocent creature.

"Who would balance your kingdom's air element?"

An important question, for which I have no answer. But I will search until my final breath to find a way for my land to exist in peace and harmony without her.

Aer's shoulder bumps mine. "Is this human girl really worth moping over in the dark of the night, Gadriel? A mortal who makes promises to your enemies?"

"I do not *mope* over any girl—fae or human. Leave me be, treacherous mage. The mortal sought to protect me from the annlagh. Unlike you, she didn't betray me and curse my line to slow and torturous deaths if we cannot find our mates. When will you give up your hopeless dream of becoming queen and let my family live in peace?"

"When the last prince of Talamh Cúig's heart thuds its final beat."

So *never* is her answer, then.

"You helped the annlagh," I say. "Another deed of a traitor."

"I will always assist those who rise against you."

"Why?"

"To hurt you, as you have hurt me."

With the weight of a kingdom pressing down on my shoulders, I shake my head, pity for the air mage softening my rage. What must it be like to live every moment of one's life motivated by jealousy and hate? I pray to the Elements I never find out.

"I may need you for now, Aer, but know this: one day, I will find a method to stabilize the magic of my land without you. Then not only will you be irrelevant, but also dispensable."

Far out in the ocean, the sea witches wail, and Aer's eyes flash red, uncertainty lining her brow. "Impossible. But if that day comes, it will be me who vanquishes all opponents and is left standing on the rubble of your kingdom."

"Then taste the dirt you're so keen to conquer." I roll away, leap into a crouch, and summon earth magic, blasting the ground beneath her.

In a spray of earth and rocks, Aer swoops into the sky, but not fast enough for me to miss the gratifying sight of her spitting dirt and stones or to hear her bitter parting words.

"Beware of the mortal, Gadriel. If you don't guard yourself well, it will be *she* who conquers *you*."

Lleu alights on my knee, and I whisper soothing words and stroke his feathers, calming both our trembling fury.

Still shaken, I decide not to return to the revel. Instead, I spend a while plotting ways to defeat Aer for good, then my thoughts wander to the human—her smile, her clear, amber eyes, the power of her touch.

As my eagle and I sit together, listening to the songs of the sea witches, I ponder the air mage's words, and one thing becomes abundantly clear.

If Aer has warned me against Holly, that is good enough cause to draw the mortal closer.

I grind my teeth in a futile attempt to stop myself from thinking about the other reasons, such as attraction, desire, longing, and something else I dare not name.

Not yet.

Not yet.

19

The Prince's Land

Holly

"Quit trying to strangle me," yells Elden, his shaggy hair standing on end and making comical shapes as we ride down the hillside toward Eerdran Bay and the shores of the Emerald Sea.

The wind whips long, yellow locks around his throat as if it is trying to strangle him. Elden's element is air, so he fights back playfully, entertaining us as our horses pick their way along the rocky path.

Stone walls rise up on either side of the pathway, tall in parts, so I cannot always see the ocean below or what lies around the corner, adding to the sense of adventure.

We giggle at Elden's story of how his father nearly choked on laughter this morning after seven magpies stole his breakfast right from under his nose. Fyarn claims to despise this band of mischievous, regular morning visitors, but his son swears they are his greatest source of joy.

Turning a corner, we almost collide with the Prince of Talamh Cúig himself, who is heading toward the castle, Wren setting a leisurely pace up the hill. We pull our horses up sharply.

For a moment, Gade's eyes flare wide, then he smooths his features into his usual mask of stoic arrogance. "Sister, Elden, Voreas," he says, nodding at them. "Good morning." His gaze rakes over me, down and up, then down and up again. "Human, what a surprise to see you outdoors and on horseback."

"You can call me Holly. And why are you so surprised? Do you believe humans are so dull that we would prefer to stay cloistered in our rooms, moping and sewing instead of investigating a new and intriguing land?"

"No, I—"

"It is day five of my *visit*, and your family is taking me to meet some members of the Sea Court. Do you object?"

Voreas snickers, and Mern shushes him.

Gade smiles, looking alarmingly pleased with himself. "Not at all. In fact, I believe I will join you." He swings Wren around and starts off down the hill. Over his shoulder he says, "Coming? Or have you suddenly remembered an urgent sewing project you must return to?"

Mern snorts and nudges Bee into a trot, the rest of us following close behind.

Frankly, I would prefer it if Gade didn't accompany us. The mere sight of him causes me to relive the drunken kiss we shared on the balcony the other night in painful and explicit detail.

Out of the two of us, I suspect I was the only inebriated partici-
pant. I wonder what his excuse was.

I waste no time and maneuver my gray pony, Calypso, alongside
Wren. "You've just come from the beach," I tell Gade. "Surely you
have more important tasks to attend to now."

The corner of his mouth twitches. "Surely."

"Well... go attend them."

He throws his head back and laughs. "Are you rejecting my
company? You hurt my feelings."

The telltale signs of a lie—a wince or a grimace—don't cross
his face, indicating I *have* offended him. Fortunately for him, he's
a faery prince and will recover soon enough. Gripping the reins
tightly, I break eye contact.

"I'm going to come anyway," he says. "As you keep reminding me,
you're leaving soon, so before you go, I'd like to spend as much
time with you as possible."

My heart leaps into my throat, beating wildly. "Why? To torment
me to death?"

I think of his mouth soft on mine, and his palms, warm and firm,
angling my face to his advantage. My limbs, melting like butter.
The hot pound of my pulse.

Stop this nonsense at once, I tell myself.

I'm nothing if not my own torturer. It is well known that, for
humans, faeries are addictive, and if I don't take care, I may find
myself a slave, beholden to the whims of the Seelie prince, lost
until he spits me out like candy that has lost all its juicy flavor. My
body and mind forever ruined.

Pulling my horse up, I huff loudly and let Gade and Mern pass,
their hair billowing behind them in the breeze like silky capes.

Annoyed, I ride the rest of the way to the cove at the rear of the party, listening to my companions discuss El Sanartha and the prospect of a war with the Merits. Gade's words are bloodthirsty, seemingly motivated by bitterness and a desperate need to avenge the death of his parents, for which he holds the Unseelie king accountable.

For someone who once believed I was a sorceress sent to destroy his kingdom, Gade is remarkably open with political information today. This can only be for one of three reasons: he has decided to trust me; this is some sort of test; or he's completely forgotten I'm here.

Before long, we arrive at the beach, which thankfully stops me fretting over Gade and his irrational and changeable personality.

Eerdran Bay is as beautiful as Mern described; a faery tale paradise where seals and merfolk recline on slick, black rocks, basking in the sunshine.

We dismount, then Mern takes a long spiral shell from her doublet and blows into it, a mournful sound floating over the waves. An answering wail comes from the cliffs behind us, and Gade directs us into the mouth of a cave set into the black rock face.

Inside, limestone and crystal walls glitter with condensation, and at the rear, two sea fae recline in a shallow aquamarine pool. At Mern's direction, we slip our boots off and sit around the pool's edge, dangling our feet in the water.

Gade introduces me to Selanthia, Queen of the Sea, and her heir, Ezili, sea witches sworn to the Land of Five as allies and protectors.

Both fae have white hair, braided with seaweed and colored glass, that undulates around their scale-covered bodies. Their feet are webbed and lips so blue they're almost black. Driftwood crowns twist around their brows, bright coral and smooth, luminous shells and pearls embedded in them.

"A human. How interesting," says the queen, eying Gade with something like suspicion.

Do they think he would bring danger into their sanctuary?

"The girl who saved my life, no less," he replies.

"Yes, we've heard the tales of your mortal healer, haven't we, Daughter?" says Selanthia. "Very diverting."

Ezili slides up to me, her webbed, claw-tipped fingers gripping my knees roughly. I try not to gasp, but fear flows through my veins regardless.

Gade smiles fondly at the sea witch, so I suppose I am in no danger. Or perhaps I am, and this is to be my fate—the Seelie prince's gift to the sea queen of a tasty meal of human.

"You have eyes of a fae creature, girl," the sea princess says. "As yellow as a selkie's, hungry as a frost wolf's, and as sharp and knowing as a sea hawk's. One day, you may be one of us. What do you think of her, future kingling?"

Gade's mouth opens then shuts. "I like her at least as well as any of the aforementioned creatures."

Ezili laughs at his typically cryptic answer.

"What tidings do you bring from the depths today?" asks Gade. "Bright or foul? Light or gloomy?"

Selanthia kneels before him in the shallow water. "Both. Three Merit druids fell from a sea vessel seven nights past; the youngest took some time to drown. Before he died, my merfolk took his dreams of war and of something else, something important to you that is hidden in the Merit lands; the answer to a mage's riddle. Methinks it is the Black Blood curse."

"What?" Gade splashes into the water and kneels to meet the queen's eyes. He grips her shoulders. "Do you recall it? If so, tell it to me now."

"I do, and it is the verse already known to you. The rest was gibberish and told of a distant future—something about a cure, a Silver King, and his right hand. If you wish to survive the Black Blood and rule, I recommend you don't waste time waging war, searching for the key to the druid's dreams, and concentrate instead on finding your bride."

Gade's hands crack into tight fists. "No. This is bad and all the more reason to march on the Merits sooner rather than later."

"And I say, it is good news because it means the future princes of your land may one day be free of the curse. But certainly I agree 'tis bad news for you and your sons, who must live out your lives ensnared in its dark grip. Before you deal with the Merits, you must marry your mate and rebuild your strength. Heed my words, Prince of Five. Mother Sea knows all."

Gade looks downcast but nods in agreement and steps from the water onto the rocky floor of the cavern. A single wave of his hand dries his leather trousers.

Talk turns to other subjects, and Gade, Mern, Elden, and Voreas express sympathy for the recent death of the sea babe before gossiping about who is courting whom under the waves and inquiring about progress on architectural additions to the ocean palace.

Ezili tells an amusing story about a light whale that chased a comet three kingdoms across the waves before realizing it wasn't a fish. Then we say our goodbyes and find the horses grazing on a patch of seaweed near a rocky outcrop.

The others mount quickly and begin up the pathway toward the castle, but Gade calls out, "Holly, wait a moment."

We stand motionless, holding our horses' reins and staring at each other.

"Here," he says gruffly, handing me a leather-wrapped parcel. "If you insist on gallivanting about the land without inviting me along, then you at least need something to protect yourself with."

I bounce the weight of the package on my palm. It feels like a weapon. "How many assassins do you expect will come for me over the next few days?

He laughs. "Oh, a handful at least."

"Will you be one of them?"

"If I were to attack you with anything, mortal, it would not be a knife."

"That's the third time today I've heard you call me human or mortal. Yesterday, I corrected you once. According to your own words, I only have to remind you to stop on two more occasions."

"Are you officially reminding me now?"

"Yes."

"Then that's only my second reminder today. So to be precise, there are three more times you must tell me."

"Or strangle you instead."

He huffs out a laugh, and his hand lifts toward my face, then falls back to rest beside the dagger strapped to his thigh. It makes me wonder what he would use to kill me. A sword? His bare hands?

The indecent smirk dimpling his face tells me that a moment ago, he likely wasn't talking about attacking me in a murderous sense.

"Open it." He tips his chin toward the parcel.

I obey.

A small knife with a jeweled, golden hilt glints prettily against the leather, almost too beautiful to be a weapon. "This is mine? I can keep it?"

Gade smiles. "As long as you promise not to stick it between my ribs or harm a member of my household with it, of course. It's yours for all time."

I wrap the knife and slip it into my pocket, wondering how long he has carried it around for, waiting to give it to me. "And you don't want anything in exchange for it?"

"Your trust is payment enough."

That shocks me.

"You want me to trust you? Why?"

His head ducks close, and he whispers, "Because I like you. And I hope you will think of me as a friend."

"A friend?" My lips twist in a wry smile. "Oh... well, it would be my pleasure to call you that, Gade. I accept your terms. Thank you."

Shaking his head, he gives me a strange look, as though I've done something unwise. Then I remember Mern's warning that in Faery, it's best not to express gratitude because it leaves you indebted to the fae you thanked and vulnerable to exploitation.

Gade holds his arms out as if he's offering to lift me into the saddle. My cheeks flushing, I shoulder past him. "I don't need help."

Mounting Wren, he sighs heavily. "Are all the humans in your village as argumentative as you?"

"If they met you, Prince Gadriel, I believe they would be."

A long screech slices the sky, and then Lleu soars from the tree-tops, landing on Gade's shoulder and remaining there, chirping and squawking the rest of the journey back to the castle as his master holds the reins with one hand and strokes the bird's golden feathers with the other.

As my horse gallops past them into the castle's main courtyard, a strange thought pops into my head, making me laugh.

Better Lleu than me.

20

Suspicion

Holly

The next morning, as Voreas and I return from my archery lesson in the forest, we come across quite a cozy scene. The royal family and a few key household members are on the tournament oval, hitting balls through hoops with long, intricately carved mallets.

"It's called crooked," Voreas informs me when I ask him to explain the game. "From a distance, it may appear elegant, but the players must employ a high degree of trickery, magic, and sometimes savagery to triumph."

"Looks fairly peaceful to me."

He snickers. "For *now.*"

Under a small pavilion bedecked with rich-colored rugs and cushions, lies an extravagant picnic feast. Finely dressed fae dot the scene, eating and applauding, and sylphs and pixies swoop through the sky, shouting encouragement and the occasional vulgarity.

The fire mage, Salamander, and her blue-haired sister, Undine, recline on cushions eating grapes, skewered on the tips of their long fingernails. Gauzy strips of material from their gowns, every color of the ocean and flames, move around their limbs as if alive, the effect mesmerizing.

Fyarn runs off with one of the mallets, and his sons, Elden and Blade, laugh as they chase after him. The spectators laugh too, including Gade, his crown glinting as he throws his head back, the sight of his light-hearted joy rendering me speechless.

By my side, Voreas debates out loud whether we should join the party or sneak into the kitchens and steal some of the honey and nut ices the cook has prepared for dessert tonight, but I am barely listening.

To regain my attention, he elbows my ribs hard. "Look, Holly. What do you think Serain is plotting, lurking there in the shadows of the third hazel tree?"

"He does look suspicious," I reply, noting his stillness and the shape of his body, hunched but poised, as if ready to strike someone. The stone in my pendant pulses against my skin, confirming that danger is close by. "But Mern told me he's always hanging about spying on everyone. Isn't that his job?"

Gade suddenly sniffs the air and looks up at Serain, who's still hovering on the outskirts like an outcast crow. Smiling, the prince shouts out his adviser's name, beckoning him to join the party.

Voreas nudges me again. "What you say is true, but Serain has looked ever-more bitter of late, and last night, I saw him in deep discussion with a púca by the Moonstone Cave, where portals to other realms sometimes open. Those meddlesome creatures are always up to no good, sticking their noses into court politics. And Serain has long resented Fyarn for coming first in Gade's favor."

"But that doesn't mean—"

"While he's otherwise engaged, I think we should inspect his quarters for incriminating correspondence and the like."

"We?" I splutter. "Why involve me? I'm a healer's daughter, not a spymaster's."

"Come," Voreas says, tugging me along the back pathway toward the castle, out of view of the picnickers. "You're human, which means, if we get caught, you can lie and offer a plausible excuse as to why we're rummaging about in Lord Serain's room."

"What could justify snooping in a High Councilor's bedchamber?"

"I can't imagine, but I'm sure you'll think of something. Fear not." He pats my shoulder reassuringly. "There is plenty of time to fabricate a reason. But I recommend you commence right away because once we enter Serain's apartments, we'll be discovered fairly quickly. Maids frequently go in and out and may alert someone."

"What? Expecting to be caught is not a very good plan."

"Who said I had a plan?" He laughs. "Chin up. I doubt you'll lose your head over this. Our prince will likely forgive you any trespass, Holly sweet. You are a prize, and he knows it well."

I roll my eyes and follow Voreas through the castle's corridors and spiraling staircases to the middle level of one of the seven high towers.

Lord Serain's apartment is a large, semi-circular room, divided by velvet drapes that hang from midair with no rails or hooks in sight. The walls are lined with panels of honey-colored wood, creating a bright, cheerful atmosphere at odds with the dour personality of the room's resident.

Thick, white furs drape the bed in the middle of the room, its four posts carved with fire-breathing dragons. Rich tapestries cover all other surfaces except for the desk that bears neat stacks of scrolls, blank parchment, and writing implements, set in front of the arched windows that overlook the mountains.

Everything is neat to a fault and, in my opinion, rather too grand for a mere adviser. But I remind myself that this is Faery—where everything is excessive and flamboyant.

"Go look over the desk while I check the bed," says Voreas. "Take care to put everything back in its place." He sweeps pillows and cushions to the floor, feeling around and under the mattress. "Don't just stand and watch. Search. *Hurry.*"

I dart over to the desk and rifle through documents covered in neat, cursive writing. I read quickly, skimming for words—like plot, spy, or murder—finding nothing remotely suspicious.

The large desk drawer contains maps of the land with no unusual markings, blank paper, and jars of ink. I flip through a huge leather-bound book called The Laws of Five, then set it down on the desk with a thud.

Frustrated, I press an elegant spyglass to my eye and peer toward the forest's distant trees, searching for unusual landmarks or obvious signals.

"What excuse did you settle upon?" says a deep voice from behind us, making me drop the eyeglass and leap ten feet off the floor.

"Oh, frog's turd. It's you," says Voreas.

Prince Gadriel smirks before he turns and closes the double doors, locking the three of us in Serain's room together.

I cross my arms over my chest. "Why do you have to turn up everywhere I go?"

Gade strides forward, his hands clasped behind his back, stopping close enough to peer deep into my soon-to-be lying eyes. "I could ask the same of you."

I smile to test if he'll return it. He doesn't.

"Well?" he says. "What is your answer?"

I swallow, then square my shoulders and tap my chin. "Let me see... if we were discovered by a servant, I'd probably tell them Lord Serain had left his cloak behind and I'd offered to retrieve it since I was on my way to collect a book from my room."

He grunts. "The servant would likely tell you Serain has fire magic and doesn't require a cloak because he can generate warmth himself."

"Oh."

"Fortunately, I am not a maid," says the prince. "What excuse would you give me?"

Voreas, the betrayer, stays silent, looking back and forth between Gade and me as if we're performing solely for his entertainment.

I take a deep breath. "Lately, Voreas has noticed Lord Serain acting strangely, meeting with wild fae in odd places, lurking more frequently in the shadows, as he was during the game of crooked, and spying."

"Like you two are doing now?" Gade asks.

"Forgive us." Voreas dips his head in a bow, picks up the eyeglass, fidgets with it, then places it back on the desk. "What we have done is wrong, but I am not the only member of our court who has noticed Serain's odd behavior."

Finally, Gade gives us a crooked smile. "Count me as one of them. He has recently made two mysterious trips to Port Neo since I've returned, and as yet, my informants haven't ascertained exactly where he went and precisely who he met with."

Relieved, I pick up cushions and place them back on the bed. "We came here to see if we could find anything incriminating; letters and the like."

"Where have you checked already?" Gade asks. "Tell me how I can help."

I point at the wooden wardrobe built into the curve of the wall. "We haven't searched that yet."

Like a common thief, the Prince of Five rustles through fine clothing, opens and shuts drawers, pulling papers out and inspecting them before placing them back with care.

"How did you know we were here?" I ask, smoothing out the bedclothes.

Gade laughs. "I rule all elements, including air. As Elden once told you, nearby whispers are easy to hear." He cracks a seal from a previously opened letter. "What is this?" Muttering as he reads, he turns toward us. "This is a lover's note from a member of the Merit Court."

Footsteps sound in the hallway, and Gade slides the correspondence into his voluminous black shirt. "Someone's coming."

"Thank you, Master of Magic," I hiss out. "Even I can hear that."

Gade grasps my arm. "I'll wrap a cloak of invisibility around us, and we can stroll out with our noses in the air. Take care not to knock anything over on the way out. Now come closer."

"Me?" I ask, pointing at my chest.

"Yes, you." He tugs me against him, and Voreas huddles close. "Sorry, Holly," Gade says. "But I need your help again."

The prince's mouth comes crashing down on mine. He kisses me quickly but no less thoroughly than the night we danced on the balcony of the Great Hall, the effect just as devastating.

Voreas's silver eyes widen as lightning flashes, blinding me. When I can see again, Gade whispers, "The spell worked," as he tugs me and Voreas through the open doors and past a green-skinned goblin carrying a basket of freshly pressed clothes.

We hurry down staircases and corridors, coming out into a council room situated behind the dais in the Great Hall.

Laughing, we lean against the oval meeting table and try to catch our breath.

"So..." Voreas shoves his glittering silver hair from his face and waves his hand between me and the prince. "Call me odd, but I tend not to think of burglaries as particularly romantic occasions. Care to explain the kissing business?"

"No," Gade and I say at the same time, bursting into laughter again.

"It's just a... a sort of magic thing," he says.

"A magical thing?" Voreas raises an eyebrow. "Interesting and perplexing."

"And you will swear on your most prized possession—your glorious silver hair—never to speak of it to anyone, including me, *ever* again," Gade says, his voice low and deep with glamor.

"Keep your gossamer shirt on. There's no need to attempt to compel me." Voreas bows deeply. "As always, Gadriel, I am your sworn servant, and I vow never to betray you, not in thought, word, or deed."

"Good enough," says Gade. "And one last thing, in case I haven't mentioned it, touch this girl and pay with your life."

Voreas swallows obvious laughter. "But surely there are exceptions to your rule."

"Such as?" Gade pours water from a jug into three goblets, passes one to me, leaves Voreas's on the table, and takes a sip from his own as he reclines back on the curved divan set against the wall.

Voreas picks his cup up. "Can I move her out of harm's way?"

"Of course," answers Gade. "You must help me protect her."

"May I brush forest debris from her hair? A leaf from her eyes?"

Gade picks up a tiny wand of smoky quartz from the arm of the sofa, rolling it between his fingers. "If absolutely necessary."

"Can I whisper secrets in her ear?"

"No." The wand snaps, crystal shards showering the black rug and his boots. "That is absolutely forbidden."

"Stop," I say. "You're both behaving like infants. Gade, what will you do about Serain?"

"I will have his Unseelie lover investigated and Serain followed at all times. I suspect I'll need to detain him at some point. Before long, most traitors provide ample proof of their schemes. Perhaps now you will wish to stay longer, Holly, and witness the end of the story you've set in motion here today. Fae justice served is quite an event and certainly worth observing."

"No thank you. I'm sure I couldn't stomach it."

"Suit yourself," says the prince.

He dismisses us, explaining he must attend to petitioners who've sailed from Port Neo to renew trade routes and defense agreements, crucial to maintaining peace while he lingers in a weak condition without his fated bride.

I don't know why he informs us of the details of his business, nor why terror ices my veins as I close the door on the sight of him, reclining against the midnight-blue sofa, his knees spread wide, dark hair tumbling around a feral gaze that rakes me from my head to my toes.

Actually, that's a lie. I *do* know why. The man—if I can call him that—disturbs and mystifies me, one day calling me his friend and the next, staring hungrily at me as if I'm his prey.

Later that night, Gade, Mern, and their uncle Fyarn are absent from dinner, and I'm left to eat and dance with Elden and Voreas and a band of charming pixies. The music is wild and intoxicating, and I whirl until my bones ache and my arms and calf muscles cramp uncomfortably.

The third time Voreas notices my glazed eyes and thrashing limbs, he pushes me from the middle of a reel, and I spin toward the edge of the dance floor, depleted and exhausted.

"Gade really should forbid you from dancing before something bad happens," he says.

"But it's such fun, and as long as my friends—that includes you by the way—make sure I don't get too carried away, there's no harm in it."

"Yes, no harm," says Elden, "until the sluaghs spin you out on the moors, never to be seen again, and Gade rips the rest of us into tiny pieces for allowing it to happen."

Voreas and Elden escort me back to my rooms, and we take the long way around, enjoying the moonlit night, while they caper around me singing outrageous songs and telling tales about the darker fae who live in the forest.

When I cover my ears and protest, they insist they're only trying to help me, so I might recognize these gruesome creatures should I ever come across them when I'm alone, which is quite unhelpful for two reasons.

One: their prince has forbidden me from going anywhere unaccompanied.

And two: it would do me no good to be able to name a creature's species in the final moments before it ate me.

As we pass through a starlit courtyard, my gaze snags on a tree in the far corner, covered in silver and black crystals that shine like thousands of glowworms, with four cages strung from its highest branches.

Other than the thorn-like protrusions that curl up from the bases and cover the bars, the cages are empty, but they serve as perfect, horrifying examples of the cruel fae justice that Gade mentioned so proudly this morning.

That night, the gilded, wicked devices haunt my dreams, and instead of unknown faces, it's the wretched eyes of Mern, Voreas, Elden, and I that peer through those unyielding bars.

And Gade stands below us, smiling serenely as we plead for mercy and swing and swing from the tree's creaking branches.

Each time I wake, I tell myself, tomorrow is the day I will go home.

Tomorrow, I'll be free of him.

21

Who Did This?

Holly

The next day, the Prince of Five doesn't grant me leave to return home. Instead, he tempts me to stay a little longer by promising to personally show me anywhere in the castle and grounds I wish to see, effectively delaying the terms of our bargain by a few days; an offer I couldn't refuse.

In his most charming guise yet, Gade proudly paraded me past the castle's astonishing sights and introduced me to kitchen staff, dressmakers, blacksmiths, guards, and grooms, but not once to any members of the nobility—the so-called high fae of his kingdom. And on the tenth day of my visit, I learn the likely reason why.

As I walk along the Seaway path, planning to eat my crisp apple on the cliffs of the tournament oval while watching the merfolk play in the waves, four elegant fae hurtle up the hill toward me.

I recognize them from court dinners—two females with iridescent wings sailing above their golden shoulders and hair that tumbles in a riot of pastel colors to their ankles, and two males with short dark hair, skin as pale as chalk, and ink-black wings of tattered leather.

When they notice me, their smiles turn to sneers as sharp as the intricate cuffs that grace their prettily pointed ears.

The sand that powders their cheeks and dusts their fancy gowns as they pass around a wineskin, laughing and setting circlets of twisted metal to rights on their smooth brows as they stumble along, tells me they're likely returning from Eerdran Bay.

"Oh, look," says the tallest of the dark-haired males who has a nose that reminds me of a deerhound's snout.

If I recall correctly, he's called Lord Cannibule, a moniker that seems to suit the cold cruelness of his gaze.

"There's the human girl," he shouts, pulling the others to a stop and tapping his pointed chin dramatically. "Now what was her name again? Was it Folly? No. Jolly? Perhaps... Dolly?"

They fall over themselves, laughing as though he's emitted the cleverest joke to ever pass through a set of self-satisfied lips.

"It's Holly," I correct, going right up to them and smiling in their haughty faces.

"By the Elements, the creature speaks," shrieks the girl with the bleakest eyes, her pretty wings fluttering like something out of a mortal child's pleasant dream.

"Yes, I speak. And I'm so smart I can even ask what your names are," I reply.

"Indeed you may ask, but we won't give them to you," says Cannibule.

Grinning as I remember the rest of their names—Dustiniel, Ziandron, and Nikitas—I take a large bite of apple instead of the fae lord's slender throat.

The smaller male with starlit eyes, Lord Dustiniel, flares his thin nostrils. "You're either very foolish or extremely brave to eat faery fruit, mortal."

"It does me no harm. Both Mern and your earth mage charmed me against its effects."

"That was a mistake, if ever Terra has made one."

Charming fellow.

"Nevertheless," I say smoothly. "It's a very tasty apple. Good day to you all."

"Enjoy our bounty while your good fortune lasts," the girl called Ziandron says as I skip past, knocking me into the low rock wall that hedges the path. "Terra has most likely rigged the charm to end at any moment."

The pain in my cheek blinds me, but unfortunately my hearing still functions fine, and the sound of their laughter mocks me all too clearly.

"Oh, dear. She has fallen," ethereal Nikitas says.

"She'll be fine," Cannibule asserts. "She is a healer... Apparently."

Their rude comments trail off as they stagger toward the castle, clearly pleased to have caused some pain and misery. I refuse to let such nasty creatures spoil my day.

Deciding to search for wild comfrey to treat my bruise with, I pick up the hem of my embroidered skirt and start back up the hill.

It would be easier to visit the apothecary, but I don't want news of the altercation finding its way back to Gade. Being known as a tattletale would only cause me more trouble with the high lords and ladies of the Seelie Court.

Wincing with each bite of fruit, I stroll past the castle grounds toward the Black Forest, concentrating on the path so I don't trip and gain further injuries.

Near the edge of the forest, I smack into a wall of hard flesh and fall backward, the apple core rolling down the hillside as Gade grips my shoulders and steadies me.

"Where are you going in such a hurry?"

"To find herbs. I fancy a cup of freshly picked tea," I lie.

"Mapona has every herb you can think of growing in the apothecary garden. Why not visit her and save yourself an unpleasant tumble down the hill?"

"I feel like a walk." Another untruth. Since I've arrived in Faerie, lying is becoming quite a habit.

My gaze roves over the constellations of gemstones on Gade's belted, indigo tunic, his dark leather pants, then the crown on his forehead, glinting in the soft afternoon light.

Today, his black hair hangs loose in shiny waves past his shoulders, rubies and diamonds braided through it. Silver shoulder armor juts at dangerous angles, studded with dark crystals in the shape of tiny thorns. Despite the finery of his clothing, only one jewel adorns his fingers; the heavy garnet ring he's always twisting whenever he speaks to me.

JUNO HEART

Although I've been in the kingdom for ten days, I'm not yet accustomed to this shining version of my captor, who looks every bit a future king of Faery. The shock of his beauty, his otherness, befuddles my mind, and distracted, I lift my hand and touch my face.

His smile dissolves as his fingers trail lightly over the bruise on my cheek. "What happened?"

A quick head shake is my response.

"I see." A muscle ticks in his jaw. "*Who?*" he demands.

"It's nothing." I brush his hand away and try not to wince.

"*Who* did this to you?"

"I... I tripped and fell."

"*Liar.*"

"It's the truth. I swear it."

"Your words may describe the circumstances, but who pushed you first?"

Biting my lip, I shuffle backward, away from the prince.

He steps forward; the ground rumbling underfoot and cracking the roots of nearby trees, his anger made manifest in the external environment.

"Gade..."

Baring his teeth, the blue of his eyes turns to ice. "Give me names, Holly, and on my life, whoever they are, they'll pay dearly for hurting you."

"They were fooling around and didn't mean for me to hit the rock wall."

His fury shimmies around his body, like heat waves above hot stone.

I've said too much, and now I'll never hear the end of it. Dread churns the apple in my stomach, souring the digesting pieces. The last thing I want is revenge on the faeries who tripped me, for Gade to deal out heavy-handed retribution. I'd much rather pretend the incident never happened.

He widens his stance and folds his arms across his chest. "I want their names."

"And if I refuse?"

"In Faery, denying a prince's request is a serious offense."

"How can that be true? Nobody, including a prince, should be granted everything they want. You're sounding like a tyrant."

He snorts. "You're calling me a tyrant now? Unbelievable."

"You take yourself far too seriously. You'd benefit greatly from learning to laugh at yourself."

"And why in the realms would I do that?" He grunts. "Ridiculous idea."

I spin on my heel and walk toward the tree line, Gade following along as if he's been invited on an outing.

"In Faery," he says, pulling me around to face him. "Fae are punished for such transgressions against royals—a term of imprisonment or bondage to any manner of cruel creatures would be fitting for your refusal to give up names, but as with all things in my land, payment can be bartered. What would you give me to release you from being punished for your errors?"

"Errors? I thought I only made one."

"One, your refusal to name your attackers. And two, your rudeness toward a prince of Faery."

I huff out a breath. "A moment ago, you wanted to protect me, and now you want to punish me. Are you joking?"

"I rarely jest."

"Why on earth do Faeries have to bargain for everything?"

Thinking fast, I study the deep blue of the afternoon sky above his shoulders. "As you know, I have no gold or special powers to offer. Would the telling of a mortal story satisfy you?"

"I have no need for human tales, tall or small. We have the finest story weavers in the realms residing in this kingdom."

I laugh and poke my finger into his shoulder armor. "Then take me to your prison, Gadriel, for I have nothing valuable to give you."

"I disagree."

I brace my hands on my hips. "What, then?"

"Since you are sober today, I'd happily take a kiss freely given and call the matter settled."

"Oh, don't remind me of the other night. I've already apologized for my behavior. It was inappropriate. I was—"

"Beautiful. Charming. Do you understand what I'm asking? If you agree to kiss me only for the sake of the bargain, then the kiss will be worthless. But if you kiss me because you want to, bargain or no, then your payment is priceless to me."

My heart thuds against my ribs. "How will you know the difference? I could lie and say I long to kiss you, and then do it under sufferance."

"I'll be in no doubt, healer. Already, a fire glows in your eyes, and the spiced scent of your blood provides tantalizing insight."

Cunning fae. This bargain he's devised forces me to declare my inner feelings—the ones that grow feverishly each night, ignited by images of the Prince of Five and stoked by the sinuous fae on the tapestries in my bedchamber, dancing in the flickering firelight.

"But I don't need to be punished for denying you anything. You're contriving nonsense solely to bend me to your will. And, yes, you're right—I *do* want to kiss you. So if you have the courage, *Prince* Gadriel, I dare you to step closer and just hurry up and do it."

He reels backward, shocked. "No one speaks to royalty with such contempt and disrespect."

"Except me. But you're wrong. I speak to you like that because I like you. Quite a lot, in fact. I will always tell you when you put a foot on the wrong path or get too big for your britches. And that's because I—"

Then, thankfully, his lips are on mine, warm and demanding, and cutting off my reckless words.

Wind rustling through leaves, birdsong, and the distant crash of waves against cliffs—all of it merges, disappearing beneath the sound of my blood rushing through my veins, my sighs, and Gade's soft groans.

Time slows and warps as my breath and body mold to his will, heat engulfing me as he draws me closer and whispers my name.

Holly.

Three times he says it, yet I could hear it from his lips a thousand more.

My hands traverse the hard planes of his chest, then my fingers lock behind his neck as I bask in the feel of his warm skin, his urgent lips.

He gently cups my bruised cheek, and light flashes behind my closed eyes. The heat increases until it scalds, and with a gasp, I step backward out of his embrace.

A vortex of elemental magic whirls around us, wind, flames, crystals, and water droplets dancing together in intricate patterns.

I press my hand against my cheek and feel no pain. I poke it with my finger. Nothing.

"What did you do?"

With a wave of Gade's hand, the spinning magic reabsorbs into his chest. "Nothing nefarious, I promise. I healed your face, that's all."

His hands curl into fists by his side as his eyes burn through me, and he looks ready to consume me whole.

And I wonder... what would that feel like—to let him devour me?

I squeeze my eyes shut and force myself to think of Mother and Rose—of how they must be struggling without me, how much they must miss me.

"Today is the tenth day of my confinement in your land. The time has come for you to help me return to my family, just as you promised."

"Confinement? Is that truly how you view it?" His head cants to the side.

I remain silent.

He blows out a hard breath. "If that is what you wish, then of course. There is nothing in the seven realms I would refuse you, human, if it were in my power to grant."

That declaration shocks a startled noise out of me. Since when? And why is he only mentioning this now?

"My name is Holly." I clear my throat. "And that makes five," I say.

"Yes, yes, only two more times you must remind me. But listen to me, Holly, stay one more night. Just one. Let me thank you for your healing work in the hut with a grand feast in your honor. Give me this last chance to convince you to remain in my service a while longer, or at the very least, to extract your promise to return to me when your mother is no longer ill."

I flinch at his careful words—how he implies my mother's *passing* without stating it outright. I think about what he wants—me to stay in his service, which can only mean to *work* for him.

"Do you kiss your servants very often?" I ask.

He blinks. "Many fae dally with their attendants... but I do not."

"Worse and worse. Am I correct in assuming that you're asking me to be a servant, attend you personally and help you perform personal tasks such as washing your hair and bathing and the like?"

Gade rubs his frown. "No. Of course not. And fae only bathe for—"

"*Pleasure.* Yes, I know. You've reminded me many times. And believe me, witnessing you take your pleasure is the very last thing I want."

"Why must you take offense at everything I say?"

"Why must you insist on causing it?"

He leans close and speaks through gritted teeth. "You are impossible, human."

"*Holly.* Now that's *six* times I've reminded you," I yell, my blood boiling over. "And you, *prince*, are intolerable. Good day."

Instead of poking my tongue out, I drop a sarcastic curtsy, then stalk off, turning to shout over my shoulder. "And, Gadriel, I'll eat my dinner in my rooms this evening, so don't bother feasting in my honor. And unless you want to discuss my departure, please don't talk to me, either."

"Holly." His deep voice booms from behind me, and I stop in my tracks, refusing to turn because I have no desire to witness the soft pout of his lips or the anger heating his gaze.

"I will find the fae who hurt you," he says, "And they will pay a terrible price."

"No, I forbid it."

He has the gall to laugh. "That will not stop me."

"Well then, Gadriel Raven Fionbharr, you're nothing but a black-hearted, wicked faery. Aren't you ashamed of yourself?"

"Why would I be?" he says, laughter lacing his tone. "I'll never regret anything that keeps you safe."

Both guilt and fear surge through me. Fear of the tortures he might inflict on those courtiers if he discovers their identities. And guilt because, even knowing what he's capable of, his protective nature makes me want to stay in Faery for as long as he keeps kissing me as though I am special to him.

If my mother didn't need me, maybe I would remain here, glamored and bewitched, drinking faery wine and dancing to the whim of Gade's desires for a year and a day or some such ridiculous and unfathomable duration of Faery time.

And if there were an accurate way to be certain he'd never tire of me, I'd be sorely tempted to stay forever.

22

Secrets and Solutions

Holly

With the afternoon sun warming my back, I take the fastest route to the edge of the Black Forest, stopping and slipping out Gade's knife at a ditch where mauve flowers sway above the hairy leaves of comfrey.

As I stuff cuttings into my pockets, laughter peals from the direction of a copse of tortured willow trees. Stilling, I listen for a moment, check that the stone in my pendant remains cool, and then pad closer to the sound.

Two voices murmur from behind a moss-covered stone obelisk surrounded by a ring of rowan trees and partially hidden by gnarled willow branches. Recognizing Mern's voice, I creep closer as a second fae answers her in a deep, scratchy rasp. It's Terra, the earth mage.

"If I were you, Princess," she says. "I would not fret over a little scrap of a human. Do you think old Mab cared overly for the welfare of her mortal playthings?"

"No. Mab delighted in their downfalls," replies Mern. "But this is different. Holly is my friend, and without her help, my brother may have died alone in a shepherd's hut. We owe her much, and at the very least, she deserves our protection."

"Then the answer to your query is simple—don't tell the girl Nestera is in the Spike Tower. What use has a mortal for this knowledge?"

"Holly made a bargain with Nestera to provide the exact items that will help her escape from a high tower. Nestera doesn't do well in captivity, and it won't be long before her mind disintegrates. I'd like to prevent that."

"If necessary, we mages can release her," says Terra.

"Of course, but there are mysterious forces at work here. By the terms of the bargain, it is clear Holly is destined to release the changeling, but I fear involving her."

"Well then, you must view the matter from a different angle, Mern. If you don't tell the girl, will you be obstructing Fate?"

"Yes, I believe I would be. But the magic in the forest encircling the Spike is unstable and dangerous to a human. Gade would have my head if I told Holly about Nestera and she did something reckless and went there alone."

"Does she not wear the Morgana pendant? It should provide some protection," says Terra.

"But it may not."

"That is true. Whoever imprisoned Nestera is blocked from my sight. But mark me, strong magic is involved."

"Who do you suspect?" asks Mern.

"'Tis likely my sister. Who else has the power and thrives on hostile machinations?"

"Aer? For what purpose?"

Terra snorts. "The threads my sister weaves are complex and impossible to unravel, but they never fail to attempt to wrap around and entrap your brother. No doubt she seeks to use the girl to harm him. But fear not, Princess, Aer may wound, but my other sisters and I will always be here to heal him."

Gadriel. Must he always be involved in everything that happens in this city?

"For that, my family is most grateful. Now, I'd best find Gade without delay," says Mern. "He needs to know about Nestera, and he'll want to keep Holly safe, no matter her role in this mess." She takes a step backward and bows, her horns catching on branches and tumbling golden willow leaves around her. "Thank you for your counsel, Terra. I'll leave you to enjoy your earth retreat."

Before the princess finds me eavesdropping in the bushes, I creep away, then hurry back to my room with the terms of Nestera's bargain racing through my mind.

When I arrive, I go straight to the desk, grab a quill, and write out the ingredients I promised to obtain for the changeling on a piece of blank parchment.

Twenty-three arm lengths of the orb spider's web, the same of the weaver's golden twine and her silken rope—one of which will hold Nestera's weight—a crested pigeon, and a biscuit soaked in the old queen's favorite honey.

Already, a plan forms in my mind. If the tower has a well-placed window, with the assistance of Nestera's magic and the items on my list, it might be possible to break her out. There must be a way to get the rope up to her, and if there's something inside the tower room to tie it to, then all going well, she can climb down to safety.

To be sure, the scheme is patchy, but I owe it to Nestera to supply the materials that I swore I would, and I have my necklace to warn me of danger.

For a moment, I consider requesting help from Mern or even Gade, but quickly dismiss the idea. They'd no doubt take over and wouldn't allow me to accompany them to the tower. The terms of the bargain were clear—it is *my* duty to help the changeling. No matter the outcome.

I think of my mother as I dress warmly in the fine leather trousers Mern gave me, a thick woolen tunic, and the heaviest cloak in my wardrobe. Then I tuck Gade's blade into a sheath in my boot where it will be more secure. I'm not particularly skilled with a fighting dagger, but having it will be better than being unarmed.

Since I've been gone, I'm certain Rose is keeping Mother comfortable. And even though I cannot bear the thought of never seeing her again, a promise is a promise, and I would never shame my mother by returning to her bedside a breaker of bargains.

First, I visit the kitchen at the bottom level of the castle and request the biscuit soaked in special honey. Featherlayne, the hobgoblin cook, huffs and puffs while searching for the old queen's honey, but as she wraps the biscuit in stiff waxed cloth, she tells me that since I saved the life of her future king, I am welcome to anything at all in her stores. I carefully place the parcel in the leather satchel that's strapped across my body.

Next, I call on the weavers and needle workers in the Bask Tower. They listen to my request, then send their swallows flitting through the air, dipping in and out of deep storage chambers set high into the room's stone walls to retrieve ropes, golden twine, and three empty spools that barely look big enough to fulfill their task. Obviously enchanted, the rope and twine contract as the birds wind them around two of the spools, leaving the third empty at my request.

"Do you know where I might find a crested pigeon and orb spiders' web?" I ask the master seamstress, a tall elf called Rhapsowen.

She speaks around a mouthful of thorn-tipped pins, blood flecking the edges of her lips. "Ask at the stores behind the tournament oval. They sell the pigeons for pie making and someone will direct you to the closest shrubs where the orb spiders live."

I hurry down to the market and follow the chirping sounds to the bird seller's stall. A hunched old woman with fiery eyes sells me a crested pigeon in a silver cage for the price of a dance at the next revel I attend, which may be tonight if Gade ignores my instructions and goes ahead with the feast in my honor.

I've already forgiven him for our argument earlier. I was partly at fault, and he was right about one thing—I often choose to find offense where none is meant, a result of growing up with not one, but two mischievous brothers.

The bird coos happily as we pass by row after row of stalls stacked with magical and handmade curiosities. Finally, I come across a woman spinning her own jet-black hair on a spinning wheel. It's one of the strangest sights I've ever seen, her slim body upright and unmoving, and the section of hair she's working on getting longer as she progresses. Even the pigeon seems in awe, growing quiet and watching.

"Excuse me," I say, stopping in front of her table. "Do you know where I might find orb spiders' webs?"

Glancing up, she smiles—the corners of her honey-colored eyes wrinkling. "I do," she answers as she grips her hair and snips it away from the wheel with a pair of shears. "It's not far from here. I will show you the place."

The faery has a light step and a free tongue as we walk side by side along the forge behind the castle, passing livestock in large pens—four-legged animals that remind me of sheep and deer with coats of unusual colors and textures. She comments on the fae we parade past, gossiping like the women in my village do each morning at the well.

When we locate the white-barked zephyr tree, we find many orb spiders, identified by their striped, purple legs, resting in the center of their diamond-shaped webs.

"Take a piece of silk from the bottom of the web, wind slowly from the outside, taking care not to disturb the center or the spider. They are slumberous creatures and shouldn't wake unless you jerk them with clumsy movements. Requiring no spinning, each thread is strong enough to carry the weight of a large hobgoblin."

I place the birdcage on the grass, then step closer to the lowest web and begin winding it carefully around the last spool, magic condensing the thread as I work.

"Tell the spool the quantity you require," the fae says.

"Twenty-three arm lengths, please."

She laughs. "How polite and very human you are."

I almost thank her, then remember that I shouldn't.

The lady watches quietly for a few moments. "Good. Move a little slower. If one bites you, you have three thousand heartbeats to receive the antidote and not one more, or you'll fall into a sleep that lasts three thousand moon turns."

"Good grief," I say. "I appreciate the warning. What's your name, so I know who to repay with equal kindness if the opportunity presents?"

"The price to know it is too high for you," she answers, disappearing into thin air before I can ask about the Spike Tower.

It takes a while before the spool stops accepting the glistening thread. Every time I take a break from winding to wipe sweat from my brow, the movement wakes the spiders who shake their long legs at me. One even dances about, gnashing its pincers, but a lullaby, softly sung, calms it instantly.

After I tuck the spool into my bag, I collect the bird and continue along the path toward the forest, studying a black spire that pokes through the treetops and is most likely the tower I seek.

At the bottom of the hill, a golden-haired girl sits on a stool out front of the dairy, milking a cow over a wooden pail.

"Good afternoon," I say, pointing at my distant quarry. "Do you know the quickest way to the tower peeking through the trees over there?"

A pair of yellow eyes greet me as she lifts her head and fixes a steady, wizened gaze on me, an ill-match for her youthful, pretty face. I press my pendant against my chest, relieved to find the stone as cool as river water.

"If you wish, I can take you there myself." The girl's soft voice is hard to hear over the bird's wings fluttering against the cage, but her smile is as gentle as the morning sun, dissolving any feelings of mistrust. "It's not far, but the path is tricky to follow." She whistles to the pigeon, and it stops fretting and settles peacefully on the perch.

"That's very kind of you. And I accept your offer." I wait for her to lay out the terms of a bargain, but she merely pats the strange cow's side, then rises and ushers it into the paddock alongside the dairy, where a pack of similar striped beasts stand bellowing.

"They're okapris," the milkmaid says. "Quite harmless, unless you threaten its young. Then the female won't hesitate to devour you whole, crunching on your bones until none remain."

She studies my horror-stricken face, mistaking it for confusion. "Okapris can unhinge their lower jaws, allowing them to eat even large-sized fae and humans."

"Useful information," I say. "I'll endeavor to always be sweet to their babies. My name is Holly. What's yours?"

"All of Talamh Cúig knows what you are called, including the forest creatures. In Faery, there are risks in gifting names so freely, which is why I will keep mine to myself."

Faeries have odd customs concerning their names, and many choose to go by aliases that refer to their appearance—such as Clawcaped and Mottlefeather—instead of the monikers their parents gave them.

We walk in silence through a thick, bramble-twined forest, the bark-rough heads of tree folk separating from trunks to peer at us as our movements wake them from their slumber.

Whispers sough through leaves, and birds call to each other from the treetops as a gold-tinged dusk falls around us. Oddly, the crested pigeon hasn't made a sound since the faery whistled it into calm.

Finally, the smooth, black surface of the tower shows itself, its thin spire spearing through the fir trees above us. The girl guides me onto a narrow path that winds through scrub and menacing-looking blackberry bushes.

"Your fragile human skin will likely bleed, but that is the quickest way through. I'll remain here a little while in case you attempt to find your way back to the castle." Which is a polite way of telling me that if I take too long, I'm on my own.

"You're very kind," I say, squaring my shoulders. "I don't plan to be gone long." Which is perhaps overly optimistic.

As the velvet night settles around me, I check my boot to make sure the knife is still snug in its sheath and stride forward, humming to the pigeon to suppress the nagging thought that something wasn't quite right with the faery who brought me here. Why didn't she inquire about my purpose?

To calm my nerves, I think of Mother, then Gade, my breathing slowing.

I'm not afraid, though deep down, I know I should be.

Stepping over an evenly spaced line of crystal geodes that circle the tower, I crane my neck until I spy a dark, shuttered window halfway up. I snatch a stone from the ground and throw it, thankful for the games I played with my brothers when it hits its mark and thuds against the shutter, Nestera immediately peering out of it.

"There you are, little human," she says. "I've been listening for you. The spiders said you would come."

The spiders told her? Seems unlikely, but who am I to question the mysterious skills of faeries and hairy arachnids?

"Quickly, unpack your bag, for he will kill me soon. Did you bring all you promised?"

I swing my satchel onto the ground and place the birdcage next to it, wondering who this nefarious *he* is. I have my suspicions, but I want to hear her confirm them. "Who did this to you?"

"The darkest one. There is no time to waste. I'll explain later. First, tie the orb spiders' thread to the pigeon's leg, then put the biscuit in its beak, and let it loose. I will call it upward with an enchantment. Hold the spool and allow it to unwind carefully as the bird flies up. When it has nearly unraveled, tie on the golden twine, then the lighter silken ropes, and after I've taken up all of the spiders' thread, attach the heaviest rope for me to climb down on."

"You're unchained?" I ask.

"Yes, but much weakened. The room is lined with iron panels, but I have saved a store of magic for your arrival."

Nestera sends three luminous balls of light to bob around me while I work. It takes some time to unwind enough web, but my fingers work deftly and nothing snags or breaks, making me wonder if the changeling's magic assisted me.

After I prepare the pigeon, I cup it in my hands, noticing tiny, glowing insects darting inside the translucent globes that bob around me. With a squawk, the bird pecks a hole in one, and the fireflies escape, a trail of sparks spiraling into the trees.

Nestera chants indecipherable words in her cracked voice, and the pigeon takes flight, the silver thread flowing behind it. She plucks the pigeon from the air, then the biscuit from its beak and pops it in her mouth, smacking her lips together happily.

"A queen's honey has magical properties," she explains, cackling as she winds the thread up while I busy myself attaching the twine and ropes as she instructed. "Also, I am very, *very* hungry. Even you look appetizing to me right now, girl."

Sudden applause comes from behind me, and I turn to see my pretty faery guide clapping her hands together, her skin shining as if lit from within. "Well done, human."

I grab my pendant, which still lies cool and dormant beneath my clothing.

The lady laughs, pacing a slow circle around me. "For your information, that wretched, mortal-made device does not work on a mage."

Without a sound or complaint, Nestera disappears into the shadows of the tower.

This girl is a mage?

"You must be Aer," I say.

She inclines her head. "Also sometimes known as the Sorceress of the Seven Winds."

"What do you want? You cannot harm me in the bounds of the city, this forest included."

"What you say is true. At *present*. However, I can do *this*..."

She raises her arms and forks of lightning arc from her fingertips, sizzling and crackling. She directs them at my boots, and I shoot into the air, spinning from head to toe until I cannot tell which way is up or down as my body travels some distance.

She screeches out a command, and I drop onto wet grass, the landscape around me dark and lit with an eerie purple glow. My hands search blindly around me, feeling high stone walls on either side of what appears to be a narrow pathway. A heavy silence permeates the space, not a bird or night creature peeping or calling from nearby.

As I stumble onto my feet, the pendant flashes, sizzling against my skin, and the back-lit figure of a man walks toward me along the passageway. When the long robes and face of Gade's uncle come into focus, relief weakens my knees, replaced by shock and fear the moment I notice the cruel twist of his mouth and frenzied glint in his eyes. With a sinking despair, I understand my predicament all too clearly.

Aer glides from the shadows, her gaze lit with delight, but she keeps her distance, stopping several steps away from me.

Despite the fact they had different-colored hair and clothing, the fae ladies who helped me today all shared the same distinct eyes of burnished gold, filled with an intensity I can now identify as hate.

Each time, the girl was Aer, glamored to deceive me.

Fyarn and the mage must have locked Nestera in the tower to entrap me. But why? How could such powerful, magical creatures view a mere human as a threat?

"I see you have met the lovely Aer," Fyarn says, striding toward me, his gray braids slapping rhythmically against his legs.

"What is this place?" I ask.

The mage smiles proudly. "It is a maze protected by my magic, not easily breached." As she floats upward, hovering in the air, her shimmering body and golden hair are thrown into stark relief against the dark sky above the maze. "This entire forest sleeps under my enchantment, not even a sylph will bear witness to tonight's events and run to your precious prince to tell the tale."

I stare up at her. "When I first saw you today, why didn't my pendant warn me?"

"I am an Elemental mage, tied to the land and nearly as old. I warned you before; devices created by the pitiful conjurings of a mortal sorceress do not affect me. Lord Fyarn is another matter."

Fyarn stands silently, now an arm's length away from me.

"Why did you lock Nestera up?" I ask.

"The changeling discovered I am not quite as benign a presence at court as I hoped to appear."

"But you cannot lie, so when Gade seeks your advice about her disappearance, he'll learn of your betrayal and turn you into a pool of blood and bone shards."

Fyarn laughs. "How delightful. It seems the little mortal hides a taste for violence beneath her mild exterior. But don't worry about me. By the time Gadriel understands my role, his opinion will be of no consequence."

Shock at how deep his ambitions run shakes me to the core.

"Will you at least send me back to my village?" Unlikely, but if they want to be rid of me, it can't hurt to present them with the least violent solution in case they haven't considered it.

"Personally, I'd like to trade you to the Unseelie king. The Merits are foolishly obsessed with your kind, and he would pay a great deal to possess you. As would my nephew. But Aer believes Gadriel might attempt to rescue you from their court, and that wouldn't suit my plans at all."

"You're going to steal the crown from your own nephew?"

"Isn't that the ambition of all those close to a throne, whether they admit it or not?" he asks.

Aer calls from above. "Fyarn, kill the girl now and Gade will die. The throne will be empty with Elden the next first-born son in line. So do not tarry. I would do this deed myself. But as the curse maker, if I end her life, Gadriel will be free from the curse with his power and strength immediately restored. Finish her now while you have the chance. Kill your son, and I will rule by your side as your queen."

While Fyarn is distracted, I duck around his legs, withdrawing my blade from my boot as I run along the passage, my body bouncing off the walls in the dark and wicked laughter chasing after me.

My heart leaps and pounds as I run for my life, refusing to listen to the voice inside me—the one that says there is no way out of this magical maze and that I couldn't defeat one, let alone two supernatural opponents.

The voice may be right and my outlook bleak, but still, I refuse to die without a fight. Another trait I can thank my dearly departed, boisterous brothers for. Silently, I vow to make it as difficult as possible for Fyarn and the mage to kill me. It's better to die a nose-punching, rib-stabbing annoyance than an easy mark.

At least then, they'll never forget me.

Filling my lungs with air, I pump my arms harder, flee faster, slamming into walls whenever the maze turns sharply. A distant roar starts up behind me, growing louder as the air crackles with heat.

The air thickens, and I struggle to breathe.

My movements slow, then with a deafening whoosh, fire breaches the corridor, rushing toward me. As I scream, it engulfs me, forks of orange and blue licking my limbs and clothing.

Disappointment fills me. It won't be easy to punch some noses while I'm burning alive.

But at least there's no pain. Only heat and noise and the cold comfort of fury. Then Fyarn is upon me.

He tugs me from the flames by my throat, dragging me against him.

"Before I give you to the fire, girl, I have a mind to taste what my nephew has been enjoying."

"I'd sooner burn." I stamp down on his boot, drawing back enough to point my knife at his ribs. A violent, unseen force deflects the blade downward. I stab, and the force intervenes again. Gade's uncle has fire magic. How can he control my knife?

Fyarn laughs. "Silly girl, wondering why your weapon fails you. It is not my doing. Given that is the knife Gade's mother gifted him, he must have warded it against use on members of his retinue or family. It's useless. What shall you do now?"

Wriggling and twisting, I tuck the knife into my boot. I can't use it on Gade's uncle, but if I survive him, it may still prove useful. I think of my sister, Rose, teasing me for being an optimist. Better that than a coward who gives up without a fight.

"My nephew is a fool and makes decisions with his heart. When his parents died, I believed I'd cleansed our bloodline of kindly fools, but alas not. Gadriel isn't worthy of the Crown of Five. What I do now, I do for my people."

"No, you're a terrible man who will find a way to justify the horrible acts you commit before I die. And I can't stop you. You asked me before what I'm going to do without a weapon. Let me tell you: if you kiss my mouth, I'll bite your tongue off. Defile my body, and I'll curse your breeding organs to never bring you pleasure again. Will you take the risk?"

"No, witch. You shall burn," he roars and shoves me back into the fire.

Heat engulfs me, and my body spins like a pig on a spit through the flames, round and round and round.

As I die, sounds grow distant. Swirling, high-pitched laughter and the staccato thud of hooves beating the earth dissolve into the forever-night that swallows me in one great big gulp.

Then it is over.

Holly is gone.

The end.

23

Spike Tower

Gade

Not long before dinner, a horrendous squawking noise rouses me from my nap where dreams of this afternoon's argument with Holly play on repeat, tormenting me with the foolish words I spoke aloud and the smart ones that I did not.

When I lift my head from the pillows, I find Lleu hopping on the balustrade outside my window as if the stone beneath his feet is on fire.

Yawning, I leap from the bed furs without bothering to throw a robe on and pad barefoot onto the balcony to admonish my eagle.

A golden moon hangs low in the sky, crowned by a purple mist—a sign of bad tidings—that I immediately attribute to Holly's departure tomorrow. Really, it should be the least of my concerns. After all, what is one mortal girl to a future king of Faery?

Nothing, I tell myself.

Everything, counters the voice of the curse.

My jaw clenches as I realize which inner voice I agree with—the curse this time, not my own rational mind, a sense of helplessness igniting my temper, which poor Lleu is about to bear the brunt of.

"Instead of making all that racket," I growl out, "why don't you come inside and shut your jabbering beak?"

Ignoring my outstretched arm, Lleu casts me an evil eye then flies around my chambers, extinguishing candles, landing on picture frames, bookshelves, my desk, picking up objects with his feet and dropping them on the inlaid-wood floor.

I cross my arms and watch. "Are you trying to tell me something by destroying my belongings or have you gone completely mad?"

Lleu lands in front of the arched doors, his wings outstretched as he bites limbs from a satyr's body that's carved into the wooden frame. Trouble brews in the kingdom, and my eagle wishes to lead me into it.

"All right, Lleu, I understand. I am to follow you without delay. But unless you're about to guide me to a forest revel, which I must advise I have no desire to attend, then please allow me a moment to get dressed."

Screeching, he hops up and down, his distress hastening my movements. "If it's so important, why don't you show me what's troubling you?"

I still my thoughts, waiting for his mind to connect with mine and images to flow, but none come. "Lleu, calm yourself and try again."

Nothing happens. He's far too agitated for the task, which sends a bolt of alarm coursing through my blood. I could cast a glamor and leave immediately, but I have a feeling that wherever we're going, I'll be glad of the protection of clothing.

I throw on a shirt while Lleu tugs at my leather trousers, dragging them off a chair, along the floor, and delivering them at my feet with another ear-splitting screech.

"That's very helpful of you," I say, tugging the pants on with rough movements. He squawks as if I've dealt him a grave insult. I laugh, then strap on arm bracers and chest armor, and sit on the bed to begin work on my boots.

The door opens, the corridor sconces casting a triangle of light on the threshold that Mern's armored body steps into. "Brother, Nestera is gone. I've been trying to find you, but a scuffle between Uncle Fyarn's new retainer and his chambermaid waylaid me. You should have seen it. What a mess. They nearly tore each other to shreds."

Lleu takes to the air again, flying in a haphazard spiral around Mern's head and shrieking as loudly as he can. At the moment, I don't care about Fyarn's servants. I have much bigger fae to fry.

"Nestera's gone?" I lace my boots quickly, barely glancing at Mern. "Where? On holiday to Port Neo?"

"This is no time for jests. Terra says she is locked in the Spike Tower."

"What? By who?"

"My fire mage's spies tell me there are fae in your kingdom who believe Nestera is in collusion with Holly against your court, and her gift of the pendant is proof."

"Absolute nonsense," I say. "The girl is harmless. You've said as much yourself."

"We know that, Gade. But there are many courtiers who don't trust her." Mern shields her face with her arms as Lleu swoops past, knocking books from shelves, knives and goblets from tables and sideboards. "What is wrong with your eagle?"

"I think he's one step ahead of you, Sister, and wants us to help Nestera. Go ahead to the stables," I tell Lleu. "We'll be right behind you."

In a flash of black and gold, Lleu swoops over my head and exits the room.

As I finish strapping my sword and numerous daggers and blades to my body, I follow Mern through the doors, telling the guards in the hallway to allow no one to enter. "You've checked on Holly? She's safe?"

Mern's footsteps falter. "No, dammit. I'm a mudbrain. Wait... Let me take a look." She stands still and closes her eyes, concentrating. My sister's earth magic allows her to cast her mind to another space if it's reasonably close by, a useful but not entirely reliable skill.

"Gade, she's not in the hall or her chambers."

Mern breaks into a run, and I follow, taking the lead as we race through the warren of hallways on the royal floor, telling myself not to lose my head. The human is ungovernable, reckless, and has most likely taken a stroll before dinner, that is all.

She is fine.

She will be fine.

Along the way, we crash into Rhapsowen, sending her sprawling.

Mern helps her up, and together they collect the pile of tumbled gowns. "Have you seen Holly, the human girl?"

"Yes," says the seamstress. "She came to me wanting ropes and twine... Mab knows what for."

I seize her shoulders. "How long ago? Did she say where she was going?"

"An hour before dusk. I directed her to the market stalls for the other items she was seeking."

"The Spike," Mern and I say then leap onto the fluorite handrail and slide down all the way to the third-floor exit that leads to the external stairs closest to the stables.

We saddle our horses and combine our magic to move earth and wind to arrive at the Spike Tower in record time, Lleu flying silently above us.

When we arrive, the tower is as solemn and bleak as usual, and all is silent and still around it, the forest strangely so.

I send Lleu to peer through the cell's open window, and in no time, he returns to show me images of the changeling alone and unchained, but no sign of Holly, *dammit.*

Leaping, I grab hold of the weaver's rope that swings some distance from the ground, then climb up and through the window. Without delay, I hoist the weakened changeling onto my back and hurry down again.

"Where is Holly?" I demand the moment our feet hit the ground. Without waiting for her answer, I vault onto Wren's back.

"Aer took her, my prince," Nestera croaks. "All three of them dissolved in a vortex of powerful air magic."

I lean forward over Wren, readying to charge back into the woods, but Mern seizes my arm and wrenches me back.

"Wait, Gade. Aer will have protected the location with a veil," she says. "Wherever they are, it won't be visible from the ground. Nestera, can you return to the castle alone?"

"At a slow pace, yes, I can," the changeling answers, already hobbling into the trees.

"Good thinking, Mern. Lleu, I need your help." My eagle lands on my bracer. "Search above the forest. I will use your sight and seek disturbances in the energy field. When you find one, return quickly and guide us as close to the location as possible."

Settling my body in the saddle, I rest my hands, palms up, on my thighs, let my consciousness merge with Lleu's, then release him to the sky. Cold wind rushes by as we fly through the velvet night, swooping over treetops. Through the eyes of my eagle, the forest is an enormous beast, teeming with elemental magic, its limbs heavy with slumber and no whispers moving through its leaves or branches.

Aer has cast a spell upon the woods, for I see no dryads or wild fae cavorting under the stars, when nighttime is their favorite time to play.

A fracture in the fabric of the air, purple-edged and roughly the shape of Talamh Cúig's tournament oval, becomes visible in the center of the forest.

"There! You've found it," I tell Lleu. "Hurry and return to us." As he wings sharply around, I let my mind fall away from his and land back in my body, opening my eyes with a painful grunt. Mind travel is not the most pleasant of experiences.

"Aer has gone deep into the trees," I tell Mern. "I know the direction. Quickly, let's meet Lleu along the way."

Forming a picture of Holly's face, her generous smile and exquisite lips, I imagine kissing her, and power sizzles through my lungs, heart, and limbs.

As I glamor the horses with wind magic to gain speed, Mern says, "Gade, wait. Nestera mentioned *three* of them disappearing in Aer's magic. She is not alone."

"I know. I suspect Serain will be with her. But I was a fool not to confirm his identity."

As we take off at speed, I prepare myself for battle. If Aer has harmed the human, she has broken her vow and risks the severest of punishment from the High Mage. Banishment from court, her powers tethered to the land and inaccessible for her own use.

And how will I punish her?

Rage clouds my mind.

If Holly is dead, I will destroy Aer, rip her to pieces, and damn the consequences.

At the edge of the magical veil, Mern and I combine powers to tear an opening through it, galloping onward until we reach a gate set deep in high walls made of crumbling, dark stone.

We dismount, and Mern asks, "Will your powers hold?"

"When I get closer to Holly, I assure you they will."

"Interesting. Next time we take wine together, Brother, you have some explaining to do."

I grunt. "Expect me to be otherwise occupied with princely duties."

We thrust our palms out and blast the gate off its hinges, clearing our way into a narrow entry passage. Drawing our swords, we run through a dark maze and follow Lleu, who flies above and directs us through the serpentine corridors toward our quarry.

Holly.

The human is alive—I feel her life force thrumming in my blood—and if anything happens to her, the fae responsible will pay the price for their crime in never-ending pain and tears.

I vow it.

Finally, we round a corner and confront a vision from my worst nightmare—Holly spinning inside a vortex of flames, her mouth gaping wide on a silent scream.

Uncle Fyarn stands in front of the fire.

"Move, Uncle, or you'll be struck," I yell as Mern and I prepare to unleash havoc, moving our hands through a series of patterns, molding the elements to our wills.

Thunder rumbles in the sky above, and I'd wager every gold coin in the treasury that it signals the air mage is fleeing the scene.

The ground shakes, and instead of moving out of the way, my uncle begins to chant. He is selfless, not caring for his own wellbeing. And now, the magic of three fae will combine to destroy Aer's malevolent sorcery.

All the elements obey and respond to my call, earth strengthened by Mern's power, the ground swaying and cracking beneath our feet. We hold strong, pushing through the agony of power coursing through our bodies, then at last, the flames gutter and disappear beneath the rubble.

Holly's body sinks with the debris, but Mern and I raise more power and lift her into the air, bringing her to rest on the ground beside the rubble. We rush toward her, but Fyarn blocks us.

"Uncle?" I say, shock and confusion icing my veins.

What is happening here?

"The Prince of Five has come to your rescue, girl," Fyarn says, picking her up and drawing her trembling body against his chest, his blade glinting at her throat.

Pain lances my heart.

I cannot believe what I see.

My uncle, my mentor these past years—a traitor, a would-be murderer of an innocent girl.

"*You*," I spit out. "Let. *Her go*. Or I shall turn you to dust."

"I don't think so, nephew. Your power isn't what it once was. You are *weak*."

Hah! The betrayer knows nothing. In Holly's presence, my magic increases a thousandfold. I slow my breathing, the pound of my pulse. I must buy time and wait for the perfect opening to make my move.

And Fyarn has always loved to boast.

"It was you all along," I say softly. "*You*, who killed my parents. *You*, who has plotted with the air mage. Your own brother, Fyarn. How could you commit so vile a crime?"

Madness sparking in his eyes, he shifts the grip on his knife, and blood beads on Holly's throat. One reason to be thankful she remains unconscious. "Yes, I wanted your parents to die because they were weak, Gadriel. *Weak*. But in the matter of their deaths, I swear I am innocent. I do not know what happened to them."

Mern spits on the ground and lowers her chin, her horns locked on Fyarn and ready to charge. "But nonetheless, you played a role in orchestrating the peril that befell them."

Fyarn gives no answer, which is as good as a confession. The desire to blast him to pieces wars with my need to keep Holly safe.

Fury boils in my blood, my mind racing, limbs trembling with the urge to attack. A quick death is too good for him.

"Let her go, and I may yet show you mercy. Drop the knife, and move away from her."

He laughs. "You think me a fool? Why would I surrender now, when I possess the most valuable bargaining piece? The key to everything."

How does he know the mortal's safety is critical? That I would kill for her, maim, and terrorize if it would keep her safe?

"You speak in riddles," I say, lightning curling from my fingertips.

"Do I? Think about the curse, Gadriel. Uniting with your fated mate is said to neutralize the poison in your blood. Look at the power circling your body. At present, you aren't the weak, brain-addled princeling who set out hunting a little over two sennights ago."

Unbidden, a bolt of my power strikes the ground in front of his boots, the walls of the maze shuddering with the force. "Enough!"

Fyarn stumbles, pulling the girl tighter against his chest, the knife pricking deeper into her flesh. I use every last bit of my willpower to restrain myself from blowing his head from his shoulders.

How dare he threaten what is mine.

Mine.

Holly is *mine*, and I will blow the realm apart to prove it if I must.

Waves of heat coil from my eyes as I lower my chin, brace my feet wide against the earth. "You have one last chance to release her," I growl out.

"And then what? You'll kill her as well? You cannot strike me without harming her." He sighs. "Nephew, do you not comprehend who she is? Has your magic not called to her blood? Has *her* blood not incensed your needs and driven you mad with lust? She is the *one*, and I will not give her to you. To defeat me, you must forsake her."

"Your crazed mind unleashes a twisted tongue, Fyarn. It is *you* who cannot survive, wagering your life on the hope that a prince of Faery holds a human in high regard."

"The trees have whispered words to me, long ago spoken by the druids, back when Aer wrought the curse from her unbridled fury. There is an end to it. A king who will come in many years' time. Another foretold girl who is his. Both hold the key to the cure of the Black Blood curse. If you kill this one," he gives my mortal a shake, "you will fall. The curse will pass to your cousin. Elden doesn't possess the temperament to rule nor the will to solve the curse's riddle. And I am not the father who will allow him the chance."

So, his nefarious plan is revealed, along with his deluded belief that Holly is my fated mate, which is a laughable assumption. It is impossible. A human could never be the Queen of Five.

"But you plan to kill her regardless," I say, struggling to form words as all five elements build within my chest. My eyes burn, no doubt glowing like liquid silver. "So what does it matter?"

A subtle movement attracts my attention—Holly's fingers flex then inch toward her boot, her body drooping into the perfect position to draw a weapon from it.

Quickly, I whisper the words to undo the binding in the knife that prevents it from causing harm to me or mine, hoping with every fiber of my being that she manages to reach it. This means, of course, if she wishes to, she can now wield it against me. But she won't. I trust the mortal with my life.

Mern shifts closer to me, her arm brushing mine. She, too, has noticed that Holly is awake. Lleu circles silently above, waiting for an opportunity to take Fyarn's eyes from their sockets. We are united and ready.

"Why do you hesitate?" I ask my uncle, balling my hands into knuckle-cracking fists to prevent my body from shaking under the force of the tremendous power building within me.

His mouth opens, brow furrowing, and as he takes a breath, the mortal withdraws the blade from her boot and plunges it through the slit in his chest plate and into his armpit.

Fyarn stumbles, and Holly dives forward out of harm's way. Shouting, Mern and I blast elemental power from our bodies, aimed at Fyarn. The walls of the maze crumble, flame and wind roaring as they whirl in a lethal maelstrom in the place where my uncle once stood.

I tug Holly and Mern into my arms and throw a shield around us, a large bubble of water, flexible and impenetrable. The world rocks and shudders while I count out Holly's heartbeats—twenty-seven of them—then I open my mouth, drawing a long breath and the excess elemental energy back inside me.

Exhausted and panting, we drop to the ground and survey the aftermath, still holding each other tightly.

Ash and snow swirl through the air, and Lleu cries as he flies through it, swooping to land at the edge of the deep hole where Fyarn the Betrayer once stood. I am numb to his loss and feel no sorrow or remorse.

Holly scrambles up next to Lleu and stares down the cavity. "He's gone. Is he dead?"

"Without a doubt," I respond, sheathing my sword and going to her side. I grip her shoulders and spin her around. Blood and grime streak her face. "Are you all right?"

Surprising me, she smiles. "Yes, no thanks to your uncle. But I'm fine. Fatigued and sore, but I'll survive."

"Come," says Mern. "We must move outside the maze and seal it up, then get Holly to her bed. She looks ready to collapse."

Watching the mortal struggle to breathe, I must agree with my sister's assessment. Holly is in dire need of rest, and even so, I wish it were *my* bed I could whisk her away to. Does that make me the evil faery she once believed me to be?

Outside the maze, I ask permission to kiss Holly briefly and boost my power while Mern watches us with a slack jaw. Then my sister and I join hands and focus on the veil of magic over the forest, shaping it and contracting it until it swallows the ruins of the maze, dragging it under the earth and sealing it up forever.

The entire forest and every living creature within it draws breath, their hearts beating again in their natural rhythms, released from Aer's spell. Animals scurry through the nearby thicket, owls hoot, and in the distance, I hear the song of a wild elf, giving thanks for her freedom.

The horses snort and whinny as we walk toward them and reward their patience with a feast of carrots from my saddlebag.

"All this time, our uncle hid his true nature." Mern scowls. "And, worse, neither of us suspected what he was capable of."

I run my gaze over her face as she mounts Bee. Purple half-moons rim her eyes, and color has leeched from her horns, leaving them the pale shade of dead autumn leaves. Tonight's efforts have sapped her strength. We must return to the castle in haste.

"Fyarn was likely drawing on another's power in order to hide his true self," I say.

"Aer," growls Mern.

"She was definitely involved," mutters Holly as I lift her onto Wren's saddle. "For unknown reasons, she wants me dead."

"Because she wishes to hurt me," I respond, adjusting Wren's bridle. I draw a quick breath as I realize I've revealed too much.

Holly clasps my forearms as I mount behind her and tug her tightly against my body. "Aer has disappeared. Will you hunt her down?"

"The air mage cannot be found unless she wishes it," Mern answers. "She lives as the breeze that tangles our hair, the wind that shakes apples from trees. We'd do better to speak to her sister, Ether. Aer's time to pay for her misdeeds will come. Perhaps not in our lifetimes, but pay she most certainly will."

We ride slowly through the twisted trees, foxes and young dryads peering out from the scrub to watch us pass. Holly twists in the saddle and looks up at me. "What did you mean before about Aer wanting me dead to hurt you?"

"She knows I value you."

Silence prevails for several moments as Holly thinks my meaning through.

"And Fyarn said I was someone or other. Did he mean the witch you thought I was when you found me by the oak?"

"I wonder," I say, evading the question. "Do not worry yourself with such things. I am most assuredly aware that you are no sorceress come to bring about my kingdom's downfall."

"You're hiding something. If not the witch, then who am I meant to be? Answer me, Gade."

I heave a sigh. "Fyarn believed you're my fated one—the girl who can lay the curse to rest."

Beneath my touch, her muscles tense. "What? That's impossible."

"Indeed. He was wrong. A mortal could never wear a crown of Faery."

"What makes you so certain of that, Brother?" asks Mern.

Instead of answering, I urge Wren into a gallop.

After we dismount, leaving the horses in the care of the stable hands, we walk through the Courtyard of Tears. Holly peers up at the gilded cages hanging from the Tree of Retribution and gasps at the sight of their inhabitants; the four fae who accosted her earlier today, their bodies crammed into them.

Their limbs protrude from the bars at odd angles, slick with a dark substance that she likely guesses correctly to be blood.

She asks no questions nor makes a sound, which worries me greatly. When has she not seized an opportunity to admonish me for my actions?

Steadying her steps, I tuck her arm through mine, wanting to protect her from all who wish her harm, but knowing the biggest risk to her wellbeing at this moment is me.

Let *her* rest, I tell myself over and over as if I can enchant the wicked thoughts from my mind.

At one of the many back entrances to the castle, Mern bids us goodnight, and Holly turns to me. "Now that we've saved each other's life, the scales are balanced. You owe me nothing. Thank you for coming tonight, Gade."

"And thank you for helping me kill my uncle, the rotten, conniving betrayer."

"My pleasure. Anytime you have foe to defeat, don't hesitate to call upon me."

Laughter rumbles from my chest. I stroke her cheek—gently, carefully. "You will go home tomorrow, Holly, and you'll be safe. This I promise you."

She twines her arms around my neck and pulls me close. "Kiss me," she whispers against my lips.

Without delay, I comply. Instantly, heat licks through my veins, need roaring to life like a creature of flame inside me. Thankfully, the mortal has more sense than I do and pushes against my chest, breaking our kiss.

"Gade?"

"Yes?"

She looks at the cobblestones around her boots, avoiding my hungry gaze. "What answer would you give if I asked you to show me all that's possible between a man and a woman?" She watches my jaw drop. "Tonight."

"To-tonight?" I stammer out. "What... Do you..."

"I am an untouched maid. Human customs demand that I must remain one until I am married. But I will never marry."

"You will never marry a *human*," I correct. "Quickly. Repeat my words. Say them back to me."

She shakes her head. "There's no point. It doesn't mean the same when humans make vows. We break them all the time."

"And still, I need to hear you speak the words. Promise me you won't marry a mortal man."

"Well, I can certainly say the words and promise you they're true. I have no plans to marry a human and will never do so. There—it's done. Are you happy?"

"Very," I answer, the word sounding close to a growl.

"Now, show me to your bedchamber. I'm eager to see it."

Desire hits me like a hammer to an anvil, my throat so dry I have trouble swallowing. "Are you certain? Swear that you want this."

"I do. More than anything."

The skin around her eyes is red. Her limbs tremble. She can hardly stand straight. Grinding my teeth, I tamp down the flames of lust. "But you need rest. You look asleep on your feet. This is not the time for—"

"Our time is *now*, Gade. There will be no other opportunity. If you promise to catch me, I'll gladly collapse into your arms. Tell me now, will you do it?"

"Yes. I will always catch you, little human. Wherever and whenever you fall, I will be there to carry you to safety."

"*Holly*," she says as I gather her in my arms. "And that makes seven. So now you must always call me Holly."

"With pleasure," I reply. "I'll call you anything you desire."

Even my queen.

24

Lover's Retreat

Holly

G ade's smile is sweeter than honey and brighter than starlight as his arms band my waist, and he takes my lips in a delicious, slow kiss.

"If you are truly sure, Holly, then I know the perfect place, my refuge from court. Only myself and a single trusted servant have ever stepped inside it. I would love to share it with you."

"I've never been more certain about anything. I want to experience love just once before I relinquish it forever," I say. "With you, Gade."

He cups my cheek. "Why relinquish it? I am a prince of Faery, soon to be a king. I can give you all you desire and more. If it pleases you, I can bring your mother here, restore her health. She can live beside you for the span of many mortal lifetimes."

I shake my head. "Your offer is generous. But I won't cheat death out of any soul, even my mother's. Lilé has devoted her life to the old gods and the new. I would never disrespect their judgment when the time comes for them to claim her."

"As you wish," he replies. "Before you leave, I will make you mine, and I'll claim you so thoroughly you will never forget who you belong to. In exchange, you must promise to return to me when you can. All I ask, is that you don't make me wait too long. Please, Holly, grant me this or destroy my every chance of happiness."

I don't know how I will bear the pain of being tossed aside when he finds his fated mate, let alone the agony of watching him marry her. Nevertheless, the idea of returning to Faery, to *him*, even for a little while thrills me.

I mirror his movements and cup his cheek with my palm. "I promise I'll do my best to visit you as soon as I can."

We kiss quickly, urgently, then saddle Wren and ride into the night—our cloaks billowing behind us as we fly along at breakneck speed, passing the place where the new city will one day lie and entering the mystical Emerald Forest.

After a time, we dismount out front of a house made of earth and stone, its facade set into the hillside and concealed by trees and rambling vines of wisteria and ivy.

In the adjoining stable, the only part of the dwelling that boasts a single spire of moss-agate crystal, Gade lifts me from Wren and doesn't set me down until we enter his retreat.

Inside, I find a magical building of immense beauty, constructed from dreams of the past, present, and future, large sections of the ceiling and walls made of a glass so seamless that I'm certain it doesn't exist in the human realm, even in the grandest of palaces.

As we wander through the rooms, hand in hand, the forest holds us in its soothing embrace. We're safe here, the rhythm of nature's beating heart and the old magic of Faery entering our lungs and thrumming through our veins.

In the bathroom, I stare up at a crystal-flecked night sky. "How is this possible?" I ask. "The house appears to merge with the hill. There shouldn't be any sky visible."

He laughs. "How do you think?"

"Elemental magic."

Spinning me around, he nods. "Yes. Now come here. Time to cease stargazing and focus on *me*."

"So arrogant," I say, melting into his kiss.

In Gade's arms, I transform from a healer's daughter into a princess. *His* princess, who is forever treasured and will never be cast aside.

When we undress each other, I'm not embarrassed or ashamed. Neither am I afraid when his teeth scrape my skin and the press of his fingers grows firm and insistent.

We bathe in a tub of black stone that could easily fit Wren, the water heated by magic from Gade's fingertips and scented with rose petals and stems of lavender, produced with a wave of his hand.

While bathing, we stare and stare, soaking up the sight of each other, Gade's touch gentle and reverent.

Silently, he exits the tub and lifts me from the perfumed water, settling me on my feet. He runs his hand along my skin, following the contours of my body, slowly drying me with air magic. Then he picks me up and carries me through dark corridors slashed with moonlight, his eyes never leaving mine.

"Careful," I tell him, playing with a lock of his water-slick hair. "You'll crash through a wall if you don't look where you're going."

He laughs, but doesn't take his gaze from my face.

A roaring fire greets us in a circular hearth sunk into the middle of the bedroom, hewn from rough stone. A glass roof sweeps above the bed that is crafted from clearest crystal and carved with elemental glyphs and creatures.

Gade throws me onto the bed furs, his expression feral as he licks his lips. "I've dreamed of this moment every night since we met."

"Surely not the first night," I tease.

"Yes, even then."

"No wonder you thought I was a sorceress," I say with a laugh.

"I am sorry, Holly, but my desire is strong, and the first time will be fast. Speak now if you do not wish this, and I'll find another way. Despite my hunger for you, if you ask me to stop, I will. Don't doubt it. Never fear me. Have faith that my most fervent wish is to please you, and above all else, to keep you safe from harm."

"I'm not afraid," I say, opening my arms.

"One thing I must tell you first; the night of the banquet when we made our second bargain, your words of thanks cast you into my debt once more, and although this gave me power over you, please know that I have never forced your feelings or used this to control you. But I must be sure you do not doubt it, so I gift these words to you: Holly O'Bannon, I release you from the binds of debt. Your will is yours now, as it has ever been. I release you."

A strange sensation flutters behind my breastbone, gentle as a bird ruffling its feathers and gone before I can study it, leaving in its place, a sense of hollow loss. Fortunately, I know how to replace it. Gade's touch will do nicely.

Watching me carefully, he swallows hard. "Tell me now, do you still want me?"

"Yes," I say. "More than anything."

Flames, ice, and molten metal trace the edges of the star glyph on the back of his hand. He examines it a moment, then laughs. As he grins at me, the elements rise and whirl around the hard planes of his chest, spinning at a mesmerizing pace.

The furs are as cool as silk beneath my bare skin until the prince crawls over me and fire sizzles along every inch of my body. Elemental magic circles the bed as he takes care to position his large body where he'll cause the least discomfort, his hands and fingertips worshiping every part of me as they caress and stroke. Then he kisses me, and his demands turn violent.

I brace for pain, but ecstasy melts my muscles, tendons, even bones. I am a river, urged to flow by the heat of his kisses. With one slow, firm movement of his hips, we breathe in and become one body, one soul, our lips and limbs seeking and gripping and trembling toward something unknown to me. Something just out of reach. I long for a terrible, beautiful end to this wild abandon, and at the same time, I never want it to stop.

"Gade," I cry out at the peak, shivering as I bite his lip.

Bone and muscles turn to stone. "You are hurt?" he asks, his voice a broken whisper.

"No. No... keep going."

The rhythm changes from controlled and steady to rough, ragged, and perfect. Heat and light coil in my stomach, my core, an unbearable tension, and then I explode, my body pulsing in time with the stars that blink down at me through the roof glass.

His arms grip my waist like bands of steel, squeezing painfully. He grunts, groans, while I struggle to breathe.

"No," he moans, his every muscle straining, fighting the end. "Please. *Holly*..." Another groan wrenches his chest, its intensity and tone prickling chills over my flesh.

Shudders rack his body, and I cling to him, whispering soothing sounds. "My love," I murmur, and his head whips up, iolite eyes glittering darkly at me.

I wait for him to return the words that will make me stay forever. But no answering declaration comes from his lips. "Mine," he growls instead. "You are mine, Holly O'Bannon. And never shall you deny it."

Certainly, at this moment, I cannot, for what he says is truer than the breath in my lungs, my blood that heats only for him, and the flesh that will one day rot from my bones.

I am human. He is not.

And all we have is this night.

Time warps, shifting and changing form, and we waste not a moment of it. When the stars sleep behind dawn's first light, Gade rolls out of bed and brings me cool water and honeyed bread and fruit. He feeds me from his fingers, like I'm a little bird, resting in his lap.

When we finish eating, he kisses me, then heaves a heavy sigh. "Would that I didn't have to speak these words, my dearest Holly, but if you must leave me, do it now or do it never."

I hesitate, and he lifts me off his lap, plucks a silken robe out of the air, and tosses it to me. "Put this on. I shall call Ether. She'll provide an update on your mother's health, and this information will either take you from my arms or keep you in them."

Pulling his clothes on, he holds his palm up in the air, chanting in a low, guttural voice. A ball of blinding light appears, hovering chest-height in the space between us. The High Mage steps out of it, her gown of layered silver as bright as the globe of energy she materialized from.

Her pale brow rises as she inspects the prince's rumpled, half-buttoned clothing. She smiles, but makes no remark on our recent activities. "How may I be of assistance, Gadriel?"

"The mortal wishes to cleave my cursed heart in two and return home. I'd prefer if she did not."

Ether inclines her head. "Understandable."

"Gade," I admonish. "I've reminded you seven times to call me Holly, yet you just called me mortal again. How can I trust your word if you cannot stick to it?"

Gripping my shoulders, he presses me to sit on the bed and drops to his knees in front of me. He takes up my hands and kisses each knuckle. "Holly, I am sorry. You can trust me with your heart, your every breath, your life; I swear it is so. If I sometimes err and fall back on calling you my mortal, please know I only do so because the term reminds me of your fragility, your value, and of how very precious you are to me."

I grab the pointed tips of his ears, draw his face close, and kiss him with raw emotion.

Laughing, Gade draws back. "Are you trying to kill me?" He turns toward the mage. "If you show Holly that her mother fares well, perhaps she'll decide to stay longer?"

Ether sits opposite me on the bed, folding her legs underneath her body like a child. Something in her bright expression tugs a memory—an image of a dark forest and a bright ring of mushrooms flashing in my mind.

Holding my hands, she closes her eyes. Pain shudders through me as I'm dragged through time and space, and I find myself floating above the foot of my mother's bed.

The room dimly lit by one lantern, my sister sits at the bedside. She wipes tears from her eyes and spoons a tincture between my mother's dry lips. Lilé's cheeks are gaunt, her skin thin and translucent.

"Mother," I say, gasping, my arms stretched toward her as I'm sucked backward through another vortex of pain, my mind fragmenting then drawing together again as I land back in my body, lying on the furs in the prince's forest hideaway.

"Lilé is dying," says Ether. "You must leave immediately."

A muscle jumps in Gade's jaw as his hands curl into tight fists. "Can you open a portal?"

Ether draws me from the bed by my hand. "Yes. The Moonstone Cave is close and its energy the strongest. Ride there now, and I will meet you."

Without another word, she disappears. Tears blinding me, I dress quickly, and Gade gives me his fur-lined cloak, insisting it's warmer than mine, drying my face with his magical kisses.

In no time, Wren delivers us to the cave behind the tournament ground, and Gade lifts me from the saddle into his arms.

"Promise me you shall return as soon as you are able. Vow it now, Holly, or I shall break all my promises this instant and keep you with me forever, my soul damned from entering the Otherworld."

"I don't understand why you want this or for what purpose, but I promise to return when I can. I have my sister to consider as well as my mother, so it may not be as soon as you'd like. By then, you'll likely have forgotten why you ever wanted me to return."

"Never." He takes my hand, and we walk into a glittering cavern, finding Ether standing at the edge of a pool of water at the center of the cave.

"Heed my words, Holly." Stepping close, Gade frames my face with his hands. "As Faery needs the mortal world to anchor it to flesh and bone, as lady night needs the moon to light its midnight canopy, I will always desire you, my mortal. *Always*."

My heart melts as he kisses me with a tenderness that nearly breaks me. I'm certain he believes his declaration because he cannot lie, but a fae prince's devotion is surely a fickle thing.

"I'm willing to risk that your interest endures, Gade. And I'll most definitely come back to find out for certain. I promise."

"Do not doubt how much I need you. Here, take the signet ring of the Land of Five's heir to remind you who you belong to." He twists his garnet ring off and puts it on me, too big, it slips and slides around my finger. When I get home, I'll braid a string of leather and wear it around my neck, close to my heart.

"Whenever you hold this in your palm and concentrate on Ether's name, her face and eyes she will come to you," he says. "Picture her as clearly as you are able, call her, and she will not fail to answer."

"Why didn't you use this when we were stuck in the hut?" I ask.

"Can you not guess? I wanted more time with you."

I grip his sharp cheekbones and kiss him hard. Tiny jewels break off from the walls and shower around us, his emotion affecting the elements. I laugh, raising my hands and collecting handfuls. I press them into his open palm.

"My gift to you, Gade. Keep these and think of me. Please tell Mern, Elden, and Voreas goodbye."

He nods, but his fingers cling to mine as Ether draws me into the pool of water. She chants a song, calling on all five Elements, spirit last and honored the most reverently.

"Gade, will you answer one question?" I say.

"Yes, you may ask for anything and consider it yours."

"The night you bargained for a dance, you told me you were only afraid of one thing. What is it?"

Deep laughter bounces off the cavern walls. "*You*, Holly, and the power you hold over me."

The sparkling cavern dims. My limbs tremble, and a terrible pressure builds inside my skull.

"Wait..." says a voice, Gade's, faint and coming from far away.

Splashes drench my clothes as he joins me in the pool, dragging me into his arms for a final, near-fatal squeeze and a vicious, teeth-scraping kiss. Already in the next world, my body only barely responds.

Ether admonishes him, and the golden light of his presence disappears, replaced by a roaring, burning thrum through my veins.

My limbs dissolve, then my torso, my head, and as the darkness takes me, a final thought flashes through my mind.

How did the High Mage know my mother's name?

25

A Mother's Bargain

Holly

I wake in a pool of brilliant moonlight at the edge of the forest next to a well-worn path that leads back to my village, amazed to find myself so close to home. A fox cries in the distance, but the surrounding undergrowth is silent. The forest creatures are asleep.

I wonder how much time has elapsed in the mortal realm since I've been gone—days, weeks, possibly months? What if the vision Ether showed me actually happened years ago?

These thoughts immobilize me and fill me with dread. But then I draw a deep, settling breath. There's no sense in lying on a pile of fern leaves if Mother is still alive and waiting to bid me goodbye. I need to shake off the disorienting pain in my head and get to her bedside as quickly as possible.

Brushing dirt and leaves from my clothes, I follow the path through the woods, thankful for the full moon above. Before long, the walls of Donore are in sight, and then the narrow street that our mud-walled cottage sits slowly sinking into. And finally, I see the red door my sister painted last spring with roses, lilies, and holly leaves, a salute to our flowery names.

Releasing a slow breath, I stride through the front door into the main room of the cottage, the comforting sights, sounds, and smells weakening my knees. It's wonderful to be home again.

The neat, white-washed walls glow a warm orange in the candlelight, the fire crackles, a tasty stew simmers over the flames, and the pungent tang of cooling herbal tea fills my nose.

"Who's there?" calls my sister from behind the linen curtain where my mother's bedchamber lies.

"It's me, your sister, Holly. Who else are you expecting at this late hour?"

"Holly!" Rose cries, rushing into the room. "Are you all right? Sweet mead, where the blazes have you been? Quickly, come here to me."

She flings her arms wide, and I step into them, the scent of rosemary in her hair tickling my nose, bitter poppy flower and henbane wafting from her clothes.

Tucking a lock of hair behind my ear, she says, "Brace yourself, Mother's last breath is nigh."

"I'm glad I made it in time." Nodding, I wipe away tears. "How long have I been gone?"

"A sennight."

"Only seven days?" I was in Faery for at least two sennights, possibly longer.

"Mother swore to me you were alive and well," Rose says, beckoning me into the tiny bedroom where a body lies on the bed, too small and frail to be the formidable force that is my mother, Lilé.

Rose grips my arm. "She promised all was well with you, but I never truly believed it until now."

I hug her tightly. "And here I am in the flesh."

"Praise the gods. I couldn't bear it if Mother passed without you. And Liam and I are to be married in a sennight. We hoped that she would be with us, but I'm so thankful that *you* will be, Holly dearest," she says, leading me to Lilé's bedside.

My throat burns as I sit beside my mother and take her hand in mine. Golden eyes the color of lightest honey open, so similar to mine.

"Darling Holly, I knew you would come," she whispers. "I've been waiting, but I'm so tired and can hold on no more."

The sound of her voice, weak and dry, hurts my heart, but I paste on a bright smile. "Mother, how I've missed you." Rough skin scratches my chin as I kiss her hollow cheek. "You think I'd let you pass through the veil to the Otherworld you've long lectured about without bearing witness to the event? Ye of little faith!"

She chuckles. "Oh, I knew. I knew you would be here. Your sister has taken great care of me, eased my suffering just as you would have bid her had you the chance."

I glance at Rose beside me, crying softly. I must remember to thank her for her hard work and devotion.

"I am sorry I haven't been with you this past week."

She smiles. "And I am grateful he would part with you so we could say our goodbyes."

More tears stream down my face, and I freeze in the action of wiping them with my sleeve as her words sink in. "Him? Who do you mean?"

"The prince of Faery. I wasn't sure if he'd risk your absence, given what you are to him."

"What I am to him..." I repeat, then swallow hard. "Mother, what on earth are you talking about?"

"A few years ago, a faery woman paid me a visit, offered you a place of comfort in their land, and—"

"Mother! You sold me to the Prince of Talamh Cúig?"

"Hush, child. No money was exchanged. Only an assurance of a good life for you, away from the hardships of the village after I'm gone." She grimaces, fighting pain. "Please... a sip to ease my throat."

I help her drink cool tea, then lay her head back, arranging her gray braids on the pillow.

"Rose has Liam," she continues. "And besides me, Holly, you have no one."

She's right. I cannot deny it.

"What am I to him? What did you mean by that?"

"The woman I bargained with was a nasty sort, but I know a thing or two about extracting the truth from a fae. You are this prince's fated one, destined to still the curse in his blood and to heal him. Daughter, I believe he will love you like no other could, and you deserve to know what it is to be treasured by a man, as your father valued me and Liam prizes Rose. After my passing, you'll return to his realm with my blessing."

The room whirls around me as I digest my mother's words. Not only does Mother know I've been to the Land of Five, but *she* is the cause of it. This revelation turns my world inside out and upside down.

Mother coughs out a laugh. "Close your mouth, Holly dearest. All is as it should be. And, Rose, come here to me. Take my hands girls and sing me to the land of peace, where we will one day be reunited."

Rose and I do as she bids and hold our mother in our arms, singing quiet songs of hope and joy as she labors over her final breaths. After her heart drums its last beat, our tears persist as we call for our friend Jasmin and, together, prepare Mother's body.

For three days, villagers traipse through our home to drink mead and share stories of Lilé's life with us. We laugh, cry, and sing, and when the grave is finally ready, we place Mother's body to rest and do it all over again, this time in reverse.

After the funeral, Rose and I walk home arm in arm.

"Holly," she says, a tremble in her voice. "Will you be leaving me now?"

"Not before I see you married to your handsome baker."

"And after you go, will you be allowed to visit us?"

"The prince has promised as much. Tell me, Sister, does Liam make you happy?"

A wide smile brightens her tear-blotched face. "I couldn't wish for a better partner to share my life with than Liam. But perhaps you have outdone me. A *faery*, Holly. How I long to meet your prince. He must be quite a delightful fellow to win *your* impenetrable heart."

I laugh. "You likely wouldn't say that if you met him."

"But I refuse to believe he's bad if you care for him."

My laughter cuts off abruptly as I ponder all I know about Gadriel Fionbharr, his fervent care of me, his gentle touch, and his endless capacity for cruelty. In my mind, I see the bodies of those who crossed me hanging in those gilded cages and wonder, will my love be enough to temper his often callous fae nature?

Over the following days, we ready the cottage for Rose's wedding and transform it into a home for the newlyweds. I immerse myself back into the rhythms of village life, ignoring the stabbing pain that knifes my chest each time my thoughts wander toward the prince of Talamh Cúig.

In the final days before the wedding, I am far too busy with arrangements and food preparations to mope overly. Only in the nights, as I lie next to my sister, do I allow myself to drift in memories of Gadriel's forest retreat, reliving in great detail what we did together during those long, feverish hours.

And I cannot help but wonder... will I ever experience such joy again?

26

Chimes for the Air Mage

Gade

A full moon turn passes in the realm of Faery, each moment since Holly left a torment to endure. Ruling a kingdom in peril keeps my mind and body occupied, but not my heart, and I begin to deeply regret the words I didn't allow myself to say to her, stubbornly believing a mortal queen of the Land of Five would be an unacceptable breach of fae law.

Each day, when I'm not planning an attack on the Merit Kingdom with the war council, I consult with Ether and faery lore advisers. Then at night, I pore over voluminous texts, seeking guidance, looking for any rules that forbid me from taking a mortal as my Queen of Five.

I find nothing and no one to divert me from my course—until Ether insists I extract a promise from her sister Aer, the curse-maker, to meddle no more in my life and to do no harm nor scheme against my future queen.

Ether and my family agree Holly is my fated one, the girl who will keep the curse dormant in my blood until my death, when it will unfortunately pass to my heir—our son.

It pains me to know he must endure the curse's madness while he seeks his fated queen, as I have done. But I hope he won't be as foolish as me, not recognize her, try to cast her aside—and pay the cost with his life.

Regardless, Ether insists I must hear the air mage confirm in her own words that she chose Holly O'Bannon to subdue the curse, so my mate will never doubt it. But from the moment our bodies became one, my heart and eyes were opened, and even in my mind, I could never, ever deny the truth of it.

As I am hers, Holly is mine, and nothing in the seven realms will change that.

Today, I have ridden to the top of the Dún Mountains, where I'll lure Aer from the cave she has dwelt in since her schemes with my uncle came to naught, with a gift of a spectacular wind chime the glassblowers created at my bidding.

Wrought in gold and silver, near colorless gemstone wands and intricately carved glass feathers jangle from the side of Wren's saddle, their magical song of air calling to the mage's deepest desires and urges.

Within moments of my arrival, she appears at the mouth of the cave, golden hair tumbling to her bare feet and swathes of shimmering veils flying around her body. Every inch of her is fair to look upon, except for her cold, merciless eyes.

"Prince of Five, how you honor me with your presence," she shouts. "My ears and heart tell me you come bearing a gift."

"I have," I say, dismounting, and then holding the ornament aloft so the wind and the light catch it to great advantage.

Avarice blazes in Aer's gaze, her hands already grasping toward the chimes. "What do you want in exchange for it?"

I reattach the chimes to Wren's saddle. "Only to hear you confirm that the human, Holly O'Bannon, is my fated one who will cure me of the poison."

"Yes, she is that. But you are a fool if you believe she'll deliver you happiness beyond relief of the poison, for you will never deserve it."

"So you have told me many times over, Mage. Do you swear that she's the chosen one?"

Ungraceful laughter snorts from her fine nostrils. "Tell me, Gadriel, in her presence, did the pain of the poison subside?"

"Yes. My power increased as well."

"No doubt you have inspected her skin from head to toes. Were there any special markings upon it?"

Frowning, I scan my memories of our night together, remembering the silk of her body, the warm, perfect taste of it, then the birthmark on her inner right thigh.

"Yes—a mark in the shape of an eagle with its wings spread wide."

"Then you have all the proof you need. Each heir's mate will bear a marking of their prince's elemental affinity or bonded creature, proof that she is the one. The only question that remains is this... do you want her for your queen?"

"I do." *More than anything*, I think, refusing to tell Aer how badly I want and need the mortal by my side.

"But a human, Gadriel? For a prince of Faery, your standards are miserably low."

"You say this, yet it was *you* who chose her. Does this explain my obsession? Does your curse compel me to love her?"

A sudden wind roars around the mountaintop, tearing at our clothes and hair.

"*Love*." She spits the word out like a mouthful of sour wine. "My power doesn't manipulate your feelings. My curse ensures only that she'll hold the poison at bay until you die when it will pass to your heir. If you don't have a son, it will transfer to the next first-born son in your line—which in your case, will be your cousin."

Relief flows through my veins. My love for Holly is real. 'Tis no faery fabrication or mage's twisted trick.

"Look at you, smiling like a besotted fool. You're meant to despise this mortal and take the better option—*me* as your Queen of Five! Do this, and I can dissolve the poison the moment you gift me with this promise and seal it with a single kiss, saving your descendants from suffering as you have done, Gadriel."

"But I want this girl and no other. You've always known it cannot be you, Aer. I've never pretended otherwise."

A violent gust of wind blows me stumbling backward, and I raise a shield of air to counter the tempest.

Aer folds her arms, her eyes hard but fixed on the glorious wind chime. "I suppose you'd like me to vow to never orchestrate or scheme against the girl, nor cause her harm myself?"

"Precisely. If I were to make her my queen, what will you require to ensure her safety?"

She huffs a self-satisfied sigh. "The price would be steep."

"What do you want?"

"*Everything.*"

I laugh, the sound harsh as the wind takes it up and spins it through the mouth of the cave, and it echoes back at me. "Impossible."

"Hear me out before you refuse." Aer snarls. "In return for her safety in our land, you must give up something dear to you, something that would cause you great pain to live without."

My boots rooted to the gray rock beneath me, I stare at the mage, waiting for her to state her terms more clearly.

"And, in addition, I will not reveal the exact item you must forsake before the bargain is struck. I can only assure you it will be a material item, not a person or an animal, favored or not."

"That is absurd. I will never—"

"Ah, but in exchange for a mere mortal, I believe you will. Don't look so worried. Do you care so much for sticks and stones and jewels and thrones?"

"You *know* I do not." My jaw clenching, I think fast, determined to wreak the least potential damage with the bargain I make. For there is no other choice but to strike it. I will give anything to have Holly by my side. "If you promise not to harm or orchestrate to do the same to a single person or being under this bargain, then I will accept."

A sly smile widens her mouth. "There is one final detail I believe it is only fair to mention. When the time comes, if you refuse to pay the price, I will take your fated one away from you, and she *will* suffer greatly for *all* eternity. Mark my words, Gadriel."

"So be it. Speak the terms, and I will accept the bargain."

Both fury and triumph glint in the air mage's golden gaze. "Prince of Five, I vow to never cause harm to your human mate Holly O'Bannon of Donore, neither by my hand, my power, my schemes, or influence as long as you give up the prized material item at the time I request. I do swear upon Mab's bones and the Seven Winds that roam the Seven Realms that what I ask you to give up will not be a being, fae or human, or even the tiniest creature of Faery."

"I accept your terms then, Sorceress of the Seven winds, Aer, curse maker mine."

The mountain shudders as she strides forward and grips my face with sharp-nailed fingers. "Seal it with a kiss, Princeling dear."

Cold lips press against mine, and as I draw back, her tongue swipes my mouth, sending images tumbling in my mind of an enormous oak tree set against a black night sky. Twelve chanting men dressed in druids' robes, swearing oaths to a curse.

I grip the mage's shoulders and shake her. "*What is this*? What did you show me?"

A cackle issues from her lips, whispering around the hillside thrice. "Merely the past and the future combined." Her fingers beckon toward the wind chime tinkling at the side of Wren's saddle. "Now give me my prize."

I unstrap the treasure, throw it in the air, twirl my fingers, and send it spinning noisily toward the mage. Her power seizes it, and she turns and walks toward her cave, the chimes floating above her head and the song of sprites accompanying them.

As the mouth of the cave swallows her form, her voice trills on the breeze. "*Your* mate may be safe from me, Gadriel, but there will be many other future brides I can meddle with. You should have thought to protect them."

Blast the Elements, but she is right. I should have. I *could* have. In my eagerness to be reunited with Holly, I was careless and thought only of her. I grind my teeth with fury, cursing my foolishness.

In penance, I will dedicate my life to solving the curse, finding the cure, and saving my descendants from the horrors I have faced.

But first, I need my mortal.

Holly promised to return to me when she could, but I already tire of waiting. The need to keep her safe gnaws like a living creature at my innards, tearing me apart, slice by slice.

No doubt, I am a man in love, who before the curse, likely possessed more than a few admirable traits, but patience was never one of them, which means...

I must journey to the human realm and retrieve my fated mate.

27

A Faery Visitor

Holly

As the sun rises on the morning of Rose's wedding, our dear friend Jasmin knocks upon the front door and our work begins in earnest.

We laugh and sing as we string garlands and hang them from walls and rafters, pull pies and cakes from the oven as neighbors arrive and arrange tables outside, weighing them down with food and drink.

Hours pass, and when the final touches are in progress, the time comes to prepare the bride in the way of our family tradition.

Jasmin, Rose, and I dress in long shifts of white and journey to the river in the woods.

In the dappled shade of a weeping willow tree, we sit on the bank, making necklaces of forget-me-nots and marsh marigolds, and weave the excess flowers through our unbound hair. Then we wade up to our waists in the cool stream and scrub Rose's skin with river stones and wash her hair with the rose and lavender soap our mother prepared specially for this day.

Jasmin squeezes water from my sister's fair hair, then tosses her own dark locks over her shoulder. "Are you excited for your wedding night, Rose?"

Laughter peals from Rose's lips. "Yes, of course. And since I've already sampled my baker's most delicious treats, I am assured of a delightful evening."

"Have you no shame?" I joke, heat rising to my cheeks as I duck my head and hide my smile.

Jasmin, who is known to enjoy a ribald tale or two, sings a shocking song about an extremely lusty bridegroom, changing the lyrics from blacksmith to baker, her voice ringing through the trees. A red-breasted robin chirps in response, and other creatures scramble off through the undergrowth in fright.

Rose and I join the final verse, laughing as we sing about the girth of the fellow's husbandly attributes. When we finish the song, a hush settles over the forest, and every bird, animal, and blade of grass stills, including us.

"I believe I know that tune," comes a deep, resonant voice from the bank behind us.

Shivers race down my spine. Looking over my shoulder, I squint into the sun and see the outline of a large man, his body positioned as if he's staring down at us.

"Or at least one quite like it," he continues. "Where I come from, such songs are greatly favored." Then the man steps forward, his face clearly visible.

"Gade!" I cry, splashing through the water onto the bank.

His arms open, and I fall into them, clinging to his waist as if my life depends upon it. My feet fly off the ground, and I'm spun around and around until I call out for mercy, dizzy with shock and joy.

"I can't believe you're here," I say, inspecting him from head to toe.

A glamor hides his pointed ears, the magical glow of his eyes, and the no doubt rich fabric of his doublet and trousers, but not the shocking beauty of his face and form.

"I could wait no longer to see you, Holly. My heart bleeds, my mind and body ache for you. I beg you to put me out of my misery and return home with me now."

Rose clears her throat as she exits the water with Jasmin, who is wide-eyed and blushing, her bawdy nature dissolving in the presence of a real-life faery.

I move next to the girls. "Gade, this is my sister, Rose, and our dear friend Jasmin. They both know who and *what* you are."

"But until this very moment, I didn't believe the tale," says Jasmin, her lovely features writ with awe and wonder. "I've never met a faery man before."

Gade's smile turns mischievous. "Would you like to meet more? I can personally arrange it if it would please you—"

"No," I shout. "Please, no. Perhaps another time."

He gives a fond chuckle.

Rose drops a curtsy, her smile broad. "You must excuse our appearance, Your Highness. I'm to be married today, and we're busy with preparations."

"A wedding," he says. "How pleasant. I find myself much occupied with thoughts of similar unions. In fact, they consume me like a fever."

I frown, and Rose giggles. "Thankfully, our Holly is an accomplished healer and can help you with your malady. You've done well to seek her out."

Grinning, Gade bows. "Indeed. I am wise."

"What a handsome man you've ensnared, Sister," she says in a none-too-quiet whisper.

I roll my eyes. "Oh, please do not call him *Your Highness* or praise his looks. Only the grovelers in his court use his title, and believe me, he's already arrogant enough. His name is Gade, and as far as I know, I'm yet to capture him."

"But you have, Holly, and I am yours, if you will but accept me. I've searched my heart a thousand times and cannot think of one reason why you would reject me." A smile spreads over his face, setting my heart pounding. "Have I not already pleased you in every way a husband should?"

"*Shush*," I scold. "We've a maiden in our company." I indicate Jasmin with my hand.

"Ah," he says. "Another fine flower. Is every girl in your village named after beings that dwell in gardens?"

"Only the succulent ones," Jasmin replies, a host of devils shining in her dark gaze.

As he laughs at her comment, his ocean eyes travel slowly along my body. "Surprising outfits that mortal maids wear. There are fae creatures that would raise a brow at the sheerness of the fabric."

I glance at the wet shift clinging to my figure, leaving nothing to the imagination. "Oh!"

Rose throws her arm across her breasts. Jasmin and I do not.

"I like it a great deal," Gade says, his smile as hungry as a wolf's.

My sister chuckles. "Clearly, you have much to discuss with my sister." She turns to me. "Holly, I'll be fine to get dressed without you, so we'll leave you to speak privately. I hope you'll stay for the ceremony, Gade. Don't be late, though. It begins in one hour. What shall I tell our neighbors about him?"

"Tell them he's a cloth trader from the east who rescued me when I was lost in the forest recently."

Rose nods. "Close your mouth, Jasmin," she says, taking her hand and pulling her through the woods in the direction of home.

"I would be honored to attend," Gade calls out, his gaze not leaving mine as the ladies' imp-like giggles echo behind them.

Gade gathers me into his arms and kisses me until my head spins. "Shall I summon a bower?" he asks, his finger trailing my breastbone.

"Absolutely not. It's my sister's wedding day. There's no time for pleasure until it is over. But, oh, I am so *glad* to see you."

His brow furrows. "Glad? That is all?"

I clasp his face and shake it. "I'm thrilled. Amazed. Overflowing with joy."

"Better," he says. "Shall we marry alongside your sister so she can bear witness to the happy event? We'll have a much grander ceremony when we return to Faery."

"Who said anything about us getting married?" I ask.

I laugh at his expression—the shock of a future king of Faery unable to believe a mortal girl might not want to wed him.

"Holly, do you truly doubt that you are mine and I am yours?"

"I don't doubt you believe it to be so, and in truth, my heart sings to hear that you want me as your wife. I never dreamed it possible."

"Then we are in agreement?" He whips off his indigo cape and wraps it around my shoulders. Taking my hand, he leads me up the bank and into the trees. "Your sister will not mind a double ceremony. She seems an amiable type."

"She is, but I won't be marrying you today."

The earth shudders beneath my feet as he stops in his tracks and takes me by the shoulders. "What?"

"I can't. I mean... I'd love nothing more than to be your bride, Gade, but I'm human. Most of us only give our hearts once in our lives. I couldn't bear to watch you take fae lovers. I'd go mad with jealousy and sorrow."

With his hands cradling my head, he kisses me sweetly, then brushes hair from my face. Reverently, he presses my palm against his heart. "My love, I swear upon the Elements, by the breath of life, the blood of flesh and bone, and the ocean's endless tears, I will never take another to my bed, bower, or even into my arms in desire. You are forever my only one, my love, and thus it shall always be."

"You love me?"

"I do. A fae prince has no need to utter such words, but I am quick to learn your human ways. And it is true; I love you, Holly." His lips touch mine. "I love you," he whispers, then kisses me again. "I love you above all else."

The temperature drops. Rain falls upon us—a sun shower. Then wind lifts and blows it away, tiny flames from out of nowhere flickering over our clothes.

I laugh, breaking our kiss. "Gade, stop that at once. Someone might see us."

"Who?" Raising a dark brow, he swirls his finger, and motes of gold twirl down, landing in our hair.

"Please, hide your magic and promise me you'll keep your glamor on or my neighbors will come for you with pitchforks."

"Would they not kneel and worship me as a god of old?"

"Well, Jasmin might and perhaps a few other ladies. But the men would chase you out of town with haste before they lost their wives forever."

He snorts as we start along the path to my village.

"You really believe I'm your fated one?" I ask, my brow pleating.

"Without question."

"Why?"

"The mark of the eagle on your thigh is visual proof. And then there is the deal Aer made with your mother. Either the chosen bride or their family must be willing, and Lilé, by all accounts, was more than happy to give you to a land where you will be respected and honored for your knowledge of healing instead of vilified for it."

I sigh, closing my eyes briefly. When I stare into Gade's face, I know he understands me as no man ever will. He is right—I am his; he is mine. But still, I can't resist teasing him.

"Hm." I tap my chin in contemplation. "And what if I insisted on staying in this realm with my sister?"

His jaw drops. "Why would you refuse me?" Flustered, his gaze scans the trees for answers, then he smiles. "Actually, you are bound by two bargains to return to Faery. The one you made with me the night you left, and Nestera has called for the pendant to be returned since you neglected to deliver every item you promised. Have you forgotten her terms?"

"I delivered all she asked for. The bargain is done and dusted."

"Oh, no, you haven't. Nestera requested the old Queen Sersia's favorite honey, not my mother's. You gave her the wrong honey."

"But that's ridiculous. I've never heard of this Sersia. Nestera didn't state *which* queen she meant."

"And *you*, poor bargainer that you are, forgot to ask."

"Faeries! I will never grow used to your sneaky ways."

He smirks, clasping his hands behind his back and dipping his face close. "But I predict you'll grow very used to *mine*."

"Well then, it's fortunate I was only teasing. Of course I'll be returning to Faery with you."

"Praise the Elements. I hoped I wouldn't have to drag you home, but know this, wife—I was quite prepared to do it."

I draw a breath to remind him we're not married yet, but think better of it. I'll let him call me *wife* as often as he wishes. It's wonderful to hear him say it.

We exit the forest onto the cart road from where a small section of the village can be seen.

"Welcome to Donore," I say with a flourish of my hand.

"You truly reside here? *This* is your village? *Here*?"

"Yes, it is."

"My poor love." He pats my hand resting on his forearm. "If only I had known, I would never have allowed you to return to this vile place."

Laughing, I shake my head at his frown and quickly change the subject. "Have you visited this realm before?"

"Me?" He points at his chest. "A fae prince? Whatever for?"

I blow out a long breath. "We must work on decreasing your arrogance."

"Why?" he asks, looking bewildered.

Giggling, I guide him onto a narrow fork in the path that leads to a discreet route behind the town and passes by the wall of my cottage garden.

Before I open the gate, I say, "Gade, remember to keep your glamor in place at all times, and please try not to look too outraged at the simplicity of our lives. This is the human realm. You come from a place where magic and miracles are as common as leaves on trees. Keep your mouth closed and your opinions to yourself."

"But surely I can use a little magic, some innocent trickery if the opportunity arises? Engage in some harmless entertainment?"

"No. I absolutely forbid it." Swallowing laughter, I kiss him quickly. "Come, let me show you how mortals live. We may not reside in palaces and possess luxuries, but we *do* know how to have a good time."

28

A Wedding

Holly

The priest entwines a velvet ribbon around Liam and Rose's wrists, speaks the ceremonial words, which they repeat, and then pronounces them man and wife.

It's both a joy and a privilege to witness my sister's happiness, but I weep tears for my mother, who would have given anything to be with us today.

As I talk with well-wishers after the ceremony, Gade watches me, and the entire village watches *him*—the *impressive cloth trader who possesses a rude amount of unearthly beauty*, which is how my next-door neighbor described him. Little does she realize how accurate her words are. If he removed his glamor and revealed his true princely visage, she'd likely have a seizure.

"Why do you cry?" the aforementioned prince asks, angling my chin up with his finger. "Has someone offended you? If so, point them out, and I'll smite them to stone where they stand."

"Gade, *no*. No smiting today, *please*. I miss my mother, that is all."

He nods and, thankfully, doesn't murder any of my neighbors.

When our turn comes, we congratulate my sister and her brawny new husband. The sour twist of Liam's mouth as he inspects Gade tells me he's not at all pleased to be upstaged by a handsome stranger. But Rose laughs and kisses his scowl away.

Sweet bread and mead are passed through the gathering. Gade swigs from my cup, then splutters and coughs. "Do not drink that. It's terrible and likely poisoned."

Beside us, the blacksmith and his family frown and whisper amongst themselves.

"He has a cold and refuses to take my remedy," I tell them. "He can't taste a thing."

They raise their eyebrows and smile.

Gade draws my back against his chest, his breath rustling the flowers in my hair. "My sweet, delicious little liar."

"Jealous of my skill?" I ask.

"Yes, and it will be an extremely useful talent for a Seelie queen to possess. Holly, I have much I wish to say to you, words of love I should have spoken long before you left my land. I need to rectify that as soon as possible."

"Yes, the sooner the better," I agree, my words drowned out by the cheers of the crowd.

Liam gives a touching speech about Rose's good heart, her steadfastness, and the deliciousness of her smile, and I break my bread in half and pass it to Gade. He chews for a long time, his face tight with disgust. I bite my lip and stifle my laughter.

Rose kisses Liam, then holds their joined hands aloft. She whoops loudly, then takes off at a run, and all the guests, including myself and a confounded fae prince, chase after her. When we catch her and begin to tear strips from her apron made for this custom, Gade steps back from the mob, gripping my hand tightly and tugging me with him.

"Must everyone have a taste of her to mark the ceremony?" he asks.

"No, it's a tradition and good luck to obtain a piece of a bride's clothing. Nobody wants to maim her."

"And I am glad of it. I was about to draw my sword and cut them all down."

Liam swings Rose onto a stone bench, kneels before her, and lifts her dress. Gade grunts in surprise, raising an eyebrow at me. As my sister's garter is removed and tossed to the crowd, he whispers, "I hope you do not expect me to do this at our wedding. In Faery, it would start a riot."

I snort a laugh and elbow his ribs. "Remind me, did I actually agree to marry you?"

"It matters not, Holly sweetest. Before long, a faery bride you shall be."

We eat and dance and sing, and as the moon rises, a procession forms that snakes its way around the village and ends in the main bedroom of our cottage.

We women divest Rose of her outer garments, and the men do the same to Liam. Flowers, dried and fresh, are strewn over the couple as they sit upright in bed, laughing and smiling back at us, then we draw the curtain and leave them to their wedding night.

Flasks of mead are passed around and jokes and songs hollered as the lovers consummate their vows. At the end of a particularly graphic song, I risk a glance at Gade, who hasn't moved from my side. His glamor flickers, and a young girl across the room stares at his crown of silver, the elongated tips of his ears poking through his raven locks. Jasmin looks on, too, her eyes wide and mouth agape.

"Gade." I clear my throat. "Your glamor."

"What about it?" Glowing eyes cut my way. "You don't like it? I specifically chose gold and crimson for the rather plain doublet because I know you are fond of me in these colors."

"How could you know that?"

He chuckles. "When I'm in your company, I pay great attention, Holly. I notice when your eyes darken. I hear every hitch in your breathing, every skipped beat of your heart, every—"

"Your glamor, Gade, it isn't holding. Do you want everyone to know a faery stands among them?"

One shoulder shrugs. "In truth, I would not mind." Then he stares at the shine of his silver-tipped black boots and the butter-soft dark leather hugging his thighs. "Oh, I see. The bedding ceremony distracted me. I lost focus."

"You're lucky everyone is drunk. Now quickly, put it back."

He inhales deeply and his glamor stabilizes. "No longer are you allowed to tell me that faeries are barbaric. Mortal marriage traditions would raise a blush on even a river nymph's cheeks."

"I suppose that's fair," I agree, laughing. "This is because mortal marriages are more often than not about property. They're business transactions. So we need proof that the girl is a maid to be certain who fathered any forthcoming children."

"I forget that humans breed like hob rabbits. But... your sister is not a—"

"How can you tell? No, don't answer that question. Many cheat by making a small cut in their skin and letting the blood drip on the sheets in advance of the bedding ceremony."

He laughs, then stops abruptly. "Come. We must leave. It's unbearable having you so close with all this talk of bedding. The desire to touch you consumes me."

Heat flushes over my skin as I realize what he means. I grip his forearm. "Perhaps I shouldn't leave Rose so soon after mother's death... I could stay a few more days."

"She is safe, and her man is strong and hale. We will visit them soon."

"We?" I ask. "You'll come with me?"

"Of course. I cannot keep you safe from another realm."

"Who killed your uncle?" I whisper. "Was it you or me?"

"Good point," he concedes as we find Jasmin. She blushes furiously as we say our goodbyes, and I instruct her to kiss Rose and Liam for me and promise her that we'll return soon. Gade kisses her hand, and her knees buckle.

As we walk into the garden, he says, "Your friend is sweet and fair, but something isn't right with her. She stares overly."

"Only at you, and probably because you terrify her. Believe me, there is nothing wrong with Jasmin Petalfeather." Of course there's another reason she quakes in Gade's presence, but I'm not about to inflate his ego any further. It's big enough already.

"With a name like Petalfeather, are you certain she has no fae blood in her veins? And why in the realms would she be scared of me?" he says with mock innocence.

"It's a mystery," I say, rubbing my cheek against his arm like a cat. "How do we return to Faery?"

"The well at the edge of the forest. Ether created a return portal and has left it open. All we need to do is jump."

"Down the *well*? No, thank you! You can travel by that dubious method and send Ether back to get me."

"There's nothing to fear. Trust me, Holly. When have I led you astray?"

"Many times."

"In the name of Dana, Mab, and the Elements Five, I would *never* allow harm to befall you. And should you choose to run, know this—I am faster than you. *Much* faster."

We arrive at the well, and he leaps onto the edge and holds his hand out to me. "Come. Take a look."

"I've been wondering... Is it possible for humans and fae to have children together?"

"What an odd question to ask at such a time. Hoping to distract me so you can make a run for it?" A devilish smile curves his lips. "But the answer is yes. And as soon as we return, we'll begin our attempts in earnest and spend much time practicing."

Gingerly, I climb up beside him and stare down at the gaping hole. No water shimmers in the moonlight. There's only a bottomless, black void below.

He huffs a breath. "Since you're having trouble committing, allow me to assist."

Without warning, his shoulder digs into my waist, he hefts me over his back, and then jumps.

"Close your eyes, mortal," he yells.

"You promised not to call me that."

"Apologies. I look forward to being punished for my transgression."

His laughter echoes until I pass out, the velvet darkness swallowing me whole.

29

The Price of Love

Gade

The moment we step outside the Moonstone Cave, my shoulders slump as I realize the much-anticipated child-making practice must be delayed.

Aer waits for us near the tournament ground, the sky dark and rumbling above her, marring the otherwise bright and sunny morning.

"Hide," I whisper roughly, sliding my body in front of Holly's.

She lifts her chin, returning to my side. "Never."

Aware there is no point arguing with her, I take her hand and hold it tightly. If Aer doesn't kill me today, it won't be long before this girl will be the death of me.

The air mage vaults into the sky from the black cliffs above the oval, her arms and legs morphing into the black-scaled limbs of an air dragon as she spirals through storm clouds, roaring as the bones in her face crack and lengthen.

"We had a bargain," I shout. "Stop posturing. Come down and speak civilly, if you're brave enough."

"Brave enough," she screeches, her snout disappearing as she partially shifts back into her fae form and drops to the ground in front of us, a spiked black tail whipping the air behind her. "Had I a mind to, I could slay every fae in the realm with ease, future kings and queens included."

It's unnerving to see Aer's lovely head enlarged and atop the body of a dragon. I draw my sword and sink into a crouch in front of Holly, ready to spring and cut the mage's tail off before it slices us to pieces.

The dragon's body makes a slithering, sucking noise as it changes, leaving the regal mage standing before us dressed in her usual layers of golden silks.

"So, Gadriel, you have truly done it. You've brought a mortal queen of Faery home. Your poor taste astounds me," she says, stalking a close circle around us.

Holly doesn't shudder or tremble, only squeezes my hand tighter.

"Well, then," continues Aer. "You've made your choice and now the price must be paid."

"What price?" asks Holly, her gaze flitting between Aer and me.

"In exchange for your safety, mortal, your future king has agreed to give up a material item that he holds dear."

Dressed in the pale-green muslin gown she wore to her sister's wedding, Holly looks vulnerable and very human, but she squares her shoulders and holds the mage's gaze. "And what might the item be?"

Aer smirks. "First, Gadriel must tell me what he plans to do about the Merits now that his uncle is gone and his treachery revealed."

"As was yours," I say. "You played a role, at least in enabling and hiding Fyarn's deceit."

She shrugs and spins on her heels, arms outstretched like a child playing a game. "That may be so, but the Merits swear they didn't murder your parents, Gadriel, and you'll likely go to your deathbed never knowing what became of fair Queen Aisheel and brave King Bryar. Since you cannot directly blame the Merits for the woes of your land, will you live in peace with them?"

"Never. Before long, I will march on their capitol with your sisters behind my banner."

"Besides me, there are others who won't support a war with the Unseelie fae."

"Name them," I demand.

"The moss elves will not fight. Many of them have made happy marriages with Merit fae and live in the forests surrounding the city. They won't use magic against their own kin."

"Then I'll banish them."

"Even Mapona, your prized healer?"

"Even her. As my queen, Holly will be made immortal and will grow into her fae powers. Herbs are her natural passion, so if she is willing to accept the position, I'll gladly make her our kingdom's healer."

"Fine. The price that you'll pay me now will make your war plans difficult. This pleases me. Now get down on your knees and kiss the earth, warrior prince of Talamh Cúig. Do it now, and say goodbye to Castle Black, your beloved home, for which all know you would give your final breath to protect."

Shock shudders through me, an animal sound of pain rumbling from my chest. "Your price is the destruction of my home? No. The cost is too high."

"You refuse to pay it?" Aer swoons, her eyes rolling back in her head as if a vision overtakes her.

"Kill her," Holly says. "Now, while you have a chance."

"Her power is linked to the land and our magic. If the air mage is destroyed, we all are."

Aer chants a song about a different human girl and another prince called Never or Ever—perhaps glimpses of future events or simply images flickering through her mind sparked by madness.

Air is a difficult element and requires a sharp, disciplined mind to control it or risk succumbing to insanity, and the Sorceress of the Seven Winds was never worthy of governing it.

Snickering, she jolts out of her trance and stalks forward. "Well, if that is truly your choice, Gadriel—a building of stone and wood over your mortal, then give her to me now. She is mine."

I lunge forward. "Stop. Wait... Of course I'll adhere to the terms of our bargain. I was shocked that your wish to hurt me also extends to harming your own people. Where will they live when their home has been destroyed?"

"That's your problem, princeling, not mine. Marry this weak girl, restore your powers, and begin rebuilding."

"No, Gade. Don't do it." Holly paces in front of me. "She asks too much. I won't let you."

"Holly... I'm so sorry," I say.

Rage shoots through my veins as tears spill down her cheeks. Pain grips my chest like a band of iron, the pain so intense I can hardly speak. Does she really think I would choose the castle over *her*? How little she knows me.

I grip her shoulders, dipping my head close. "I will *always* choose you, Holly O'Bannon. Above all things; it will *always* be you."

Surprise flickers over her face. "But, Gade, your people…"

"The only reason I'm sorry is because I know you'll always blame yourself for the destruction of the city. But this is *my* choice, and I choose *you*. I never thought I could love anyone, and you've proved me wrong. Our love will temper a curse, restore my power and the health of our kingdom, and we will always have each other. What is a castle but reformed earth and rubble, when what we have will last forever? We'll rebuild a better city. *Together*."

Aer snarls as I take Holly in my arms, press a soft kiss against her mouth and dry her tears.

Holly nods. "Then do what you must, Gade. I will always stand beside you."

Without warning, the mage shoots air magic from her palm, knocking me several feet away from my mortal. "Your life is joined to the earth, Prince of Five. Kiss the ground, and give me your blessing to destroy the castle that sits upon it."

"My blessing wasn't bargained for." Magic kindles in my chest, but I push it down.

Without a doubt, my next words will infuriate Aer. She will retaliate, and I can only stand by and watch until the terms of the bargain have been settled.

"Do your worst to my castle, but know this; you will never have our respect or love. You will never beat us down, never cower us. And one day you will realize, that you will never, *ever win*."

The mage releases a long, drawn-out moan, a storm gathering above her halo of yellow hair. "Oh, Gadriel, why must you always choose the most difficult path?" She howls, and her lower jaw unhinges, opening wide to the sky as elemental power pours down her throat and shudders through her shaking limbs.

"What's happening?" Holly asks, attempting to weave her fingers through mine.

"Move. Quickly!" I push her away just as the air mage flicks her hands out in front of her chest.

My body flips and shoots off the ground, and I'm dragged back and forth over grass and rocks, then thrown hard against the black cliffs below the castle. Unseen hands hold me upside down by a boot as Aer twirls her fingers, her gold eyes turned black with rage.

I hear Holly's voice, urging me to fight, but I can't. I won't risk Aer turning her wrath on my human. Let the mage use me instead. I'll do anything to keep Holly safe. *Anything.*

I'm flung this way, then the other, until finally Aer tires of the game, dumping me on the grass and wiping her hands in satisfaction.

Holly rushes over and checks my body for broken bones, but only my dignity has been injured, a small price to pay for her safety.

Aer watches us with disgust. "Unless you prefer to see your people perish, Gadriel, call them from the castle, then watch every happy memory collapse before your eyes—your carefree childhood, life with your loving parents, the once-flourishing city. Watch me destroy it all."

I cup my shaking hands around my mouth and call Lleu, who is fishing far out over the ocean. When he feels my distress, he arrives in a flash of golden air magic and circles above me. I concentrate on images, indicating what I need him to do, which is to find my sister, show her that the castle is about to fall, and help her guide our people into the Emerald Forest.

He takes to the sky, and before long, fae can be seen pouring down the hillside to take cover in the forest caves.

"It is time," says Aer, pushing on my shoulders until my palms brace against the earth.

She presses her hands over mine and begins to hum. Immediately, the earth quakes and rolls, and with a terrible roar, my home disintegrates, slabs of shiny, black stone turning to glittering dust before my eyes in the space of seven heartbeats.

Above my people's screams and the groans of a falling kingdom, Holly and I whisper words of love and hold each other tightly, tears painting our faces, while the mage laughs and taunts, dancing in rhapsodic glee.

We hold our heads high and ignore her.

"Love is priceless," I tell Holly. "I would pay the same over and over again to have you with me."

Memories rush by—the iolite hallways Mern and I raced through as children, my parents' massive bed of gold in their equally gilded chambers, the mirrored music room, the marble bathhouse, our laughter that I presumed would echo through each beloved room for all eternity—all of it destroyed by bitterness and jealousy.

When only the ruined foundation walls of the city remain standing and dust chokes our lungs, Holly says, "Kiss me, Gade. Strengthen your power and wash away the horror."

We kiss, our bodies spinning slowly through a whirlwind of debris. As we turn, rain falls, drenching our hair and clothes, then snowflakes cascade from the sky, sparkling on our eyelashes and shoulders. I conjure tiny flames that lick us dry, then use the heat to turn the fine dirt and dust to gemstones of every shade, transforming ruin into beauty.

Laughing, Holly opens her arms, jewels falling between her fingers as she dances around and around. "Jewels and fine palaces matter not, only people and dear creatures of land, sea, sky, and flame do," she shouts like a glorious madwoman, a formidable future queen of Faery, who understands the nature of all.

I join her in the jubilant dance, and we twirl in each other's arms around the edges of the tournament oval. We ignore Aer when she calls us names, the mage's fury at our unbroken spirits evident in the black cloud above her head that pelts her skin with hail and sleet.

"We must reassure our people," I tell Holly. "With magic and an army of enthusiastic fae, we will have a new home in no time."

Ether appears in a mist of white light, striding toward Aer who is huffing and howling on a boulder below the ruins, her hair a wet tangle and her fine silks in muddy tatters.

"Sister," says the High Mage, "when will you learn that destruction begets naught but pain and suffering, and bitterness brings only loneliness? You seek to be esteemed above all others, as Queen Mab of old was, but only through acts of love that bring your subjects joy and happiness will they grant you a place in their hearts."

Aer rises, her fists twisted into the muddy fabric of her gown. "And will you punish me for what I have done this day?"

"As you well know, our power is connected, and the five elements balance the whole. Aer, you remind me of a child who screams and rails against the very people you seek approval from. Living with the results of your actions will be punishment enough. Your exile in the mountains will continue, and when I have done all I can to set things right here, I will come to you, and you'll swear so many vows of protection toward the city, land, and people that you won't have leave to scratch your nose without my permission."

Aer's knuckles crack, but she makes no reply. How can she? Ether is all powerful, and none can stand against her.

"In the meantime, I will give a gift to Gade and his future bride, something to ease their people's sorrow. And, Aer, you must vow that you will never interfere with it, ruin, or harm it in any way."

"Can I refuse?" Aer asks.

Ether shakes her head, and her sister repeats the words of the vow. Then the High Mage turns to Holly. "What is your favorite gemstone?"

Without a second thought, she says, "Emerald. If Father could've afforded it, that's what my mother would have had for her wedding ring."

"Lovely," says Ether. "That shall do nicely."

Power radiates from the High Mage's body. The trees in the distance blur and shake, the ground rocking and rumbling as if the entire realm is folding in on itself. My jaw drops as emerald spires spear through the trees atop the mountain on the site where we had always planned to build the new city of Talamh Cúig.

Beside me, Holly gasps and claps. "Ether's magic is astounding."

"She is truly a goddess among fae, and all will be well in our land as long as she stands with us."

Aer rocks back and forth, her face flickering between the scaly skin of the dragon's, then back to the ethereal mage's. Red swallows her golden irises as madness overtakes her mind.

Ether calls Lleu down from a nearby fir tree and instructs him to lead my people to their new home. Holly and I will join them soon.

Then Ether turns to her sister. "Your powers will be stripped in their entirety if you break your vow and interfere with the Emerald Castle."

"You cannot do that," Aer says. "My power is joined with the land and—"

"*For now...*" warns Ether, her body glowing silver. "One day, it will not be so. I will continue to help you bring the fated girls to Faery to save the future princes, for one of them will be the cure to the curse, and unlike you, Sister, I want the Land of Five and its people to thrive. Cross me on this matter, and mark me, you will regret it."

"Gade?" Holly whispers, drawing me toward the cliff edge overlooking the sea. "If we have a son, he will bear the same horror you've endured—the transformation of his personality from light to dark, the pain. How can we dream of happiness when we know this fate awaits him?"

"My love, we must make the best of all circumstances, even terrible ones. We'll learn the girl's mark from the mages and help our son find his mate, and he will do the same for his heir, and so on until the curse no longer lives in the blood of our line."

I take Holly over to Ether, and we kiss the mage's cheeks in turn. "I thank you, High Mage, for your wondrous gift and for all that you do for our kingdom," I say. "In your honor, we vow to rule over it with love and kindness."

Bowing, I kiss her hand.

"Rise, Prince of Five. I cannot remove the curse from your veins, but I can offer further protection, a boon like none ever bestowed upon your line. As compensation for the heirs' affliction, each male after you, including your son, will be born with the ability to shift into magnificent creatures aligned with their element—dragons, griffins, phoenixes, and the like."

Aer screeches as Ether seizes my blade and slices it across her palm, mine, then Holly's, letting our blood flow together and drip into the earth.

"By wind and soil, tears and rage, and never-ending love,
Creatures of Five from below and above,
Enter these vessels, this bloodline of fate,
Earth, Air, Water, Fire, Spirit make haste,
As love sets us free,
So mote it be."

At the exact same moment, Holly and I double over with the force of the spell as it tears through our flesh and bones.

When we recover, I kneel before Ether. "How can I ever repay you for the gifts you've given us today?"

Her long talon of gold tips my chin up. "Gadriel, when the Silver One and his right hand end the curse, you and your queen will have long reigned together in the Otherworld. That day will be thanks enough, and although I can say no more about the answer to the cure, which Aer has hidden where none would think to seek it, know this: the two keys will find each other. Their paths will not be easy to navigate, but walk upon them they shall. One day, there will be peace within for the Heirs of Five; I swear it upon the source of all things."

"Thank you, High Mage," says Holly, dropping into a low curtsy.

Ether places her palm over Holly's forehead. "Child of earth and bone, share your kindness and wisdom with Faery. The folk have much to learn from you." A purple halo appears above Holly's tawny head, then dissolves into her body.

The High Mage has blessed her with fae powers before our marriage ceremony, a great honor. I squeeze Holly's hand, grateful that she can now defend herself from any who seek to harm her. I grin at her trembling form, her stunned expression, eager to find out which element Ether gifted her with.

We bow to Ether and amble up the hill toward the forest that leads to our new home. We turn as Ether picks up her sister's unconscious body and calls out, "After you've inspected the Emerald Castle, no doubt you'll be busy planning a grand feast for me to attend tonight."

"Indeed, but first, we must practice," I reply.

"Practice what?" asks Ether.

"I dare not say. But there is one thing in particular we aim to perfect before we leave our chambers today."

The High Mage harrumphs, and Holly and I laugh as we make our way through the forest, our arms wrapped tightly around each other.

30

Epilogue – Ever After

Holly

I scoot my children from the bathroom with instructions to visit their aunt Mern who is tending the falcon chicks in the mews. Then from a jar in my bedchamber, I take five honey-soaked biscuits and give one to each child before they flee through the door, their laughter echoing behind them.

"Holly, my skin is shriveling off," booms a deep voice from the bathing room. "What are you doing out there?"

"Tending to your naughty sons and daughters." I lean against the carved doorway, a faun's arrow digging into my arm. "Simply reheat it," I say, laughing when I take in the glorious sight of my husband. "Must you wear your crown in the bathtub, Gade? Not all crystals fare well with a soaking."

Wearing a wicked grin, his wet hair frames his sharp cheek-bones, then spills over broad shoulders and his muscular chest. "Of course I must. Come join me, and I'll explain why."

I sashay closer to the copper tub, making a show of peering down through rose petals and bubbles. "It *does* look enticing."

"A surprising comment." His expression turns reflective. "If I remember correctly, early in our acquaintance, you declared you'd never enjoy witnessing me take my pleasure in my bath. Perhaps you should turn away."

The sound of his smug laughter cuts off the moment my robe slips from my shoulders, pooling like crimson blood on the floor.

I take his outstretched hand. "You're correct. I did foolishly say that. But recall what my greatest skill is, my love."

"Lying?"

"Yes."

With a quick tug of his arm, I fall into his embrace, water splashing the stone floor.

"The water *is* cold," I say. "Why didn't you fix it?"

Slowly, he licks his lips. "You know I love nothing more than watching you use your powers."

"Because I'm always making a muddle with them?" I tease. "Or because of this?" I raise my palms and throw my head back, letting all four elements blaze for his entertainment.

Flames dance about the edges of the water, while snow swirls in the air around us, air magic moving our hair like serpents, entwining black and darkest gold together.

Emerald dust merges with flakes of ice, and I open my mouth, allowing a large ice crystal to land on my tongue.

Taking Gade's face between my palms, I kiss my love, the King of Faery, and share the magic with him.

Thank you for reading Prince of Then. I hope you enjoyed it!

Keep turning to read an excerpt from Book 1, Prince of Never, the story of the thirteenth Black Blood heir, Prince Ever, and a modern-day mortal waitress with a magical voice, called Lara.

If you've read the prequel last and have already read the rest of the series, stayed tuned for upcoming steamy re-writes and of course, Wyn and Aodhan's stories.

Prince of Never Excerpt

Prologue

With a sound like rolling thunder, the horse canters onto the ridge of Waylan's Tor, his midnight coat shining in the soft dawn light.

The black steed's rolling eyes are fearsome, but his nature is warm and calm. In contrast, the rider's beauty shines bright and fair, but *his* heart is as dark as coal.

The barren hill has a perfect view of the Crystalline Oak—distant and removed—and exactly how the golden prince prefers it.

Brow furrowed, he scans the grassy earth beneath the tree's metallic roots.

Searching. Searching.

After long minutes, his broad shoulders drop, and he exhales a heavy sigh, white puffs of air swirling to join the mist.

An amber moon sinks low in the lightening sky and, once again, the girl is nowhere to be seen. Thank the Elements. His lids fall closed, the pounding of his black heart slowing.

More times than he cares to remember, he has held his breath, standing on this rocky outcrop, silver eyes seeking—always looking for someone who never arrives.

Forever waiting.

Waiting.

Waiting for her...

He tears his gaze away from the hated tree, twisting the garnet ring on his left hand that proves he is the kingdom's heir, for no other fae can wear it. Then, even though he has no desire to view the tree and what may lie below, he forces his gaze to return—to be certain she isn't there.

She isn't.

Relief flows warm through his fouled blood.

Drawing wild lengths of hair from sharp cheekbones, he sneers as he ponders his people's prophecy. Perhaps the legends of his court are no more than tales to entertain children, stories spun from fanciful lies about *him* and the one who has the power to end his pain. *She* who is foretold to come.

One day.

The girl he doesn't want.

Every day.

The girl he already hates.

Forever...

He recalls what happened to his older brother, Rain, the horror—and he knows the stories of the curse are true.

The cold bites through gaps in shiny armor, nibbling around snug leather, but it doesn't matter; his veins are already filled with icy winter.

Why, then, does he shiver?

Maybe it's the poison slithering its way toward his heart—the creeping magic from which only *she*, his fated queen, can save him.

He leans forward in the saddle, fingers stroking warm horse flesh, and squints over the dusty plain below. Checking—to be absolutely certain.

All is well. Not a creature stirs. This morning, no girl lies dew-covered beneath the oak's grasping branches.

Brilliant. He won't be saved today. Instead, he will ride far and ride hard. And be at peace...as much as a cruel heart can be.

But one day—one very unfortunate day—under that tree is where he shall find her, the queen who can make him king.

And when he does...under that tree is exactly where he'll kill her.

For Everend Fionbharr will never be king.

Never.

Never. Ever. After.

Chapter 1 – LEGS

Lara

Whenever I remember Mom, I think about how her legs looked the last time I saw her—thin, grotesque branches covered in striped stockings and red boots, twisted and broken beneath the wheels of an inner-city delivery truck. Like the Wicked Witch of the East in that old kids' film, The Wizard of Oz.

I'd just turned fifteen.

She'd just turned dead.

Even though we were complete opposites, my mother, Ella, was my happiness, my home. My everything. Now four years after her death, I rely on photos and videos to remind me of what she looked like because staring in the mirror doesn't help.

She had black hair and serene dark eyes. Her face was tanned, and she was always, *always* calm. And, me, I've got strawberry-colored hair, freckled skin, moss-green eyes, a quick laugh, and an even quicker temper. We were summer and winter.

At least once a day, I long for her so badly I clutch my stomach to ease the ache, like I'm doing right now as I make my way to work, crossing from one end of the city to the other, imprisoned in a metal firecracker.

The train goes clack, clack, clack, wheels shooting sparks as it hurtles over a bridge and slices through the sky like a curved silver blade.

I stare at my reflection in the dark window, my pale face merging with the city buildings we pass, and I allow memories of Ella to fill the cold spaces inside my body.

Mom was a game coder obsessed with fantasy games about fae kingdoms where elven warriors and all manner of strange creatures got up to no good. She justified her obsession as work, which in a way it kind of was. My father never justified anything. He's just a loser I've never met—a sperm donor. If I sound like a sad sack little orphan girl, trust me, I'm not. After I found singing, everything made sense again.

More on that later.

Ella was also a digital artist, and the walls of the house I grew up in were lined with magical paintings of fae kings and queens, ethereal creatures with flowing limbs, dancing hair, and frighteningly pretty smiles. Each one a beautiful, terrible nightmare.

"It's real you know, Lara," she told me when I was thirteen.

"What is?" I'd asked, not glancing away from the jigsaw puzzle of the emerald castle she'd made, a gift for my twelfth birthday.

341

"The castle, the king and queen—all of them."

A bright-green piece of jigsaw grass held suspended in my fingers, I asked, "Honestly?" At the time, I was still naive enough to believe in faery tales.

Mom's smile was steady. "Honest, Peanut. Their world is just as real as ours, separated by a mere shimmering veil that's as easy to look inside as peeling back a layer of onion skin. Don't be surprised if one day you trip down a forest pathway and find yourself falling into their world. Believe me, some people are prone to it."

"That sounds fun. I hope I do go and visit someday." I giggled, and she tickled my ribs.

"Well, I hope you don't. But if it ever *does* happen, remember these three things: One, never be fooled by fae beauty because they're all jerks. Every last one of them. Two, don't ever promise them anything. And, three, no matter how much they'd like to, they can't lie. That last point is important. They will twist and omit and evade until the cows come home. So listen carefully to every single word the sly snakes hiss at you, because doing so may save your life."

The jigsaw piece slid from my fingers, plunging into my glass of milk.

Mom laughed at my goggle-eyed expression and ruffled my hair. "Don't worry too much, sweetheart. I'll tell you more about them when you're older—when you're in greater danger."

"In danger of what?"

"Falling," she said, whisking away my empty bowl of popcorn and heading for our cramped and messy kitchen.

No matter how hard I begged her, she never spoke of the Elemental fae as if they were real-live beings again. When she died,

I hid her seductively spooky pictures in the basement and tried to pretend they'd never existed. I wanted to forget them. But, of course, I didn't.

After the accident, I moved into Aunt Clare's uptown apartment where I've lived with her and my cousin, Isla, ever since. They're both great people, and I love them dearly. But, as I said, not a day goes by where I don't long for my mom's special brand of kindness and warmth. The smell of her jasmine perfume.

With a loud rumble, the train pulls into a grimy subway station. *Finally.* I check the time on my cell as I leap out of my seat. Seven thirty. My cousin is going to murder me. I'm so freaking late.

Zigzagging around a drunk guy who's swaying in the middle of the doorway, I swing my backpack over my shoulder and bounce down onto the platform.

I trudge along graffiti and tile-covered passages until I climb stairs and exit onto a cracked sidewalk. The scent of piss and misery from Forest Stand Station is replaced by the pleasant aromas of garlic and basil and something else I don't recognize, reminding me I skipped lunch today because I was feeling out of sorts. Wired and jittery.

Smoothing the purple waitress's uniform over my jeans and my loudly rumbling stomach, I prepare lame excuses to offer my co-workers.

My singing lesson went over time.

That's a lie.

Stan, my elderly teacher with the drooping mustache, is as punctual as a sunset, just nowhere near as pretty.

My train was late.

Nope, it had been early.

On the journey to the station, I'd had headphones clamped over my ears. I got lost in a dreamy tune, dawdled, and arrived just in time to watch the train I should have been on pull away from the platform. Darn things, they're only on time when you don't want them to be.

Across the road, a green and red neon sign flashing the words Max's Vinyl City blinks a warning on top of the diner where I should have started my shift twenty minutes ago. I hate being late.

Oh, well, there's no other option but to get in there and face the wrath of Isla and a long, tedious lecture from my boss.

As I dart down the steps and then over the crosswalk, I can't help noticing how packed the booths are inside the brightly lit interior.

Crap. Max is going to baste me alive and then stuff me into the pulled-pork sandwiches.

Cheeks flaming with guilt, I trip through the door, greeted by the sounds of clattering dishes, a retro rock and roll song distorting out of the speakers, and the smell of frying bacon. My belly grumbles again.

Shabby art deco is the vibe inside Max's joint. It's like a 1940s movie theater faded several decades past its glory days. The floor is checkered, the booths and barstools ruby red, flashy metal trim decorates most surfaces, and the overhead lighting is garishly bright.

"You're late, Lara," calls Max through the kitchen hutch, steam rising around his barrel-shaped body. A Neanderthal brow is framed by messy hair, the dark tips curling around his grin as he works the grill with finesse.

"Hey, you'd better put a hairnet on, or you'll get busted by the food inspectors again," I tease, before offering an apologetic smile.

"I'm sorry, Max. I got lost in a song and a dream, dragged my feet and ended up missing the train," I admit, going with the truth. It's simpler. "I won't do it again."

Across the floor, my cousin, Isla, tucks buttery-blonde hair behind her ears and sets a plate of waffles in front of a customer whose tongue practically lolls out onto his necktie. Not sure if he's slobbering over his dinner or the pretty waitress who's serving it. "You'd better not make a habit of this, late-girl," Isla says. "Remember who got you this job."

"How can I possibly forget when you remind me so often?" The swing door whacks my butt as I escape into the kitchen, and Isla's laughter washes over my back like a balm.

"Okay, Princess," says Max. "Cease the trash talking and take over the fryer. Joe, now that Lara's deigned to join us, you can get your ass back to the sink and wash those pots like your life depends on it."

I dump my coat and bag and greet our regular kitchen hand, a sixteen-year-old local kid who somehow supports his terminally sick mom and younger sister on his barely minimum wage. "Hi, Joe. I know it's going to be hard to leave behind the excitement of dangerously sizzling fat and charred animal remains, but I need you to move aside."

"No problem," he says, sweeping a regal bow toward the deep fryer. "It's all yours, Scary Slayer of Burgers. You know I find cooking too stressful anyway."

"You'll get a handle on it soon. Sorry for being late."

"It's cool." He plunges his nail-bitten fingers into soapy dishwater and attacks the soup pot with gusto. "But you owe me a song during pack-up. One of those weird ye olde medieval things where you sound like an angel."

"Okay." I laugh. "I've just learned a spooky new one about crazed lovebirds who go on a gory murder spree. You'll like it."

He snickers as our assistant cook, Mandy, strides out of the freezer and dumps a tray of frozen meat on the stainless-steel bench.

"Oh, hey, Lara," she says, waving a frozen chicken wing in greeting.

"Hi," I say. "I like your new hair. Are you taking it out partying after your shift tonight?"

Shaking her platinum pixie cut, she says, "I've got term papers to work on this weekend, so I can't—"

"Hey, you two, is this some kind of cheese and wine night or your place of employment?" Max scowls over his shoulder. "Table five's order needs plating. Now would be a good time to hop to it."

We quit socializing and start working our butts off.

Busy is great. Busy makes the shift fly by, and in only four hours' time, I'm wiping down the grill. My back, feet, and head all ache, but I'm so close to going home I don't mind.

Out of nowhere, warm breath gusts over my ear and bony fingers dig into my waist, making me squeak like a trodden-on kid's toy. "So, tell me about the dream you got lost in on your way here, Lara," demands Isla, turning me around to face her. "Hope it wasn't another one about those creepy faery things again."

Damn. Isla knows me too well. She's aware I've been plagued by those dreams since Mom's death. They may frighten and unsettle me, but I've never admitted to her how much I like them.

"Um..." Stalling, I flip a stack of frozen burger patties into a plastic container. "How can you call them creepy? Those fae boys are hotter than these here ghost peppers." I flap a bright red example of the pain-inducing chilies under her nose.

Blue eyes narrow at the pepper. "And they're probably just as fatal." Cranky frown in place, my cousin folds her arms between us. "Your mother never should have stuffed your head full of all that fantasy land garbage. Babbling incessantly about Elementals this, Court of Five that. No wonder you're not interested in any normal guys, Lara."

"Hey, that's not fair. I go on dates every now and again."

"True—when I line someone up for you, choose your outfit, and push your disinterested butt out the front door."

As my mouth opens to remind her I had an actual boyfriend for three whole months last year, my head spins like a pinwheel, and I have to clutch the bench to stay upright.

Isla steadies me. "Lara! Are you okay?"

"I'm fine. Never better," I fib. The whole day long, my brain's been in a pressure cooker, and it feels like it's about to explode.

Looking skeptical, Isla raises an eyebrow.

"I promise I'm okay. It's only hunger. All I ate at break time was a piece of buttered toast, and I skipped lunch."

She sighs. "You'd forget to eat entirely if Mom and I didn't remind you. Listen, I've got a date with Sam tonight, and he's picking me up here after work. I've got time to kill before he arrives. Joe and I will cover cleanup for you. You should go home and rest."

I swallow a moan of relief. It's not just the lack of food affecting me. I *do* feel strange. I must be getting sick.

"Hey," yells Joe, furiously mopping the floor as I make a dash past him to collect my bag from the storeroom. "What about my song?"

I hold back a groan. I'm too worn out to do the murder ballad I'd hyped him up on earlier. I'll have to think of something else to sing. "Sure. Give me a minute."

When I return, I stand in the center of the room and grip my belongings tightly. As I close my eyes, my heart pounds faster, the sound drowning out the clatter and clang of the kitchen. I wait for inspiration. Unfortunately, none comes. Okay, seems like I'll have to wing it, then.

Joe leans on his mop handle. Isla and Mandy smile. And even Max stops scrubbing to lean back on a bench and watch.

Mouth opening wide, I draw in a long breath that spirals through my body, chest to feet, then back up again, soothing my headache and bringing peace and calm.

My boot stomps the floor. Once. Twice. And I sing in a low creepy voice, aiming to make them laugh.

Sorry, Joe.
Tomorrow.
I'll bewitch you with a scary song.
But tonight, I have such a headache that it's sure to all go wrong.
Tonight.
I'll probably sing the wrong spell.
And it may not go very well.
Tonight.
You'll cry and cry a river, if I turn you into a snake.
Hush, I'm so sorry, Joe.
Tomorrow.
I surely won't make that mistake.

Cracking my eyes open, I laugh at Joe's dopey grin and struggle into my snug autumn coat.

"Don't worry, Lara," he says, dancing the mop over the floor once again. "If you're singing to me, I don't think I'd care if you turned me into a rat and kept me in one of those cages with a hamster wheel."

"And then who'd look after your family if that happened?" I scold.

Joe's dark eyebrows draw tight. "Oh, yeah. Maybe don't make me a rodent, then." He turns to Max. "Yo, boss. Gonna walk Lara to the station. I'll be back before you even notice I've left."

Grabbing his arm, I stop him from dumping the mop in the bucket. "Don't bother. It's barely a five-minute walk and loads of people are out partying at this hour. It's busy. Safe."

Everyone rolls their eyes. They know there's no point arguing with me.

I give the crew quick hugs, and before Isla can start up another lecture, I exit the diner at the speed of light.

Relieved to be outside, I inhale a big breath of fresh air. Gone are the tangy food odors from earlier. The night smells earthy and crisp, like rotting leaves blown in on a sea breeze. It's strange.

My temples pound in sync with the beat of my boots as I head for the subway, still smiling at how Joe is always keen to hear me sing. He's convinced I'm part magic, that I've got a witch for an ancestor somewhere in my bloodlines.

But, unfortunately, I can't cast spells or turn people into animals, although, sometimes, I really wish I could. The diner's resident ass-pincher, who haunts table seven, coincidentally on the nights either Isla or I work, would look a little nicer as a beaver or a raccoon.

A car horn beeps as I cross the street, then climb concrete steps leading up to the station's entrance, the night air brisk and energizing. Hands stuffed deep inside my coat pockets, I stare up at the swirling wrought-iron patterns on the arched gates and the sign that reads *Forest Stand Station*, wishing I were as special as Joe imagines.

Magical.

Powerful.

But I'm not. I'm an average, passably pretty nineteen-year-old who's boringly practical and sensible, *most* of the time. I'm neither too loud nor too quiet. And even though, at times, I can be snappy, I try hard to be kind.

Week to week, my life is fairly uneventful. Most nights, I work shifts at the diner, only to spend all my hard-earned money on singing lessons. And that's basically my world in a nutshell.

Work. Sing. Work. Repeat.

On the singing front, I join amateur vocal groups and choirs, always searching for the perfect fit, seeking people I can unleash my unusual voice on. Ethereal yet strong, it can be quite a shock on first listen.

So, yeah, all I want to do is sing. From retro rock-and-roll classics to ancient tunes about forest creatures and lands beyond the veil, I love them all. Wow. Listen to me sounding as eccentric as my poor dead mother!

The wind collects my ponytail, fluttering it over my eyes. Sighing, I drag it away and gaze up at the station's clock tower. It's nearly midnight, and I have at least fifteen minutes to fill until the next train arrives.

Out of nowhere, a girl's screech rips through the air, causing me to flinch. I tug my coat tighter around my body and search for the source of the noise. When I find it, I breathe a sigh of relief.

Gathered around a bench at the top of the steps, four girls huddle close, laughing as they take selfies, a long gauzy veil whipping around their bodies. They're a bachelorette party getting giddy in the wind.

I heave myself up the stairs. The bride-to-be spies me passing, and her mouth gapes open.

"Hello?" she calls out. "Excuse me, miss, can you help us? Please come here."

Miss? No one's called me that in...well, I don't think I've ever been called that. They must be drunk.

I stop walking. I'm too darned tired to take happy snaps for them, but still I force a smile and head over.

The wispy beauty covered in white grins at me, tottering on her heels as if she's not used to wearing them. Her cool fingers grip my coat sleeves and pull me close.

She dips a strange curtsy. "Hello! Please allow me to make introductions. That's Terra down there playing in the dirt, Undine bathed in blue, Salamander with her hair on fire, and I, of course, am the bride, Aer. Did you notice we look alike, you and I?"

"Er... no. Do we? Hi, I'm Lara." I wave awkwardly while I hear my name repeated, little whispers slithering on the breeze.

Lara. Lara. Lara.

Dramatically dressed and pouting scarlet-painted mouths, they look the same as a million other party girls—but not quite. There's something disturbing about them. Something wrong.

"We need your help," repeats Aer. "When we passed through the alley beside the station, our sister, Ether, cut herself on a piece of old tin. See over there?" She points to the empty, lamp-lit alleyway that, in the daytime, is full of city suits eating lunch in trendy cafes. "We can't bear the sight of blood," Aer continues. "And Ether needs tending to."

"Red blood. Red blood," says dark-haired Terra, nodding furiously. "I don't like red blood."

Blue-haired Undine smiles sweetly. "Don't worry about her. She's lost nearly every one of her marbles."

Okay.

"It might be best if you call 911," I suggest.

"No. No. No. It's just a small cut seeping tiny threads of blood. She needs a little bandage, that's all. You can use this." Ruthlessly, Aer tears a strip from her veil and thrusts it at me. "You, Lara, can put it on her. We've drunk too much, and we don't like blood. We might faint and hit our heads."

I glance around. A few people are trudging up the steps, and some are entering the station. The streets aren't busy anymore, but it's hardly deserted. These girls seem pretty helpless, and they don't look like muggers.

"Please?" begs Aer, the breeze blowing her golden locks from her face, revealing a kind and hopeful expression.

"Okay, sure," I say, taking the makeshift bandage.

"Oh, thank you. Once you enter, she's not far in. You'll see her quite easily." Salamander claps like I've done something amazing, and I wonder what her real name is. It's probably Sally or Susan.

"Ether?" Aer yells. "Our new friend, Lara, is coming to see you. You'll be very happy to meet her. You will. You will."

Well, I don't know if I have the power to make her *happy*, but I can definitely slap on a bandage and try to cheer her up a little.

"Ether?" I call. "What's your actual name? Is it Esme or Elaine?"

I hear a whimper followed by a cough. That's encouraging. At least it wasn't a guy's voice, the girls' pimp hovering nearby preparing to attack me.

"Hold on, I'm bringing a bandage."

Warm light pools around the cobblestones, illuminating my path. A bell tolls in the distance. That's weird. Must be a local church ringing in the midnight mass.

Or something...

I keep walking, but there's still no sight of the injured girl.

"Ether?" I try again.

Silence. Maybe I imagined the whimper before.

I stop and glance behind me.

"Hey, Aer?" I call toward the street. "I can't see your sister. She's not—"

"Go farther. Go father," the girls cry in unison. "Help her. We can't bear the blood."

Carried on the rising breeze, their voices sound shrill and not so sweet anymore. Shivers roll over my skin as my boots fall softly on the ground.

Shuffle. Shuffle. Shuffle.

Suddenly a girl appears out of the shadows. Dressed in silver, she raises elegant arms toward me. "Hello, Lara. It's so very nice to meet you."

Wow. Okay. She shines like a diamond in the sun, and it's currently nighttime.

"Hi." Standing two yards away, I ask, "Are you all right? You don't look hurt, but your sisters insisted you need this bandage for a cut."

A smile dances over her face. "Oh, yes, I'm fine. Come hither. Bring me your medical aid, and I shall show you I am well."

What?

Dread churning in my gut, I hobble forward. I don't want to go any closer to this shining girl but can't stop my legs moving. The sound of my heavy steps bounces off the brick walls, echoing around us.

Clomp. Clomp. Clomp.

As I walk, my eyes skim her body, searching for a wound. I don't find one, so I smile dumbly and keep moving forward.

Need to help her. Need to touch the shine. Feel if it's—

What the hell is wrong with me?

Raising her arms toward the stars, she smirks, purses her lips, and blows out a long breath.

And then keeps blowing.

My hair takes sudden flight, strawberry-colored ribbons streaming behind me. My coat becomes a cape, billowing like a wet sail, nearly toppling me over.

In a panic, I turn back toward the sisters, blinking furiously to clear my vision. What I see just cannot be right... They look...*changed.* They've grown taller, elongated into willowy, stick-limbed creatures, half beauties, half horror show. I must be seeing things.

Okay. I really, *really* need to get out of here. *Now.*

But I don't move. Instead, my feet sprout roots into the ground as I'm buffeted by the wind still blustering through silver-girl's lips. Angry now, it spins like a mini cyclone around my limbs.

Winding faster and faster, it lifts my arms, spreading my feet, my legs—wider and wider—until I'm raised aloft, speeding through the air while stretched out like I'm relaxing on a comfortable bed, toward the glittery sky.

I am freaking flying.

Or dreaming.

Or crazy.

I should be terrified, screaming, howling, wailing. But, no, I simply open my eyes wider and wider to take in the glory of the stars as they rush to greet me.

Oh, they're so pretty.

This is lovely.

Lovely.

So *lovely.*

The wind surges around me, but I'm not cold. I feel perfectly warm. Perfectly safe. Perfectly happy.

Perfect.

A voice like a bell rings in my ears. It says something that sounds like, "Say hello to *forever* for us, won't you, Lara dear? Sing him a pretty song. Aer's very jealous, you know. She wanted to be the one."

What? How can I say hello to forever. What does that even mean?

"Who's Forever?" I cry to the planets spinning by.

Someone laughs, the sound like violently shattering glass.

Then everything is black. My mind, my heart, my soul.

Black.

Black.

Black...

Also By Juno Heart

Prince of Then: Gadriel and Holly's story, the prequel.

Prince of Never: Ever and Lara's story.

King of Always: Raff & Isla's story.
King of Merits: Riven and Merri's tale.

Ebook & paperback covers

Hardcovers

I also write about damaged heroes and the girls who heal them under a steamy romance pen name. Stay tuned for steamy fae books coming soon and Wyn & Aodhan's stories!

Join my newsletter list and be the first to hear of new releases, read-first opportunities, and other sweet deals.
You can sign up at my website: junoheartfaeromance.com

And don't forget to have a listen to the Prince of Never audiobook! Available at all retailers.

About the Author

Juno Heart writes enemies-to-lovers romances about cursed fae princes and the feisty mortal girls they fall hard for.

When she's not busy writing, she's chatting with her magical talking cat, spilling coffee on her keyboard, or searching local alleyways for a portal into Faery.

She also publishes books about damaged heroes under her spicy contemporary romance pen name.

For release news and sales alerts, join Juno's newsletter!

Website: Junoheartfaeromance.com

Email: juno@junoheartfaeromance.com

Come say hi on Tik Tok!

Acknowledgments

Thanks for reading Gade and Holly's story! I hope you enjoyed it.

Endless thanks to Ken, the guy who read the whole of Pride and Prejudice out loud to me as a bedtime story each night and who continues to make my dreams come true.

Thank you so much Rosemary P, Saskia, and Amelie for your amazing feedback, Susanna B for naming Holly's mom, Lilé, and to Jasmin E, the inspiration for Holly and Rose's best friend, for claiming Gade as her book boyfriend long before his story had been finished, and to Anna T for her ongoing support and friendship.

Massive thanks to the awesome designers for the beautiful covers, saintjupit3rgr4phic for the eBooks and paperbacks and Covers by Juan for the hardbacks!

Until next time,

Juno.
X

Printed in Great Britain
by Amazon